Praise for **Clarence Nero's** previous novel,
Cheekie: A Child Out of the Desire

"Cheekie offers a little bit of everything: humor, drama, tragedy, and mostly an uplifting sense of entertainment. Highly recommended."
                                                        –Harpo Productions

"The novel sensitively reflects the lives of the less fortunate who are left behind."
                                                        –*Publishers Weekly*

"A lively, indiscreet, sometimes hilarious, often poignant narrator, who paints a vibrant, emotionally intense picture of his family and neighbors. Nero evokes both the humorous and the more horrific aspects of what it's like to grow up as the child of parents who are only just starting to grow up themselves."
                                                        –*Christian Science Monitor*

"The author shows the triumphs and tragedies of living in the ghetto."
                                                        –*Ebony*

"Nero's account of a boy growing up in a New Orleans housing project is both witty and refreshing."
                                                        –*Booklist*

"So well written that you feel as if you're peering through the window of Cheekie's life."
                                                        –*Sister 2 Sister*

Also by Clarence Nero

Cheekie: A Child Out of the Desire

THR3E SIDES
TO EVERY STORY

—— a novel ——

Clarence Nero

HARLEM MOON
Broadway Books
New York

PUBLISHED BY HARLEM MOON

Copyright © 2006 by Clarence Nero

Published in the United States by Harlem Moon, an imprint of The Doubleday
Broadway Publishing Group, a division of Random House, Inc., New York.
www.harlemmoon.com

HARLEM MOON, BROADWAY BOOKS, and the HARLEM MOON logo, depicting a moon
and a woman, are trademarks of Random House, Inc. The figure in the Harlem Moon
logo is inspired by a graphic design by Aaron Douglas (1899–1979).

Reading Group Companion by La Marr J. Bruce

Book design by Michael Collica

Cataloging-in-Publication Data is on file with the Library of Congress.

ISBN-13: 978-0-7679-2136-7
ISBN-10: 0-7679-2136-4

First Edition

146866421

To the Holy Spirit:
For guiding me along the way.

To James Tyrone Cooper:
For never letting me fall and for always having my back.

To all those who have ever been trapped in one way or another:
This is your time to break free!

"How was I caught in this game?"

—Dionne Warwick, "Theme from *Valley of the Dolls*"

ACKNOWLEDGMENTS

To my mother, Katie, who brought me into this world. Thanks for paying for my Web site and for all your love.

To Grandma Emelda, an unsung writer in her own right, for the support and inspiration.

To Elton D. Pullett, my rock, my friend, a rising star.

To all my family members, whom I love with my whole heart. These have been difficult times, but we will make it through. The spirit of New Orleans is within us.

To other family members: Roz, Monique, Aunt Lillie, Aunt Dolly, Aunt Marion, Debra, and I can't forget my talented cousin this time around, Sherika Mahdi: you guys were right there on the front lines with me. I couldn't have gotten through any of this without you, too.

To all my friends who came through for me and my family during the storm. I will never forget your generosity, prayers, and love: William Nyaho Chapman and all of his friends (too many to name, but you know who you are); Michael Webster; Lynette, Andrea, and all of your friends; Pearl and Brian Cremins; Corliss; Marie Dutton Brown; Mondella Jones; Qevin

Oji; Ryan Johnson; Douglas Pineda; Kent Nichols; Ms. Wanda (the tax lady), and so many strangers whom I don't even know. Thank you, thank you, thank you.

To Dr. Maya Angelou, Auntie Maya, for just being the awesome person you are and for opening your heart to me and mine. Crossing paths with you in this lifetime has been a true highlight for me.

To Dr. Ernest Gaines, for his guidance and advice during much earlier drafts and the entire workshop at the University of Lafayette.

To Willie Burton, the only African American with the most Oscar nominations (quiet as it's kept), you've been a true friend and inspiration. You're a class act and a wonderful human being.

To Victoria Sanders, my wonderful literary agent, who came on board and got the job done. Thank you for standing with me through it all.

To E. Lynn Harris, for opening the door for me. You're a beautiful person and one talented brother. Thank you so much.

To Keith Boykin, my writer friend whom I'm just so goddamn proud of! Thanks for posting my letter and inspiring me.

To Janet Hill, for giving me a chance and being so nice about everything.

To Clarence Haynes, my namesake and one of the best in the business, for pushing me beyond my own limitations and helping my family, too.

To James Wilcox, my mentor at LSU, a great writer and wonderful person. Thank you for being my teacher, motivator, and at times even my counselor. I couldn't have gotten through this process without your expertise and solid advice.

To the National Endowment for the Arts, for the lovely grant to keep my writing afloat during the storm.

To Amanda Briggs, a talented and classy woman who has just been a wonderful friend and supporter.

To Ms. Jamey Hatley, who often cries because she's so happy for me. Your warm and sweet spirit lifts me up high. I'm looking forward to seeing you out there one day soon.

To Emilie Stat, my next-door neighbor, for coming on board and agreeing to assist me with such enthusiasm. It means a lot. Thank you.

To all of those in workshops at LSU, colleagues, and friends who have read drafts of the novel and/or screenplay along the way or supported me on some level: Melinda Young; Omar Tyree; Vincent Tolliver; Kamal Dorsey; Scott Widdon; Scott Gage; Dr. Suzanne D. Greene; Dr. Julie Kane; Marcus Battley; Michelle Benoit; Zena Brooks, at D.C. CAP; Mari Kornhauser; Frank White; Derrick Hampton; Chris; Dan Mangiavellano, my office mate; Bobby, Penelope, Andrew, Brock, Carolyn, Shane— the workshop crew who are all so talented in their own right; Tussy; Li'l Ann; my cuz Toya; Delvin; and my sister li'l Katie (thanks for being so excited about the book).

And last but most certainly not least, my Father in heaven, who kept me! Period.

PREFACE

Now that the sexy, sizzling cover has caught your attention, I would like to thank you for picking up my novel and being curious enough to read this preface.

I grew up in the Ninth Ward of New Orleans–an area that became well known in the wake of Hurricane Katrina. My grandmother raised fourteen children–seven girls and seven boys–in this community. I am a third-generation Ninth Ward resident. Some of my most pressing memories and recollections of growing up there were of hardworking people trying to raise their children in less-than-ideal circumstances. It was in the Ninth Ward where I lost two brothers to violence and drugs, and a close female cousin to AIDS. They were all under the age of thirty when they died.

While covering the storm, the media only scraped the surface of the terrible conditions that existed within the city's largely black population. As a result, I was reminded of why it was so important for me to continue writing this book (I had already started the novel before Katrina) and to give voice to this once-forgotten community. Many people here at home and even abroad were shocked and horrified at the large number of poor, black folks trapped in the Superdome. But the truth is, a lot of the citizens of New Orleans had been trapped long before the floodwaters held them captive: trapped by grinding poverty, failing school systems, and an alarming homicide rate that plagued the city. But given such harsh realities and sad circumstances, I have also experienced an abundance of hope from witnessing the courage and great spirit of New Orleans folk. From the jazz halls of Bourbon Street to the celebration of Mardi Gras, we are a people who know how to have a good time and rise above our hardships. So it is from this bastion of pain, heartache, and joy that I put the pen to paper.

Although this novel is a work of fiction and set in pre–Hurricane Katrina New Orleans, the characters represent true depictions of a particular aspect of the Ninth Ward. What was washed away in the brutal storm was a community with quite a unique makeup of poor working-class folk, single mothers, thugs, educators, middle-class families, gays, preachers, politicians, and so on. This is a place I called my home and have been writing about for many years. In 1998, my first novel, *Cheekie: A Child Out of the Desire*, was published. It's the story of a boy growing up in the Desire Housing Project, set against the backdrop of poverty, crime, homicide, drugs, and other perils often synonymous with inner-city dwelling. I now feel more passionate than ever about that novel, given the social climate in New Orleans. Moreover, the story of Cheekie, his family, and his friends has historical significance, since that area has now been emptied of most of its inhabitants following the after-effects of the storm.

In the wake of Katrina, my family, like most families from the Ninth Ward, lost everything and relocated to various parts of the United States. These have been extremely difficult times, and we have some long and hard days ahead. My prayers and thoughts are with the people from this region as they try to rebuild, reclaim their lives, and make sense out of the devastation.

With such a large proportion of black men in prison, with drugs controlling generations, with the down-low issue, and with HIV and AIDS threatening our communities, we have to discover better ways of communicating and working together to solve our common issues. Our future is at stake. We can no longer afford to turn the other way.

THR&&**SIDES**
TO EVERY STORY

Tonya

I don't know where to begin with this nightmare, so I'm just gone start right around the time Johnny got his get-out-of-jail card, because that was when all the goddamn drama started going down between us. And I know everybody probably gone have something to say about the situation, but nobody knows what happened like I know.

To begin with, I loved Johnny with my whole heart, so whoever tried to say I was using him or that I was some gold digger, they can kiss my black you know what for real. All the sistahs out there who've ever had a brother on lockdown will be able to relate to what I was going through back then: that sometimes it gets hard for a girl when your man is miles away in some jail and you still got needs.

Don't misunderstand me. While Johnny was away in jail I was committed to him, but just not completely faithful. But the hard-core fact was, *he* was the one who got sent upstate for five years, not me. I still had shit I had to take care of on the outside, although Johnny was deep inside my heart and forever on my mind. Everyone knows that a sistah from the hood gotta get hers for herself, because ain't nobody really trying to give you a damn thing out here in these streets but the blues.

So, yeah, I'll straight-up admit that I was laying the pussy down on Rico, an NO rapper who held down the dirty South like Lil' Wayne and Juvenile.

If I don't say nothing else good about that lying, cheating nigga, I have to give Rico his props. He had mad skills on the mic and wasn't like some of those fake-ass rappers out there who talk about living the game and coming up from the cut because it helps them sell more records. Rico lived every bit of the street life. The shit he rapped about, I felt it deep down in my bones like a cold fucking breeze on a zero-degree day.

I came from nothing, y'all, for real. My mama raised me and my two brothers in the Florida Project off of Desire Street without nobody's help but the good Lord's. Not to sound all broke-down or try to get some kind of sympathy either, but I have seen some shit out there in the world that could last me a lifetime. Although nothing beats seeing my own brother Eric get shot down like an animal in the streets by some crazy-ass nigga who was jealous over the fact that his woman had lust in her eyes for my brother.

Niggas know they be killing one another for nothing. Took my brother's life for simply looking at his woman, but that ain't even half the shit me and my family been through in that lower Nine. I'm talking about the Ninth Ward, that is. And I for damn sure have a lot to say and to get off my chest, but some things you just gotta take your time with.

Like I was saying, Rico was rapping about life in the projects, which I could relate to, so that's one of the reasons our friendship was so special. The other reason was the fact that we was both artists. Where Rico was a rapper, I could work a goddamn stage and dance a nigga right out of his drawers.

Yeah, I was a stripper. Babee, ain't no shame in my game. And I ain't even trying to hide or deny it either. You see, I'm not ashamed of my past at all, because the past has only made me the strong woman I am today.

I was stripping down at this spot called Club Circus in the French Quarter, right off of Bourbon Street when Rico first saw me doing my thing, shaking and clapping my ass for dollars. My stage name was Booty. You know that song "Bootylicious" by Destiny's Child? It was like they were singing about me.

"Oh baby, you so hot, girl, you sizzle!" some corny nigga with a played-out Jheri curl and a mouthful of gold teeth hollered. Jheri Curl—what I would come to call him—was a regular at Club Circus who got on my last fucking nerve. "And, girl, you got the kind of ass that a make a nigga go bankrupt. Just booty on top of booty!"

Jheri Curl would show up every night, sit up front near the stage, and say the exact same line to me until him and all of his li'l podnuhs started joking around and calling me Booty, which I didn't have any problem with. Them niggas were breaking me off with a li'l change every night and every li'l bit helps when you broke. It was my booty that attracted Rico to me in the first place.

After I got offstage one night, Rico informed the manager that he wanted to meet the girl with the big, sexy booty, but I quickly shut him down. I passed the word along that I was not interested in anything he was offering. Rico was a player, and every woman from the Third to the Ninth wards knew he was the biggest whore this side of the Mississippi, so I was not even about to set myself up to take a hard fall like some trick with no goddamn sense.

Besides, I had Johnny–a real soldier–and I knew one day he was coming home to love me again. We was once high school sweethearts and so in love with each other that everyone just knew we would be together forever. No man had ever loved or been committed to me the way Johnny had. He made me feel safe and secure in those strong-ass muscly arms of his. So, nobody can't say it wasn't true love. Me and Johnny had that kind of strong love that people wrote songs and made movies about. Damn, y'all got me thinking way back. It was no fairy-tale meeting, but I fell for that nigga the first time I looked into his eyes.

Me and my girls was walking home from school when we heard these dudes behind us cracking jokes. One of them, Johnny, was talking about my sexy ass, but I was trying to ignore him. Sometimes I liked the attention niggas showed me over my body, but other times I just wanted to be left alone. Johnny caught me on one of my off days when I just wasn't feeling it.

"Girl, you got the kinda ass that make a nigga fall down on his knees and thank Jesus!" His strong and deep voice blended in with a laughing crowd of kids from around the old neighborhood. Latisha and Tamika, my girls for real, grabbed hold of my arms. They wasn't about to let some niggas disrespect me. Latisha and Tamika always did have my back, which they've proved time and time again since middle school.

"Come on, nah, baby," another dude shouted. "Why y'all gon' be like dat? My man just tryin' to holler at the one with the big booty." More laughter.

"Girl, just ignore them," Latisha said, dragging me by the arm.

"They so damn ignorant," Tamika added, flipping her long hair out of her face and pulling at me, too. She was the prim and proper one in the crew. Tamika was also conceited, stuck-up, and didn't take crap from nobody. We was walking as fast as we could, but them fools stayed behind us the entire way home. I don't know why niggas think we love this kind of shit, anyway. We don't want nobody whistling, honking, and shouting at us like we some stray dogs or runaway cats. Step up to us like men and maybe we might take your asses seriously.

"Hey, li'l mama, why don't you do like Juvy," Johnny called out, "and back that ass up fa' me."

"You know what?" I pulled away from Tamika and Latisha, swung around to face the crowd, and went off. "Y'all are so fucking immature!"

"Oh, so you feisty and hot." Johnny made his way to the front of the crowd and stared me in my face. I noticed he was wearing a football jersey with a big number thirty-two on his right sleeve, which was the winning number that year. Johnny was our school's football star, and he had broken more records than any athlete in Higgins High's history. But I didn't give a damn who he was.

"You got something to say?" I got right up in Johnny's face and gave him a piece of my mind, sister style: hands on my hips, neck twirling, and everything. His boys was cheering, roaring, and trying to get some shit started. Latisha and Tamika stepped to my side and got into kick-ass mode.

"Then be a man and say it to my face," I said.

After which, Johnny did something that shocked the entire crowd, including me. He got down on one knee like he was about to propose. All of a sudden you couldn't hear nothing, and everyone stopped dead in their tracks.

"What I was tryin' to say was..." Johnny took hold of my hand. He was staring me in my face with those dark brown eyes of his that made a bitch like me melt. But I was holding on with a tight face and trying my best not to give in to his charm and good looks. Johnny had done pissed me completely off, and I wanted him to know it, too.

"I was wonderin'"–he cleared his throat, like what he had to say was really hard to get out–"if you would go to the home-coming dance with a nigga."

"Girl, forget him," Tamika said, nudging me in the back. "Tonya, didn't you hear me?"

"Yeah, I heard you." I looked into Johnny's eyes. It was like he had a hold on me or something. For a brief moment I couldn't think, move, or speak.

"So, what's up?" Johnny asked with the widest grin on his face. He had me eating out of the palm of his hand, but I tried to keep it together. "You gon' let a nigga take you to the dance or what?"

"Okay," I heard myself say, cracking a smile and shaking my head from side to side. You know every woman wants to be swept off her feet, and Johnny had done just that. It was the perfect sunny day for falling in love.

You see, Johnny's charm got him what he wanted, but his anger often kept him in a whole lot of trouble on the other hand. Now, that brings me back to the story.

Johnny waited until our senior year of high school to do something completely stupid, even though I admit that my ex-boyfriend Greg was a jerk and deserved to get his ass kicked for trying to manhandle me.

It all went down one night after a high school football game, and I was waiting at the front gate for Johnny. Greg drove up in his daddy's BMW, trying to impress me and claiming how badly he wanted me to be his girlfriend again. I told him to get lost, and that was when one thing led to another. Greg tried to force me inside the car. Said he just wanted to take me somewhere so we could talk. I was kicking and screaming when Johnny came flying out of the school gate like Superman. It must have looked like Greg was attacking me or trying to rape me or something. Johnny went too far, although I understand how it may have looked from his perspective. He fucked Greg up so bad, the boy ended up in the hospital for weeks with multiple bruises on his chest and face. Doctors didn't think he would make it, which totally freaked me out. Our high school romance turned into a nightmare overnight. Johnny wound up in jail for almost killing Greg.

Whatever the case, I didn't turn my back on Johnny or look at him any different. Part of me understood that he was only trying to look out for my best interests. So, you damn right, I stood by my man, despite what other people thought: taking three-hour bus rides to visit him in Sierra Leone, Louisiana, and writing love letters to him into the early morning, until my fingers would ache. Although it was hard, and sometimes a sistah got lonely, I wasn't out there looking for someone to take his place. Even though Rico slowly made his move on me by showing up at the club night after night and showering me with expensive gifts, I continued to remain faithful to Johnny.

I stripped at the club every chance I got and tried to make ends meet every which way I could. But the shit wasn't easy, y'all. That li'l change them niggas was giving me at the club wasn't enough to buy a Happy Meal at McDonald's. It seemed like the more I stripped and shook my ass, the farther I seemed from getting anywhere. Here I was, living with my mama in a run-down two-bedroom house off of Louisa Street and trying to help her pay the bills, but every month it seemed like we never had enough–like we could never get ahead of the game.

Although stripping at Club Circus paid some of the bills, I had this one dream of dancing in music videos on BET and touring the country with some famous rapper like P. Diddy or Jay-Z. I was just as talented as some of those dancers on TV in Diddy's and Jay-Z's videos, but unlike me, they wasn't shaking and clapping their asses for some li'l change in some smoky, dark club, but getting top dollar for their skills.

Well, the big dream did come true for this girl from the lower Nine who a lot of people probably thought wasn't gone be nothing in life because I was poor and black from the projects. But I showed all of their hating asses. One day Rico introduced me to a lifestyle and made me an offer that I could no longer resist, a once-in-a-lifetime chance to become a music video dancer and tour the world with him. I know some folks would try to say I was only with Rico for the fame and money, but it wasn't even like that.

Dancing for Rico's company was a chance for me to be somebody in life. Sometimes you gotta rewrite your own story and not live the one that was written for you at birth. My grandma had it hard in life, raising five girls and six boys on the strength of her back without nobody's help, including this shameless-ass government or that low-line handout they call welfare. And some of my aunties, uncles, and cousins also had it hard, burying sons and daughters before the age of twenty-two, but I was gone be damned if I was gone struggle all my life, too. I had seen my mama work all of her life to keep food on the table with minimum wages that was like a goddamn slap in the face. I knew that was not the life I wanted for myself. God had something better in store for me. I just thought that better life was with Rico, especially since he was lavishing me with all the material things I had always wanted.

Who wouldn't get caught up in that kind of fantasy?

The best part about dancing in music videos was the thrill and high it gave me. I felt special, wanted and needed. You know, like I was making a difference and connecting to something big that the whole world would see.

The pay was good, too. Before long I had diamonds, furs, and even a sports car, which I pulled into the driveway of an upscale apartment around the white folks in the Garden District of New Orleans, another one of Rico's little gifts to me. Since I was Rico's girlfriend, I got paid top dollar just to shake my ass in front of the camera, a long way from my days of stripping at Club Circus.

Don't misunderstand, though. It was nice having beautiful things and lots of money, but the truth is I never asked Rico to do none of that shit for me. All I really wanted from him was a job and a fresh start. That's it! Everything else that happened between us was just as much of a surprise to me as anyone.

Once I started dancing for him, our romance took off like a train heading east. Shit, everything was happening so fast I barely had time to stop and think about what I was doing. You know, just so happy that I was doing something different with my life and not the same old tired routine of getting up and going to shake my ass at the club. I knew so many girls who danced at Club Circus until they got old, played out, and used up with nothing to fall back on. I was not trying to be that kind of sistah, for real.

I have to be honest, though. Although I had stopped going to see Johnny in jail and writing letters to him, I couldn't get him out of my system. Here I was, living the life of luxury and having a good time with Rico, but still thinking about another nigga.

Of course, it broke my heart to cut Johnny off the way I did, but I had no other choice. If I had continued to write or visit him in jail, things would have gotten more complicated. So, I did Johnny a favor and walked out of his life for the time being. The way I saw it, we would have our time together again once he got out of jail. In the back of my mind, I knew he was the nigga for me, but I had to do what I had to do in the meantime.

You see, Johnny was my first, and Mama said you never truly get over your first, especially if he was putting down wood the way Johnny was. Babee, that nigga knew how to hit all my spots and fuck a piece of pussy right out of its cage. Sistahs, you know once you get a good piece of dick, you ain't never gone forget that shit. Johnny made love to the pussy as if it was his mission and purpose in life. Damn! I get wet all over again just thinking about that fat, curved dick of his.

But on the other hand, sistahs, if you get some bad dick, you ain't likely to forget that shit either. I ain't gone even cut corners about what I have to say. Rico had a small-ass dick that messed me up in my head, because I couldn't believe that dicks could even be small like somebody's finger. (And that's when it was hard!) Being with him was like suddenly going from a fat-ass pork sausage to an Oscar Mayer wiener. And I don't know anyone who can get filled up off a damn Oscar Mayer wiener. But that nigga could eat, so that at least was a plus in his favor.

Anyway, on a serious note, the entire time I was with Rico, I felt like something was missing. And I'm not just talking about in a sexual way, either, because it wasn't all about sex with me. Yeah, it was important, but what a sistah really wants is to be made to feel special, like she's the only woman on earth for the man she's with. I never felt like that with Rico. His career always came first with him.

Yeah, me and Rico was traveling the world together, and I was meeting all of these famous people, but at the end of the day I would come home feeling empty inside. Rico must have sensed that I didn't love him, because eventually his eyes started roaming to some white chick from New York who worshipped the ground he walked on. You know how it is, sistahs. When niggas get a li'l cheese and status in life, they eventually leave our asses for the blue-eyed blonde, so it wasn't like I was that surprised. Rico wasn't a nigga you could trust or bet your life on anyway, so that's why I never truly gave him my heart. No matter how famous Rico was or how much money he spent on me, Johnny was the nigga inside my heart. This I swear to God on my brother's grave, and I don't usually say the Lord's name in vain.

So, let it be known, Rico did dump me for the white girl and took back his promises to love me forever—along with all the expensive gifts, like the apartment in the Garden District and the sports car. You heard me right. He left me with just the clothes on my back and a few dollars I had saved up in the bank for a rainy day, which was kind of strange. One minute I was on top of the world, meeting and greeting celebrities, and the next thing I was back in the hood where I started from.

Of course, I was hurt and disappointed to lose everything, but I was not in love with Rico, so I got over him. What scared me the most about the situation was not having a fallback plan or some other nigga to lean on. Since I could remember, there had always been a nigga trying to holler at me, and now I had nobody in my life.

When I heard that Johnny was getting out of jail a couple of months earlier than originally expected, I was beaming with joy and so happy. I took him coming home as some sort of sign from above that we was destined to be together. You know, that God allowed things to end with Rico in preparation for a future with Johnny. I was such a fool for believing in dumb-ass Barbie-doll fantasies.

Up to this point I've been reminiscing about old times and telling about this great love between me and Johnny, and I haven't even gotten down to the gutter of what happened once Johnny finally came home. Babee, when I finish telling you everything about Johnny and James and a list of other punks he was running around town with, you probably gone end up just how I was a year ago: scared, and don't trust anything with a bat and two balls swinging between his legs. Johnny may have been the love of my life when he went to jail, but that nigga was on some other shit when he got out, for real!

2

James

Two years in confinement at Sierra Leone Correctional Facility and here I thought I had seen and heard it all. But apparently I was wrong, honey. Doing hard time was nothing compared to the hot mess I got into the year Johnny came home for good.

First of all, let me set the record straight on a few things before I even get into the business about what happened or didn't happen between me and Johnny.

Tonya, Booty, or whatever Ms. Girl called herself was indeed a gold-digging, trifling ghetto slut. Yeah, I called her out of her name, and I don't mean no disrespect to black women, because I have a strong black woman for a mother who I love and admire for standing by me through all of this nonsense. But sometimes you just have to call a spade a spade, and tell it like it is. Ms. Girl wouldn't know what true love is even if it was written across her big-ass forehead. Chile, don't even get me started with reading her, because I'm a Christian and I really don't like putting other people down.

However, I knew of Ms. Girl long before I even heard of the name Johnny Lomack, so this thing between us went back a long ways. When I met Booty, she was a low-class stripper over at this club called Circus where I used to hang out from time to time.

Wednesday night was gay night at Club Circus, and the children would take over, honey. When I say the children, I'm referring to the gay children, that is, and we ran Wednesdays at the Circus. And, of course, mademoiselle was your ringleader, queen bee of the pack. All the children knew James Santiago, because I was fierce. Moreover, I was a designer girl, a runway supermodel.

Walking the runway at the Circus was nothing like a fashion show in Milan. You had to command attention. It was never given to you on a silver platter. If you wanted to get noticed, you had to walk through the club like you owned that bitch, with your chest pushed out and head raised up in the air like an AKA sorority girl. Make no mistake about it: The children can be some of your toughest critics, so I served them runway every time I made my grand entrance.

Back in those days I wasn't giving the children drag, because I didn't have to. I was naturally beautiful and didn't need a wig or makeup to enhance what I already had: soft, silky black hair and lovely tan skin for your mama, honey. Every week, I would serve the children different designers: Versace, Dolce & Gabbana, just to name a couple. Going to a gay club was like performing in Las Vegas: You had to give them children inside the club your best performance every night, because competition was always fierce. You best believe that.

My sidekick was this gorgeous piece of fish, Ebony Sinclair, who wasn't a lesbian or anything. She just liked hanging out with the fags, so we called her a fag hag. And, honey, the chil-

THREE**SIDES**TO**EVERY**STORY

dren lived for Ms. Ebony, because her face was flawless like a top model on the cover of *Vogue*.

But beauty didn't necessarily guarantee a winning scorecard. I knew Ebony better than any of those children, and life wasn't all that easy for her either. Like everyone else, that girl got her heart broken, had to sit down on the toilet to shit, and had to work to pay her bills. Her biggest problem was choosing the wrong kind of men to date–the ones who used her face as a punching bag, but I ain't even trying to get all up in that girl's personal business, at least not right now, anyway.

Ebony worked as a stripper, too. But come on now, everyone who strips ain't necessarily a whore like Ms. Girl, Booty. Ebony was a college student at Delgado trying to pay her tuition bill. I could respect a girl who was willing to work for her coins, no matter what her profession or vocation was.

Ebony and I actually met at Delgado in a freshman English class, of all places. We hit it off immediately. Some people might look at me today and not even know that I was a college student at one time. Even if it was for only two semesters, at least I went. I know some girls who ain't never stepped foot in somebody's college to try to educate themselves.

Besides, I ain't ashamed to say that I'm a college dropout. Kanye West dropped out of college and wrote a whole damn album about it, and look where his ass is at today. People like me and Kanye West understand that college can't offer superstars what they need on the spot: instant success and glorification. I found my stardom in the club scene, where I was free to be anything I wanted to be. But I was young, and there was still a lot I didn't know about the children or the gay lifestyle. What I needed was a mentor, someone to groom me into fierceness. That person would ultimately find me. I now say it was fate.

Ms. Alexandria Pandora "Razor" Craft, a six-foot man dressed in exotic outfits who gave RuPaul a run for her money, was the legendary mother of the House of Craft and prima donna of drag queens. Pandora sent word among some of the children that she wanted me to join the House of Craft because of my talents and skills on the runway. A lifetime friendship was born, and I now had a new mother who nurtured me in the gay world.

Being a black man, feminine, and gay wasn't easy by any stretch of the imagination. On a daily basis I had to put up with insults from ignorant-ass people on the street who couldn't accept me for being myself. But chile, it wasn't white folks, but my own damn people trying to pull me down. Yeah, I said it. Some black folks act like they don't have any love for the children, honey, but we are human beings and was part of the struggle, too. Moreover, we come from the same history and got the same black blood running through our veins, so that shit hurts, having your own race treating you like an alien from outer space or something.

Pandora understood the pain of being openly gay when everyone from preachers to politicians be hating on us. So, therefore, she made it her mission in life to be there for all of us with unconditional love, protection, and guidance that we couldn't get from the black straight world.

Not to say my birth mother didn't provide me with moral support, but Pandora was older—twenty years my elder—and gay herself, so she understood me in ways that my real mother couldn't. When Pandora's family discovered she was a flaming gay queen, they turned their backs on her. She had no other choice but to leave. Pandora ran away from home when she was a teenager and has never looked back since. As a result, she knew what it was like to feel unwanted and rejected, and Pandora never wanted any of the children to experience that kind of pain or loneliness.

Like the name suggested, the House of Craft meant you had to be creative and crafty to be a member. Pandora could be just as tough on the children as she was loving. Not just anybody was getting up inside her house. Besides, in order to get into somebody's house you had to have something to offer the children in addition to your good looks. Some type of talent that made you a showpiece.

You see, it was all about illusions. Even if you didn't have a lot of money, you had to act like you did. Most of the children didn't have a quarter in their pockets, but the house made them feel special and important—a place they could go to be seen and heard like a sorority, but for gay men—a society within a society with its own rules.

Oh, it was always about competition, too. Houses competed against one another in one of many categories at an event we called the ball. Usually held at a hotel ballroom, the ball was an extravaganza that was like Mardi Gras all over again. Of course, there was a long catwalk for the children to parade around on in their exotic costumes. The competition was judged by a community of our own peers, and we competed against one another with sweat and tears like it was the Oscars: Best butch queen, best business executive, best runway model were some of the many categories that were up for grabs at the ball.

In those days, the House of Chanel and the House of Flying Daggers were also popular houses, but they had nothing on us, honey. We were beautiful and talented and ghetto all rolled up in one. You just can't find a winning combination like that these days. I walked in the best-designer category, because fashion was indeed my forte. Since I worked part-time at Saks, it was so easy for me to stay on top of the latest fashions.

Basically, I was stealing from them. I was a thief, honey. And I'm not proud of my former lifestyle, but at the time I did what I had to do to survive and keep ahead of the game. Winning the category for my house gave me a chance to feel rich and successful for a day, an indescribable joy for someone who was born dirt-poor.

One night, me and Pandora were at the Marriott Hotel on Canal Street preparing for one such ball when we got this hysterical phone call from Ebony that some bitches at Club Circus were planning to jump and attack her. Me and Pandora, along with Noxzema Cartell, a drag queen friend of ours who was known for her seductive catwalk, immediately headed for the club. No questions asked. Fighting came with the membership. House sisters always had one another's back. Since Ebony was a dear friend of mine, she had the full support of the house, too.

When we arrived on the scene, Ebony and Booty were fighting outside the club over some dirty-ass rapper named Rico, who was ugly as a pit bull, if you really wanted to know the truth. But for some reason, the straight women loved his short, red ass. It probably was his color, because light-skinned dudes still rule the South, quiet as it's kept.

Anyway, they were fighting over this red nigga and Booty's girlfriends—five of them, to be exact—jumped in and started helping her. Oh, baby, that was when all hell broke loose. We scooped them bitches up one by one. Me, Pandora, and Noxzema were fighting and tossing whores around so that you would have thought we were inside a boxing ring, tag-teaming their asses. But you have to believe me when I tell you this: It was never our intention for someone to die that night.

When all the fighting was over, there was one stripper left stretched out on the ground with her throat slit wide open. The finger was pointed straight toward our mother. Everyone knew that Pandora had a reputation for cutting girls and taking no mercy. That's how she gained the nickname Razor in the first place, because she would actually leave a cut behind on a girl's face with a razor as some victory mark. But on the occasion of the fight between five bitches and one whore named Booty, Pandora maintained her innocence the whole time.

The DA, this redneck named Mr. Wallace, was all too eager to send another black man to Sierra Leone, a hellhole the state of Louisiana had the nerve to call a prison. The name alone lets you know exactly what type of place it was, a modern-day version of slavery. That's why inmates called Sierra Leone "the plantation."

Sierra Leone is actually a real place off the coast of Africa where they used to take slaves from before bringing them to America. Now tell me that shit ain't foul—to name a prison after something that used to be connected to slavery and then fill it up with nothing but black men.

When the trial was over, Pandora got life without the possibility of parole and was shipped off to Sierra Leone without so much as a good-bye. The DA didn't even hear testimony from everyone who was at the club that night. Some people claimed they saw Noxzema slit that girl's throat. But during the trial Noxzema disappeared and was never heard from again. She must have been scared or guilty of something, because why run off if you are innocent? I had a hit out on that bitch, but she was good at hiding, wherever she was.

Anyway, Pandora took the fall for the stripper's murder and everything went downhill from that point on. With our mother locked away, the House of Craft fell apart. And you know what's fucked up about it? Ebony still didn't end up with Rico after all–Ms. Girl did.

That's right. While Johnny was away in jail pining away for the love of his life, Booty was running around town living the glamorous life with a thugged-out rapper with no cut. But she was dead wrong for how she treated Johnny. If it wasn't for her ass, Johnny wouldn't have gotten sent to prison in the first place. Oh, I bet she would never mention that li'l detail when talking about her deep love and respect for Johnny.

What happened was some jealous-hearted nigga she used to mess around with was trying to rape her one night and Johnny jumped in and saved her ass. Johnny beat him so badly that he almost killed the dude. The same redneck DA who prosecuted Pandora didn't want to hear nothing about how Johnny was trying to protect his girlfriend. As far as Mr. Wallace was concerned, he was ridding the streets of New Orleans of another "nigger"; at least, that was the impression I got of him at Pandora's trial.

Needless to say, Mr. Wallace sent Johnny upstate for five years, with the possibility of parole in four. Everything came full circle for me when I ended up in the same predicament as Pandora and Johnny. Years of stealing from my employer caught up with my ass.

Mr. Wallace wasn't the prosecuting attorney on my case–a small miracle in an already extremely fucked up situation–but a sistah by the name of Debra Boudreaux, who wanted to give me a second chance in life. I thank God for her, because theft was something retail store owners take very seriously these days. That's why I tell these young children every day that they better know what they're doing out there in those streets, because white folks ain't playing with us. They will send your ass upstate, throw away the key, and forget your black ass ever existed in the world. Ain't nothing fierce or cute about going to prison, honey.

Since this was my first crime, Ms. Boudreaux got my sentence reduced from three years down to two, with parole in one. Originally I was supposed to do that year in New Orleans lockup over on Tulane and Broad. But, see, when I got there, they wanted to test me. I'm talking about some of the other male prisoners. Just because you have a dick between your legs don't mean shit in prison, honey.

Some of the hardest, most thuggish niggas will try to turn you out, even if you weren't down with dudes. But when they know or suspect you're already gay, it's like open season. Everybody wants a piece of your ass. But I showed them bastards one by one that I was not to be fucked with. They thought because I was feminine and gay that I was weak or a bitch, but I wasn't having it. Unlike some of the children, I can count on one hand how many men done run up inside of me. I was never a promiscuous girl and wasn't gone start being one in prison.

When I almost choked a six-foot, rusty-looking nigga to death for trying to have his way with me, nobody messed with me after that—a small victory on one hand, and a big, huge mistake on the other. Because of bad behavior and violence, I got sent to Sierra Leone to do two years of hard-core time.

Of course, I was scared. I had heard so many horror stories about that prison. How the majority of the men there had murdered someone and were either on death row or imprisoned for life. Moreover, that there were more killings and rapes inside of

Sierra Leone than on the streets of New Orleans. But once again, fate would have it that I would end up on the same tier with my mother, Pandora, who was already running the joint by the time I arrived.

She was the prison's den mother who took care of everyone, and in return they gave her due respect. If you needed a special favor, Pandora could make it happen. She even helped with shuffling drugs in and out of prison. The power that Pandora had acquired in such a short period of time was unbelievable, but when you're well connected on the street, it pays off behind bars. She had to cut a few people in the process, leaving her victory mark behind as a warning to other inmates not to take her looks as a sign of weakness.

Yes, Pandora was a flaming, full-blown drag queen, but she could be as brutal and cutthroat as any hard-core criminal. But that's how you had to be in prison: Show your strength or risk being hunted down and killed like an animal.

As tough as Pandora was on the outside, I knew a softer and more loving side to her, too. Pandora was the type of person who would give you the clothes off her back if you needed them. Just so loyal and protective of me. Nothing about our friendship had changed either. Inside the joint she looked out for me as if we were back at home running the club scene at Club Circus.

First day on the tier, Pandora sent word out that I was her daughter in training and that no one was to ever lay a hand on me or she would kill them. And she meant it, too. So no one bothered me at all. Now, that brings me to where I've been trying to get to this whole time—to me and Johnny. Pandora was the one who first introduced the two of us.

You see, one of the duties of the den mother was to take care of the inmates' personal needs as well. She would braid their hair for five dollars, which was really a nice deal. On the outside, it might have cost almost forty dollars to get your hair braided by someone. Johnny was one of her clients.

Honey, let me take my time with this, because I don't wanna mess it up when I describe to you how fine and off-the-hook Johnny was. Picture this: a tall, chocolate specimen, six-four to be exact; lean, muscled arms with tattoos; long legs; a wide, solid chest; a nice, gorgeous ass; and a set of perfect white teeth. And he had the nerve to have dimples, honey. Being gay and having been around lots of fine men in my life, I thought I had seen them all. However, I ain't met a nigga yet who could touch the likes of Johnny Lomack. He was sexy, sexy, sexy. I can't even think of any other words to describe him. And I loved Johnny from the very first day we met.

"So, Pandora tells me that you went to college," I recall him saying, and looking at me straight in the eyes with an intense stare. Johnny was a very serious person, and it came across in the way he would look at you. Behind those dark brown eyes of his was a man holding back a lot of pain. Just by looking into Johnny's eyes, I knew that boy had been through something traumatic in his life. He rarely ever smiled—just a dark and gloomy figure.

"Yes, this is one of my smart daughters who done been to college and everything," Pandora said. Me, her, and Johnny were in the yard having a smoke during one of our few break times at Sierra Leone. "That's why I thought y'all should meet."

The sun was beaming down over us, and Johnny gave me one good lookover. I could tell he was sizing me up. He didn't trust many people, and I guess he was trying to figure out where I was coming from.

"What the fuck you looking at?" I asked. It didn't take Johnny long to figure out that I was spicy and rough around the edges, just like my mother, Pandora. "You see something you like?"

"Nah, I don't get down like that," Johnny said. He meant it, too. Pandora had already filled me in on who was down and who wasn't at Sierra Leone, but I was testing him just to make sure. You know, I was having some fun with him, but I didn't mean any harm by it. I wasn't one of those children who try to turn straight dudes into being gay. As far as I was concerned, if you're down, then we can float. If you're not, then there's the door.

Besides, the last thing I wanted was to get myself involved with some confused, down-low nigga who couldn't decide on any given day if he wanted meat or fish for an entrée. Been there and had done that, honey. Those type of niggas break your heart, and I had run across my fair share of noncommittal men who dibbed and dabbed on both sides of the fence.

"I don't fuck around with dudes," he went on, blowing circles of smoke out of his mouth. Johnny was rough, but not thuggish. I picked up on the fact that he was a bad boy who had come from a good family. His intelligent accent often gave him away.

At times, Johnny spoke like a man who was in charge of a Fortune 500 business, and sometimes like he was just a regular nigga off the block. He for damn sure had hopes and dreams that stretched far beyond prison walls.

"I never said you did," I said, looking away for a moment. Johnny's gaze was so intense that it made me nervous. "So let me guess. You're interested in my brain and not my body?"

"Actually, I am," Johnny said. He took me completely by surprise, but not Pandora. The two of them had set this meeting up for a reason.

"You know Johnny's enrolled in GED classes up here," said

Pandora. She smashed a cigarette underneath her shoe like it was her worst enemy. "I told him how you was Ms. Math Whiz extraordinaire."

"I don't know about all that," I said. "A girl like me ain't cracked a book open in quite some time."

"What's the word? You think you can help out a nigga or what?" asked Johnny. He was serious as a heart attack. "I have English down pat, but I can't figure out math for a damn thing."

"So, you're really serious about this?" I was definitely surprised and taken aback by his determination.

Like Johnny, though, you had some smart dudes up there on the plantation who wanted to do something positive with their lives but felt trapped. Men who could have been good husbands and fathers—doctors, strong businessmen, preachers, and lawyers. But the system now had them, and most of these dudes were going to end up being nothing but a prisoner for life, which was the saddest thing to see.

"I wanna make my moms proud," Johnny said. I found him to not only be a determined individual, but extremely charming—two qualities that I like in a man. From that moment on, he had me in more ways than I could say.

I started tutoring Johnny in math right away, which was kind of cute, honey—spending all of that time with Johnny and helping him make a dream of his come true. If nothing else, it sure brought us closer together. We quickly became friends. Johnny didn't have a problem with me being gay either, but he always made it clear that he wasn't into "any shit like that." He once broke a dude's nose for coming on to him in the shower, so I wasn't about to take any chances with him.

Besides, Johnny was in love with Tonya, and he talked about her all the time. He even had a tattoo of her name on his arm, so you know that nigga was crazy about Ms. Girl. I didn't put two and two together until much later that Tonya and Booty were one and the same person—the slut from Club Circus who was fucking around with Rico.

But it wouldn't have mattered anyway, because to Johnny, Tonya was the love of his life, so he thought. It was the most devastating thing to hear how she broke his heart. I wasn't there with him in prison at the time of their breakup, but Pandora had filled me in on all the details.

When Tonya stopped coming to see him and writing letters, Johnny became so depressed that he lost weight and got so skinny. That boy really went through something over Ms. Girl. Johnny suddenly didn't wanna do anything but grieve. He stopped speaking to everyone and became extremely violent. Johnny ended up in the hole, a dark box they put you in for days, with little food and water. He went to the hole just about every other week. Pandora said that the rage behind Johnny's eyes was a serious matter. To tell you the truth, I don't know how it happened or what changed him, but after one of his visits to the hole, Johnny came back a totally different person, which was right around the time I came into the picture.

When he got out of the hole, Johnny was on a quest for knowledge. I would see him reading book after book and studying his ass off. That boy really wanted to better his life, and I enjoyed hanging around him and feeding off his energy. He was a genius with English and science, but he couldn't pass the math section of the GED for nothing in the world. But it didn't matter to the other inmates whether he had a GED or not. Johnny just made everybody up there at Sierra Leone feel special. You know, like we could accomplish anything that we set our minds to. By learning the law and through reading books, Johnny helped all of us take some kind of control and responsibility over our lives.

He started talking to inmates on the plantation about their crimes and discovered that the law had been discriminating against us. I'm talking about black men, honey. Because many of us didn't have the money or the means to seek good legal counsel, they were locking our asses up and throwing away the key without proper justification.

Johnny researched everything from misdemeanors to the death penalty, and it was soon revealed that most of those dudes up there at Sierra Leone didn't even belong there. Moreover, most of the inmates on the plantation were given longer sentences than the law actually allotted for. Honey, when some of them dudes heard about that shit, they wanted Johnny to represent them. You know, become their lawyer. Johnny didn't have a law degree, but he didn't need one. Those inmates trusted and believed in him, and that was inspiration enough for Johnny to do a good job.

He picked three dudes to work with who he felt had been dealt the worst hand out of everybody. The idea was to help those three and then see what would come of it. If he won an appeal for three, there was no telling what he could do for the rest of us. Therefore, Johnny started reading up on every last one of those dudes' cases and writing appeal letters to the powers that be on their behalf. Once Johnny knew the legal terminology and the law inside out, he could speak their language in order to make things happen.

Most of the time, Johnny's hard work was for nothing, because nobody was really trying to take a bunch of prisoners seriously. But every once in a while, he would receive a letter indicating that his request for an appeal was being strongly considered, which would end up being nothing more than another letdown. It was hard cracking the law and getting those judges and lawyers to change their minds. No matter how good your behavior was in prison or what level of education you obtained, you were gonna always be a criminal in their eyes, and that was just the harsh reality of the situation.

But Johnny was a fighter, and that's what I loved about him. He was a real straight-up nigga, honey, who wasn't about to let anyone push him around. The more they said no, the more Johnny wrote letters. Now, the way I got involved in this legal business was when Johnny started trying to get an appeal on Pandora's case, which I had firsthand knowledge of, since I was at the scene of the crime.

Before long, you should have seen us—me and Johnny inside of the prison library doing research, studying, and making our stay on the plantation count for something. Although we never obtained an appeal for anybody while I was still an inmate, the time spent was worthwhile. Me and Johnny would meet up and spend hours upon hours together inside that library, so you could imagine, being in such close proximity with each other, something was bound to happen between us. The attraction had been building for months.

"Man, you would not believe this!" Johnny had read something very interesting in one of those law books and he just couldn't contain himself. I sat across the table in a chair opposite him. "Don't you know that more death penalties have occurred in the South than in the North?"

"You don't say." I smiled at him. Johnny was so hot and appealing to me when he displayed his knowledge of the law. "Do tell me more."

"It says so right here." He pointed directly at the page. "That not only are there more death penalties in the South, but that most of the ones handed down have been for a black man killing a white person. Now, you tell me that shit ain't discrimination when they got more black-on-black crimes occurring every day of the damn week?"

"So, what are you saying, hon?" I asked. "That they should be killing more black men up in this bitch?"

I loved debating Johnny and seeing him get all worked up and heated. It was so cute and sweet how his eyes would flare up with passion and he would start stumbling over his words and trying to get his point across.

"Nah, you know I ain't saying some shit like that," Johnny said. "But I'm just trying to show you how some of these white folks think."

"Here we go again." I shook my head. Johnny often talked about white people being prejudiced toward blacks, but he sometimes could be the most racist of them all. "Blaming white folks for all of our troubles. They ain't the ones pushing drugs in our neighborhoods to our own people or neglecting our children. We're destroying each other all by ourselves."

"And there you go," he said. "Not thinking beyond the big picture."

"Fuck you, nigga," I said tartly. Me and Johnny had our own special way of speaking to each other, so he wasn't turned off by my sharp tongue. "I got my motherfucking high school diploma."

"Okay." Johnny smiled. I had won round one. "You got me.

But anyway, this is some serious shit I just read. If this is true, don't you realize what's going on?"

"I'm sure you're going to tell me," I said. "So go right ahead."

"That what we're seeing down here in the South is just another form of lynching, man," Johnny said. "They lynching our asses on the sly. Think about it."

"You're really tripping now," I said. "Ain't nobody being lynched around here."

"Look at it this way then," he said. "If they're killing black dudes for murdering white people more than they do it the other way around, then somebody out there thinks that a white person's life is more valuable than a black one's."

"Okay," I said. "You got a point there, but you know I don't believe nothing I don't read for myself, honey."

"Here it is, right there." Johnny walked around to my side of the table and pushed the law book in front of me. "Take a look at it for yourself."

"Okay, but could you please give me some space, hon." I couldn't get too close to Johnny without becoming nervous and getting excited—emotions that I wasn't even trying to feel for any man at that present moment. Don't ask me why. But when I landed my ass in prison, I wasn't feeling nothing sexual. It was strange, but my body just shut down, and a girl simply wasn't feeling any sex, honey.

Now don't get me wrong. They had some fine motherfuckers up there on the plantation who turned my pages quite a bit. But like I said, I just wasn't trying to get into anything too heavy or deep. Yeah, I'm sure a lot of it had to do with my issues of being hurt by other dudes.

Isn't that what keeps all of us connected to our fears and

from taking chances in life? Fucked-up shit that we've been through in our past?

Each gay relationship that I had ever tried to cultivate began and ended in the exact same manner. The encounter would start off with great conversation and a strong connection that would lead to hot sex for about three months. By the fourth month, things would start to unravel. I would discover that the deep relationship was based on nothing more than sex. The fleeting passion ended any hope of a serious romance, and a girl was simply tired of getting her heart broken. A lot of these men just weren't into chivalry and romance anymore.

Whatever the case, I had an animalistic attraction for Johnny that scared the hell out of me, and that I was not trying to let out of the cage.

"So, what do you think, nigga? Was I right?" asked Johnny. He had a seductive look in his eyes, which I avoided. Johnny once told me that he was straight, and I had believed him. Like I said earlier, I wasn't into trying to turn somebody gay. Hell, I was too fabulous, honey, to be chasing behind a nigga, anyway. "Let them motherfuckers chase you," Pandora would often say to me.

"You think I'm gon' bite you or something?" Johnny had a nervous but serious grin on his face, like a child with his hand in the cookie jar. The chemistry was unbelievable between us.

"I see you have jokes today." I shifted his attention back toward the book and off of me. "Now, show me what you were talking about."

"It's right here in the second paragraph." Johnny pointed toward the page and brushed his hand up against my arm so gently that if I wasn't paying close attention, it was something I would have missed. His hand felt warm and tingly.

"And there's some much more interesting stuff on page twenty-two that might actually help us with Pandora's appeal." He leaned over my shoulder, and I could suddenly feel his hot breath on the back of my neck, which made the hairs on my body stand up.

"Okay. That's a wrap for today." I jumped up from the table. Honey, I couldn't stand the heat any longer, so it was time for mama to get her ass out of the kitchen.

Besides, Johnny was my friend, and I wasn't supposed to be having those kind of sexual feelings toward him, anyway. Chile, you would not believe what freaky gutter thoughts I had going on inside my head. If I had my way, Johnny was already butter-ball naked and fucking me up against the table, old-school style. Honey, he was fucking me up against the table and knocking them law books on the floor with one leg of mine on the table and the other one somewhere on the bookshelf.

"What's wrong?" Johnny grabbed hold of my wrist before I could even make it out the door. Once again his eyes told me exactly how he felt, and I was scared of what I saw. "Don't run from me."

Those four simple but powerful words changed everything for us that day in the library. I stopped running from him, and something magical happened between me and Johnny on the plantation. We fell in love. And what started with us in that library over textbooks and research didn't end there.

When Johnny finally came home from prison was when the fire really started to heat up between us. And nobody, not even Ms. Girl, could put out the raging flames.

3

Johnny

I know there ain't–I mean isn't–any easy way to get into what went down, but I have to jump right into it head-on. First thing I would like to say, though, is that there's definitely three sides to this story. I'm just hoping you hear me out and don't pass judgment until you heard it all. Man, this shit is so much fucking harder than I initially thought, 'cause a nigga like me isn't used to opening up and expressing my true feelings to everyone.

I loved Tonya with all of my heart and thought we would be together forever. That girl was so fucking special to me–and still is–so all of this gossip about how I messed her over with some dude is nothing more than a bunch of talk and hearsay by some nosy motherfuckers who don't know a damn thing about me. But I'll tell you straight out that this ain't no down-low shit about how some nigga left his girl for a fag, 'cause what happened between me, Tonya, and James wasn't as cut-and-dried as that melodrama bullshit made for shows like *Jerry Springer*. This was a real-life situation, with people's feelings and emotions caught up in the mix, so you can't just break matters of the heart down to simple arithmetic when it's on the level of college algebra.

Even though high school seems so long ago, this all started when I was the star running back of my high school football team, the Higgins Wildcats. My record was unbelievable. I was averaging one hundred yards and running six touchdowns per game, so fast and unstoppable I became known as "T-Mack." Yeah, boy, I was built like a motherfucking truck, and strong. Nobody could catch my black ass.

Moreover, I had every college out there wanting me, and everyone in the city of New Orleans knowing Johnny Lomack from that dirty Nine. No doubt, I was on top of the world, but with that kind of attention often came a whole lot of trouble.

Man, niggas be hating and shit. They smile in your face, but at the same time they're trying to figure out ways to bring you down. Nothing I couldn't handle, though, 'cause I know there is always gonna be crabs in the barrel. The biggest problem I had was with all the women. I had beaucoup honies and was getting more ass than I could imagine.

There was Lisa, the hottest and most popular girl at Higgins High, who I boned on the regular; Tina, the captain of the cheerleading squad, who I fucked when I couldn't find Lisa; this li'l hottie Helene, who got off on sucking dick, and finally Stacey, a quiet, churchgoing type who I was trying my hardest to break in, but she wasn't going for it. Now, Tonya wasn't even in the picture as of yet, but I had my eyes on that piece of sexy booty, too.

But to tell you the truth, man, I was screwing one hottie after another, 'cause I was trying to prevent something inside of me from coming out into the open. Fucking a lot of women was my way of convincing myself that I wasn't gay or didn't have these feelings for dudes. There you have it. Johnny, Mr. Ladies' Man himself, was checking out other niggas on the sly. It still feels funny to admit that to anyone.

It wasn't something I would ever have acted upon. Just a part of me, like a person's hands and feet. Sometimes the desire to be with other dudes got so strong that it even scared me. Those would be the worst days, 'cause the craving would get so profound that I would have to go and release myself.

I would lock myself in the bedroom in the dark. I would lock myself in and beat my meat until I was bone-dry and couldn't even feel myself nutting any longer. You tell me that shit ain't wild. Here my pops–who's a preacher, mind you–his bedroom was only two doors down from mine, and I'm inside my bedroom jerking off with the lights out. You damn right I felt like a freak, 'cause I thought that shit wasn't normal.

Being raised in a strict Christian home, I had been taught that homosexuality was sinful–the worst sin out there–and I didn't wanna do something that was like a direct slap in the face of God. When you have these gay feelings inside of you, it's a constant struggle to do what everyone else thinks is the right and moral thing to do, especially if you have religion down in your blood the way I did.

Pops had no mercy when it came to that gay shit. When he preached on the subject of homosexuality, I saw a fire in his eyes that was just downright passionate. Pops instilled in me–and all of his sons, for that matter–that men were supposed to act like and conduct themselves as men. None of that sissy bullshit of crying and hanging on Moms's skirt like a li'l soft pussy.

That's why I couldn't understand how these feelings grew inside of me. I hadn't been molested or raped or anything twisted like that. I was the son of a preacher, for God's sake, although

I must admit that I was a bad motherfucker back then. Such a knucklehead, in fact, that I was labeled the black sheep of the family.

I was the youngest out of three boys, and the one who caused Moms and Pops the most worries. My ass stayed in hot water. I once got kicked out of school for smoking weed in the bathroom, and was caught fucking my second cousin, Rana, in our upstairs bedroom. And it was at our family reunion picnic, so you know that shit didn't go over well. Now, my brothers Ronnie and Carl weren't perfect, but them niggas just never got caught in the act. I guess you could say I was the stupid one.

I'm real proud of them, though. Carl ran track for LSU, and Ronnie was a star quarterback at USC. Athletics for damn sure run in the family. During their high school years, Pops played football, and Moms ran track. No doubt, we aren't like most of these black families out here today. Our family's real tight. No matter what happened, I knew one thing for sure–that I could always count on Moms, Pops, Ronnie, and Carl being there for me.

Moreover, Pops wasn't one of those dudes who made babies and left 'em. He put that time in with us, worked hard, and took care of his family like a man's supposed to do. The only problem me and Pops had–he was forever trying to run my life. He wouldn't let me do me. Pops stayed on my ass about every li'l thing.

When I was a freshman in high school, I wanted to join the drama club, but Pops didn't like that idea. He wanted me to play football, like he had done in high school, but what I truly wanted to do was try my hand at acting.

Don't laugh, man, but that shit was true. I thought I could be the next Jamie Foxx or Will Smith. Those niggas were doing it big and handling their business out there in Hollywood. Pops fought me tooth and nail about joining that drama club. He thought acting was for sissies—and those were his exact words.

I think Pops always knew that something was different about me from my other brothers, and that's why he drove me so fucking hard. Didn't want one of his sons to turn out gay or something. But no matter how hard Pops pushed me to play ball, I defied him. If he told me to go left, I went right. Instead of playing by his rules and following God, I turned to the streets and hung out with an older cuz of mine, Kojack, which drove Pops even crazier.

Kojack was your basic hood nigga with gold teeth, baggy pants hanging off his ass, and dreams of making it rich. He slung drugs from the cut and made a pretty good living at it, too. I thought he was so gangster, 'cause Kojack ran the block, and niggas gave him his respect. Nobody crossed him either, 'cause their asses would get smoked if they did.

Damn right. Kojack had killed a couple of niggas out there in the streets. Like I said, he was slinging drugs, and in that type of business, you have to be ruthless. Kojack even had me making runs for him. You know, selling dope, and I thought I was so cool, but it was just another cover-up. Being on the block was another way for me to prove my manhood and squash any ideas of me being a sissy. But the truth was, my life had been easy compared to the one Kojack had.

My cuz didn't grow up with his moms or pops. Aunt Tina, Pops's youngest sister, died of breast cancer when Kojack and his sister, Nettie, were still kids. After Aunt Tina died, their pops, who was a small-time drug dealer in his own right, just took off. The kinfolks said he couldn't handle the pressure of Aunt Tina's death. As a result, Kojack and Nettie were raised up with me, Ronnie, and Carl. Although Moms and Pops did everything in their power to make Kojack and Nettie feel like part of our family, he never did. Instead of leaning on his peeps for support, Kojack turned to the streets and became well known for it.

As for me, I thought it was so cool how my cuz turned things around in his life and made a way out there in those streets despite such a fucked-up childhood. He was my hero. I respected that dude so much that after a while I wanted to be just like him—but not if my parents had anything to say about it. Moms and Pops did everything from praying over me with holy water to sending my ass to counseling two and three times a week. But none of that shit worked. The issues I had ran way too deep, and no amount of counseling was going to change me.

When Kojack got shot and ended up in Charity Hospital fighting for his life, I woke up. I came off the block and got out of the game real quick, reminding me of that story of the prodigal son, that dude in the Bible. Moms and Pops got their son back, and I started focusing more on playing ball than running the streets.

Even though Kojack survived the shooting, I wasn't going back on the block with him. You couldn't get me to go out there in those streets and risk ending up in the same situation as Kojack. Man, I was scared of dying, and I knew there had to be a better way than thugging. If I was going to make it out of the hood, it was not going to be by selling drugs or rapping. Football had always come easy to me, and I was determined to be the best player out there. Since I had wasted my first year of high school running the streets with Kojack, I had a lot of making up to do. But it didn't take me long.

By the time junior year rolled around, I was at the top of my

game. Everyone knew my name, and I was on my way to doing big things. This was the same year I met Tonya and fell in
love with her.

Man, I don't know what more I can say about this girl. She
was a strong-ass sistah who had been through so much in her
life, losing her brother to violence and growing up without her
pops around. But Tonya never allowed any of that shit to break
her spirit. She was determined to be something in life, and not
let the hood hold her back from her dreams.

Moreover, what I liked about Tonya was that she shared in
my dreams of making it as a football star. Most women don't
get off on sports, but Tonya was different. She would come and
watch me practice on the field and would cheer me on even
when I made dumb-ass mistakes out there. She never missed a
game. And when the hard work was over and the scores had
been totaled, she gave me some much-needed loving and good
cooking. That girl knew she could cook her ass off.

Yeah, Tonya could fuck, too. She had some juicy sweetness
that made my dick sing love songs. Even though I had that feeling inside of me for dudes, there was nothing better than getting inside some good pussy. I enjoyed making love to a woman
and feeling her soft and sexy body up against mine. Tonya was
my baby girl, and I got her name tattooed on my right arm, so
you know a nigga was basically hooked.

No sooner had me and Tonya gotten thick, I found out that
her ex-boyfriend Greg was trying to come back into the picture.
You know how some niggas are. They see you got a good thing
going on, and they want to come in and try to mess that shit
up. Greg was that type of dude, but I pumped his brakes real
quick. Let that nigga know who was the boss.

Dude was on some crazy bullshit and started stalking Tonya.

At first I tried to keep my cool and fall back on what my pops taught me: When another man do you wrong, you supposed to turn the other cheek and let God fight your battles. "Vengeance is mine, saith the Lord," Pops would tell me and my brothers when we got into an altercation with other dudes and wanted to fight. But you already know I was an unruly type li'l nigga with a strong mind of my own.

Man, I don't know what was wrong with me sometimes. It was like I was always doing stupid shit to get my ass into serious trouble. When I got into a heated situation, I would lose all control. Moms often said that my bad temper would be my downfall. And, man, was she ever right.

When that dude Greg tried to manhandle Tonya one night, I rode up on his ass like the Hulk and handled my business. He was trying to force her inside of his car, and Tonya was screaming and hollering. Her blouse was torn. You know, it just didn't look right, so we started fighting and throwing blows one after another until Greg slipped on a bottle or something and landed headfirst on the pavement. He passed out cold and had to be rushed to the hospital. Part of me was scared, 'cause I thought the dude was dead. You know, I had never killed anybody; but another side of me was thinking that nigga got what he deserved. From how it looked to me, he was trying to rape Tonya, and my big black dick was the only dick that was going up inside of her.

They got me on charges of attempted murder when that shit was an accident. I got sent upstate to the pen at Sierra Leone to do hard time, working in somebody's fields like a damn slave instead of playing football at a top college. But the most fucked-up part about the situation was that my own pops got on the stand and basically testified against me. You heard me right, man. When my lawyer called Pops to testify on my behalf, that dude got up there and sold my ass out. Told them motherfucking people I needed to be taught some kind of lesson.

How was sending me to the pen for something that was an accident gone teach me anything?

Man, of course, that shit hurt and went deep into my chest like a sharp razor blade. Since Pops was a preacher, he was the one person who could have helped me beat those charges. I'll never forget how he betrayed me as long as I live. What Pops did to me was almost worse than being sentenced to the pen for five years. Nothing beats doing time. It was torture how they treated a nigga up there at Sierra Leone—or rather, what we called the fucking "plantation." They worked you from sunup to sundown picking vegetables and crops in that hot-ass fucking heat for forty cents an hour. Now, you tell me that shit ain't slave labor.

When I first got there, the only thing that kept me going was knowing that me and Tonya would be back together one day. Doing time for the woman I loved was like a badge of honor. I gotta say, the first year everything went smoothly, too. Me and Tonya wrote love letters and talked on the phone every free moment we had. She even took that three-hour bus ride, along with Moms, to come and see me from time to time.

Pops never once came, which was fine by me, 'cause after what that dude did, I for damn sure didn't wanna see his face. He wrote letters and sent prayers to me through Moms, but it still wasn't enough to erase that hate I had developed inside of my heart for him. The way I saw it, it was gonna take a whole lot of years for me to get over what happened, if I ever could get over it. Family loyalty wasn't worth shit to me anymore. At the time, the only love I thought I could count on was my girl's.

So, you could imagine how a nigga felt when I eventually lost that, too.

Second year rolled around and that girl started tripping. Tonya stopped writing and visiting me. It seemed like mother-fuckers were turning their backs and betraying me all over the damn place.

Of course, I was devastated, man. Tonya's love was something I had depended on while I was inside that hellhole, and now it was taken away from me without warning. I wanted to hurt somebody for real—that's just how mad I was. When I found out from my homies on the street that Tonya left me for some rich nigga, I went completely ballistic. I didn't care about nothing anymore and became the most violent nigga up there at Sierra Leone. My ass stayed in trouble.

The one incident that stands out in my mind was jumping a gay dude in the shower. I jumped his ass for looking at my butt the wrong way. Inside the joint, you always had niggas checking you out, and I wasn't about to let some dude run up inside of me like a bitch. So, I kicked his ass, and I didn't feel any remorse about it either. You gotta let them niggas in the pen know that you ain't no weak-ass punk motherfucker.

Man, fuck what you heard: The hardest niggas up in there be screwing around with one another, acting like husbands and wives when they got women and children back at home in the hood. You'd be surprised how many of them niggas get down with one another. It's like the most normal shit in the world, just nobody talks about it in the open daylight. All the fucking and screwing and sucking goes down at night. That prison jones will mess with your head inside the pen if you're not real careful.

I would be inside my cell trying to sleep and would hear

dudes moaning and groaning and screaming out in the middle of the night like bitches in heat. They be screaming and mas-turbating—the entire tier full of niggas—and I'd hold on to fleet-ing memories of Tonya and try not to give in to the jones.

Don't get me wrong. I had that feeling inside of me for dudes, but I was still denying that shit. My manhood was the only thing left of me that was honorable, and I would have done anything to hold on to it. I thought being gay meant you weren't a man. Besides, what them niggas were doing up in there was disgusting to me. The sad part about it was them nig-gas wake up the next morning and walk around the pen with their chests sticking out like the night before they weren't shov-ing or getting shoved with a fat piece of dick inside their ass.

Not me, man. I wasn't going for that crap. Whatever attrac-tion I had for dudes, I kept that shit under tight wraps. The pen was the last place you wanted a nigga to think you were soft. They would attack your ass like a pack of wolves.

So, I broke that dude's nose and got my ass sent to the hole—the one area in the pen you don't wanna be when you got issues and demons eating away at your flesh. The hole is this small rectangular room that's completely dark and cut off from everything and everyone. It's like hell on earth, and I was so fucking scared, man. I was scared and hungry. They barely feed your ass when you down in the hole, too. After a while I could feel myself getting weaker and weaker by the day, to the point where I started hallucinating down there and going into con-vulsions like a seizure patient. I was catching seizures and see-ing images of Tonya and that rich dude inside my head—both of them laughing, pointing, and making fun of my ass.

No doubt I was cracking up, and sometimes the only way to stop from going completely mad was to fall asleep, but that was when the nightmares would creep in and disturb my rest. It was awful, man. Just really awful how those nightmares seemed so fucking real to me. They would always start and end the exact same way, too. I'm five years old, 'cause I see pictures of *Star Wars* on the walls and ceiling. I loved everything about *Star Wars* when I was that age.

Anyway, I'm lying there in my bed and sleeping in the pitch-black when someone snatches me out of my bed. Someone snatches my li'l ass and drags me out of the room kicking and fighting. I'm carried off to some unknown place and the next thing I know I'm in church with the face of Jesus staring down at me. How bizarre was that?

At first I didn't know what to make of any of this, but then I figured that God must have been trying to tell me something important about the way I had been living my life. He wanted me to get my act together.

All I can say is that the last time I got out of that hole, I was a changed man and determined to find a way to keep that anger inside of me from becoming rotten and destructive. I had to channel all that negative stuff into something more positive before it destroyed me. Huh, that brings me to James Santiago. He was one of the most positive dudes up there at Sierra Leone, so we were bound to run into each other eventually.

It just so happened that this drag queen, Pandora, who was like the pen's den mother, knew James from their days on the streets. Nobody could touch or come between the strong bond they had, and no one would have even tried either. We all respected our den mother, 'cause she took care of a nigga and made sure our stay up in the pen was a comfortable one.

Of course, I never thought in my wildest dreams that I would look to a gay dude to take care of anything for me. When you're in the pen, though, all the rules change. What you did on the outside doesn't apply on the inside. You become close friends with the people you least expect to bond with.

Pandora introduced me and James, and the two of us hit it off like we had known each other for years. I found James to be a cool, straightforward li'l motherfucker. He had no problem telling you exactly what was on his mind, and I liked that strength I peeped inside of him. Being around James and Pandora for damn sure changed my views about gay dudes.

I often took their feminine ways as a sign of weakness, but I was wrong. Gay dudes were some strong-ass people who went through a lot of shit being open about themselves. You think on the streets they call them all kinds of cruel names—inside the pen, they were called even worse. Those same hard-core niggas I was telling you about earlier who liked to fuck gay dudes when nobody was looking were some of the sickest, cruelest motherfuckers. They liked to fuck gay dudes on the sly, and at the same time beat the living daylights out of them for being who they were in the open.

Pandora and James were the exceptions to the rule, though. Nobody fucked with either of them, especially Pandora. During a fight in the yard, I once saw Pandora slit a dude's throat wide open without flinching a damn muscle. The den mother lived up to her name Razor. She would cut a motherfucker down to the ground and not shed a tear. Sometimes you had to be that way in order to get your respect in the pen. Pandora's rise to power was something else to witness up close. Hard-core niggas were terrified of dying at the hands of this drag queen, and that shit was real funny to see.

What struck me about James was how smart he was. I figured out right away that he didn't belong inside a place like

Sierra Leone. This dude had gone to college and could have easily been a professor at some high-society university. Growing up in the Ninth Ward, I was lucky to see a nigga finish middle school, let alone go to college. I thought James would make a good friend and be a positive dude to be around. That's it! I wasn't trying to fuck him or anything, at least not at first. Although Tonya had left a nigga bitter and tormented inside the pen, I still wasn't ready to test the waters with dudes. What I wanted from James was his knowledge and book sense. Basically, I was lying to myself. That nigga caught my eye from day one.

Before long, James started tutoring me in mathematics. When I got into trouble with the law, I had just started my senior year of high school. All I had to do was tighten up a few things in order to get my GED. One good thing I could say about Sierra Leone was that they offered niggas opportunities to educate themselves if they wanted to. If nothing else, it took a nigga out of the fields picking vegetables for forty cents an hour. Enrolling in the GED program instantly put me on another level from the other inmates. And I took full advantage of every one of them educational programs, 'cause I wanted to prove motherfuckers wrong who said that just 'cause I was a black man in the pen I wouldn't amount to anything. Man, I even started reading books on black history and our fucked-up legal system. It was amazing how much important information was out there in the world. Once I got that knowledge base, I started using what I knew to help other motherfuckers. I started helping inmates understand the law in order to help themselves out of a jam.

Most of them dudes were good people who had simply been dealt a bad hand in life, like our den mother, Pandora. Man, no matter what wrong shit she had done on the streets, she didn't deserve to be in the pen for life. Her case was a prime example of a failed judicial system that sometimes worked against poor people. As a result, I took a special interest in Pandora's case— me and James both—'cause she looked out for all of us in a special way. With me and James working so closely together, I couldn't help but find him interesting.

The more time I spent with James, the more I started to like the dude. He wasn't only a smart whiz kid, but just fun to be around. I would look forward to getting up every day, so we could spend our li'l special time together during recreation. In a short while, James had become more than just my tutor, but my friend, too. I could confide in him about personal shit.

Yeah, I told James all about Tonya and how she dumped me for some rapper with cheese. But you know what? James never said anything bad about Tonya. He wasn't that type of dude. All James was concerned about was making sure I was okay and that I was not about to turn into some fucking basket case. You just can't find those type of genuinely nice people in the world anymore. No doubt, I knew I had somebody special in my life, and I thanked God for him.

After a while, I admit that I was curious about James. I wanted to fuck around with him—that prison jones had taken a bite out of my ass for damn sure. I was finally ready to act upon those feelings I had been holding back for years. And it wasn't something I had to tell James, either. He said the passion and desire in my eyes told him everything he needed to know.

Cutting straight to the chase, me and James became lovers inside the pen. I know that shit must sound weird, given everything that's been said about Tonya, but I cared about that nigga. And I still do. After a while I just got tired of denying how I felt.

James was an attractive dude with a nice attitude. He never allowed his good looks to go to his head. The way I saw it, I was torturing myself for no reason.

Tonya was long gone and out of my life, so me and James weren't hurting anybody. We were two grown-ass men who were both consenting adults. I'm just gone be flat-out honest with myself: If it hadn't been for James coming into the picture when he did, I don't think I would have survived life inside the pen. That dude gave me hope and something to hold on to when I felt like the bottom had fallen out.

So, basically, I don't care what anybody thinks about what went down between us or how nasty it may have looked in their eyes for two dudes to be together sexually. 'Cause what I shared with James was just as real as anything else that I had with a woman. And not to belittle my love for Tonya, 'cause as you know, that was special, too. What me and James had, though, was on a totally different level. Gay love is an intense kind of love, 'cause for the most part you gotta keep it hidden from everyone else. And that's what makes it even more special. It's like being on another planet with no one else around to judge you or to say you're doing something wrong. I would have done anything to hold on to what we had and to keep the outside world from hurting us. No doubt, seeing James leave the plantation was one of the hardest days of my life.

We were in the prison shower—a spot reserved just for us, thanks to Pandora, who always made the impossible happen with the prison guards. She kept order in the place, and in return they allowed her a few favors.

Anyway, me and James were up in that joint saying a long good-bye, with our feelings and emotions wide open. James had done his stint and was leaving Sierra Leone at midnight–a fact I couldn't change or deny.

Of course, I was happy James was getting out, but I was going to miss him. If you don't learn anything else about me, you should know that I hated for someone to leave me. That shit drove me insane. When Tonya ran off with that rich dude I was devastated, but when James left me inside the pen all alone, there was this huge hole inside my heart.

"Man, I can't believe you leaving me," I said. James was leaning against the wall with a white towel wrapped around his slender waist. He was a tall, sexy dude with soft, tan skin and a curvy body so much like a woman's that sometimes I forgot he was actually a dude.

"I'm gon' miss you too, baby," James said. He had a light voice that he hardly ever raised beyond a whisper unless you pissed him off. James could be a loud mouth dude when he needed to, and sweet as a kitten at other times. "But I'll be waiting for you on the outside."

"Yeah, right," I said, looking at him straight in the eyes and being playful. "Two years from now, you probably be seeing some other nigga out there. Forget all about me."

The towel around James's waist suddenly fell to the floor, and he was standing before me naked. He leaned against the wall and placed a finger in his mouth like he was sucking on a lollipop–hinting to me that he wanted to suck on my knob, so I thought.

No doubt, James liked to play sex games with me, and I for damn sure enjoyed the ride. That nigga turned me out in ways I couldn't imagine in my freaky dreams, and showed me a whole new way of getting down. My dick was as hard as a damn rock sitting on a sunny beach, but what James wanted wasn't even about the dick. Sometimes he wanted to fuck non-stop, and at other times James just wanted to be held and caressed. This was one of those times.

"Tell me how much you love me," James said. He had suddenly gotten so serious and quiet on a nigga that it made me a li'l uncomfortable and nervous. It was the intense look in his eyes that showed me just how he felt about me. Although I cared about him, too, I knew I could never match the same level of emotion. The four-letter L-word wasn't something I could ever see myself saying to another dude. It was too weird and out-there for me.

Don't get me wrong: I had always known that James had deep feelings for me, but it was another thing to stare into somebody's eyes and see a gateway straight to their soul. Instead of telling him how much I loved him with words, I showed him with actions.

I held James close to me, and his head rested upon my shoulder. It was the best memory I had of us being together before all the rules of the game would change. The shit you did in the pen, you couldn't bring out with you on the streets without asking for trouble.

PART ONE

Dangerously in Love

4

Tonya

"Turn that shit up, baby!" Peaches's punk ass screamed loud enough to get everyone's attention inside the salon. Rico had a new hit song on the radio that was tearing up the Billboard charts, and Peaches knew our bitter history all too well and was simply being messy. I couldn't stand his wanna-be-a-real-woman ass, for real.

"That's my motherfucking song, girl," he said, all the while moving his butt up and down like he was shaking for dollars at a strip club. Most of the women inside Queen's Beauty Salon thought Peaches was funny, like a comedian on BET *Comic View*, but to me he was disgusting and forever saying shit out of his mouth that was just downright wrong and disrespectful to sistahs. The only reason I tolerated him and bit my tongue was because he was Tamika's first cousin, and she was my boss.

After things fell apart with Rico, a bitch still had to pay bills, so I started doing nails at the salon instead of going back to my old profession at Club Circus. Doing nails was an easy job where I could sit on my ass and look cute and not have to worry about a bunch of drunk-ass niggas touching and feeling all over my body. That was one part of the job I hated with a passion, and why I never wanted to go back to stripping.

Me and Tamika had known each other since middle school, so she had no problem with hiring me, although I had little or no experience doing nails. But I was a fast learner, and Tamika believed in me—one of the reasons why she was still my girl after all those years. Unlike some bitches out there who be hating on a light-skinned sistah, Tamika didn't have a jealous bone in her body toward me, and I loved her for loving me without strings attached.

"Okay, turn that music down and get your ass back to work," Tamika told Peaches as she styled a dark-skinned sistah's hair into a work of art. If you can't tell, I was so proud of my girl for all she had accomplished since we graduated from high school.

Tamika had gone to college, obtained both her business degree and hairdresser's license, and opened up shop in the old neighborhood when she could have easily taken her business uptown around middle-class folks. Tamika was a downtown sistah who may have been stuck-up at times, but loved being around her own people.

Moreover, she was also a member of Delta Kappa Zeta sorority, incorporated, and she was so goddamn proud of it. As a matter of fact, the salon was founded on the principles of Tamika's sorority—to uplift and inspire women of color. At every turn and corner of the place there was African masks, statues, and pictures of Nefertiti on the walls. The chairs was also decorated with kente cloth.

Delta Kappa Zeta was a strong sisterhood sorority that honored African American culture. That's why Tamika named the salon Queen's, because in her eyes all black women were royalty who deserved to be treated as such. If nothing else, Tamika was a good and positive person for me to be around, since I often had so much negative shit going on in my own personal life–but I ain't even trying to go there right now. After me and Rico broke up, I promised myself that I wouldn't let anything in the past hold me back, not even my own doubts and insecurities.

One of the things I regretted was not going to college myself, because me and Tamika shared just about everything in our friendship except the sorority. And honestly, sometimes I felt left out, but it was something I kept to myself. Tamika had been too good a friend over the years for me to be worrying her over some petty mess like that. Besides, she wasn't the type of person who allowed what she called "negative vibes" in her personal space or workplace. When she realized what Peaches was up to trying to dredge up my past dealings with Rico, she shut his ass down with a quickness. Of course, he was still showing off for the customers and being his usual outrageous self.

" 'Get down on it, hell, yeah! Get down on it.' " Peaches sang the tune to Rico's song, which was basically a rip-off from an old seventies tune by Kool and the Gang. But I wasn't that surprised to hear Rico had gone that route with his music, since P. Diddy was his role model–one of many things me and him had in common. We both thought Diddy was on point when it came to mixing old music with the new shit and then turning the tune into a world-class hit.

Anyway, the last thing I wanted to do was drag up old feelings and be reminiscing about that sellout. As far as I knew, Rico was still dating that white girl, which gave me yet another reason to dislike his ass–the first one being how he dumped me without warning just because I wouldn't give him what he wanted in bed. I know I told you part of it was because of my feelings for Johnny, but that wasn't all of it.

Rico was a whorish, freaky nigga who wanted me to service him with blow jobs as payback for allowing me into the business. Babee, I wasn't about to put my lips around that small-ass dick of his for the simple pleasure of kissing up to him.

There was this one girl in the business who was known as "Superhead" because she gave niggas good blow jobs. I would listen to Rico and his boys—fellow rappers, athletes, and movie stars—talk about this girl like a dog, and there was no way I was going out like that. Shit, I had some pride about myself for real. Yeah, I loved being a video girl and hanging out on the social scene, but not at any cost. I was Vivian Thibodaux's only daughter, and she didn't raise no slut, for real. When I went down on a nigga, it was because I wanted to. So, therefore, I tuned Rico and his hit song out of my head and focused completely on my client's fingernails.

"What color do you want, baby?" I asked my client. She was an older woman with some fucked-up hands and nails that definitely needed my attention right away. Ms. Gloria did housekeeping at the Holiday Inn, and she had rough hands to prove it.

"Give me red, sweetheart!" Ms. Gloria shouted over the music that was bouncing off the walls, but she didn't seem to mind at all. Ms. Gloria was a spunky woman for her early fifties, nodding her head to the music and really getting into the groove. I was just glad to hook her up and put a smile across her face. Doing nails wasn't simply about making money but doing a service for other people that made them feel good about themselves, too.

"I'm not going to tell you again, Peaches!" Tamika said, pointing a curling iron in his direction. "Turn it off. You know we don't mess with no wanna-be-down niggas who got a thing for white girls."

Tamika reached over and gave me a high five as Peaches lowered the volume on the CD player. His mission for the day had been accomplished. I knew it was coming, so I braced myself for the fallout.

"Why y'all hatin' on that boy?" asked Peaches with one hand on his hip. His tight pair of booty shorts showed his greasy dark-skinned legs. He was such a tired and broke-down drag queen with those long braids in his head that made him look more like a skinny, worn-out mop instead of the African queen he thought he was. The only reason Peaches took the job working in the salon was because of the name on the door. In his sick mind, he was the "queen" in Queen's Salon. And babee, you couldn't tell that troll he wasn't cute with his ugly ass.

Hell, yeah, I had issues with men dressing up like women and trying to be down with us. It just didn't make any damn sense to me why a dude would want to carry himself that way. Don't get me wrong: I didn't necessarily have problems with gay people, because it wasn't my place to judge anybody. The way I saw it, everyone has to answer to God for themselves. But what you do in your bedroom, let that shit stay in the bedroom. To me, Peaches simply went over the top dressing like a woman and putting his gayness all up in other people's faces.

"And no shade against you, Booty." He nodded at me.

Peaches may have had a hot tongue, but I didn't scare easily. For the record, I grew up in a house with two brothers and was every bit a tomboy, so I would fight a nigga straight up if I had to, for real.

"And there's none taken," I said, preparing Ms. Gloria's fingernails to be polished. First you had to soak and clean the fingernails, then remove the old polish before applying a fresh new coat. "Me and Rico been over and done with a long time.

It's not his music I have a problem with, but that white bitch he got on his arm."

"Here we go," Peaches said. This was the drama he was seeking all along, and we was about to give it to him. "Another angry black woman who can't deal with the fact that yet another black man don't want her. Maybe that should tell y'all angry heifers something."

"Fuck you," Latisha said. She had been pretty much quiet up to this point, braiding a client's hair in the back of the salon.

Latisha was another one of my girls from middle school who I could call a true friend for always being there for me during hard times. When Rico left me for that white girl, I went and stayed at Latisha's place for a couple of months before returning home to live with my mama.

"Ain't nobody bitter over shit," Latisha said. "These niggas just got it all wrong."

"Exactly," Tamika said. She had finished one client's head and started preparing for her next appointment. You see, Tamika was not only a smart businesswoman, but a hardworking stylist as well. Just about every sistah from the Fifth to the Ninth wards wanted her hair styled at Queen's. We kept a full house, so Tamika was definitely making that paper.

"Brothers need to wake up and smell the damn coffee," she said while setting up beauty supplies on the counter. "Black women have always stood by their asses since the beginning of time, and we always will. Let 'em keep on choosing white women over us. You see what happened to Kobe Bryant?"

"Got his ass played on national TV." I took the words right out of Tamika's mouth. Me and her was so close that we often finished each other's sentences. "And for what? All so he can have his li'l prized white blonde for one night. Shit, even his wife ain't a sistah, so you know I don't have any sympathy for that nigga."

"Like I said..." Peaches sat down and rested his sorry behind. "A bunch of angry black bitches."

"Okay, we ain't gon' have none of that in here," Tamika said. "I told you about using that word inside my shop."

"Calm down, Tamika," Peaches said. "Damn, y'all take this shit way too serious."

" 'Cause it is serious!" Latisha snapped. Black men dating white women always ends up causing way too heated a conversation for my taste.

"Black women have already been through too much shit," Latisha went on. She was a heavyset chocolate sistah with small Chinese-looking eyes who had also gone to college like Tamika, but dropped out in her second semester. After Latisha got pregnant with her son, Chris, she never went back.

When she started dating this Nation of Islam brother, Hakeem, I knew Latisha would become an Afrocentric and empowered sistah. From her beautiful dreadlocks to her long dresses, Latisha was a totally different person from the overweight girl who lacked confidence in herself in high school. It's so interesting to see how people change for the better over the years. Although Latisha still had a li'l weight on her, she was damn sure not shy or lacking in self-esteem. She stood up and represented for all the sistahs out there and set the record straight about black women and our history.

"As sistahs, we have had it hard," Latisha said, pulling long strands of dreadlocks out of her face. "First slavery, where our men was taken away from us, then prisons, which is just another form of slavery, and now we have to worry about our men choosing a white girl over us and slapping us in the damn face with it."

"Now, baby, I've been listening to y'all young girls in here." Ms. Gloria couldn't resist jumping in on the conversation. "And as hard as it is to see a white woman on the arm of a black man, you gotta let people choose for themselves who they want. Love don't have no color. It's for everybody."

"I hear what you saying, Ms. Gloria, and I respect you," I said. "But that still don't make it right. There's a whole new generation out there, and it's hard on a sistah, for real."

"See, that's the problem with too many black folks," Peaches cut me off. He was packing up his things to leave. He loved to get the shit started and then take off at the height of the drama. "They always bringing up the past shit about slavery. This is a whole new time and day. Ain't nobody worrying about that. We all need to be more color-blind."

"Now your ass just sound ignorant," Tamika said. "We'll start being color-blind when they stop treating us like second-class citizens, building jailhouses for our brothers and racial profiling and all that other shit."

"Tell 'em, girl," I said real proudly. Even Ms. Gloria was nodding her head in agreement. Latisha and Tamika was simply saying what was already inside our hearts and on the tips of our tongues. As black women, we could relate to being mistreated and abused by our own brothers.

"On that note"—Peaches grabbed his duffel bag and headed toward the door—"I'm out of here. I have a hot date with a sexy-ass Puerto Rican. Is that black enough for y'all angry bitches?"

"Get your ass out of here, boy." Tamika waved him off, shaking her head and laughing.

"That'll be twenty dollars, but you can give me fifteen," I said to Ms. Gloria. All that talk about sistahs sticking together got me into a generous and giving mood.

"Thank you, sweetheart." Ms. Gloria handed me a twenty. When I reached inside my wallet to get her change, a picture of my brother Ricky, in his army uniform, fell to the floor and reminded me of why my day had started off on the wrong foot in the first place. Here I thought I was being a bitch because of Rico and Peaches, but the two of them ain't had nothing to do with my foul attitude. The bad feeling inside my chest was a family thing between me and Mama.

What happened was, Mama was going through it because Ricky was being sent to Iraq to fight in what she called a "white man's war." Those were Mama's words, not mine. And she ain't never been inside anybody's college classroom either, but Mama knew just as much about politics as Hillary Clinton. And the way Mama talked about President Bush, you would have sworn she knew the man like one of them hoodlums on the street corner. She said the war in Iraq was about money, oil, and President Bush trying to finish what his father started during the Gulf War. Mama was even using big words like *conspiracy*, and *hypocrisy* to make her point stick like crazy glue.

When I woke up that morning, I found Mama inside her bedroom crying on the phone and talking to Ricky. She was trying to convince him not to go to Iraq. What you don't know is that Mama lost my daddy in the Gulf War, and she ain't never got over it. Poor Mama was so afraid that Ricky was heading down that same deadly road.

"Please don't go, son," she begged. I stood outside her bedroom door, peeping and listening in. Mama was still in her nightclothes and rollers. "I'm so afraid for you. I can't lose another son."

I couldn't hear what Ricky was saying on the other end of the phone, but it wasn't making Mama feel any better. Ricky was a strong, determined person with a mind of his own. He was the only one of Mama's children that was trying to make something out of hisself.

Don't misunderstand me: I had my dreams and all, but Ricky was really trying to make a difference in the world by representing his country in the war. He thought going into the army was his way out of the ghetto. But Mama saw the army only as a death sentence for our young black men and poor people. Whatever the case may be, I loved my brother and was so proud of him for following his heart, despite what Mama said. She was way too controlling, anyway.

"Who's that, your boyfriend?" asked Ms. Gloria. She was looking over my shoulder at Ricky's picture.

"Oh, no," I said, pushing the photograph back inside my wallet. "That's my brother."

"Who, Ricky?" asked Tamika. She'd had the biggest crush on my brother since we was li'l girls running around the hood.

"Yeah, Ricky, but look at you all in our conversation," I said, waving good-bye to Ms. Gloria. "See you in a couple of weeks."

"Don't act like you don't know how much I want that," said Tamika. " 'Cause your brother is too fine for his own good."

"Yes, he is," I said, cleaning off my counter and getting ready for my next customer. "But he don't want your fast, hot-mama ass."

"Whatever, girl," Tamika said. We was basically joking around and having fun with each other when that bitch Ebony walked in and changed the entire mood inside the salon. Me and her for damn sure didn't like each other, because of some

---

female drama that happened many years ago when I used to be a stripper at Club Circus.

Once upon a time she and Rico used to kick it, so the hate between us was over some nigga we both wasn't even with anymore. We even got into a fight outside the club one night over him, and this stripper who went by the name of Pussy Cat got killed trying to defend me. Although Ebony wasn't on the other end of the blade that killed Pussy Cat, I always blamed her for that girl's death, nonetheless. So, you damn right: I felt like me and Ebony was long overdue for a rematch. And the only reason I hadn't kicked her ass up to this point was because she and Tamika were sorority sisters, if you could believe that shit.

"Geeeeeee Phi," Ebony screamed. It was a call and response that her and Tamika gave every time they saw each other.

Of course, part of me was jealous of their friendship, but Tamika did everything she could to make sure we all got along. One time she invited us both to dinner, so we could actually sit down and work out our differences. But her plan didn't work. Me and Ebony both still hated each other way too much. I had my reasons, and little did I know, that bitch had her own, too.

"Phi Geeeeee." Tamika fell into Ebony's arms. I couldn't deny the two of them was close, so I kept my cool and minded my own business.

"What's up, soror?" Ebony asked. She was wearing dark sunglasses on a cloudy-ass day with not a peep of sunshine in the sky. Ebony was definitely wack, but this was strange even for her.

"Girl, what happened to you?" Tamika asked when Ebony took off the sunglasses. She had a dark ring around her right eye, like somebody had been using her face as a punching bag.

"Girl, nothing. I just had an accident." Every woman inside

the salon knew she was lying. Ebony was getting the beat down by her boyfriend at the time, Kojack, this ruthless gangster, drug-dealing nigga who just happened to be related to one of my exes. I'm talking about Johnny, but thank God the two of them was nothing alike. Kojack was dirty and low-down, a man who abused and mistreated women like the back of somebody's shoes on a muddy-ass rainy day.

"An accident?" asked Tamika with a frown on her face. "Is that nigga hitting on you?"

"Of course not, girl," Ebony said. She was obviously uncomfortable talking about her personal business in front of everyone. I almost felt sorry for her, but not really. Ebony thought she was too cute, anyway. Now some nigga was turning her beautiful face into something monstrous. "But stop it. You're embarrassing me."

"I'm just worried about you, soror," Tamika said. "But I'll leave it alone, if that's what you want me to do."

"Thank you," Ebony said. "Now can I please get a perm, because a sistah's hair is long overdue."

"Yo, Ebony." Kojack stuck his head inside the door. All the ladies inside the salon turned and looked directly at him. Boy, if the walls could talk, they would say just how much everybody hated his black ass. The way these women saw it, Kojack was a lowlife who was pushing drugs in his own community and destroying a lot of innocent people in the process. And for what? All so he could put money in his damn pockets.

"How long your ass gon' be?" he asked. Although he was a jerk, Kojack was a good-looking dark-skinned nigga with a nice build and a baldhead. And he could dress, too. Kojack wore nothing but designer clothes and always had on expensive gold jewelry.

"Give me about an hour," Ebony said. She was sitting down in Tamika's chair with a pitiful and scared look on her face. Ooh, I hated to see weak-ass women who couldn't stand up for themselves.

"I'll send the limo to pick you up," Kojack said. He loved boasting and putting up a front. You know, letting everybody know how much money he had, but I wasn't impressed. I knew Kojack's type all too well. Behind that shiny grille in his mouth and those nice clothes on his body was just an insecure and weak nigga who enjoyed putting women down to make himself feel better.

"Yo, Tonya," he said. "Can I holla at you outside?"

"What?" I asked him with attitude. I couldn't imagine what he wanted to talk to me about. "You're talking to me?"

"Yeah, I'm talking to you," he said. "I just wanna tell you something. So, can you please step outside?"

"What is this about?" I followed him out onto the street and waited for an answer. The last thing I wanted was for anyone to think the two of us was down with each other.

"I just wanted to tell you about Johnny," he said.

"What about Johnny?" I was cold and stiff, like frozen chicken.

"If you would cut the fucking attitude," he said, "I'll tell you."

"Okay, I'm listening." Although I was acting like a first-rate bitch, I was curious as hell to learn any information I could about Johnny. I had never gotten that boy out of my heart, no matter how many years had passed since he went away. "Now, what is this business about Johnny?"

"He's coming home tonight." Kojack's smile gave me the chills. I hated men with grilles in their mouth. That shit was downright ugly and scary, if you ask me. "My cuz getting out tonight, and I thought you might wanna know."

"Thanks for telling me." I tried to keep my cool and not show any reaction one way or another. But it was definitely a front. The truth was, my heart was beating out of my chest, and my mind was floating somewhere in the clouds. A picture of me and Johnny running on the lake during happier times flashed in my head. Back in the day, the Pontchartrain had been our favorite spot.

"I see I done put somethin' in your li'l mind," Kojack said. "I guess I know how to shut your ass up in the future."

"Whatever, nigga." I came out of my daydream and back to the present moment. "Don't give yourself too much credit."

"But give my man a call." Kojack opened the door to a white stretch limo and hopped inside. "I'm sure he'll love to hear from you."

I stood on the sidewalk for a hot minute and watched the limo disappear up the street. It started to rain. And my next client was running her ass way behind. But it was all good. Her tardiness only gave me some extra time to fantasize about Johnny. My pussy got wet as the rain.

5

James

"You better work that runway!" When I heard the lyrics to Ru-Paul's "Supermodel" rise out of the speakers, that was all I needed in order for me to work those children, honey. I hit the tip of the runway and threw both of my arms into the air like a dream girl on Broadway. There was a bright spotlight on me. "You better work (cover girl) ... Do your thing on the runway!"

Besides the spotlight, the rest of the club was in darkness, and I couldn't see a damn thing. But I didn't need to, because I was in full control. As smoke rose out of the stage like fog rising over an ocean of water, I took off down the runway like a seductive cat, gliding and turning and spinning in step to the beat until it felt as if I was floating on thin air. Knowing that I was working the children with my beauty and poise, style and grace was intoxicating. You see, I was just as legendary as Ru-Paul's song, and the children had come from near and far to see what I called my "Wonder Woman circus of gay fun."

Yes, indeed, it was a well-known fact. On Wednesday nights at Club Circus, James Santiago gave the children drag and became Armari St. James, mother of the House of St. James. It was also no secret that I was well-known for my extraordinary cat-walk, so it was only fitting that I would become the mother of my own house. The House of St. James was all about fashion, beauty, and class, and I was the epitome of all three. Not to come across as being cocky either, but you had to have confi-dence in order to be somebody else's mother—one of the many lessons Pandora taught me on my rise to the top of the gay in-ner circle.

"Geeeee Phi!" I shouted into the microphone at the end of the runway, and the children started cheering and going ba-nanas. Every one of my shows started with a long stride down the catwalk, and the children expected nothing less of me.

"Phi Geeeee!" they screamed back to me in unison. For every performance I would serve them from my hip and allow the children to come inside my world for a couple of hours with-out inhibition. Most of them wanted to do drag anyway, but didn't have the courage to actually put on women's dress and makeup, at least not in the public domain. So, they lived vicar-iously through me, and I was all too aware of the power and in-fluence I had over them.

"Oh, shit, I think we have some Delta Kappa Zetas in the motherfucking house," I said. "You children ain't gon' work me up in here tonight!"

Delta Kappa was a straight female college sorority that none of us were truly members of, but that didn't matter. Most of the children in the club were Delta Kappas at heart, and our iden-tification with the college sorority was a way for us to show unity and gay sisterhood. Delta Kappa was founded on African principles and history that we appreciated and could relate to.

"Okay, then. Let's get this show started," I said. "But before we do, can somebody please turn on these lights, honey? I wanna see the children's faces up in here."

I snapped my fingers together, and right on cue there was light inside the club. When the children got a closer look at my entire outfit, they started gagging and clapping while my enemies cringed in disbelief.

Of course, I was flawless, serving them children a hug-your-mama beaded, handmade gold-brown strapless dress with a low cut that stopped right above my knees. Moreover, I had on a pair of black boots, and my hair was long and curly with weave down my back like silk.

On Wednesdays I would mix things up so that the children wouldn't know what to expect from me. Sometimes I came dressed like Whitney Houston in a long gown and a short curly wig like she was looking in *The Bodyguard*, and then at other times I wanted to get raunchy and home-girlish. On those days I would come in a scandalous dress and red boots, giving Lil' Kim. But on the night I titled "Dreams"–there was always a theme for the night–I was serving the children Beyoncé, so I knew I was in for a long night of hard work and fun.

A girl can't simply do Beyoncé and not think she was going to perform and work for her coins. Everyone knew she did a little bit of everything onstage, from singing and dancing to strutting up and down the runway like the diva she was. Honey, I was in rare form when I would imitate Ms. Glamour Girl, Movie Star, Destiny's Child.

What more can I say? Beyoncé was fierce, and I wanted to become that girl for one night, anyway. So I did. I was Beyoncé in long Shirley Temple curls, and was loving every minute of it. But leave it to some ugly-ass jealous queen to try to read me for doing Beyoncé in drag.

"Ms. Armari, girl, don't you think you a little tall, dark, and old to be doing Beyoncé?" someone in the crowd said as I stood onstage with the microphone in my hand.

"Who said that?" Yes, I admit that I was a skyscraper, particularly in high heels. And maybe even a little older than Beyoncé—I was pushing close to thirty. But whatever the case, I wasn't about to let some girl mishandle me at my own show. She was about to get read like only I could read her.

"Tell me who said it!" The children started pointing at this tired, broke-down person in the middle of the crowd. And, chile, when I saw who it was, I wasn't even that surprised.

The person who tried to read me was none other than Peaches, this wannabe drag queen who didn't have the looks or class to pull it off successfully. In fact, she was so underrated that I had rejected her request so many times to join the House of St. James. I'm sure that girl must have hated my guts, honey, because she would come after me again before it was all said and done.

"Peaches." I went straight into reading Ms. Girl without hesitation. "Or should I say Ms. Celie from *The Color Purple*, honey. Me and my sister will never part."

All the children started laughing and cheering me on. They loved nothing more than a good game of the old dirty dozen, but at the gay club we called it a read. And reading was a form of expression that I am damn good at.

" 'Oh, sister . . .' " I began to sing the classic tune from *The Color Purple*, changing the words around to fit the occasion. "We're two of a kind . . ."

At this point, the crowd was gagging again, and Ms. Peaches had a horrified look on her face. She knew I was coming after her with everything in me.

"If you don't stop coming to my show and trying to read me"–I wasn't singing this part, but actually speaking the words into a melody–"I'm gon' come off this stage, sister, and bash your motherfucking head in. So, sister, you better know what you're doing."

Of course, this number was followed by thunderous applause. Oh, I must say it was one of my better days for reading. However, when I saw Ms. Peaches looking like she was about to break down and cry in front of everyone, I went all soft on the child and added another line of the song to let Ms. Girl know that there wasn't any hate or hard feelings between us.

"But sister, girl, I still love you, 'cause we sure gotta whole lot of style." I leaned across the stage and even gave that girl a hug, honey. Nobody knows like I know how hard it is being gay and open, trying to live life on your own terms without the support and acceptance from the straight world. And when you're ugly, too, I imagine it must have been double hard on Ms. Girl. Okay. Let me stop reading Ms. Peaches and get back to being serious.

One thing you need to know is that this drag queen gig was not something I took into my everyday world–it was only for my performance inside the club–for the children. Unlike some girls who want to be full-fledged women with real titties and a pussy, I was very comfortable with the body parts I was born with. I didn't wanna be a woman twenty-four/seven. Not that I have anything against the children who take hormone pills and have surgeries to look like real women, but that simply isn't my desire.

Doing drag was a way for me to make coins on the side. When I wasn't onstage performing, I was serving drinks at the bar. Yes, indeed, honey. I was a girl with skills. Performer on Wednesdays. Bartender on every other night of the week. But all of the hard work was done to honor the memory of my mother, who, mind you, was still serving time in prison for a crime she didn't commit. Everyone knew it, so that's why the children supported Wednesday nights at Club Circus. I was using some of the money from my performances to pay for Pandora's defense. Once I got sprung from the plantation, I hired Pandora a lawyer and together, we were going to prove her innocence, one way or the other.

However, I never gave up hope of finding Ms. Noxzema, who really killed that stripper outside the club that fatal and unforgettable night. Some of the children claimed Noxzema was living in Atlanta and doing drugs. Many times I thought about flying to Georgia and tracking her down, so I could kick Ms. Crackhead's ass in person, but soon reality would sink in. I had way too many responsibilities here at home to be going on some wild-goose chase. Being the mother of my own house and performing inside of a club kept me extremely busy.

"Come on, everybody," Tony Lee said as he joined me onstage. He was the owner of Club Circus and he always made sure the children gave me my due respect. "Put your hands together for Ms. Armari St. James!"

Tony Lee wasn't even gay. Shit, he wasn't even black, but that's how it was on Bourbon Street. Poor black folks like myself provided the talent and service, and Mr. White Man owned everything and collected the money. Every time I walked through the French Quarter and saw an old man blowing his horn on a street corner or some black kids from the projects tap dancing, it made me feel good, honey, because I knew we were the ones who made this fucking town come alive every day of the week. From the good home-cooked food to the music and Mardi Gras, New Orleans would not be New Orleans without black folks running things right alongside white folks—not behind them, like back in the day, but beside them, honey, the way it should be.

Don't get me wrong: I'm not prejudiced or anything like that. I love all races of people, and really appreciated the fact that Tony Lee gave me a job and took a chance on me in the first place. The truth of the matter was, nobody else would even hire a girl like me. I was black and openly gay, and an ex-felon on top of that, so I might as well have been dead in some people's eyes. With Tony Lee's support, I was able to make a name for myself and bring Wednesdays back at Club Circus, the only night exclusively reserved for the children.

"Armari's going to change for the next number," Tony Lee said. He was an attractive older man with a hard edge to him.

Tony Lee dabbled in drugs—the exporting and selling of narcotics—but that wasn't any of my business. I only worked for the man. As long as he was paying me my coins, he could have been head of the Mafia, for all I cared.

"Meanwhile we have three-dollar shots and one-dollar beers!" he went on. Tony Lee sported a light beard and mustache. His hair was slick and coal black, and he often wore it in a ponytail. Everything about the man was sexy, even his strong baritone voice. "So let's have a good time and all get along tonight. That means no fighting in here, or I will put your asses out on the street."

I found Jerome, one of my house daughters, in my private dressing room. He was a young kid who had run away from home because his parents couldn't accept him being gay—the same story I had heard a million times.

That's why a lot of these children end up on the streets, homeless and on drugs. Jerome was too sweet a guy for me to allow something like that to happen to him. When I discovered he was from California and was sleeping in a homeless shelter here, I took him into my home until he got on his feet. In return, he became my personal hairstylist and wardrobe consultant while juggling being a full-time student at Dianne Kerry's Hair and Barber School.

"Take a seat, love, and have a drink," he said, handing me a bottle of water. Jerome knew what I needed without me even having to ask him. "And let me freshen up that hair."

I plopped down in the chair and took a long pull from the bottle. My hair was sticking straight up on top of my head. I could see myself in the mirror. "Those children are feeling it tonight, hon. Got Mama working in overdrive."

"Well, then, we can't have you looking a mess, love." Jerome brushed my hair.

I talked to him through the mirror. "The mother has to always be on point if nobody else is."

I took to Jerome's kind spirit from the very first day we met inside the club over cocktails. He was having one for the road, and I was wrapping things up at the bar. We struck up a conversation, and what do you know, we became the best of friends.

Well, but of course, Jerome was cute, too. He couldn't have been a member of the House of St. James if he wasn't, honey. His skin that always looked tan glowed with such youthfulness. Jerome also had thick eyebrows and Asian-looking eyes that gave him an exotic appeal. And his body was ripped and cut like top-of-the-line filet mignon. Yes, indeed, the boy had it going on, and that was the only way I could put it.

"What would I do without you?" I pulled at my hair in the

mirror. Jerome had tightened my curls and was now ironing my outfit for the next number.

"Hopefully, you never have to find out," he said.

Sometimes I thought he was too kind for his own good. People took his niceness as a sign of weakness, especially men. I can't tell you how many times he had gotten his heart broken. The problem was, Jerome often fell too fast and too hard. Elizabeth Taylor had a better track record than this girl, and she had been married how many times?

"As far as I'm concerned, love"–Jerome handed me a pair of big hoop earrings–"you're stuck with me, 'cause I ain't going anywhere."

"I love you, too, girl." I slapped him on the butt. "Now, hurry up with my outfit. And where's Ms. Flo, honey? That girl can never get her ass here on time."

One thing about me and my mama, Flo: We were real close. If nobody else in the world cared about me, I knew Flo did. She was so supportive of my Wednesday-night gigs at the club that I don't think she ever missed one of my performances.

"Hold on to your wig." Flo swung the door open right on cue. "I can hear you going down for me from the hallway."

"What's up, Ms. Flo, girl?" I teased her. Me and Flo kicked it with each other as if we were friends rather than mother and son–or daughter, depending on the situation, but you know what I mean. Don't ask me why. But that was just how it was. Flo had me when she was fifteen years old, and we sorta grew up together.

"Chile, broke down and worn-out." Flo sat her tired behind on the chair. She had just gotten off from work and was still dressed in her black security guard uniform. "I literally ran my ass over here from Harrah's Casino. Hey, Jerome."

"What's up, love?" Jerome said. "I'm glad to see you made it out tonight."

"Wouldn't miss it for the world."

Flo totally accepted me being gay and would tear the roof off the building in a minute if someone tried to step to me in the wrong way about my sexuality. One thing about Flo: She didn't mess with anybody, and she didn't start any trouble. But if you fucked with her or her child, she would go into beast mode and kick your ass without questions.

Flo was raised in the hood in the Third Ward Magnolia Projects. You know the one that rapper Juvenile be rapping about in his songs? Well, before there was a Juvenile or a Lil' Wayne, there was Flo, and she held down the hood with a set of brass knuckles.

Back in the day I heard my mama, along with her five brothers and six sisters, ruled the Third Ward. Since Mama had so many kinfolks, nobody would even think about fucking with any of them. The Santiagos stuck together, and everyone knew that about our family. Flo carried that tradition over to me.

Yes, indeed, my mama loved me. And that's saying a lot these days. I think about Jerome and how his parents disowned him for being gay, and I can't even imagine walking in his shoes.

Of course, there was a time when Flo had a hard time accepting me being gay. When I was growing up, she would see me trying on her clothes and high-heeled pumps in the mirror and would beat my li'l black ass until I turned red. Flo didn't want no sissy for a son, but as time went on, she started to see there was no changing me. She had no other choice but to accept it if she didn't want to lose me.

Flo often blamed my daddy, Cleveland, for my turning out to be gay, but that wasn't the case at all. I was gay because I was born this way, not because my daddy wasn't around to show me how to be a man. I know some children who have both their parents in their lives and they still ended up being gay.

Like most deadbeat fathers, my daddy split when I was still in diapers. Flo said he ran off with some middle-class black woman and now lives in Chicago. Me and my daddy never had any kind of relationship, so I didn't care where his ass was living at. As far as I was concerned, Flo had always been both my mother and father, and that was the way it was going to stay.

"Girl, you missed my opening number." I slipped out of my clothes straight into my next outfit—a long, sexy blue gown with feathers on the shoulders. There wasn't much time to waste. Tony Lee would be bringing me back onstage at any moment.

"Shit, I got here as fast as I could," Flo said, searching through her purse for something. "Damn it! I'm out of cigarettes."

"Well, you're in luck." Jerome took a long white Kool from behind his ear and handed it to Flo, which made her day, honey. Kools were her favorite brand.

"Thank you, sweetheart." Flo held the cigarette to her mouth. Jerome struck a match. "I knew there was a reason I liked you."

"You know I got you, love." He turned his attention toward me. "If you won't be needing me . . ."

"Hot date?" I said.

"Actually, I do." He beamed. Jerome's entire existence revolved around men. Trying to find a man was like a hobby to him. "This time with a corporate lawyer. I'm betting he has major cheese."

"Now you're talking." Flo blew smoke into the air real theatrically, like she was onstage at the Saenger Theatre. "Get you a rich man, and leave them losers alone."

I could feel Flo's eyes burning a hole in my head as I applied makeup to my face in the mirror. Her conversation often led back to the same place: hating on Johnny.

"Maybe you can find somebody for your friend over there"– Flo held the cigarette between her fingers–"who would rather be with a criminal than a decent somebody."

"Don't you start with me, Ms. Girl." I turned around to face her. "Johnny is no damn criminal."

"I think that's my cue to leave." Jerome opened the door. "I'll catch y'all later."

"Be safe," I said. "And don't give it up too quick."

"Spoken like a true mother." Jerome closed the door behind him.

"At least Jerome got the right idea." Flo smashed the cigarette underneath her shoe and snatched a photograph of Johnny that I had taped to the mirror. "You need to follow his lead and forget about this Johnny character."

There's no way to sugarcoat it: Flo simply didn't like Johnny. And why? Because he was still in prison, and she thought I could do much better for a boyfriend. No matter how much I loved Flo, though, I was not about to allow her or anyone to run my personal life. I would pump Ms. Girl's brakes in a New York minute.

"I'm dedicating tonight's performance to him." I pulled at my hair in the mirror and applied more makeup around my eyes and lips. "Do you have a problem with that, girl?"

"No, I don't have a problem at all," Flo said with major attitude. "If you wanna throw your life away on some boy who's probably not even thinking about you, go right ahead. But don't say I didn't warn you."

"I won't," I said. "Now, can I please have my picture? Thank you." I tucked the photograph inside my bra. I was getting ready to perform "Dangerously in Love" by Beyoncé, and I wanted Johnny to be as close to me as possible. I had even written to tell him all about tonight's performance and dedication.

"You can be such a sap," Flo said.

"Don't hate, girl." I pulled out of the drawer a letter that Johnny had written in response to mine. Rereading his letter made me feel close to him, especially tonight of all nights. "Appreciate it."

Suddenly there was nothing else in the room but the words on the paper.

Dear James,

What's up, dude? It's another lonely, rainy night in the pen, and the rain has me thinking about you, boo. I don't know what it is about rain, but it be getting a nigga horny as hell. Got me thinking about all the li'l freaky things I'm gonna do to you when I get out of here. Stop smiling, nigga. But seriously, though, I can't stop thinking about you. If anybody would have told me three or even four years ago that I could feel this way for another dude, I would have popped a cap in their ass. But you know what I mean. I just didn't think I could feel this way about some other dude. Man, I miss you so much and been counting down the days till we will be together again.

That rain also got me thinking about how I want our first time together outside of the pen to be like. I want it to be pouring down outside the window when I'm inside you. I want that rain to be singing our song when I explode and our bodies become one. I ain't God, so I can't control when it rains and shit. But I'm just dreaming about what I want it to be like. That's all I got right now is my dreams, and they say if you dream hard enough the shit can come true.

Yo, lights about to go out in here, so I'm signing out for now. But I want to make a promise to you on this rainy night. When I get sprung from this joint, you and I got a date. In fact, you're the first person I wanna see as soon as I get out of here, 'cause I'm feeling you, dude. Just remember what I said and hold on to that. I'll be dreaming about you tonight.

Straight from the heart,
Johnny

"I don't know what's so special about some criminal writing you a letter," Flo said. She had such a jealous heart when it came to me dating dudes like Johnny. In the back of Flo's mind, she probably thought he should have been with her instead of me—a real woman. Flo may have been my mama, but no matter what, women gone be women. They think that every fine-ass brother is straight, and are always shocked when they find out otherwise.

"I don't expect you to understand," I said, getting up to leave, "since you haven't had a man in how long?"

"Whatever!" Flo said. She waved me off like what I had just said didn't even bother her that much. But she was hurting—I could see the pain in her face. Of course, I felt bad for reading my own mama, but she had it coming.

Although Flo wasn't a bad-looking woman, she had gotten

fat over the years. She was short, and had a cute round face and a nice grain of hair on her head, but that belly of hers was simply growing out of control. No matter how pretty she was in the face, most men don't want no woman who looks pregnant all year round. The bottom line was that Flo needed to take better care of herself if she had any hope of finding a man in these tough times of superficial dating and lustful loving.

"Okay. Girl, I'm outta here." I swung the door open and found some strange man waiting on the outside of the door for me. His tall, slender presence caught me completely off guard.

"Damn," I said, clutching a strand of white pearls around my neck. "You scared the fuck out of me. What are you doing back here? This part of the club is off-limits."

"I'm sorry if I scared you," this guy said. He was dressed very professionally, with a pair of eyeglasses and a silk tie. At first I thought he was with the IRS or something, because the truth was, a girl wasn't paying any taxes on all of that money I was collecting from my Wednesday-night performances. Chile, I was some scared, because a girl wasn't trying to go back to prison.

"But I just wanted to give you these." He pulled a dozen roses from behind his back and handed them over to me. Of course, he took my breath away. I didn't even have words for him, honey.

"I'm really enjoying your show tonight," he said with a warm, inviting smile. I sensed he was good people. Just charming and cute, but totally not my type.

I've never been into the straitlaced type of man with that professional, nerdy, businesslike look. Like most everyone else these days, I wanted me a thug, honey, a hard-core nigga who was gonna throw me up against the wall and fuck me with his Timberlands still on.

"This is really sweet. Thank you," I said. "What's your name, hon?"

"Marvin," he said. By the shaky tone of his voice, I sensed Marvin was nervous, which made him appear even cuter. "Marvin Holmes."

"Well, Marvin. It was nice meeting you, and thank you so much." I handed the flowers over to Flo, whose entire face was glowing. Mama thought she had a new son-in-law for sure. But it was going to take more than flowers to make me forget about Johnny. "I hope you stick around and see the rest of the show."

"Well, actually, I'm due back at the hospital," Marvin said. I could now see Flo's eyes popping out of her damn head. She had to be thinking Marvin was a doctor who had lots of money. Quiet as it was kept, Flo was nothing but a gold digger like Jerome, and was always looking for some rich man to take care of her.

"I'll catch up with you another time," he said. "Once again, nice to meet you and hope to see you around."

"Please come again. I'm here every Wednesday." I stood in the doorway and watched Marvin make his way down the long hallway. If nothing else, he had a nice round butt.

"Now that's someone you need to be trying to get to know—somebody with money and education," Flo said. "Instead of some nigga in prison who can't do a damn thing for you."

"Johnny will be home one day soon," I said, and immediately went into fierce mode on her, tossing my hair over my shoulders. "And when he does, we will be together forever, honey. Now I have a show to go and do. So please hold my calls."

"Wait just a minute," Flo said. "I might as well tell you, 'cause you gon' find out anyway."

"Tell me what, girl?" I was losing my patience. Flo was really beginning to work on my last nerve. "Out with it. I don't have all day."

"Don't forget I'm your mama," she said. "And no matter how bad you think you are, you can't beat my ass."

"Okay, Flo, girl," I said. "Whatever. Now what's going on?"

"Your friend Ebony called," Flo finally said.

"Is she on her way?"

Ebony rarely missed a performance of mine. The only time she did was when she was caught up in some drama with her drug-dealing boyfriend, Kojack, who was whipping her ass on the DL. The only reason I hadn't rode up on that trifling nigga was because he was Johnny's cousin, and the two of them were very close. The last thing I wanted to do was piss Johnny off. His family meant the world to him.

"Come on, Ma," I said.

When I wanted something from Flo really badly, I would have a slip of the tongue and refer to her as my mama. But just so you will know, Flo was the one who wanted me to call her by her first name out of fear of feeling old. That girl always wanted to feel young and beautiful, so you know where I got my ego from.

"Tell me what's up and stop playing around," I insisted.

"Ebony mentioned something about Johnny getting out of jail tonight," Flo said nonchalantly. "And to call her later. Oh, my gosh. Sweetheart, you're okay?"

Don't ask me why my ass ended up on the floor. Looking back, I say it was all the excitement of the day. If nothing else, I gave Flo something memorable to tell her grandchildren when she got old and gray.

6

Johnny

"Talk to me, man," Kojack said as we drove down I-10 to New Orleans in his black SUV with the car bouncing up and down like a cowboy on a rodeo ride. We were listening to that nigga Tupac and getting high on some good-ass weed that Kojack had stashed away just for me.

"How does it feel to be out of prison, nigga?" He squeezed that joint in between his fingers, took a hit off of it before passing that shit over to me. Man, that was some slamming-ass weed that had my head spinning in circles.

"I don't know," I said, exhaling like smoking weed was an art form or something. "That shit ain't hit me yet."

Kojack had picked me up right after midnight, and we had about a three-hour ride before we got to my parents' crib. I rolled down the window and took in a breath of fresh air.

"Man, it just feels so strange being out," I said. It's funny how you miss the small things in life when you're inside the pen, like riding inside of a car and feeling God's air up against your cheeks. "I thought this day would never come."

I had spent the entire night before getting my shit together and saying my final good-byes to dudes I probably wasn't gone ever see again. Most of them niggas were up in Sierra Leone for life and was never gone know what real freedom felt like. Them dudes had come to depend on me, and the hardest part was not being able to help with their appeals. No matter how many letters I wrote, I couldn't crack a system that wasn't in a black man's favor.

"What I'm curious to know," I said, tossing what was left of the joint outside the window, "is how did you convince everybody, especially Pops, to let you—of all niggas—pick me up?"

A lot may have changed in the world since I had been locked up in the pen for the past four and a half years, but one thing remained the same: Pops couldn't get down with Kojack or his drug-dealing lifestyle. Where Pops served the one true living God, Kojack looked to the streets for his salvation.

The two of them had never seen eye-to-eye on anything, and that's why I was so surprised when I heard Kojack had gotten the gig that I knew Pops wanted. But I told Moms straight up that I didn't want Pops coming to pick me up, anyway. Although the years had healed a lot of pain and issues between us, I still never forgot the hand Pops played in getting me sent to the pen in the first place. Just thinking about that crap made me hurt and mad all over again.

"It wasn't an easy sale," Kojack said.

Over the years, he had earned his gangster stripes on the streets. Kojack's reputation for killing, stealing, and destroying was what made him infamous. Fuck what you see in the movies; Kojack had that fire, man. He once showed me a gun that could burn a hole in a dude's chest with just one shot.

"I had to do a lot of begging and convincing to your old man," Kojack explained. "You know Auntie was cool, but your pops . . . that dude ain't changed. But in the end, I got my way. Kojack always gets what he wants, baby."

Kojack worked for this white dude, Tony Lee, who owned a club in the French Quarter. The way I understood it was that Tony Lee got the supplies from the big shots upstate, and Kojack was his man on the streets. If nothing else, selling drugs had made Kojack a wealthy-ass nigga.

My cuz was rolling in paper and living large. You should have seen this dude, man. He was rocking diamonds on just about every other finger, and had a sparkling-ass grille in his mouth that could blind a motherfucker even with shades on. Besides his SUV, Kojack had a Mercedes and a BMW with a fat crib on the lakefront, where mostly rich white folks lived. Part of me was proud of my cuz for how successful he had become over the years, but another side of me was worried about him, too. A lot of niggas hated Kojack on the streets, and I always feared for his life. The way I saw it, the last thing we needed was another soldier dead and gone. I tried not to judge my cuz for how he made his paper, but taking another human being's life was something I couldn't get down with.

"What did you tell Pops?" I rolled my window up and turned the volume down on the radio, so I could focus completely on my conversation with him. Me and that nigga had a lot of catching up to do, for damn sure. "Tell him you were going to join church or something?"

"Man, Uncle Lonnie be tripping," Kojack said. "But I know he still has that love inside his heart for me. We blood, and ain't nothing much thicker than that."

I gave him a look like, "Nigga, please."

"Basically, I told him," Kojack said, "that I wouldn't have any

THREE SIDES TO EVERY STORY

contact with you or Nettie after tonight. That dude is trying to keep me from my li'l nephew."

Nettie and Kojack were so close, they were like twins. Growing up she was like his shadow. You couldn't find a better example of a li'l sister looking up to her big brother. But I guess when your pops abandons you and your moms dies of cancer, you can't help but be a close brother and sister. I don't think either of them had ever gotten over losing Aunt Tina at such a young age.

"Man, I know you got to be kidding about Pops." I just couldn't believe the words that came out of Kojack's mouth. I had been out of jail less than an hour, and Pops was already trying to control my fucking life. Sometimes I think that dude actually thought he was God, trying to tell niggas what they could and could not do. I was a grown-ass man, and me and Pops were definitely overdue for a long talk. I couldn't wait to get home and confront his ass over that shit.

"Please tell me you're lying, man," I said, "and that my old man ain't at it again."

"I'm not lying, dude," Kojack said. "He told me the only way I could pick you up is to never have contact with you, Nettie, or the baby again."

One thing Nettie and Kojack had in common was that they were forever getting their asses in some kind of trouble, no matter how much Pops tried to steer them in the right direction. Here Nettie was only sixteen years old, and she'd already had a baby. Man, she was just a child herself.

"And he fell for that shit?" I wondered.

"Yep." Kojack smiled in my direction, showing his grille that was probably worth more than everything I owned. "Like a damn fool, but you know I ain't gon' never give Nettie up, especially now that she just had my li'l nephew."

"So how does it feel to be an uncle?" I asked.

Kojack shook his head. "It's deep, man. You know, to see that li'l joker and to know that's my blood. I love that li'l dude already. Ain't nothing like family. That's why I want you to come work for me."

"You talking about slanging from the cut?"

"No, nigga, I'm talking about selling Avon," he said. "You know what I mean. I need you out there on the block with me so you can watch my back like old times. A lot has changed on the scene since you've been away. Niggas be hating on me out here, for real. Can't trust motherfuckers for nothing. So, what do you say?"

"I don't know, man," I said. "I just got out. Let me get myself together and get back at you later."

"Fair enough." Kojack seemed satisfied with my answer–for the time being, anyway. But he was a persistent li'l motherfucker, so I knew he would be back again. And to be honest, at the time I couldn't tell you for sure that I wasn't going to go back to that lifestyle either. I wasn't certain about nothing when I came home.

Kojack pulled off the interstate once we got to Baton Rouge. His SUV may have been a nice-ass, smooth ride, but it for damn sure ate up a lotta gas. We pulled into an Exxon, and then that's when things really got interesting.

"Yo," Kojack said as he pumped gas. "You need anything to eat or drink?"

"Nah, I'm straight." I turned the volume up on the radio, mostly out of curiosity. That nigga Rico–you know that rapper dude Tonya was fucking around with? Well, his song was on the radio, and it was like someone shocked the hell out of me with a bolt of electricity. Hearing that nigga's song was bringing me back in time to a place that I was trying so fucking hard to forget. The truth was, I had never gotten over Tonya, and any li'l reminder of her brought on chest pains and the worst damn headaches.

"Don't worry, dude. That nigga is wack," Kojack said. He must have caught that sadness in my eyes. "He can't touch what the two of y'all had."

I had spent a lot of time thinking about Tonya in the pen, but days before I was to be released my thoughts and feelings got even more intense. I couldn't stop thinking about how happy we were at one time. Man, I had to know what went wrong and why she chose some rich dude over me.

Come on, man—I know a lot of years had passed, but I couldn't stop wondering about that shit. What if your high school sweetheart broke your heart? Wouldn't you wanna know what happened? If she really loved you or not?

Well, that's how a nigga was feeling about the situation, and I was gone get to the bottom of it one way or another. The only problem with this scenario was that it created the possibility for all kinds of other complications.

Yeah, now I'm talking about James. I had that nigga on my mind, too, but I couldn't talk to my cuz about him. After what happened at that gas station the night I got out of the pen, I knew for damn sure Kojack wasn't the one to open up to about me loving and having feelings for some other dude.

"What the fuck you lookin' at?" Kojack asked this dude who was walking, or rather switching, by and looking directly in his face. Man, this dude was obviously gay, and he looked like he was on crack or something with a dirty-ass, greasy face.

"I'll suck your dick for a dollar," this dude said out of his mouth to Kojack. Drugs will have a nigga out of his goddamn mind and doing some bold and bizarre antics that seem gutter and inhumane.

"What the fuck your li'l faggot ass said to me?" Kojack grabbed this dude around the neck and threw him up against the SUV. He pulled his gun out and held it up against his head. Man, of course I was shitting bricks, 'cause I thought Kojack was about to shoot that dude in the head.

"Answer me, you faggot!" Kojack shouted in the dude's face. "Suck on this, you low-life piece of trash!"

Kojack put the gun to that dude's head. He put that gun to his head, and there was an old man working inside the gas station, looking real hard and trying to figure out what was going on. And I was some scared, 'cause I thought that old man was going to call the cops. And going back to life on the plantation was not ever in the cards for me. I had gotten out on early release for good behavior. One wrong move could send my ass back to slavery.

"Please don't shoot, mister!" this dude shouted with both his hands in front of him, begging and crying for his life. "I don't wanna die!"

"Don't do it, Kojack, man." I leaped out of the car when he cocked the trigger. "They got this shit on tape."

Kojack looked over his shoulder at the old man and then back at the gay dude. I couldn't figure out what was going on inside of cuz's head, but I knew it was something pure evil. Kojack's eyes turned bloodshot red as he held a steady hand on the gun.

"Get your li'l punk ass out of here," Kojack finally said. And that gay dude took off running up the street as if he was a number one sprinter in the Olympics or something.

To be honest, I really don't know what it was that made cuz have a change of heart. I was just so relieved he freed that dude that I didn't give a damn what the reasons were.

"What's wrong with you, man?" Kojack asked once we got back inside the car. My fucking hands were shaking and trembling like a dope fiend on crack.

"Don't ever scare me like that, man," I said. "I thought you were gon' shoot that dude."

"Maybe I should have," Kojack said, pushing his gun underneath the seat. "Do the world a favor and get rid of one faggot. I say kill all of them motherfuckers that make manhood look weak."

The rest of the way home I didn't have much to say, just looked out of the window at nothing but darkness and trees lined up along I-10.

"Surprise!" Moms's voice was the loudest one that rose out of the darkness. "Welcome home, my son!"

Man, my family got me real good with a li'l surprise party in the wee hours of the morning—the last thing I expected when Kojack dropped me off in front of the door. I should have known, though, that something was up when that nigga said, "Have a good time."

Before he could say anything else to me, I had jumped out of the car and run inside the house. You know I was still kind of shaken up over what happened at that gas station in Baton Rouge and wasn't feeling like making small talk. All I wanted to do was crawl inside of my own bed and forget about that shit. But that wasn't happening anytime soon if my peeps had anything to say about it.

"What's up, son?" Pops hugged me for what seemed like forever, but I rested my arms at my sides. I didn't even wanna touch the dude, no matter how joyous of an occasion it was.

Back in the day, I had always looked up to Pops, as if he was a larger-than-life action figure. Maybe 'cause Pops was a preacher, I simply put him in an entirely different league when he was just an ordinary man like everyone else. Man, I basically lost that respect for him.

"This is the day the Lord has made," Pops said. He was a tall and handsome old dude standing six feet, four inches tall and sporting a headful of gray hair and a mustache. Pops had also put on a li'l extra weight over the years and had a potbelly that hung over his pants. I have to say in spite of everything, Pops showed me love, but so did everyone else.

I had relatives at that homecoming dinner who I hadn't seen since childhood: Moms's sisters and brothers and their children and grandchildren came up from Texas. My brother Ronnie, his wife, Karen, and their twins, Ericka and Eric. My other brother, Carl, came down from Baton Rouge. And, I can't leave out Pops's side of the family, because they were representing strong, too.

Pops's only remaining sister, Aunt Celeste, was there with her special friend, Aunt Lula. Pops's three brothers, Lee, Tyrone, and Roger, were all there, too, and like a dozen or so first, second, and third cousins that would take up an entire page if I started naming them all. Even Nettie was there with her baby, a li'l fat chubby nigga with a headful of curly hair.

"What's up, cuz?" Nettie wrapped one arm around me and held the baby with her other. "I'm so glad you're home. Meet my son, Lionel, but we already calling him Ali, 'cause he's some bad and mean."

"What's up li'l man?" When I reached for him, Ali made that baby noise, and then smacked my ass clean in the face. Man, I'm not kidding. This li'l dude wasn't even one year old yet and had a set of hands on him like a champ. I couldn't help but think that Ali was the perfect name for him.

"I told you he was bad," Nettie said. Everyone laughed.

From what I heard, the baby's daddy was some older cat who didn't want anything else to do with Nettie. You know some niggas just don't have no cut about them, getting these li'l girls pregnant out here and then running off like thieves in the night. But of all days, I wasn't even trying to let that shit ruin my homecoming celebration.

"You think I can get some of that love? Come here, my son." Moms threw her arms around my neck and wailed. Man, she was crying so hard, her entire face turned red. No doubt, Moms was a beautiful light-skinned woman, but when she cried, Moms turned all ugly on a nigga. "I've missed you so much. And boy, you look good."

"Good gracious, Liz, let that boy up for some air," Aunt Celeste said, snatching me straight out of Moms's arms and landing a fat kiss on my left cheek.

Aunt Celeste was a lot bigger than Moms, so when she hugged me it felt like something inside of me was breaking into pieces. She was talking to me like I was a two-year-old. "Now give your auntie Celeste some sugar."

On the real, though, I think Aunt Celeste is a lesbian. Nobody in the family ever said so, but her and Aunt Lula ain't never been married, never had children, or been with any men as far as I could tell. They just had each other since I was little.

Hands down, Aunt Celeste was my favorite aunt, so none of that other shit even mattered. Maybe she peeped something in me, too, 'cause I was always her "favorite one" of my brothers.

Anyway, it was funny how Aunt Celeste and Moms would always compete for my love and shit. You know it was those li'l special things that let a nigga know that he was definitely back in the crib.

"Let 'im go, Celeste," Moms said. "You ain't the only one who wants to see 'im."

Aunt Celeste rolled her eyes and then gave me another kiss before turning me loose. I started making my way around the room, giving high fives and dapping up my brothers, uncles, and cousins and kissing my female relatives on the cheeks like a stately gentleman. Then, out of nowhere, I heard a set of bells ringing like it was Sunday morning at church.

Afterward, my brothers opened the wooden doors that divided the living and dining rooms from each other. When I looked over my shoulder there was a Thanksgiving feast, with a big juicy turkey in the center of the table. And at the head of the same table was my crippled Grandma Eve, who had waited up for me, too. Man, it was wild and some crazy how everyone stayed up real late and had cooked all of that food for me.

"Welcome," she said in a deep, raspy voice. Everyone immediately took their places at the table. Grandma Eve may have been paralyzed due to a car accident in her youth, but that never stopped her from doing what she had to do in life. Grandma Eve got married, had children, and even held down a full-time job for many years. Man, she was such a strong woman, and those bells had been with her for years. Since Grandma Eve couldn't walk, it was her way of getting our attention when she needed something.

"What's up, Grandma?" I said. She kissed me on the cheek and directed my attention to the empty seat beside her.

"It was Mama's idea," Moms said. "She wanted us to welcome you home in grand fashion."

I felt like a king, sitting at the dinner table and knowing all that good food had been prepared with me in mind. Ain't nothing like New Orleans down-home cooking either. It's the best food in the land. You heard me. Let me break it down for y'all. There was Moms's collard greens, and Aunt Celeste's homemade sweet-potato pies, and Grandma Eve's biscuits. You know a nigga like me was in heaven and ready to dig in so I could get my eat on. Grandma Eve rang those bells just in time to stop me. No one was to lay a hand on the food without proper prayer and blessing the food.

"The Lord has been mighty good to us today," Grandma Eve said. She was struggling with her words like old age was weighing down on her something hard. "Them prisons done got a lot of our young men, and it's a crime on the black race."

"That's right. That's right," Uncle Roger interrupted. He was Pops's oldest brother and had a love for black people that shone all over his dark face. When I was little, Uncle Roger would drop that knowledge on me about black history—the real black history, and not the limited stuff you read about in high school books, like slavery and the civil rights movement.

"Preach that word, Mama!" Uncle Roger shouted like a deacon from a Sunday-morning pew. He couldn't keep himself still when he heard someone dropping knowledge about black folks' history. "Preach that word early this morning!"

"But one of our sons done come home," Grandma Eve said. "And thank God, 'cause a lot of them dying in those jails up there."

Grandma Eve put the spotlight on a serious problem that was going on up at Sierra Leone, with the inmates getting sick and dying off like dead leaves. And these deaths weren't at the hands of another brother or some black-on-black crime bullshit like you be hearing about on the news. These dudes had gotten sick with some kind of bacteria that was causing motherfuckers to get a bad case of tuberculosis that was spreading around the pen like wildfire. Man, that shit was scary, but real.

There were three and four dudes dying each month. And they weren't doing nothing to stop the spread of that shit up in there. You know they could have cleaned, sanitized, and tested the damn joint. Just letting motherfuckers die off one by one like they wanted that shit to happen. The hardest part for me was when Pandora got sick, 'cause that took a toll on all of us to see our den mother—the strongest and toughest soldier on the plantation—get taken down like a weak-ass chump.

Two days before I was to be released, I went to see her in that hellhole they actually had the nerve to call a hospital. That damn place was just as run-down and raggedy as a cell block, with busted-out windows, dirty-ass linen, and shit. And the funk up in that jailhouse hospital just didn't make any goddamn sense either. It smelled like horse shit mixed with peroxide and rubbing alcohol. Some crazy-ass smells that I didn't even know existed in the world. Man, that was the kind of place Pandora and a lot of other dudes were lying sick in, and I was hurting real bad 'cause of it.

"You ain't never lying about that, Grandma," I cut in on her prayer. "Just yesterday I had to say good-bye to a friend who was dying up in there."

"Oh, I'm so sorry to hear that, son." Moms placed her hand on top of mine. "I hope he'll be okay. We'll lift him up in prayer."

Pandora was a trooper, though. She didn't want anybody feeling sorry for her, especially James. Before I stepped foot off the plantation, I had to make Pandora a solid promise: that I would never tell James how sick she really was. I didn't really understand why she wanted to keep her illness a secret from James.

Maybe it had something to do with pride, which Pandora had a lot of. She didn't want James, who Pandora considered a daughter, looking down on her with pity. Either way you look at the situation it was bad, but I had planned to keep my word to Pandora and not speak a word of her sickness to anybody, especially James.

Who ever would have thought that the time would come when going to the pen was literally a death sentence?

"What's wrong, Johnny?" Moms asked. Everyone must have noticed how sad I had gotten. It was hard for me to hide my true feelings and hurt.

"I'm just thinking about how lucky I am," I said. It took every ounce of strength for me not to break down and cry or tell someone what I was really going through. But I couldn't imagine them understanding. You know, that I was torn up over some drag queen friend of mine. "Man, it just feels so good to be home. And I just wanna thank everybody for being here."

"Oh, sugar." Aunt Celeste reached across the table and took hold of my hand. "You don't have to thank us. We thank you. Thank you for bringing us together in good times. Too often we get together for funerals and not for good times. And we're glad you're home. Now, can we please eat before the food gets cold?"

Everyone immediately started digging in. It was time to eat, and I wanted a taste of every animal on the table, from fish to turkey.

"Slow down, dude," Carl said, "before you hurt something."

Everyone laughed. Besides being a track star at LSU and in training for the Olympics, Carl had lots of jokes. That nigga never ate that much, anyway. When we were kids, I used to eat his food and mine. I guess old habits die hard. Everyone got a real good kick out of watching me eat.

"Ma, can I go to the bathroom?" asked Eric. He was my li'l nephew, and I couldn't believe how big he had gotten. Ronnie and Karen started their family while they were still students in college. Eric and his twin sister, Ericka, were barely three years old when I went into the pen.

"Hurry back," Karen said. She was a pretty chocolate sister with that natural look—no makeup or weave. There was nothing fake about Karen, and I liked that. Too many sisters focus more on their nails and makeup than having a down-to-earth attitude.

"Look like you put on some weight inside that joint," Ronnie said, tapping me lightly on the arm. "You've been hitting that iron, huh nigga?"

"Yeah man, I've been doing a li'l somethin'," I joked, but Moms suddenly wasn't in a playing mood.

"Hey, watch it," Moms said. "You know better than using the N-word in this house."

"Come on nah, Ma," Ronnie said. He hated when Moms treated him like a child, but that's how she was with us, man. No matter how grown we were, Moms would still get our black asses in line. She was the glue that held our family together. "It's just a word. Lighten up."

"No, you young folk have to understand," Moms said, "and be sensitive with what older people went through over the use of that word."

"Listen to your mama, son," Grandma Eve said. "We black folks done went through a lot of stuff in this country not to be called that word."

"Okay." Ronnie threw both of his hands into the air. "Y'all win. I guess I'm outnumbered."

After Ronnie graduated from USC, he came back to New Orleans to coach football at the local high school. His wife, Karen, was a math teacher at the same school. Their children were straight-A students, from what I had heard. Ronnie had the perfect family, and I was real proud of my man.

"Uncle Johnny," Ericka said. Her li'l seven-year-old voice was so sweet and innocent. "What was it like in prison?"

"Now, baby," Aunt Celeste scolded her. "Don't go and ask your uncle something like that."

"It's okay, Aunt Celeste," I said. "I don't mind talking about being in the slammer."

"Forgive her, man," Ronnie said. "My Ericka is just too smart and curious for her own good."

"Well, to answer the question," I said, "at first it was hell, but after a while it wasn't that bad. I got off into positive stuff and did a lot of reading. You know a black man gotta educate himself about the white man."

"Yeah, but it ain't the white man hurting us today," Pops said. "We doing it to ourselves with drugs, violence, sex, and lack of education. This is your chance to get yourself straight, son."

"No need to worry about me," I said. There was suddenly a mounting tension inside the room. "I'm gon' be all right and get mine the right way."

"Well, anyway, I'm so glad you're home, cuz," Nettie cut in on the two of us, which was a good thing. Me and Pops were about to go at each other for damn sure. "You get to see my baby grow up."

"So, has everyone had enough to eat?" Aunt Celeste cut Nettie off. I guess Aunt Celeste wasn't ready to deal with the fact that her li'l teenage niece had a baby out of wedlock. Man, nobody was trying to face the reality of the situation, 'cause it was a shame on the Lomacks' good name.

You have to understand how it is. Folks in my family are doctors, lawyers, and educators and shit, and they frown on anyone who don't measure up to their idea of being successful. Besides, Pops had promised Aunt Tina before she died of breast cancer all those years ago that he would look after Nettie and Kojack. With Kojack being a thug and Nettie ending up pregnant, Pops—and the rest of the family, for that matter—must have felt like they had disappointed Aunt Tina. Nettie was the first Lomack woman to get pregnant without being married.

"Look what I found." Eric returned from the bathroom with a football in his hand. It was my football, the one that I'd run the winning touchdown with in the final game between Higgins High and St. Augustine. It was the biggest game of my high school football career. All of a sudden, the homecoming dinner went sour. When I saw that football again, it felt like my heart was being ripped apart.

"Eric," Karen said, "what did I tell you about touching things?"

"Let me see," I said. Eric wasn't sure what he should do, since everyone was looking at him like he was the family curse. I knew that feeling all too well. "Where did you get this?"

"Inside the living room beside the sofa," Eric said. Poor kid looked as scared as he sounded.

"Why don't you let me take that?" Moms said.

"It's okay!" I shouted. "I'm not going to fall apart seeing a football."

But it wasn't just any football. Moms knew that, 'cause she was at the game when I ran that touchdown. It was strange how I could feel that moment beating inside my body—the blood rushing toward my brain as I thought about how I ran into the end zone and won the championship for my school. The football still had my teammates' signatures on it.

Man, who was I fooling? I couldn't take that shit—that pain was too hard to sit on. I jumped up from the table and shot out of that room so fast you would have thought I was reliving history.

I ran out on the family dinner and went upstairs to my old bedroom, feeling the need to be alone. But no sooner had I closed the bedroom door than I heard Pops coming down the hall. The heels on his shoes made the loudest noise against our good cedarwood floors. He opened the door.

"I remember that game," Pops said. When he walked into the room, I was sitting on the edge of the bed with the football still in my hand.

"I was so proud of you that day," he went on. "My boy had won the game for his team."

"Too bad I couldn't keep making you proud," I said, looking around the room at all of my football awards. I had my football jerseys and certificates pinned to the plain white walls, and my trophies stacked up on the dresser like a million-dollar treasure. That shit meant the world to me.

"Look, son," Pops said, sitting beside me on the bed. His extra weight made the bedsprings sing. I moved to the other side of the bed, away from him.

"I'm sorry about the football," he said. "We should have been more careful, and not have had something like that lying around."

"It's okay, Pops," I said. "It's just a football."

"I know it is," he said. "But I know how much the game meant to you."

"Let's just drop it. Okay?"

"What do you wanna talk about, son?" asked Pops. He must have sensed something on my mind. Pops was real good at sensing a person's spirit.

"Kojack told me all about y'all's li'l deal," I said. "You know, the one where he promised to cut his losses and stay the hell away from me, Nettie, and the baby."

"Look, son." Pops cleared his throat. "I was only looking out for your best interests. The last thing you need—"

"You had no right, man," I cut Pops off. "And how you gon' keep that man from the only real family he got? You know him and Nettie have always been close."

"He's scum, Johnny," Pops shot back at me like a bullet. "And I just pray that my poor sister isn't up there in heaven watching what's going on down here. Because her heart would definitely be broken."

"Man, you're tripping," I said. "As usual."

"I know this is not what you wanna hear," Pops said. "But hanging around with Kojack is just asking for trouble, which you and I will both agree you don't need."

"What happened to 'judge not lest ye be judged'?" I loved turning the Holy Scripture back on Pops and watching him squirm his way out of a tight spot. "Doesn't Kojack deserve God's love just as much as anyone?"

"Of course he does," Pops said. "God's love is unconditional. But you can't serve two gods, because the wages of sin are death. Do you wanna die, son? 'Cause running with Kojack will be the death of you."

"You make him sound like the devil or something."

"Satan isn't some man in a red suit and horns underneath the earth," Pops said. "He's living and breathing in some of us."

"Man, I don't know how you can say that about your own blood," I said. "That's your baby sister's only son, who you promised to look out for. But then again, you're used to turning your back on your own people."

Pops looked me straight in the eyes and shook his head. "So, is this what all the anger's been about? You still mad at me for not putting in a good word for you at your trial?"

"Man, you left me!" The blood rushed to my head and my heart was pounding. "Sent me off to that damn hellhole without as much as a good-bye!"

"I did what I thought was best at the time, son," Pops said. "You kept making one bad choice after another. Me and your mother were afraid for your life. We thought prison was the safest place for you to get yourself together."

"Oh, don't even try to bring Moms into this," I said. "She wasn't the one who sold me out. You did."

"I don't wanna argue with you, son," Pops said. "Let's not waste this time going over things that happened so long ago. We have the future to look forward to. I wanna get to know my son all over again. What are your plans now that you're home?"

"My plans?"

"For work," Pops said. "Have you thought about what you wanna do with your life?"

"I'm going to play ball again," I said. "Maybe be a walk-on at one of the local colleges."

"Son, don't you think you need to be more realistic?" he asked. "You've been away from the game for quite a long time."

"I'm in better shape than I've ever been." I held on to the football real tight and squeezed it in between my hands. "So, I'll be all right."

"I was going to ask your uncle Roger to get you on at his shop," said Pops. "I know how good you are under the hood."

"No, thanks," I said with a cocky attitude. Although Pops was trying his hardest to make things right between us, I wasn't feeling him or his bullshit concern. I hated the way he was always trying to control my fucking life, man. "I can find my own job."

"When are you going to stop looking at me as the enemy and start thinking of me as your father? I love you, son, and simply want what's best for you," Pops said with water in his eyes; it was almost touching. "That's all I wanted for all my sons, was for them to be happy and to fear God. But you gotta want that for yourself. You're at the age, son, where you need to get a good job, join a church, and find yourself a beautiful woman to settle down with. Have you spoken to Tonya?"

"I don't wanna talk about it," I said. "Whatever happens or doesn't happen between me and Tonya is none of your business."

"I know she's the only girl you've ever loved," Pops said. He was steadily pushing his own agenda. "Maybe y'all can get back together and come work in the church with the young people."

"Don't you mean put on a good front for your li'l church members?"

"I see you're not going to make this easy." Pops stood up to leave. He had finally lost his patience with me. "So, I'm going to give it to you straight up."

"I knew it was coming," I said, playing around with the football and throwing it up in the air. "The good Reverend Lonnie Lomack reporting for holy church service."

"Don't you mock the Lord in this house," Pops said. "You will show respect as long as you're under my roof. Is that clear?"

"Crystal." I saluted him like a soldier. Man, I was just being a first-rate asshole and trying to work on Pops's last fucking nerve. It was the only way I knew how to get under his skin and make him feel something toward me, even if it was hate and disgust. "You don't have to worry about me causing any trouble."

"Good," Pops said. "And you may not want any help from me, and that's your choice, but I do expect you to find a job before the month's out. And one last thing."

I stretched out across the bed with a half-ass smile on my face and held the football with a tight grip. You know, basically trying to ignore Pops and acting like what he was saying didn't matter to me at all.

"If you make your mother cry"—Pops turned the knob and opened the door—"there won't be a prison big enough to save you from me. I'll tell everyone downstairs you're tired and need to get some rest. But you think long and hard about what I said, son."

When Pops closed the door behind him, I just lay across the bed holding the football, staring at the ceiling, and thinking about a lot of shit. Man, I was thinking so fucking hard that before I knew what was even happening, I was crying and sobbing like somebody had died on me or something.

Don't ask me why I was crying either, 'cause I didn't know what the hell was wrong with me. Being back inside my old room was bringing on bad feelings, like the walls inside the room was trying to speak to me. The price of freedom wasn't gone come without a great amount of pain and suffering.

7

Tonya

"If you can't say anything positive around this bitch, then you know what the fuck you can do for me," said Mama. And you wonder where I get my foul mouth from? Me and her was going at it over Ricky's decision to go to war in Iraq. I had finally told Mama exactly how I felt about my brother serving his country, and she simply didn't like what I had to say. "Get the hell out of my damn house!"

"Well, you shouldn't have asked me what I thought then," I said, searching the hole in our sofa for my car keys that were misplaced the previous night. Things had gotten way too overheated between me and Mama, and it was definitely time for me to bounce before something went down that we both would have regretted much later.

One thing you need to know about Mama is that when she lost her temper, she would haul off and slap my ass no matter what the circumstances was. Some folks today might call that shit abuse, but Mama had been that way since I was a child. She was hard on all three of us: me, Ricky, and Eric. Mama would beat our asses like we was criminals or something. Sometimes she went too far, but there was times we really deserved it, especially me.

I know I was a handful, running these streets out here and growing up way before my time. Babee, you couldn't tell me I wasn't a bad bitch who knew everything there was about life. I was too stupid to see that in many situations Mama was only trying to protect me from harm. She had already buried one son and a husband. Mama had to be worried about her only daughter, too. The tough streets of the NO would take a girl's innocence. You see, I'm woman enough to admit all of this, but me and Mama just had a hard time finding the right balance.

"You and me both know, Mama, there ain't nothing out here in them streets of New Orleans for Ricky to come back to but more death and violence." I pulled my purse over my shoulder and looked Mama dead in her face. She was already dressed for work in a white uniform and a pair of black no-name sneakers, and she had her hair pulled back in a bun. Mama worked the night shift, looking after patients in a retirement home, which was a far cry from the hardworking jobs she held down in the past.

One good thing about Mama was that she always kept a job and earned an honest, decent living, even when my daddy was alive, and took care of things around the house. Mama had been a cook on a ship, a janitor in an office building, and even a custodian at a middle school. Even though Mama was small and petite, with a nice, slamming figure that made young niggas gawk after her, she had wrinkled hands like an old woman, which was a clear sign that Mama needed some time off, for real. I think she had way too much stress on her, and that shit was starting to take its toll and show up in other areas of her life.

"You have to let Ricky live his own life, Mama." I noticed a picture of my daddy on the living room wall that I couldn't take my eyes off. He was dressed in a military uniform, and the photograph had been taken months before Daddy was gunned down by an Iraqi soldier in the first Gulf War.

Yesterday would have been Daddy's birthday. Mama had to be thinking about what happened to him in that war, and it was one of the main reasons why she was so worried about Ricky. I'm not a cold bitch. I understood her fears, and I was scared for my brother, too. But you can't live your life based on what happened in the past. What Mama needed to do was let go of all the pain and bad memories, so she could be completely happy and free in the present. And there was no other way of putting it: Sadness hung from the ceiling like mildew under our roof.

Mama had pictures of our dead relatives hanging on every wall inside the house as some kind of homemade memorial in honor of them, and that shit simply wasn't healthy. She even had a banner over the pictures that read, IN LOVING MEMORY. From my great-grandma Frances who had died way back in the sixties to Eric and Dad, Mama made sure she never forgot the life and times of her people.

Don't misunderstand me: I loved my dead relatives just as much as Mama did, but I didn't want to constantly be reminded of them being dead and gone. It was just too much pain and sadness thinking about how some of them died. Most of my cousins on that wall of hers had been shot and killed on the same streets that took my brother Eric. Stupid niggas be out there in the world fighting and killing one another, when most of us from the Nine was just trying to survive and keep a roof over our heads with drugs and shit on every corner and talk of war and terrorist attacks on the local news stations.

Like everything else, though, me and Mama constantly fought over those pictures being on the wall. And every time I complained about the pictures or anything else she didn't agree with, Mama would say: "Get out of my damn house then!" But this particular time she was in rare form.

"I'm the mama and you're the child," Mama said. Here I was in my twenties, and she was treating me like a dumb teenager. She snatched her car keys off the living room table.

"Sometimes I think you forget that," Mama said. "But as long as you're under my roof, your ass gon' respect me. And what that means is, that boy is not welcome in my house either."

"What boy you're talking about?" I played it cool, although I knew exactly what Mama meant.

"I'm talking about Johnny," she said. "I heard you on the phone talking to one of your friends about him getting out of jail."

You heard right. Mama even tried to control the niggas I dated, too. Babee, that woman was a trip, and she never liked Johnny from the beginning. Mama said there was something about him she just didn't trust. I hate when people make blanket statements like that without anything to back it up. Johnny had never disrespected me or Mama, and she had no reason to dislike that boy. If anything, I was to blame for being young and stupid back then, walking out on Johnny while he was in jail and running off with Rico with some pipe dream of making it big in Hollywood.

"So, now you eavesdropping on me, too," I said to Mama with a twisted and disgusted face. "Man, I really need to get my own place, for real."

"Be my guest." She opened the door to leave. "But until you do, I don't want that ex-con in my house."

Mama slammed the door in my face and left me with a headache.

I immediately picked up the phone and called the one person who I knew would understand. "Hey, girl. I need to talk to you for real. I'm on my way."

"Girl, don't even worry about your mama tonight." Tamika stood behind me, brushing my hair and looking into the mirror. It was after hours at the salon, and she was giving me the hookup.

Tamika was the only one I had told about me and Johnny. How the two of us had planned to meet up while Mama was at work. Me and Johnny would have the entire place to ourselves, and Tamika was gonna make sure I looked my damn best when he arrived.

Thank God we was all alone, because the last thing I needed was to bump into Peaches and get my nerves any more upset with his drama and bullshit. After what I had gone through with Mama, all I needed was the company of a good girlfriend, for real.

"You go home and put on your sexiest outfit," Tamika said. "And remind that man of what the two of y'all once had."

Johnny called me the very next day after he got out of jail, and I took that as a good sign, for all it was worth—although I knew I had a lot of explaining and making up to do. Johnny was nobody's fool, and he was bound to have questions about me and Rico. But the point of tonight was not for us to be doing a lot of talking, but using what I had to get what I wanted. I'll just be blunt: I ain't come this far to be sugarcoating anything for y'all or making this into a rated-PG movie or something when it wasn't one.

I was planning to fuck Johnny and lay this pussy of mine on him like it was the World Series, New Year's Eve, and the goddamn Super Bowl all rolled up in one. As Missy says on her *Under Construction* album, "Pussy, don't fail me now." Shit, I hadn't had a good piece of dick since Johnny went to jail, so you know a sistah needed a tune-up and was long overdue to get her freak on. Was Johnny going to bite? was the million-dollar question at hand.

"Girl, I'm so nervous about tonight that my fucking stomach is in knots." I pulled at my hair, looking in the mirror, making sure that Tamika had bumped my hair right and that it was sticking the way I liked it. Back in high school, Johnny often said that long hair made a woman beautiful, and I think that was one of the reasons I had never cut my hair above my shoulders.

Without a doubt, that nigga was the reason behind a lot of the decisions I had made in my life, although he was in jail and we wasn't together. Johnny was the main reason I hadn't truly committed to another man at this point in my life or why I never left New Orleans in search of better opportunities in the first place. The truth was, I had never stopped loving him. While he was in jail, I felt like part of me was on lockdown, too. My whole life and dreams was wrapped up in Johnny.

After high school, we was supposed to get married and have children and live happily ever after. Prison took that away from us. But tonight was all about new beginnings and reminding Johnny of the passion we once shared. My plan was to get on top of that big fat dick of his and show him like James Bond that "love never dies." Babee, ain't no shame in my game, but you already know that.

"Just relax and be yourself," Tamika said. She started cleaning up the salon and closing down for the night. "You and Johnny will find your way back to each other. Let him see inside your heart and he'll fall madly in love with you again."

"What if he doesn't want me anymore?" I must have sounded like a pathetic schoolgirl, but I didn't give a damn. If I couldn't talk about my fears and insecurities with my best friend, then I couldn't open up to anybody. "Or he hates me for leaving him while he was in jail?"

"Just stop it," Tamika said. She sat down in a chair beside me and placed her manicured hands on top of mine. Tamika was so beautiful and such a class act that I secretly wanted to be just like her. You know, she had gone to college and made something of her life, and I was still living at home with my mama and working for minimum wage inside of *her* salon. I was thinking there had to be more to life than this, but at the time I just didn't know which way to go, up or down. Nothing had gone right in my life once Johnny was sent to jail. Even my dancing career was a thing of the past.

"You are a beautiful, intelligent woman." She caressed my hand, looking me directly in the eyes. She often lifted me up when I was down and depressed. "And it's high time you start to realize that."

"Thank you for saying that, girl," I said. "But I don't feel so smart when I think about some of the dumb shit I've done over the years."

"We've all made mistakes. None of us is perfect, honey," Tamika said. A couple of years ago Tamika had gotten her heart broken by a wannabe playboy who was more interested in her bank account than their relationship. I don't know what's wrong with some of these niggas out here today, thinking they can use a sistah without any regard for her feelings. That's some bullshit, for real. So, needless to say, Tamika got rid of his broke ass quick, and I stood right beside her when she sent that loser packing with his tail strapped between his legs.

"You were young and fresh out of high school," continued Tamika. She was on some kind of serious mission, that was for damn sure—making a sistah feel good about herself. "You had just lost your brother and Johnny went to jail. To be honest, girl, I don't know how you did it. You're stronger than you realize."

"Girl, sometimes I don't know either," I admitted to her and myself. "It was definitely hard on me, but I got through it with the help of the good Lord and you and Latisha. Y'all are my motherfucking bitches, for real. I love you so much, girl."

"Oh, sweetheart." Tamika leaned over and squeezed me tightly. "I love you, too, girl. Now pull yourself together so you can go home and lay it down like a bad bitch Ninth Ward shaker."

"I know that's right, girl." I gave Tamika a high five and grabbed my purse and belongings to leave. "With Mama working tonight, me and Johnny won't have no interruptions."

"Don't hurt nobody tonight, girl," Tamika said on my way out the door. Johnny didn't stand a chance. That nigga had no idea how I was about to put it down for real, for real.

Mama was long gone to work, and I lit the entire house with candles and took a nice, long bubble bath. Afterward I cut some fruit into small pieces and placed them in a bowl beside the bed. This was not my usual style, but I was copying a scene straight out of *Sex and the City*. I knew how to serve it up just like those white bitches. The idea was to treat Johnny like a king–to feed, fuck, and suck him all in one swoop. Moreover, I poured two glasses of wine and made a picnic spread on the living room floor. Johnny and I would start the evening off with wine and cheese and then move to the full-course meal. Of course, I would be dessert. Johnny always did like how I tasted on the inside.

Those pictures on the wall of my dead relatives was looming over me and ruining the entire mood. So, I did what I had to do despite what Mama felt. I took down the pictures and placed them underneath the sofa. I figured what Mama didn't know wasn't gone hurt her. I had the hardest time removing Daddy's pictures off the wall. Although I was young when my daddy passed away, I remember he had a huge smile that would light up the entire room. Daddy had a big laugh, too–he was always laughing and telling jokes. He would sit me on his knee and tell stories about his life that sometimes sounded too far out there in left field to even be true.

Daddy once told me a story about when he was fighting in the Vietnam War and his boat capsized in an ocean of water. His boat flipped over, but he was able to swim back to shore through a river of crocodiles and sharks. Shit, at the time I didn't care if he was telling me the truth or not. Daddy was my hero, and I worshipped the ground he walked on. Still, Daddy and Eric wasn't coming back, and I had accepted that fact a long time ago. Tonight it was all about looking toward the future, not reliving the past.

When I heard the doorbell ring, I took in a deep breath and checked myself one last time in the mirror. I was wearing a hot and sexy red robe from Victoria's Secret with a pair of expensive high-heeled black pumps that made me look taller than I actually was. Moreover, my hair was long and flowing, and I had on just a touch of makeup and some sweet-smelling, seductive perfume.

"What's up with you, girl?" Johnny immediately asked when I opened the door and greeted him in my sexy getup. The first thing I noticed was that he had put on some extra weight, but it was all muscle. That nigga knew he looked fine. I was some wet and nervous.

"Oh, Johnny." I threw myself into his arms and squeezed my titties against his chest. Johnny smelled like a man with a rough edge to him, and that made me even hornier. "I'm so happy to see you!"

When Johnny wrapped his arms around me, I knew something was wrong. There was a coldness in his hug and a blank look in his eyes, but I was determined not to let anything ruin our special evening together.

"I missed you so much." I kissed him again and left a smudge of lipstick on his jaw.

"Damn, girl, you gon' let a nigga catch his breath?" asked Johnny. He took my arms from around his neck and looked me over. So, I struck a pose and even did a Wonder Woman spin for him.

Johnny cracked a smile. "Are you gon' invite me in or what?"

"I don't know what's wrong with me." I opened the door wider and allowed him inside the house. "I'm tripping."

I wish you could have seen the look on Johnny's face when he saw the candles and wine on the living room floor. That nigga was definitely blown away, but you know he was the typical dude. Johnny remained cool and tried not to show too much excitment.

"So, what's all this?" asked Johnny. The entire room was lit with candles. "Did somebody die or something?"

"No, silly." I tapped him on the arm and then handed him a glass of wine. "All of this is for you, baby. I wanted this evening to be special."

"Look, I think there's been some kind of misunderstanding." Johnny set the wineglass on the end table. His negative attitude caught me off guard. I expected some tension, but what he was giving me was something way over the top. "I didn't come here for any of this."

"Of course you didn't." I smiled through the obvious disappointment and hurt on my face. "I made dinner for you anyway."

"I'm not hungry," he said. "If I wanted to eat, I would have ate at home."

Babee, at this point I was really about to let that nigga have it. Throw in the towel and say forget it. You know, he was talking to me like I was a nobody or some stranger off the motherfucking street, and I wasn't that type of girl to take shit off a nigga. Still, I had to remind myself that this wasn't supposed to be easy, so I tried another approach.

"Okay, then. We don't have to eat." I opened my robe and went straight to dessert. Underneath the robe was nothing but my bare skin. Yeah, you heard me right. I was standing in front of Johnny butterball naked with high-heeled pumps on and sipping on a glass of white wine.

"Any more questions?" I asked him.

"Nah, I think you made your point," Johnny said, trying his hardest not to smile or show any reaction, but I could see his dick was blazing hard. No matter how much that nigga tried to resist, he couldn't deny all of the ass and titties I had up in his face.

"Then what you gon' do about it?" I stood directly in front of Johnny and brushed up against him. His dick poked me in my stomach.

"Damn." Johnny grabbed hold of my titties with his huge, manly hands. He was looking at my titties as if they was a slab of barbecue ribs.

"Don't be afraid, nigga," I started taunting, and was shaking in front of him like I was a dancer back at Club Circus. I was moving and singing a Mardi Gras tune. "Do what you wanna. Yeah, do you wanna, nigga?"

"Is that right?" asked Johnny. He was now blushing. "You know you wrong for how you tryin' to seduce a nigga right out of jail?"

"I just wanna make you happy, baby." I kissed Johnny's full and sexy lips, but he wasn't giving any kisses in return. So, I grabbed his dick and started stroking it inside his pants. I was stroking his dick and kissing him behind the ear.

"Stop it!" He pushed me off of him and I almost fell over our raggedy-ass couch. "I told you, man! I didn't come here for any of that!"

"What the fuck is wrong with you?" That nigga must have lost his goddamn mind, pushing me the way he did. Talking was over and done with. I grabbed that wine bottle inside my hand and was about to knock his ass across the head with it. "You don't put your motherfucking hands on me!"

"You weren't trying to listen." Johnny handed my robe over to me. "And here, put some clothes on and put that bottle down. It ain't even that kind of party. You know I would never lay a hand on you."

"Your ass really know how to ruin a good mood." I wrapped the robe around my body and set the bottle on the table. My blood pressure shot through the roof, and I could actually hear myself breathing hard. "I planned this special evening for your ass, and this is how you treat me."

"Look, I'm sorry if you got the wrong idea," he said. "But after everything that has happened between us, I didn't think you would try some shit like this."

"Just get the hell out of my house." I blew out the candles and hit the light switch. My feelings was really hurt, and a bitch was in a lot of pain. It took everything in me not to break down and cry in front of him. "I don't wanna see your face anymore."

"Oh, so you angry?" asked Johnny. I could tell this thing between us was really emotional for him as well. His voice started cracking and shaking like an earthquake. "Well, now you know how I felt being locked up and having to hear about you fucking around with some other nigga!"

"I don't wanna hear this shit!" I shouted, and opened the door for him to leave. "Get the hell out of my house!"

"I'm not going any-fucking-where!" Johnny slammed the door in my face. To be honest, his anger was really starting to scare me. Don't get me wrong; I knew Johnny wasn't gonna hit me or anything, but I had seen him mad before, and it wasn't nothing nice. All the veins inside of Johnny's neck was popping and standing up. "I waited over three years to tell your ass how I felt!"

Next thing I knew, I was bawling, y'all. I started crying and sobbing right there in front of him. Seeing that look in Johnny's eyes and the pain on his face made me realize just how much I had hurt that boy.

"I went through hell up in that bitch," Johnny went on as I sat on the couch and listened to him. "After you stopped writing and coming to see me, I couldn't do shit. There were some days I didn't even eat, let alone sleep. How do you think I felt, knowing that I had sacrificed everything for the woman I loved, only to hear she left me for some rich nigga? Answer me, man!"

"I don't know!" I said. "But I'm sorry. You gotta believe me, baby. I never meant to hurt you. I love you so much."

"Oh, I'm supposed to believe that shit?" Johnny said. "You don't know what love is. Only thing you concerned about is that paper. What, I didn't have enough money for you or something? That's why you was putting out to ol' dude?"

"What are you trying to say?" I stood up in Johnny's face. "Go ahead and say it. You've been wanting to from the moment you walked through that door."

"You know, I could show you better than I could say it." Johnny took a couple of dollar bills out of his pocket and threw the money at me. "Now, bring on Tonya–or should I say Booty–to the stage. I heard she gives the best lap dances this town has ever seen."

"Fuck you!" I hauled off and slapped the piss out of Johnny. I slapped his ass and started punching him in the face.

"Just get the hell out of here!" I said with tears and black eyeliner running down my face that made me look like a stupid-ass clown. But I didn't give a fuck how I looked. Johnny had finally pushed all of the wrong buttons. If he wanted drama, I was just the bitch to give it to him. "I'm not gon' tell your ass again. Get the fuck out of my house before I call the police or do something in this bitch I might later regret."

Johnny grabbed hold of me by both my wrists and threw me up against the door. He threw me against the door and stared me in my face. I could hardly stand to look him in the eyes and see how much pain he was in. And to know that I was the cause of it.

All of a sudden Johnny started crying, y'all, and I didn't know what the hell to do next. There's nothing worse than seeing a grown-ass man cry, because you know that shit's coming from somewhere deep down within.

"Don't you know how much I loved you, girl?" He grabbed hold of me real tight. I felt the bones in my body shiver. "I would have done anything for you."

"I'm so sorry, baby," I said. "Give me another chance. I was so young and stupid back then. But I know what I want. And it's you, baby. Rico never meant nothing to me."

"Man, I don't wanna hear this shit." Johnny closed his eyes and leaned his head against the door. He was trying everything in his power to fight the attraction and chemistry between us.

"Don't hold back your feelings, baby." I kissed Johnny on the lips, behind his ears, and then on top of his chest. His heart was beating and his dick was rubbing up against my leg.

"I don't wanna do this." Johnny pushed me off of him, but not really. He wanted me just as much as I wanted him. I unzipped his pants and pulled out his dick. It was hanging and swinging long. I started sucking and giving him a blow job right there inside of my living room.

"I love you so much, baby." I sucked him off until the muscles inside my jaw swelled.

Afterward, I stood on my feet and saw that Johnny had a look in his eyes like he was about to rip my ass apart. And I don't mean in a physical, violent way.

He grabbed hold of my arm, pulled my body close to his, and tongued the shit out of me. Next thing, Johnny took me in his strong-ass arms and carried me to the bedroom like a damsel in distress. Johnny had taken complete control of the situation, which was not exactly how I'd wanted the evening to

go at first. The plan was for me to lead and for that nigga to follow, but I wasn't about to fight the flow of things. Nothing had
gone the way I had intended, anyway.

"You have any music?" Johnny asked, searching the CD rack
for something nice and slow to set things off. I was stretched
out across the bed and waiting for him to make me feel real
good. I never knew how much I missed Johnny's dick until he
appeared at my front door. A bitch was crawling the walls and
in serious heat.

"Just hit the play button," I said. Suddenly all of the tension
between us had melted away like ice fighting with a hundred-
degree temperature, and I was looking at him with nothing but
lust in my eyes. Once Johnny got the music going, he peeled off
his hoodie, slipped out of those black jeans, and got straight
down to his boxers. His dick was rock-solid hard and poking
out at me and curving to the right like I had remembered it.
The muscles in his stomach was ripped and flat as a washboard.

"You sure you can take all of this?" he asked, as if this was our
first time together or something. Johnny definitely had a big
dick, but I was not afraid of it. Unlike some of my girls, I could
take wood lying down, standing up, or whatever freaky way a
nigga wanted to give it to me. My goal was to please my man
whichever way I could.

"Why don't you come here and see," I said, rising up from
the mattress and shaking my titties in front of him. I had borrowed one of Mama's CDs, so Peaches and Herb's "Reunited"
was setting the perfect mood. I can't speak for Johnny, but I was
for damn sure excited to see him with his clothes off. I took a
piece of kiwi out of the fruit bowl and rubbed it across my nipples.

Johnny got down on the bed and started nibbling my titties

and eating kiwi. Johnny was definitely a titties man. He was sucking my nipples and caressing my titties in his hand when all of sudden he knocked the fruit bowl to the floor.

"Damn, I'm sorry," he said, looking and acting all nervous and shit. I could actually hear that nigga's heart beating.

"What's wrong?" I asked. "You ain't used to be scared of this pussy. What done happened to you in jail?"

"What the fuck you trying to say?" asked Johnny. "I ain't scared of no pussy. Open them legs and let me show you."

Johnny parted my legs and stuck his finger deep inside of my canal. I started shaking and shivering like an addict.

"Just relax." Johnny licked his lips. He was trying really hard not to come off as being nervous, but I could still tell he was. Sweat was popping off his forehead. "I'm not gon' hurt you."

"I am relaxed, nigga." I noticed my name was still on his right arm and got turned on even more. "You're the one who look nervous and shit."

"Man, you tripping." Johnny held his dick in his hand. "I ain't never been scared of no pussy."

"Then show me what you can do, nigga," I said, running my hands across his chest. Johnny was built like a bodybuilder, with thick arms and muscled legs. "Instead of talking all of that shit."

Johnny went down between my legs and started eating me out like it was feeding time at the Audubon Zoo. I moaned and groaned as he bit and chewed me.

He looked up at me with sexy eyes. "What's up? I don't hear your ass talking no more. You like that?"

"It was all right." I bit down on my lips to hold back from screaming. Although that shit was good, I wasn't trying to make his job easy. If Johnny wanted my pussy wet, he was going to have to work at it. "Why? That's all you got, nigga?"

Johnny then kicked things into full force. He got on top, slid inside of me, and started rocking my walls. At first Johnny took it slow, but then he started thrusting his ass real hard. Babee, when I tell you that nigga was rocking my interior walls, he was rocking my goddamn walls; you heard me. If you have ever been fucked by a man straight out of jail, then you know what the fuck I'm talking about, sistahs. That dick was so good that it felt like my pussy was about to open up and explode all over my bedroom walls.

"Whose pussy is this?" Johnny asked, flipping and turning my ass all over the mattress and pushing that dick deeper and deeper inside of me.

"It's yours!" I yelled like I was saluting a commander in the United States Army. "This pussy is all yours, baby!"

"Don't lie to me!" Johnny flipped me over, slapped my ass, and started pulling my hair. He was playing rough with me, but I liked every minute of it.

"Whose is it?" he sounded like he was really into it, but then again, part of it felt like an act. Something was offbeat.

"I told you, baby," I screamed. "It's all yours!"

I had already hit my orgasm and was going for another one when Johnny suddenly fell numb. Hell, yeah, I was surprised. Johnny had never gone soft inside my pussy, especially not before getting his own nut. I figured it had to be the pressure and excitement and buildup surrounding the entire evening. Because it damn sure couldn't have been my pussy that was on fire.

"Everything all right, baby?" I asked.

Johnny slipped out of me and lay across the bed. When I saw his dick soft, it dawned on me that we had forgotten to use a condom. But you know I wasn't that concerned, since I was on the pill and Johnny looked healthy as a damn horse.

"I'm okay," Johnny said. But I sensed that he wasn't. "I don't know what went wrong. Ain't no shit like that ever happened to me before."

"Don't worry about it, baby," I said, but a sistah was disappointed, for real. Johnny hadn't hit my spot the way he had done in past years. But it was all good, though, because I was just so glad to be inside of his arms again that nothing else mattered.

As I lay across Johnny's chest and listened to the beat of his overworked heart, I felt like I was on my own li'l island paradise. Moreover, me and Johnny was like Peaches and Herb, "We both are so excited/'cause we're reunited, hey, hey."

8

James

One thing about me, honey, is that I've never been one of these children to run behind no man. Well, maybe once I did, when I was dating this dude Keith, but I was young and naive back then and didn't know any better. I actually thought if I ran and begged and threw myself at this man's mercy then maybe he might just notice me. Chile, please. If anything it pushed him farther away and made me look extremely pathetic and weak. I learned the hard way that you can't make somebody feel something inside their heart that they just don't. I think that's a song somebody already wrote, but you know what I mean. All of this nonsense because it had been almost a week and I hadn't heard a word from Mr. Johnny Lomack.

Of course I felt played and hurt, because Johnny promised me himself–in a three-page letter–that I would be one of the main people he saw on his first day out of prison. I understood he had his immediate family and close relatives to catch up with, but I thought a girl would at least be in the top ten. When I realized that wasn't happening, I pulled my depressed ass up out of bed and decided to keep it moving. Like I said, there was no time for me to be sitting around and moping over some nigga. I tell these children all the time that if he doesn't love you, then somebody else will. Let his ass go. You gotta be strong and not let people break your spirit out here in this cold and cruel-ass world. I just don't understand some of these children out there who be contemplating suicide and using drugs, all because some man dumped them for someone else. If you can't love me the way I deserve to be loved, I say good riddance and good evening. My mama ain't raised no fool or some helpless weakling. She taught me above all else that you gotta love yourself first. Both of my mamas taught me that, honey, and I got that lesson big-time.

After the fifth day had passed and I realized that Johnny was a no-show, I prayed for strength from a higher power. You heard me correctly. I called on God and looked to the heavens from whence my help cometh. The problem is that some of these children don't have the Lord in their lives, and that's why they be cracking up and losing their minds and giving their bodies to anyone with a long and thick stick. Yeah, I said it. Some of these children out here today are too loose and fast and carefree with the sex thing for my taste. Just fucking every moving, breathing, and living thing on earth, and that BS has to stop before AIDS take all of us out of here, honey.

Moreover, you gotta get some kind of religion in your life, and I ain't necessarily talking about going to church, where there isn't a lot of love and acceptance for the children either. I'm talking about that old-time religion the slaves used to call upon from the soul, lifting their voices up with praise and song from the spot whence they stood. Honey, they didn't need music and instruments to praise God. All those slaves had was their faith and belief in something greater than themselves to pull them out of the hellish situations they were in. Don't have me preach a sermon up in here, because queens got love for Jesus, too. You best believe that, honey. This is the new millennium, and the children are claiming the victory and proclaiming that God loves us just the way we are.

So, therefore, since I was feeling much better with my soul praised from the floor up, I got Ms. Ebony on the line. Me and that girl had business to take care of downtown pertaining to Pandora's case, and there was really no time to waste. If you're not careful, a man will make you lose all focus and perspective. Not me, honey. I wasn't about to let Johnny—or any man, for that matter—throw me farther off track from helping my mother get out of jail.

"Honey, what took you so long?" I had been standing outside of the court building on Tulane and Poydras across the street from the Superdome waiting for Ebony, who was running late. And she knew how much I hated to wait on someone, especially when I was trying to make my coins or handling my business.

"I'm so sorry," Ebony said, swinging a long ponytail over her shoulders and strutting in a pair of tight jeans and a loose tank top. Her titties were round and ripe for the spring season. "You know how Justin is. I had to run down my entire schedule for the day before he let me out of his sight. Girl, he just loves me so much."

Justin was Kojack's real name, and you already know how much I hated his black ass. But what I disliked even more was the way Ebony allowed this man to treat her like she hadn't already been raised by good parents or had any goddamn common sense. I know from seeing with my own two eyes that Ebony came from a loving and supportive family, because I would spend my semester breaks vacationing at her parents' home in Alabama. So I don't know what her deal was.

"What do you mean?" I asked, trying to see her light brown eyes that were hidden behind a pair of dark sunglasses. Since that day was overcast and the entire sky was pitch-black like hell was about to invade earth, I knew something was strange about Ebony wearing dark shades. But she wasn't fooling me, honey. I knew that nigga was beating her ass, and she had a black eye. One of the children had seen Ebony in the mall and had already given me the lowdown.

"He let you go?" I said, like I couldn't believe it myself. "Chile, you make it sound like he owns you or something."

"Don't start with me, Ms. Thang," Ebony said, clutching hold of a fierce Hermès bag and throwing that ponytail around in my face like that donkey's hair was really her own when she probably brought it from the Chinese store over on Canal Street.

Ebony was such a big disappointment. I never thought when we met in college all those years ago that she would end up in this predicament. At Delgado, Ebony was a smart and bright girl with so much promise and ambition. She was studying to become a nurse, and I figured she would end up working in a hospital one day and dating some handsome doctor.

Why would she allow herself to get hooked up with the likes of somebody like Kojack? I will never understand as long as I live, but all I could say was that Ebony was never the same after her mother died from a stroke.

As can be expected, she took the loss real hard, but what caught me off guard was how reckless Ebony became afterward. Before long, she was cutting classes, stripping at Club Circus, and hanging out with losers like Kojack. Needless to say, it was some sad to see my girl go from being a straight-A student to living an unfulfilling life with someone like Kojack. That nigga definitely had Ebony under his thumb, but on the upside, I have to say, he took care of Ms. Girl and had her looking good in designer this or that every day of the week—even when it rained, honey, like it had started doing that day we were standing outside the court building and going back and forth over nothing.

"Let's get out of this rain." Ebony ran inside the building to avoid getting wet. I followed close behind.

"Before I ruin these Jimmy Choo pumps that Justin paid over fifteen hundred dollars for, mind you, on our last trip to New York," she said. "Besides, you can finish reading me later, because right now we need to stay focused on the matter at hand. Pandora is counting on us."

Ebony felt a sense of guilt for Pandora's imprisonment. After all, it was her fight with Booty and some other strippers that brought Pandora to the club that unforgettable night when a young woman lost her life. Behind that gorgeous smile and designer wardrobe was a woman with a lot of hurt and regrets. Pandora was the biggest of them.

"We're here to see Ms. Boudreaux," Ebony told the receptionist at the front desk, a middle-aged white woman wearing eyeglasses and sporting a short, curly hairdo.

"Yes, Ms. Sinclair and Mr. Santiago," the receptionist said. "Ms. Boudreaux is in a meeting upstairs, but she told me to have both of you wait inside of her office. Please follow me."

All I can say is, you know you're a big-time success when you have a white receptionist and a laid-out office with your entire name and title on the front door and you're a person of color on top of that, honey. Ms. Boudreaux was a sister at the top of her game with a reputation for representing the poor and underprivileged and taking home a win in every case.

Remember, Ms. Girl was the one who got my case reduced to almost nothing all those years ago. That was back when she was prosecuting for the state, but Ms. Boudreaux was now on the other side of the courtroom defending the accused criminals, which she seemed to have more passion for, and which was one of the main reasons why I wanted her on Pandora's case.

Like myself, Ms. Boudreaux strongly believed that the criminal justice system was a joke and totally biased when it came to poor people and, minorities, especially black men. I was counting on Ms. Girl's legal expertise and passionate heart to get Pandora's sentence reduced from life to something less harsh, or maybe even have the matter thrown out altogether. They never had enough evidence and shouldn't have prosecuted Pandora in the first place.

"If you guys need anything," the receptionist said as Ebony and I took a seat in the empty chairs in front of Ms. Boudreaux's desk, "please let me know. Make yourselves comfortable. Ms. Boudreaux will be right with you."

"Thank you, ma'am," I said.

"You're very welcome." She closed the door. Ebony and I took in the room. This was our first meeting inside of Ms. Boudreaux's office. Most of the time we would meet her for lunch at a mutually specified location.

"Harvard University," Ebony said as she noticed the various degrees on the wall. Besides the Harvard University law degree, Ms. Boudreaux had a BS degree in political science from Southern University in Baton Rouge, her hometown and birthplace. Along the back wall she had law and various other books neatly laid out inside of bookshelves.

"How impressive." Ebony finally removed the shades and I

was able to see with my own eyes what the children had been gossiping about for days. And just as I thought, she had a dark ring around her right eye that she'd tried to cover up with a heavy coating of makeup. "I knew she was bad, but Harvard and Southern? What a fierce background."

"So, were you going to ever tell me?" I immediately shifted the conversation in another direction.

"What are you talking about now?" Ebony sounded disgusted with me, but she always did when I was pulling her together.

"I'm talking about that nigga and how he's beating your ass," I said. "What the hell is wrong with you, Ebony?"

"Just leave it alone," she said. "It's nothing that concerns you."

"Honey, if I could just get one good round in the ring with that weak nigga," I said, "I would show his ass a thing or two."

"That's exactly why I didn't tell you," Ebony said. "The last thing I need is you and Justin going at it, so you can mess up things for me even more."

"Chile, what could be any worse than somebody punching your ass in the eye?"

"He didn't mean it." She gave me the same dumb line that most abused women in denial say: "It wasn't his fault. He–"

"Girl, just stop," I cut her off, "before I lean over and punch you in your other eye for being so stupid."

Ebony's cell phone rang in the middle of our conversation, and it was none other than the devil himself.

"I told you I had a meeting downtown," she said to him, as I stared and shook my head. "I'm not hollering at you, Justin. I'm just saying."

"Give me that phone." I snatched the cellular out of her hand. "She's in a meeting, and she'll call your ass later!"

I hung up on Kojack before he could get a word in edgewise. Although it felt good hanging up on him, I had never seen Ebony more terrified before in my life. The look on her face would have scared anybody, but not me, honey. I wanted that nigga to ride up on me, so I could show his ass who was really the boss.

"Oh, my God," she said. "You have no idea what you have just done. Give me my phone so I can call him back before it be some shit."

I slipped the phone in my pocket. "I don't think so. His black ass can wait until our meeting is over, if it ever begins—"

"I am so sorry for keeping the two of you waiting." Debra Boudreaux walked in and interrupted us right on cue. She was wearing a blue power suit and carrying a black leather briefcase. Her hair was full of energy and bounce, falling right above her shoulders. What I liked about Ms. Boudreaux was that she was a very feminine and sexy lawyer who simply enjoyed being a woman.

"I got tied up in a meeting upstairs that went longer than I expected," she said as she pulled strands of hair behind her ears. "Are you guys okay? Hope you haven't been waiting that long."

She placed her briefcase on top of the desk and smiled in our direction. Her teeth were white as snow and a perfect fit behind her full and sexy lips.

"Don't worry about it. You're okay," Ebony answered for both of us.

Ms. Boudreaux sat behind the desk and threw her keys across a pile of folders and looseleaf papers. There was a picture on her key chain that caught my immediate attention. It was a photograph of a woman and a distinguished-looking man who looked very familiar to me.

"Is there something wrong, Mr. Santiago?" asked Ms. Boudreaux. She noticed the expression on my face and couldn't help but wonder.

"I know this man." I picked up her keys and pointed at the picture. "He came to my show and even brought me flowers."

"Who, Marvin?" asked Ms. Boudreaux. She looked really surprised. "The two of y'all know each other?"

"Well, not really." I proceeded with caution. Marvin could have been one of those down-low dudes who wasn't completely open about his sexuality to everyone, and the last thing I would have wanted to do was call somebody else out of the closet. It wasn't my place, and I just wasn't that kind of girl. Coming out and being openly gay in the public eye wasn't an easy thing to do in this society, and I respected anyone who chose not to. But, nonetheless, I was still quite curious about the picture.

"He just looked familiar." I choked on my words. "But you know, everyone has a twin."

"I'm sure we all do," Ms. Boudreaux said. "But if you're into drag or anything, I know for a fact it was Marvin. He loves drag shows and has been trying to get me and my partner, Diane, down to Club Circus for years."

Of course, honey, I was gagging to find out that my fine, sexy, and smart attorney was what we children call a lipstick lesbian. Not to say lesbians can't be cute or smart, but this woman was so gorgeous and feminine that I just knew she was straight. You have to understand: The kind of lesbians I knew from my days at Club Circus weren't called lesbians, but real straight-up dykes who acted, looked, and even carried themselves like dudes.

And, ooh, honey, some of them dykes loved to fight. They

could close a club down if someone even thought about look-ing at their woman in the wrong way. Not a feminine bone in their bodies. So, you better believe finding out this news was somewhat of a shock to me, and I was beaming like the sunlight at high noon.

"So, you're family, too?" I said with an air of grandeur. Know-ing Ms. Boudreaux was one of the children made me sit up taller and proud, because she was an embodiment and repre-sentation of the many layers and diversity within the gay com-munity—everything that was positive and good.

"Diane and I have been together for over ten years." She gazed at the photograph, and I saw nothing but genuine love and affection in Ms. Boudreaux's eyes. "Marvin is one of our dearest and closest friends. Just such a nice and intelligent guy. He's actually our personal physician, too."

"A doctor," I said. "How interesting."

I was now thinking about Flo, and how happy she would be to learn that her suspicions were right about Marvin. If she had her way, you know I would have forgotten all about Johnny and taken Marvin as my new man. Seeing the way Ms. Boudreaux stared at the photograph of him and Diane with such love and intensity only made me think about what me and Johnny once had on the plantation. It was sickening to think that we might not ever capture that feeling again.

"All of this has been so very sweet," Ebony said. "Can we please get back to business? I do have another appointment this evening." Ebony could be quite the little bitch at times, espe-cially when it came to the topic of lesbianism. Although Ebony enjoyed hanging out with gay men for fun, she wasn't down for "dyking," as she would often say. For some reason, gay women made Ebony feel very uncomfortable. Maybe she was a closet lesbian herself.

"Please forgive me," Ms. Boudreaux said. Her professionalism was something to behold. She pulled up her sleeves and immediately got down to business. "I don't know what got into me. I'm not usually that open and personal with my clients."

I rolled my eyes at Ebony for making the woman suddenly feel awkward in her own office. "It's all good. You're amongst friends."

"Well, nevertheless, I do have some good news about your friend's case." Ms. Boudreaux said. "After going back and forth with the judge, I was able to get him to at least take a closer look at Ms. Alexandria's case to see if he would agree to a retrial."

"Thank you so much." I squeezed Ebony's hand. This was such good news to both of us. "You don't know how happy we are."

"Let's not get ahead of ourselves, however," Ms. Boudreaux said. "We still have a long way to go. The judge only agreed to take a closer look. That's it. I'll be honest with both of you. In order for us to win a case like this, we need more concrete evidence. Have you made any progress in finding this Noxzema person?"

"Honestly, I haven't," I said with a devious grin on my face. "But believe me, before it's all said and done, I will find her, and she will confess or she'll end up six feet underground. You can take that to the bank and cash the check on it."

"I'll pretend I didn't hear that," Ms. Boudreaux said. "But whatever you do, please make sure it's within the confines of the law. You've made such great strides since getting out of prison, and I would hate for you to do anything that might jeopardize your progress."

During the rest of the meeting we laid out our plan in black and white for Ms. Boudreaux. Since Noxzema wasn't officially charged with anything, it was going to be up to us to get the evidence. Me and Ebony came up with the idea of getting her confession on tape, but Ms. Boudreaux said it wouldn't hold up in court. Noxzema's attorneys could argue she was forced at gunpoint to confess or that the recording was fabricated. There was just so much red tape and legalities to the judicial system that sometimes it was frustrating and mind-boggling.

"Like I said," Ms. Boudreaux warned us. "Don't do anything that might do greater harm than good to your friend's case."

After which, we came up with a better scheme to trap Noxzema into a confession. The tape would only be used as a means to an end. Once we had Noxzema's admittance to the murder on tape, we would simply call the police and have her say exactly what was on it word for word. Of course, I knew our plan was a long shot. But there was no other way if we had any hope of getting Pandora freed from prison.

"It could work," Ms. Boudreaux said. "But just be careful."

"Oh, don't worry about us." I stood up and shook her hand. The meeting had finally come to a satisfying conclusion, and it was now time for me and Ebony to be on our merry way. "If I was you, I would save my prayers for Noxzema."

"Thanks for coming in." Ms. Boudreaux tried to contain her laughter, but a huge smile was plastered across her face. Shit, she knew I was being silly and humorous, but somewhat serious at the same time. Behind every joke is the truth.

She held the door for us. "Be safe and try to keep dry, because from what I understand"—and Ebony, who hadn't said much of anything after learning that Ms. Boudreaux was gay, couldn't escape fast enough, like the woman was gonna suddenly try to lick her pussy or something–"it's raining very hard outside."

Boy, was she ever right about that fact, honey. When me and Ebony opened the front door of that court building, rain fell so hard and continuously from the sky, it made me think twice and wonder about something old folks often said about New Orleans being way below sea level and one day going underwater.

"Talk your shit now!" Kojack yelled as he jumped out of the car and got up in my face, pointing his finger and making threats. That crazy-ass nigga suddenly came screeching up to the court building and almost ran both me and Ebony over on the curb with his BMW. Although he caught me off guard, you know I wasn't scared. Shit, I had been waiting for an opportunity like this one.

"You punk-ass motherfucker." Kojack gritted words between his teeth and continued to mouth off. "So, what you gon' do? Talk your shit now!"

"Get back in the car!" said Ebony. She stood in between the two of us, looking like a hot motorcycle chief with her sunglasses on. "Don't do this, Justin! Please get back in the car!"

When I reached in my pocket, Ebony really started going hysterical and trying to convince Kojack to chill. She knew I always carried a switchblade, like Pandora, and had no problem with splitting a motherfucker in half if I had to.

"Why you not saying anything now?" asked Kojack. I think my silence was making him more nervous than anything. But what that dumb-ass nigga didn't know was that I was being silent for a reason.

"When in the middle of some shit," Pandora said to me

many years ago after an incident outside the club one night, during a fight with a tall, butch-looking drag queen, "stay calm and find your position. And then strike with force and without a conscience."

I reached for the switchblade and was about to drop Kojack's ass on the curb inside a pool of his own blood when we got interrupted.

"Is there a problem?" A police officer drove up alongside the sidewalk as a heavy rain pounded us. Ebony continued to watch me real closely with my hand inside of my pocket on the switchblade.

"No, there's no problem, Officer." Kojack spoke for the three of us. The last thing he wanted was trouble with the law. Most cops knew Kojack by face, since he was one of the biggest drug dealers in New Orleans. But this cop looked as if he could have been a rookie, with his boyish face.

"Me and my man was just having a li'l conversation." Kojack turned away from me and squeezed hold of Ebony by her shoulders. But I never once took my hand out of my pocket.

"Well, have your conversation somewhere else," the cop said. He waited until Ebony and Kojack were safely inside the BMW. As for me, I stood out on the curb and said nothing, with the rain pouring down over me like a running faucet.

"This ain't over, punk," Kojack whispered to me before pulling off with Ebony in the car. By the look in his eyes I knew Kojack meant it, because he was just that kind of nigga. This meant that I would have to watch my back.

"Get home safely." The cop winked at me and drove off. I thought he might have been one of the children, with his wide grin and curious eyes, but I wasn't certain. Sometimes even my gaydar didn't work.

I headed toward Canal Street to catch the Desire bus to that five-four, otherwise known as that mighty Nine, where I had this bad feeling that trouble might be awaiting me.

"Hey, Ms. Armari," Kelly greeted me when I got off the bus. She was a chubby red girl with a pie face who I had adopted as one of my "play" kids around the neighborhood. One thing about those kids on my street, honey, was that they had nothing but love inside their hearts for Ms. Armari. So, I couldn't help but love them back in return. Unlike some adults, who kept their distance and looked at me like an alien from outer space or something, those kids accepted me for me, and I really took that shit to heart.

"Hey back to you, Ms. Kelly." I kissed her fat cheeks. A light drizzle fell from the sky. "And don't forget to call Ms. Armari James when she's not dressed up."

Kelly suddenly had a blank look on her face, like someone caught her hand in the cookie jar. Sometimes I confused that poor child, honey. One day she might catch me in drag, and another time I'm looking like a regular dude from around the block with baggy jeans and a baseball cap.

"I'm sorry," she said with a frown on her cute little face. "I forgot the rules."

"Don't worry about it, hon. We're still friends." I squeezed her cheeks like they were lemons. "Now tell me. What are you doing playing out here in the rain?"

"I was waiting for you to get off the bus," she said with a wide grin. Kelly's mom and dad were both crackheads, so her grandmother was raising her in a one bedroom apartment down the hall from me.

The apartment building we lived in was right off Galvez Street next to the Claiborne Avenue Bridge and less than a mile from the Florida Projects. It wasn't paradise, but it was a far cry from residing in the hood, where a child's innocence could be taken away at any moment and without notice. I was so thrilled knowing that Kelly had gotten out of the projects, from having been around such decay and hopelessness, and now had a solid chance of making something out of her life while living with her grandmother, who loved her. All I could say was, thank God for grandmothers. Without many of them, I don't even wanna think about where some of these children would be to-day.

"That was so sweet of you to wait for me." I handed Kelly a five-dollar bill. Ms. Girl always wanted money, too, but I knew she genuinely loved me, so I didn't mind giving it to her. "Buy yourself something sweet."

"Thank you, Ms. Armari. I mean James." She ran off, but stopped dead in her tracks like she suddenly remembered something important or some earth-shattering news.

"Is something wrong, honey?" I wiped water out of my face so I could see her li'l Chinese-looking eyes up close.

"I forgot to tell you," she said. "There's a man waiting for you by your door, and he looks *real* mad."

I watched Kelly skip away to the corner grocery store before starting my journey home in the rain with that switchblade itching inside of my pocket and burning up against my right leg like fire.

9

Johnny

"Good morning to you!" a sweet, singing, and soulful voice woke a nigga up out of his sleep to bright sunlight with the chirping of birds outside the window. Although that particular day was as beautiful as mornings could get, it for damn sure couldn't touch what went down the previous night under a full moon and storming weather.

While I was still inside the pen doing hard time, I had written this dream letter to James about us having sex with the rain falling outside the window and the two of us fucking and getting our freak on. All I could say now was that the dream had nothing on actual reality. A nigga's dick was still solid hard just thinking about last night's session during the pouring-down rain as me and James got our grind on.

"Wake up, hon." James lay across my chest wearing a white-collared Sunday-school shirt and a pair of sexy black Calvin Klein briefs. His skin was so soft and tender that it felt like silk up against my body. You heard right. I was stretched out on the bed like a king ruling over his castle, and James was right there beside me like my prince on a throne. This was our first time sleeping in the same bed together, a long cry from our days on the plantation when we had to sneak and hide just to fuck around.

"Good morning to you too, nigga," I said to him, rubbing that crappy stuff out of my eyes and trying to wake my ass up completely. It took me a moment to fully get my wits about me and to realize what had happened between us. When I looked underneath the covers and saw my naked body and dick staring back at me, everything suddenly made perfect sense to me. I had showed up at James's door unannounced and had gotten a motherfucking surprise out of this world.

I was standing outside of his door, and James came rushing up the stairs with a switchblade in his hand like he was about to slice my black ass into little pieces. Man, it was some scary and crazy bullshit, which I thought had to do with that letter I had written him from the pen. I had made James a promise that he'd be the first person I would come to see the moment I got released off the plantation. I had broken my word to him, and I thought that was the reason for him coming after me with a switchblade.

But come to find out, it was over some other shit that had to do with my cuz Kojack, which was the biggest fucking surprise of all. James and Kojack already knew each other through a mutual friend. You talking about two worlds colliding? All I could say was that a lot had changed since a nigga had been in the pen, and I had some much-needed catching up to do with everyone.

"So, you all right, hon?" asked James. He kissed the top of my chest and sucked my nipples bone-dry like a little baby at his mother's breast. James was basically trying to finish what we started last night and at the same time soften me up. When he touched me, he had a way of making me forget all about the problems and troubles of the world. His kiss alone made me feel like I was really connected to somebody on this planet, and that was something I never felt with anybody—not even Tonya.

No doubt, things had gotten pretty intense and heated between me and James last night, and it was gone take more than sex to set things right. James had lied to me about knowing Tonya, and a nigga like me hated surprises. The way I saw it, his ass should have come clean with that type of information long before I got out of the pen.

"Am I now completely forgiven about everything?" He looked up into my face with sexy eyes and a slight grin. He had such a sweet nature written all over his beautiful face that it was hard to stay mad at him for too long.

"It's all good." I caressed his face as he lay on the muscle of my arm. His eyebrows were thick, and he had a wide grin on his face. I could hardly take my eyes off of him. He was prettier than some women I had fucked around with in the past. "I'm just glad we got everything out in the open—at least, I hope. A nigga don't need any more surprises."

"I swear, baby. I told you everything." James crossed his heart and hoped to die—a cute way of letting me know that he was being sincere and honest. "I don't want there to be any more secrets between us. But how you gon' handle everything with Tonya?"

I discovered that James and Tonya knew each other from back in the day, when they both were hitting the club scene real heavily. Man, you're talking about too close for fucking comfort. I couldn't believe it.

"What do you mean?" I suddenly got defensive. No matter how much I cared for that nigga, it was still hard for me to talk about Tonya with him. I preferred to keep the two worlds separate.

"You can't go on the way you have," James said. "And why should you? We love each other, and there's nothing wrong with that, hon."

I turned away from him and stared out of the window at the morning sun that was peeping through the blinds. Reality had finally sunk in, and it was weighing on my soul, like a sorrowful hymn on Sunday morning. Me and James were no longer on the plantation inside of our own li'l world with our own set of rules. The love game we played in the pen was now up against a whole lot of other bullshit, and man, I truly didn't know how I was gone handle all of it.

Here I was, lying in bed with some dude that I couldn't get enough of, when only days before I was fucking around with the girl I had loved since high school. Man, it was some twisted and complicated shit, I know, how I was feeling James more than my own girl. But in all honesty, James got my dick to stand up in ways that Tonya never could. And I'm not just talking about sex either, but something deeper that I felt down in my heart for James, although at the time I couldn't admit that shit to myself, let alone to him or Tonya.

"Talk to me, hon." James held me from behind and squeezed hold of my shoulders. "What are you thinking about? I love you, and there's nothing you can't tell me."

I looked him in the face. "I just need for you to be patient with me. You know a lot of this shit is still new for me."

"What?" asked James. "You don't love me, too?"

"That's not what I'm saying, man." I felt nervous and started sweating like a damn horse. "I just need a li'l time to sort things out."

"You can't even say it, can you?"

"Say what?"

"That you love me," he said, searching my eyes for the answer.

"Man, get out of here with all that." I played it off, but the truth was, I was very uncomfortable. Using the four-letter L-word with another dude felt strange to me. "You need to lighten up and just relax."

"Look, Johnny," he said. "I can only be me and say what's on my mind."

Man, it was something else how open James was with his sexuality and how he couldn't have cared less about what other people thought about him. That strength inside of James was what turned me on to him the most.

"And I can only be myself, too," I said. "You got your way of saying and doing things, and I got my way. We two different people."

"And I understand that, hon," he said. "But what I don't want is for you to start beating yourself up again and feeling guilty. When you were inside of that hellhole of a jailhouse, they turned their backs on you without thinking twice. So, you don't owe a damn thing to anybody, especially Ms. Girl Tonya."

"I feel what you're saying," I said. "But I'm not just thinking about Tonya right now, but my entire family, man. You know my pops is a preacher, and he would never accept this shit. None of my peeps would, especially a nigga like Kojack."

"Well, you already know what I think about his ass." He hated my cuz's guts and the very ground he walked on, which wasn't that surprising to me. You already know Kojack was the type of hard-core nigga who wasn't feeling anything homosexual or otherwise, and James was an in-your-face type of li'l dude. So, they were bound not to get along or like each other. I just couldn't believe that I was now smack-dab in the middle of their hatred.

"I know he's your cousin," James went on, "but he's a jerk who has no respect for women—or anybody else, for that matter. He's a low-life drug dealer, and the way he treats my girl Ebony is just dead wrong."

"I feel you on that," I said. "No man should be putting his hands on a woman. I don't know what the fuck my cuz was thinking, but you have to understand that dude been through some shit growing up."

"Whatever, hon. We all done been through some shit in this life, especially black folk, but that's no excuse for bad behavior and ignorance. But, anyway, you don't have to worry about me or Ebony saying anything to him about you and me and this life. As far as I'm concerned, I hope I never run into his ass ever again. But what about your dad?"

"What do you mean?"

"I know the two of you have had y'all's issues, too," he said. "I think you need to deal with that head-on. The tension between y'all may be the reason why you still having those nightmares. You tossed and turned all night long."

No matter how hard I tried to block shit out of my head, I kept coming back to the same exact place. I'm five years old inside of a dark-ass room and someone snatches me up out of my bed, kicking and fighting. I want to scream out for help, but there's a hand over my mouth. Before I awake from my dream, I look up and see the face of Jesus staring down at me.

"I'm sorry if I woke you." I sat straight up in the bed and banged my head against the bedpost like a damn idiot without any sense. I started to rub my head, feeling kinda embarrassed.

"I don't know what the hell is wrong with me sometimes. Why do I keep having the same fucking dream? And why can't I get the face of Jesus out of my head?"

"Maybe it has something do with you not going to church and feeling guilty about it," said James. He lay across me and put his head in the middle of my stomach.

"And?" I said with a li'l cocky attitude. "What the fuck that has to do with anything?"

"I'm not a psychiatrist," he said. "But I think you need to do two things in order to stop these nightmares from haunting you."

"I'm listening."

"First, go back to the church where you grew up," James said. He was real good at giving advice. I wasn't that good at taking it. I turned my face toward the window. "And then find your dad and forgive him. I think that's the only way you gon' deal with that anger inside of you."

"Okay, moving right along." I dismissed him like a bad habit. The last thing I wanted to hear was advice about how me and Pops needed to fix things between us. But going back to church was something I could deal with, 'cause honestly I had no problems with the Big Man upstairs. The only reason I hadn't gone to church in years, anyway, was to spite Pops. Man, I know that must sound childish, but I wanted to do Pops the way he did me when he got up on that court stand and sold me down the river. I wanted him to hurt and feel pain, so he'd know how that motherfucking shit felt.

"I don't wanna talk about nothin' dealing with my old man," I said with a mean-ass look on my face. James was now barking up the wrong fucking tree.

"Well, I guess we won't be inviting him to our wedding either, huh?" James held my face inside of his hand. "Come on, loosen up and smile, hon. You know I hate when you get angry with me."

I finally cracked a smile. "Nah, none of them ain't gon' be coming to our wedding. This thing here is just between me and you."

Afterward, James rubbed his entire face up against my arm like a small kitten giving attention and showing affection to its owner. He was such a touchy-feely li'l dude, but I didn't have any complaints.

"What is this?" I suddenly noticed a beautiful heart-shaped pendant around James's neck and immediately became curious. "You been accepting gifts from some other nigga?"

"Of course not." He ran his hand across my nipples. My dick was poking him in his chest as he lay across my body sideways on the bed. "You know you're the only man for me, hon. Pandora sent this to me in the mail a couple of months ago. She wanted me to have it, which I thought was the strangest thing."

"Why is that?"

"It was the only thing she had from her birth mother," he said. I got nervous and bloated. "You know the two of them have been estranged for many years. Don't get me wrong—I love it, but why would Pandora part with something so special to her? Her letters and phone conversations have been really bizarre, too, like she's given up on life. How was she the last time you saw her?"

"She seemed fine to me." I cleared my throat and quickly felt the muscles inside my stomach tighten up. "You know, running the place and keeping niggas in line. What I do know is how much she loves and misses you, man. That's all she talked about."

"I miss her, too. She's everything to me, and I really don't know what I'd do if she wasn't in my life." James smiled while admiring his necklace. Now, I understood why Pandora held me to secrecy. Knowing the truth about Pandora lying sick in the pen's infirmary was only gonna break James's heart, man.

"I miss my motherfucking girl," said James with a huge grin on his face. "And I've been counting down the days until she comes back home. You know I've been working with a lawyer. We gon' try to get her out of that fucking hellhole, honey. Now that you're home maybe you can help us? It'll be like old times, me and you working together and doing research."

I turned away from him and stared out of the window once again.

"What's wrong, hon?" he asked. "Don't shut down. Talk to me."

"I just hate talking about that place." I stared him in the eyes and shook my head. "Man, after you left, shit got worse for everybody. Dudes started dropping like flies."

"I heard about that," he said. "That shit's been all over the news, how some bacteria got inside the prison and was knocking off inmates left and right. I'm so happy you got out, and to hear that Pandora's doing fine as well."

"I don't understand," I said. Part of me was hoping that it was a miracle. That Pandora had bounced back. That the strain of tuberculosis that was killing dudes on the plantation hadn't taken a turn for the worse. "You heard from Pandora?"

"She wrote me a letter a couple of weeks ago," James said, "letting me know that she was doing okay, and for me not to worry about her, which was a big relief. It must have gotten pretty scary for y'all inside of that place, huh?"

"Man, you don't know the half of it," I said, but quickly

caught myself. James had no idea how close to home he was hitting. Over forty dudes had already died from that shit.

"But let's change the subject," I said. "Talk about something less sad."

Suddenly James leaped out of the bed with a seductive and devious grin on his face. Moreover, I could tell by the look in his eyes that he had something else on his mind besides talking. What he now wanted was some dick. And I was just the right Ninth Ward nigga to lay it down for him.

"What's up, man?" I pulled my arms behind my head and flexed my chest muscles for him. I stroked my dick so James could see all nine inches of what he was going to be getting.

"You don't wanna do that," James said, peeling off his clothes like he was stripteasing in some goddamn club, which wasn't that much of a surprise to me. James loved performing and putting on a show, and all you had to do was look at the pictures on his bedroom wall to prove it.

Covering every inch of the wall were photos of just about every black woman singer, from Beyoncé to Patti LaBelle, Whitney Houston, Diana Ross, Mary J. Blige, and the Queen of Soul herself, Aretha Franklin. He called that wall his "diva wall," and the funny part about it was, James could perform every last one of those ladies' songs with his eyes closed.

James did drag part-time at this club in the French Quarter, which I had no real problem with. As long as he carried and conducted himself like a dude in the public eye, it was fine by me. You know I wasn't down for walking down the street with some dude dressed like a woman. Not that I was ashamed of James or anything, but I had always been private with my shit.

"You think I can get a repeat performance of last night?" James tossed the white shirt on the floor and then slipped out of his briefs. His dick was hard, moving up and down like it was on vibrate.

No doubt, James was a sexy li'l motherfucker with a slender body and a nicely toned chest. Sometimes it blew me away how he looked like such a solid nigga on the outside that if you saw him on the street you would never suspect he was a gay dude who did drag. Until he opened his mouth, that is. James's body may have been masculine-looking, but his voice was for damn sure feminine. But it was all good, 'cause I liked both sides of him.

"You think you can handle all of this?" My dick saluted his like they were both old-time friends or war buddies.

"No, the question is"—James turned around and gave me a front-row view of his sexy, round ass—"can you handle all of this?"

The veins inside my dick looked like railroad tracks. Blood rushed to my head.

"Bring that sexy ass here," I said, holding my dick in my hand and waiting for him to mount me. But if you could believe, the phone rang and interrupted us.

"Hold that thought," James said, picking up the phone. "What's up, Jerome? I can't talk—I'm in the middle of something, hon."

Jerome was one of James's daughters from the "House of St. James": James was the mother of the house. It was interesting to me how gay dudes had their own sorority and shit. In fact, everything about this world was interesting to me. Sometimes I felt like a kid in a candy store.

"Calm down, hon." James looked serious. "It's going to be all right. Come and see me later and we'll talk about it. Try not to worry. Men are just dogs. And remember I love you.

"Sorry about that." He disconnected and quickly went back into his seductive mode.

"Is everything all right with your friend?" I stroked my dick.

"Chile, she'll be all right," he said. "That girl is always going through it over some man. Now, where were we?"

James leaned against the bed and started sucking my toes. Man, my entire body started shivering and shaking. Nobody could suck motherfucking toes like that nigga. Then he ran his tongue up my entire body until he found my weak spot: James rested his tongue inside the circle of my navel.

"Come on, man," I said trying to push him off of me, but not really. His damn tongue felt good. "Stop playing around."

James lifted my right hand and started sucking my fingers one by one.

"If you keep this up, I'm gon' nut all over your ass," I said, biting down on my bottom lip to stop from screaming out loud like a rooster at the dawn of early morning. My ass got hot and sizzled like fajitas over an open flame. And my dick had a tangy itch that felt like an unbelievable sensation of pure fucking joy.

"Okay. Now that I've had my appetizers I'm ready for the main course." James snatched a condom off the top of his dresser and tossed it over to me. "But first you need to handle your business, player."

No doubt, James was a responsible li'l dude when it came to safe sex, which I hadn't always been good about. When a nigga like me got into a heated situation or felt that joyful feeling on the tip of my dick, I would sometimes forget about strapping up. I know that must sound stupid with these diseases and AIDS killing motherfuckers out there in the world today, but I'm just being truthful. Some niggas just think they are invincible and shit. And I guess I was no different.

I slipped the condom on and smiled. "You ready to take Big Willie for a ride?"

James suddenly jumped on top of my dick and straddled me like he was fixing to take a full-grown horse out to pasture.

"It's time for you to show Mama what you working with, hon," he said, spreading his entire ass over my dick. A warm, unbelievable feeling came over me, like I was about to go somewhere I had never been before. That's how I felt with that nigga—like we were meant for each other. Man, we rocked those bedsprings and slammed the bedpost against the wall so hard it sounded like a damn earthquake.

"Work that shit out, baby," I said, moving and thrusting my ass as hard as I could. James rode my dick like a Western cowboy as we fucked long and hard.

Me and James were in the bed working them box springs and getting our motherfucking groove on when someone rang the doorbell and interrupted us.

"I'll be right back." James slid off of me and ran out of the room.

Hell, yeah, a nigga like me was mad. First Jerome called, and now someone else stopped me from exploding and nutting into ecstasy. Leaving me with a hard dick and a set of tight balls full of cum was like torture.

"I'm so sorry, hon." James rushed back into the room and started putting his clothes on in a hurry. "One of my kids' grandmother just collapsed in her apartment, and I need to get her to the hospital."

"Is she all right?" I threw the covers off of me. "You need me to go with you?"

"No, hon," James said. "That won't be necessary. I'll call you later."

Before I could say another word James was already out of the door, which wasn't that surprising to me. James had a big heart, and he truly cared about those kids around his neighborhood, which I found very interesting. You just didn't find human beings today who worried about other folks' problems the way James cared about people. I couldn't help but respect that dude. But I wasn't at all happy that he ran out on me and Big Willie. "I guess it's just me and you, nigga," I said to my own dick.

The sheets on the bed made for a perfect tent while I handled my business with the bedsprings singing to me and the morning sun blazing in my eyes.

10

Tonya

"I think Johnny's gonna ask me to marry him," I said to both Latisha and Tamika, who listened to me go on and on about Johnny. Early morning at the salon was a time for gossip before getting our asses ready for a long day of work and grind.

"Girl, I'm so happy for you." Latisha hugged me and rocked me from side to side.

"Me, too, girl," Tamika said from across the room. She was setting up beauty supplies on the front counter. Besides the three of us, there was two other ladies waiting to get their hair done and watching the *Ellen* show on TV. They were Peaches's clients, and for some reason he was running late that morning, which wasn't no skin off my back. Some days I actually wished he wouldn't have showed up at all. The mood inside of the salon was so peaceful and quiet when his loudmouth ass wasn't around.

"Girl, you must have laid it down the other night," Latisha said, "for that nigga to now wanna walk you down the aisle."

Of course, I wasn't sure whether Johnny was going to ask me to marry him or not, but it was just a feeling I had. You know a girl has a sixth sense when it comes to certain things. When Johnny called me last night and told me that he had something important to tell me, I figured, What else could it have been? Niggas just don't be calling you up out of the blue and saying shit like that unless they be about to open their hearts and express their true feelings for real. One of my girlfriends had gotten a similar phone call from her man five years ago and now she was happily married with three children.

"Baby, you don't know the half of it," I said. "He was knocking down my walls like it was nobody's business. Banged me up so badly, I could hardly get out of the bed the next day."

"Damn, girl," Latisha said. "Was he trying to kill you or what?"

"I heard that get-out-of-prison dick ain't nothing nice," Tamika said. "Although I would never know, since I've never dated a criminal or anything."

"Hold up, bitch." I pumped Tamika's brakes real quick. "My man ain't no motherfucking criminal."

"Oh, my bad," Tamika joked. She actually thought that shit was funny. "I must have gotten him mixed up with someone else. Because the Johnny I knew did hard time in that slave prison upstate."

"For trying to protect me," I corrected her. Although Tamika was often supportive of me, she could sometimes be the most judgmental person of all. For some reason, Tamika couldn't really understand why I had such strong feelings for Johnny when he was nothing but a loser in her eyes. She never came out and said those words, but I knew it to be true by the way Tamika would make wisecracks at Johnny on the sly.

"That's the only reason why he went to jail," I went on. "Looking out for me."

"Okay, girl, you don't have to get your cage all rattled,"

Tamika said. "I know how much you love Johnny, and I've always supported y'all's relationship. Haven't I?"

"I know you have, but y'all don't understand how much I love this dude," I said. Maybe Tamika was on her period or something, but she picked the wrong damn morning to challenge me about my love for Johnny. Mama had already beat her to the punch.

Since she found out about Johnny being out of jail, Mama had been on my case every day about seeing him.

"He ain't gon' do nothing but bring you down," Mama said the morning after I fucked Johnny in her house. Of course, Mama had no idea about that shit going down under her roof, but it was my own personal secret of sweet revenge. "There's just something about that boy that I don't trust."

Rico was the man Mama had chosen for me, if you could believe. And the only reason she liked Rico was because he was rich and famous. Now you tell me who was more screwed up in the head—me or Mama? Here she knew better than anyone else how badly that nigga had treated me, and yet she still wanted us to end up together, which wasn't happening, whether Johnny was in the picture or not. Rico was too much of a whore for me to be trying to settle down with him, for real.

"I've loved that nigga since high school," I said with dreamy eyes. As far as I was concerned, me and Johnny was already inside of the church standing in front of the minister and saying our vows. Babee, my head was so in the clouds—you hear me—that I could hardly stand up straight for being so damn happy. "You know y'all gotta be in my wedding."

"What colors would we have to wear?" asked Latisha. She was really catching on to the idea, but not Tamika, who was more like a dark cloud over my sunshine.

"Could you at least wait until the man popped the question first?" Tamika said to Latisha with nothing but attitude. Whatever the fuck her problem was, it was beginning to get on my last nerve. But Tamika's sour mood only got worse when Peaches walked in on the scene, being his usual faggot and messy self.

"Phi Geeeee," Peaches shouted with his index finger in the air, as if his ugly, troll ass could ever be mistaken for a Delta Kappa. He was making fun of Tamika's sorority, which set her completely off.

"Hey! Hold the fuck up." Tamika's entire face turned demonic. She pointed her finger at Peaches. "I told your ass about playing with my sorority."

"I was just clowning around with you, cuz," Peaches said with a dumb-ass look on his face. I was very surprised by Tamika's reaction toward him. She rarely ever lost her cool, especially with Peaches—her favorite cousin.

"I told you in the past about taking my sorority for some fucking joke," Tamika said. "Me and my line sisters went through too much shit getting our letters to have someone like you play around with our traditions."

"What do you mean, someone like me?" asked Peaches.

"Just get to work," Tamika said. "Your customers have been waiting on you for over thirty minutes. I'm not going to tell you about your tardiness again."

"They can wait," Peaches said. He swung a Chanel bag off his shoulders and threw it across the chair. "You obviously have something on your mind, Tamika, and I wanna know what it is."

"I already told you how I felt," she said. "Don't fuck around with my sorority business or you and me gon' have major problems."

"You act like I'm the only one," he said. "I know so many of the children out there who are Delta Kappa Zetas at heart and don't mind letting you know it either."

"What the hell's that supposed to mean?" asked Tamika. Me and Latisha took a front-row seat to the drama.

"I'm talking about the gay children," Peaches said. "At the club, it's like the in thing to say that you're a Delta Kappa Zeta. In fact, there's this drag queen I know who starts every one of her shows with the Delta Kappa Zetas' call."

"Oh, yeah?" Tamika said. "Then I'm just gon' have to come down to that club and set them straight. Because ain't nobody gon' be disrespecting my sorority. When does this so-called drag queen perform?"

"This coming Wednesday," Peaches said. "Are you really coming down to Club Circus to confront the children?"

"Do I look like I'm fucking playing?" Tamika rolled her eyes.

"Girl, we got your back." Latisha gave Tamika a high five. "Just let us know the place and the time and you ain't saying nothing but a thing."

"You can count me in too, girl," I said. "If them punks want some drama then we're just the three bitches to give it to 'em."

"Well, I guess that solves that problem." Peaches removed his Chanel bag from the chair and called over his first client. "Come on over here, Ms. Precious. Let me beat that hair of yours, girl, 'cause my fellow coworkers done worked my nerves this morning."

Everyone returned back to work. One thing that was clear, though, was that we was going down to that gay club, and it was gonna be some shit when we got there, for real. Tamika had made that crystal-clear before continuing with her morning chores.

"Can you please turn that volume up for me, baby?" I said to one of our clients who was controlling the remote control to the TV.

The morning news was now on the tube, and I was hoping to hear something about the war in Iraq. You know my brother was over there in that country and that shit was constantly on my mind—the one thing me and Mama did have in common: We was both worried about Ricky's safe return home.

"Now more breaking news just coming in to us this morning," Angela Hill said. She had been the lead anchorwoman for Channel Four News for years. I wasn't prepared for the words that came out of her mouth next.

"We just got word that local millionaire rapper Rico collapsed onstage during a promotional concert for his latest CD," she reported. "No other information is available at this time."

"Hey," Latisha said to me. "Where you think you're going?"

I took off running and left the front door swinging behind me.

"What the hell are you doing here?" Beverly immediately asked upon answering the door. She was Rico's mom and business manager, who couldn't stand the ground I walked on.

Don't ask me why. I never did this woman a damn thing but tried to love her son with all of my heart. The problem with Beverly was that she thought nobody was good enough for Rico, although nine times out of ten he was the one out there breaking hearts and doing somebody else wrong. That boy was terrible, but you couldn't tell Beverly nothing when it came to her precious son.

"Hello to you, too, Ms. Beverly," I said. "I need to see Rico. Is he home?"

"First of all, follow me." She swung the door open and headed back down the long driveway in search of Rico's bodyguards, who watched over his property like hound dogs. I tagged along beside her. "How did you get past security?"

Rico's house—or should I say mansion—was something out of a fairy-tale book: five thousand square feet of beautiful white brick marble that gave the White House a run for its money. Rico had six bedrooms, seven bathrooms, a six-acre lake, a Jacuzzi, a poolhouse, basketball and tennis courts, and a movie theater all on one piece of land that overlooked Lake Pontchartrain. Although I had been to his house many times over the years, it always took my breath away.

"Why did you allow her past security?" Beverly asked Chuck at the front gate. He was one of Rico's most trusted and personal bodyguards. When me and Rico was an item, me and Chuck had always gotten along well, so he was on my side from the beginning.

"I thought it was okay." Chuck choked over his words. Beverly had a way of intimidating people with her deep, raspy voice and strong black-woman presence.

Don't get me wrong. Beverly was a beautiful dark-skinned sistah who was a force to be taken seriously in the rap and entertainment world—a far cry from her days growing up in the Desire Project that was once the most ruthless hood in the NO. That's right. Ms. Beverly was from the hood, too, and even though she tried to cover that shit up with designer suits, long weaves, and makeup, her ghetto side came through loud and clear.

"You thought it was okay?" she scolded Chuck like he was a child or something. "My son doesn't pay you to think," she said. "Don't let something like this happen again."

"Whatever you say, ma'am." Chuck walked away, leaving me and Beverly alone with each other, which was a dangerous thing to do. The two of us had never gotten along and was prone to go at each other's throat. A couple of years ago, we was on the set shooting one of Rico's music videos, and she hauled off and slapped the piss out of me for raising my voice to her. At the time I walked away because I was afraid of putting my hands on her and losing Rico. But, babee, I was now waiting for her ass to try me.

"Why don't you leave Chuck alone," I said. "It wasn't his fault."

"Don't you talk back to me, young lady." Beverly grabbed hold of me by the arm and squeezed tightly. "Let me show you out of the gate."

"Get your hands off of me, woman!" I wasn't weak. So, you damn right I pushed Beverly off of me so hard that she fell on the front lawn in her Roberto Cavalli suit.

"You ghetto bitch!" Beverly jumped off the lawn and launched toward me, but Rico came out of nowhere in his house robe and slippers and caught Beverly's hand in just the nick of time. We was about to be some Crystal-and-Alexis, *Dynasty*, catfighting bitches out there on that lovely and beautiful estate of Rico's.

"That's enough, Mama," Rico said. He held Beverly by her arm and stood in between us. "I could hear y'all way from the main house. What the hell is going on out here?"

"She attacked me, son," Beverly said, out of breath. "I'm calling the police."

"She's a lying witch," I said. "Ain't nobody attacked her. I came here in peace, because I heard on the news about what happened to you. But I see coming here was a big mistake."

I turned to walk away, but Rico caught hold of me by the hand. His eyes was suddenly talking and begging me not to leave. In that moment, I felt a rush of feelings come over me that was kind of scary. Me and Rico had a connection, and I couldn't deny it no matter how fucking hard I tried.

"I don't want you to leave," he said with my hand in his. "You came all of this way. You might as well stay awhile."

"Son, are you completely out of your mind?" asked Beverly. "Dr. Rivers told you to stay in bed and rest. That means no visitors, especially of the gold-digging kind."

"Put a lid on it, Ma." Rico led me up the walkway to the main house. "She's staying, and that's all there is to it."

"Please give us some privacy," Rico told his housekeeper as we entered his bedroom. "Damn, I still can't believe you're here." He snuggled a white teddy bear underneath the gold-and-black silk sheets on his king-size bed. Rico's crib may have been off the hook, but his bedroom was like a palace all in itself, with black and gold everywhere—his favorite two colors in the world.

"Have a seat." Rico had the cutest dimples and the prettiest teeth that I had ever seen, especially on a dude. But that was the way Rico was: well-groomed with a low fade cut, and always sharp from head to toe. "I promise not to bite," he said.

"Thank you for taking up for me with your mom." I sat next to him on the bed and took in the entire bedroom. On the walls was pictures of just about every male and female rapper on the planet, alive or dead. Although Rico was a superstar himself, he was a fan of Lil' Kim, the Game, Kanye West, Tupac, Biggie, and so many other legends in the rap game.

"True dat," he said. "You know you can't pay her any mind. She just be trying to look out for a nigga."

Rico started with a coughing fit like he had the worst flu. Of course it caught me off guard. I had never seen him weak and helpless like that before. In my eyes, Rico had always been the tough-ass, invincible rapper. You never think about celebrities getting sick and being down for the count.

"Are you all right?" I rubbed his leg. "Have you seen a doctor about that cough? It doesn't sound good."

"Don't worry about me, girl. I'm gonna be all right," he said. I could tell he was trying hard to fight whatever was ailing him. You know how niggas are. Hate to appear weak and shit, especially in front of us women.

"And yes, I've seen a doctor. Just got a li'l bug," he went on. "Nothing a couple of days of rest and relaxation won't cure. But damn, I still can't believe you came to see me."

"Why you say it like that?"

"You know," he said. "It wasn't like we ended on the best of terms."

"Don't remind me," I said. Part of me had never gotten over him dating that white chick. "How's your li'l white girlfriend, anyway?"

"We been over and done with." He slid his hand underneath the covers and started playing with his dick to let me know exactly what was on his mind. But I wasn't that surprised. Rico was well-known for being a nasty and horny bastard, and no amount of sickness was going to stop a nigga like him from trying to hit the pussy.

"She wasn't strong enough to handle a brother like me," he said. "What I need is an African queen by my side."

"How long it took your dumb ass to figure that shit out?"

"Damn, that's cold. But you know what?" Rico lay across his

gold pillow and stared at me with the most intense look on his face. "Let's not talk about her."

"Why you looking at me like that?"

"I see you put on a few extra pounds," he said, still holding his dick underneath the covers. "But that shit looks good on you."

"Thank you," I said. "I try to take care of myself and look good for my man, Johnny."

Shit, I had to say or do something to set that nigga straight. Rico was beginning to get the wrong idea about my visit. He had sex on his brain when I was just basically trying to be a concerned friend. That was it. I swear.

"Now, that's some fucked-up shit to say," he said. "Throwing that jailbird nigga up in my face."

"Don't call him that," I said. "I never called your white girlfriend out of her name."

"True dat," he said. There was a long pause between us.

"What you been up to?" he asked. "Besides fucking around with that loser."

"I'm working at my girlfriend's salon," I said real proudly.

"I'm happy for you." Rico let out another loud cough. It hung in the room over us, but he quickly got hold of himself.

"You sound horrible," I said. "You gotta start taking better care of yourself."

"If I knew I was going to get this kind of love and attention from you," he said, "I would have gotten sick a whole lot sooner."

"Don't joke around like that." I rubbed the top of his leg once again. "You can't be playing with your health. Your fans are counting on you to be around for some years."

"Okay, Mommy," Rico joked. "I promise to take better care of myself."

"Good." I smiled. "Now I feel a whole lot better."

My eyes caught an old picture sitting on top of his dresser of the two of us. We was on the set of one of his videos in New York City, one of my favorite places to hang out. When I was in the Big Apple, I felt so alive and full of life. You just don't get that kind of rush growing up in the Ninth Ward.

"I can't believe you kept this picture of us." I held the frame in my hand. It took me back to one of those rare days when me and Rico actually got along working together on a project. "We had the best time shooting this video."

"Yeah, it was a lot of fun." Rico stroked his dick underneath the covers. "We definitely made a good team. You been doing any dancing?"

"Not really." I straightened the picture frame on the dresser. "I don't have much time for dancing anymore. I'm just trying to keep a roof over my head and pay the bills."

"Now, I think that's a shame," he said. "To have a body like yours and not be sharing it with the world. Why don't you come back on the road?"

"Okay. Now I know you're sick in the head," I said, "to be asking me back when we did nothing but fight like cats and dogs on the road."

"I was young and bigheaded back then," Rico confessed. This was definitely a different side of him that I hadn't seen when we was dating. If he was running game, I damn sure couldn't tell.

"Just starting my career," he said. "So many women around that I couldn't see what I had right there in front of me."

"Stop tripping," I said. Part of me wanted to believe in him, but another side of me couldn't forget how full of shit he was. Rico had always been a smooth-talking nigga with charm coming out of his ass. "You know you don't mean that shit."

"I'm being serious," he said. "We shooting this project in South Africa in a couple of weeks to help stop the spread of AIDS. It's gonna be real big with 50, Diddy, Ciara, and a lot of other big-name players in the game. I want you to join us. Come on. Say yes. It'll be like old times, and you'll be helping to make a difference. If you don't do it for me, think about all of them children in Africa who need you."

Of course, I was blown away by Rico's offer. His desire to help the children of Africa was kinda touching, too. You just don't see too many young rappers caring about other people in the world besides themselves. Rico had grown over the years and I liked the new him.

"So, this is strictly on the up-and-up?" I said.

"Scouts honor," said Rico. He held his hand in the air like a proud soldier. "This is business, and you know I don't be kidding when it comes to my motherfucking career."

"And you understand that I'm now with Johnny?"

"You don't have to rub that shit in my face," he said. "But, yeah, I understand where you coming from. As long as you understand that I scratch your back and you gotta scratch mine, too. You feel what I'm saying?"

"I thought you said it was on the up-and-up." I got defensive. "No strings attached."

"Come on, nah." Rico stroked his dick underneath the covers. "You know how this business is. Besides, I know you miss me or else you wouldn't be here."

"I should have known"–I shook my head. Rico may have been a changed man in some ways, but not when it came to using other people to get what he wanted—"that it was too good to be true, and you wasn't playing it straight."

"Come on. It'll be our little secret," he said. "Nobody has to know. Besides, I know you ain't happy working in some salon."

"I don't know about any of this," I said. "I just came here to check on you. Now everything is happening so fast."

"Stop thinking about it and just go for that shit." Rico pulled the covers back on the bed and made room for me beside him. "Oh, did I mention how much a gig like this is paying?"

He lay back against the pillow and watched me closely.

"Okay, I'm listening, nigga."

11

James

"You're a lucky woman, Ms. Wilson," Dr. Cramer said to Kelly's grandma as she lay in the bed with tubes and machines attached to her body on the fourth floor of Charity Hospital. Ms. Wilson had suffered a mild stroke, and we were all just thankful she was alive. Three days ago we thought that girl wasn't gonna make it, honey.

"Your pressure is down," the doctor went on. "And you're getting stronger every day."

Apparently Ms. Wilson was a diabetic with high blood pressure who hadn't been taking good care of herself. Part of it had to do with her health insurance policy, which didn't cover a lot of her medical expenses. Now, you tell me something ain't wrong with that picture. Ms. Wilson was in her late sixties and far too old to be worrying about deductibles and all of that other bullshit. Reading all of those law books when I was doing my time on the plantation, I had learned a lot about Ms. Health Care in this country and how she was nothing more than another form of racism against the poor and underprivileged.

"Thank you, Doctor," said Ms. Wilson with a strained and

weak voice. No matter how grim her reality was, she tried to put on a positive and strong front. "You did good by me, and I'll never forget it, sugar."

"Don't mention it," Dr. Cramer said. "I'm just doing my job. You're the real hero. The way you fought back from this stroke in record time is amazing."

"But I still thank you, sugar," Ms. Wilson said. It sometimes hurt her just to speak. The pain was in the grin of her cheekbones. "Over the years y'all been good to me up here at this hospital."

Charity had some of the best doctors in the world who truly cared about the poor people. But, shit, they saw just about everything imaginable under one roof. From gunshot wounds to pregnant women and AIDS patients, Charity doctors were some of the hardest-working people in the medical profession, across the color line. You heard me. Black and white doctors were on the front line in that damn hospital taking care of the elderly and poor folks who oftentimes didn't have a pot to piss in or a window to throw it out. So the fact that Dr. Cramer was a white woman doctor wasn't that much of a surprise to me at all.

"Don't thank me." Dr. Cramer squeezed Ms. Wilson's wrinkled hands. "Thank your granddaughter for calling in help, and this lovely man for getting you to the hospital in time."

Ms. Wilson looked over at me with the tubes running through her nose. She smiled. "Oh, I can't forget my man. That's my little sexy and sweet friend. He would be my boyfriend," she said, "if he was old enough to hang with me."

"All right, now," I said. "Don't start nothing up in here you can't finish."

"I see the two of you are already well acquainted with each other," said Dr. Cramer. She was a tall and slender lady with round glasses and a genuinely sweet personality. "So, I'll leave you two lovebirds alone."

"Don't worry, Doc." I smiled over at Ms. Wilson. "She's in good hands."

"I'll be leaving early today, but Dr. Holmes will fill in for me for the rest of the day." Dr. Cramer signed Ms. Wilson's medical chart and dropped it in a slot at the foot of the bed. "He's an excellent physician."

"Did you say Dr. Holmes?" I couldn't resist asking.

"Yes. Dr. Marvin Holmes," Dr. Cramer said. "Do you know him?"

"Sort of," I said. "He knows a friend of mine."

To tell you the truth, the man had been on my mind ever since I found out that he and my lawyer were friends. You know, it was such a small world how all of us were connected.

"Such a fine young man," Dr. Cramer said. She turned her attention back toward Ms. Wilson. "And he's going to take real good care of you. Take it easy now, and don't overdo it."

"Yes, ma'am," Ms. Wilson said. "Don't you be worrying about this old girl. She's gotta lot of trouble to be getting into."

Dr. Cramer immediately took off without commenting. Once Ms. Wilson got started, there was no stopping that girl, honey.

"Come here, baby," she whispered to me. I moved in a little closer to her bed.

"What you need, hon?"

"Why don't you run down the street and get me some pig lips and a bag of red-hot potato chips to go with it," she said. "They killing me up in here with this hospital food."

"Now, come on, Ms. Wilson," I said. "You know better than that. That kind of food ain't good for your high blood pressure."

"Oh, shit," she said. "I'm getting older every day, and I can eat what I damn well please. All of us are gonna die of something, anyway."

Ms. Wilson had made a good point, but what she was hinting at was a real serious problem with many black folks. Chile, we put too much of everything inside of our mouths without thinking about the health risks.

Don't get a girl wrong. I love soul food just like the next person, but black people got the highest blood pressure, and highest rates of diabetes, strokes, and clogged arteries than any other race. The truth was, though, I was heading home myself to eat a big pot of collard greens, pig tails, and corn bread. Shit, I didn't say I was perfect, but I was simply trying to inform you what I know about the medical situations of my black folks.

"You're right about us all having to die." I held Ms. Wilson's hand. She gave me a warm feeling inside. "But I'm not about to be the one to help you get there faster. Besides, you have a little cute granddaughter who needs you to stick around for a long time."

"I hate when you're so damn right," she joked. "Where's my little angel, anyway?"

I walked over to the door and stuck my head out into the corridor. Kelly was sitting in a chair and playing with her black Barbie doll. For the past couple of days while Ms. Wilson was in recovery, I had been responsible for Kelly. They didn't have much family in the immediate vicinity besides Kelly's crackhead mama.

"Hey, you," I called over to Kelly. She was in her own little seven-year-old fantasy world with Barbie. "Someone in this room wants to see you. You think Barbie would mind if you stepped away for a moment?"

Kelly tossed that Barbie doll to the side and ran into the room without any shame or hesitation.

"Hey, Grandma!" She lay across Ms. Wilson and immediately started crying.

"Don't cry, my little angel." Ms. Wilson caught the tears from her granddaughter's eyes in the strength and wisdom of those wrinkled hands. There was some deep history in every last one of those wrinkles, I figured.

Kelly would often tell me stories about how her grandma had to clean and scrub floors for white folks in some rich neighborhood uptown just to keep a roof over their heads and food on the table.

"Grandma is going to be just fine," Ms. Wilson went on. She ran her hands through Kelly's coarse and long hair. I quietly slipped out into the hallway.

"Excuse me." I stopped a nurse in the corridor. "Can you tell me where I can find a pay phone around here?"

Chile, Ms. Sprint had gotten me together after not paying my cell phone bill for over two months. And one thing about Ms. Sprint, honey, is that she don't play when it comes down to her coins. That girl will cut your ass off without a moment's notice and introduce you to Ms. Operator, who will gladly tell you in a hot minute, "Your service has been interrupted because you have failed to pay your invoice on time."

Of course, it was embarrassing, but every extra dime I had was going toward Pandora's case. Doing drag one day out of the week and bartending just wasn't bringing in enough money. And I was dreading the fact of going out there and getting a third job.

"You have to go down to the first floor," the nurse said. She held her eyes on me longer than normal. But it was nothing I wasn't used to, though. Women often came on to me. When I was out of drag, I guess you could say I was a handsome dude. At least, that was what I had been told, anyway. But, chile, if them women only knew that I was after the same thing they were after–a fine piece of trade for your mama, honey.

"Thank you, sweetheart," I said with my voice raised to a higher register. "You've been such a doll."

Honey, you should have seen that girl pushing down the hallway when she heard me speak in what I called my "queer voice."

Sometimes I enjoyed playing games and messing with straight women on the sly, but only to a certain extent. Lying and using women for your own personal pleasure is just dead wrong, and too many of the children are doing it out there today.

But some men are seriously struggling with their sexuality and too afraid to come out of the closet for fear of being rejected by this fucked-up society that can't accept and love people for who they are. And for those brothers I say, get some help and seek counseling, but don't drag these unsuspecting women into your crazy bullshit. That's why I pushed Johnny from the very beginning to come clean with Ms. Girl, Tonya, because the fallout ain't even worth all of the heartache and drama.

"Hey, hon." I held the receiver to my ear while talking on the pay phone. "What you up to?"

"On my way home," said Johnny. "I got good news."

"What is it, baby?"

"I just took my GED," he said. "And passed that shit with flying colors."

I was suddenly overcome with emotion and felt dizzy. No one knew more than me how hard Johnny had worked toward getting his GED.

"I'm so happy for you, hon," I said. "You did that shit, and this is only the beginning."

"Yeah, thanks to you, nigga," he said. "I ain't forgot all of that tutoring you gave me for free. Everything you taught me, I ended up using."

"We have to celebrate later on after I leave this hospital," I said. "I'm still up at Charity."

"How's Kelly's grandma doing, anyway?"

"A lot better," I said. "Thank God she's going to pull through, so everybody's happy on this end. What you up to later?"

"Man, I'm so pumped up," he said, "that I'm heading to UNO to fill out a college application as we speak. Then, later, I'm meeting up with my man Kojack. We got some running around to do."

My stomach started to churn at the mention of a certain person's name. It took everything in me not to blast Johnny's cousin and tell him exactly how I felt about that motherfucking loser.

"I know that's your cousin." I bit my tongue to keep from saying what was really on my mind. "So, I'm not gon' bad-mouth him, but just please be careful. I don't trust his ass, hon. Something about your cuz just ain't right."

"Stop worrying over nothing," Johnny said. "We just hanging out together, not robbing a fucking bank or anything. I wish people would cut my man some slack, anyway."

"Well, you know how I feel," I said. "And that's all I have to say about it. But right now I wanna focus on you, baby. This is so exciting."

"I know," he said. "I'm a motherfucking king. So go ahead and tell me."

"Yes, you are, honey," I said. "And it's nothing but going up from here. What you doing after you hang out with your cousin?"

Johnny suddenly got quiet and took a deep breath. "I'm supposed to be meeting with Tonya."

"About . . . ?"

"I'm finally gon' tell her," he said. "About me and you and everything. Life is too short for me to be walking around here and worrying about what other people think."

Of course, I was taken back by his revelation. When I met Johnny all those years ago on the plantation, he was so uptight and totally against anything gay related. But now he had come full circle to embracing his sexuality, and it was amazing.

"Are you sure about this?" I asked.

"Yeah, nigga. I'm sure," he said. "You know I wouldn't say some shit like that if I wasn't."

"Calm down," I said. "I just wanted to make sure you were okay with everything. What about your kinfolks? Are you planning to talk to them, too?"

"Yeah, but not right now," he said. "Everyone is getting ready for the christening of my cousin's baby, so this might not be the right time to hit them with something like that."

"I understand," I said. "Whatever you decide, you know I'm right here for you, hon. Ain't no mountain high enough or valley low enough to keep me from that big, fat piece of yours."

"Stop being silly," he said.

Shit, I had to find some way to lighten the mood. "I thought you liked my singing?" I said. "You need to stop being scared and come down to the club and catch my show tonight."

"You know I really wanna see you perform and shit," he said. "But I can't get down at no gay club. It's too wide open for me."

"Whatever," I said with a slight attitude.

"Call me later then," I went on, "and we'll find some other way to celebrate. I love you."

"Yeah, me too," he said. And it was as close as I was going to get to Johnny saying the L-word to me. "Keep the fire burning. Peace."

After we disconnected, I stood in the hallway in one spot and soaked up the moment. Everything that I had ever wanted and wished for was coming true, and I couldn't believe this type of joy had found me at such a wonderful time in my life. Me and Johnny were going to finally be together as a couple without restrictions or limitations. Being gay was such a tough existence, and to find somebody out here in this world to love you for you ain't no easy thing to come by. So I for damn sure counted my blessings.

"Well, well, well, if it isn't James Santiago." When I heard that voice, I turned around in slow motion because I knew it was someone from my past. Someone I didn't really want to see or run into.

"Collen," I said. He looked feeble and malnourished, pushing himself in a wheelchair. "Is that you?"

Collen was one of the first dudes I messed around with when I started hanging out at gay clubs. He broke my heart, and it took me a long time to get over him.

"Is it really you?" I said once again in disbelief.

"Yeah, it's me." He coughed. His skin was so pale and white that he looked like a ghost. "In the flesh."

Collen was once a hot piece of a specimen with muscles on every inch of his body and a tight and sexy ass, too. He was one

of those children who would enter the club and demand immediate attention. His smile was his calling card that drew you in
unsuspectingly. And let's not even talk about Collen's sex, honey.
He was working with one old fat piece of iron that I could never
get enough of. Yes, indeed, Collen's sex was off the chain, and he
was once a force of nature, so it caught me off guard to see him
looking like a skeleton and sitting in a wheelchair.

"What are you doing here?" I asked, which was perhaps one
of the silliest questions I had ever asked before in my life. But I
didn't know what else to say. That poor child looked bad,
honey. Real bad.

"This is my new home." He smiled through uncontrollable
coughing and shortness of breath. There was suddenly a pink
elephant in the room, and I was afraid to say the four-letter
A-word out loud.

"At least until I kick the bucket," Collen went on. If he was
afraid of dying, he damn sure wasn't showing it. Collen acted
like a man who had accepted his fate head-on.

"I'm glad I ran into you, though," he said. "I had been trying
to track you down for quite some time."

My stomach started to churn for the second time in one day.
Maybe I had loose bowels or something, because I felt like I had
to go to the bathroom and take a nice, long shit.

"Why you been trying to reach me?" I forced an anxious grin.
The truth was, when we were an item, me and Collen hadn't always practiced safe sex. I was so young, stupid, and naive back
then and actually thought I was invincible, like Superman.

"You might wanna have a seat," he said. A feeling of absolute
fear overtook my body, running through me like electricity.
"Because what I have to tell you, I know you ain't gonna even
wanna hear it."

12

Johnny

"Congratulations, my son!" Moms wrapped her arms around me in a tight grip. She was so proud of me, man, and it felt good putting a smile on her face and knowing that I was the reason for it. Over the years I had caused Moms way too much stress and worry, and getting my GED was my way of letting her know that I was sorry for everything and was trying to do something positive with my life.

"I'm so happy for you." She stared me directly in my face, and her eyes quickly filled up with water. "You're now officially a high school graduate. This is so wonderful, son."

"Come on, Ma," I said. "Don't start crying on me. It's just a piece of paper."

"Don't say that." Moms took the GED certificate out of my hand. She had been a high school teacher for many years, and nothing was more important than her children's education. "This piece of paper proves what I've known all along."

"What's that?"

Moms pinched the side of my jaw like I was a three-year-old or something. "That you're just as smart and talented as your brothers. If you put your mind to it, son, you can accomplish anything in this world. And that's the real lesson, given everything you've been through. So, what's next?"

"I applied to UNO," I said. "I wanna play ball and major in prelaw."

"You want to be a lawyer?"

Moms seemed really surprised by the idea. She and I hadn't spoken much about my stint on the plantation and how I helped out my fellow inmates with their individual cases. Reading law books and learning all about the legal system was one of the most memorable experiences I had up there at Sierra Leone. Studying law gave me a sense of purpose in life, and at one time brought me and James closer together. The way I saw it, I was simply returning home to something that gave me real joy.

"I had no idea," Moms said. "You're just full of surprises today, aren't you?"

"What's all the excitement about down here?" my cousin Nettie interrupted us. She had Lionel in her arms.

"Johnny now has his GED and plans to major in prelaw." Moms turned her attention to Nettie. "Which makes a strong statement, young lady, that it's never too late to get your act together."

After Nettie had gotten pregnant with Lionel, she dropped out of school with no job or plans for the future. Life is hard enough just trying to stand on your own two feet, and when you add a baby to the equation, shit gets even more complicated. Thank God she had Moms and Pops to look after her, though. Rondell, the baby's daddy, was nowhere to be find, so you could imagine the kind of stress on Nettie, being a teenage mom.

"I'm so proud of you, T-Mack," Nettie said. She was the only one in the family who still called me by my nickname from high school, and I loved her even more for it. "You're on your way, man."

"I know you heard me, young lady," Moms said. "Don't act like you didn't."

"I heard you, Aunt Liz." Nettie rocked the baby in her arms. "I'm gon' get myself together. If not for myself, for my baby's sake."

"I know you are, sweetheart," Moms said. "I just want the best for all of you. But at least we now have two things to celebrate on Sunday."

Ali was having his christening on the first Sunday of the month, which was a tradition in our family. No matter where you stood with God in your adult life, every child in the Lomack family was christened before turning one year old. With Pops being the pastor of his own church, he wouldn't have had it any other way. Being christened was the most sacred and holiest moment in his eye.

"This is so great," Moms said, reaching for the telephone. "I have to call your father down at the church and tell him the good news. I'm sure he wouldn't mind having his Bible class interrupted for something like this."

"Wait, Ma." I took the receiver out of her hand. "Why don't you hold off on calling Pops?"

"What's the matter, son?"

Both Moms and Nettie stared at me with curious looks on their faces. I must have been acting really strange to them.

"Kojack is waiting for me outside in the car," I said. "He wanted to come in and see the baby. I knew Pops had his Bible class on Wednesdays, so I told him it'd be okay."

"My brother is outside?" Nettie switched the baby to her other hip.

"Yep," I said. "And he really wants to see you and the baby."

"Please let him come in, Aunt Liz," Nettie said. "Uncle Lonnie isn't here, and I miss my brother so much."

"You know I can't do that, Nettie," Moms said. "You know how your uncle feels about Kojack's lifestyle, and I can't go against my husband's wishes. Now, I'm sorry, but that's just the way it has to be as long as you're living under our roof."

"Man, that's so unfair," Nettie said. "Regardless of what y'all think, that's still my brother, and I love him."

Suddenly the sound of bells interrupted and saved us from one awkward and uncomfortable moment. Those bells were like the most precious sound in our house, 'cause it let us know that Grandma Eve was still breathing and kicking in her upstairs bedroom.

"I'm coming, Mama Eve." Moms took the flight of stairs. She suddenly stopped and looked back at me and Nettie. "And don't the two of you go anywhere. We're not finished with this."

"Whatever you say, Aunt Liz," Nettie said. But soon as Moms was out of sight, I immediately turned to Nettie with a wide grin.

"Are you thinking what I'm thinking?" asked Nettie.

"Fa' sho'." I opened the front door and waved my hand to get Kojack's attention.

Since me and Nettie were the two outcasts in the family anyway, we figured we'd live up to our terrible reputations and allow Kojack inside the house to see his li'l nephew despite what Pops said.

"Hurry up, nigga," I said to him. "Before my old man gets home."

"I owe you big-time for this shit, man." He gripped my hand. "Now, where's my li'l nephew at?"

"Right here," Nettie said, hugging Kojack with one arm and holding Ali with the other one. "Hey, boy. It's so good to finally see your ass in person."

Although Pops kept Nettie and Kojack from seeing each other, they had their own way of keeping in touch with each other over the telephone.

"Good to see you, too, sis," said Kojack. He took the baby out of Nettie's arms and held him in the air. "Damn, this dude is big."

"That's why we call that li'l joker Ali," I said proudly. "Don't you think he's built like a motherfucking boxer?"

"I don't know about that," Nettie said. "But he sure the fuck came out of me already grown and ready to take on the world with his bad ass."

"What's up, li'l man?" Kojack smiled at Ali with all thirty-two of his teeth sparkling through a plateful of grille.

Man, that dude was so happy to see his nephew and Nettie in one swoop. No matter what the family thought about Kojack selling drugs, they couldn't deny he cared about his peeps.

"I'm trying to figure out who my man looks like," Kojack said. " 'Cause he for damn sure don't look like none of us."

"That's 'cause he's a spitting image of his pa," Nettie said. "With his trifling ass."

Although I had never met Rondell in person, I heard he was an attractive red-skinned dude with light brown eyes. And you know how women be loving on niggas with pretty eyes.

"You don't have to worry about that nigga anymore," Kojack said with an evil-ass look on his face. "Your big brother took care of everything."

Me and Nettie stared at each other.

"What did you do, cuz?" I asked the question that was on both Nettie's and my minds. But before Kojack could answer me, the evening took an unexpected turn.

"What the hell are you doing up in my house?" Pops slammed the door behind him and interrupted our conversation. And I wish you could have seen the look on our faces. It was one of complete horror.

Dead silence swept the room. For a brief moment I think the three of us were in total shock seeing Pops walk through our front door instead of being at his Bible-study meeting, like we had initially thought.

"Somebody'd better answer me!" Pops was shouting at the top of his lungs like a goddamn demon. "What is this low-life, murdering crook doing in my house?"

"Look, Uncle Lonnie, man, I respect you," Kojack said, pushing the baby into Nettie's arms. The tension in the room had risen to an all-time high. The baby was crying and screaming from the pit of his lungs.

"But I'm not gon' have you call me out of my name," Kojack went on, "like I'm some punk nigga."

"Let's get out of here, man." I pushed Kojack toward the door.

"Let go of me, man!" Kojack said. "I'm tired of this dude treating me like shit. Like this not my family, too!"

"Don't you use that type of language in my house," Pops said. "You murderer!"

"What are you talking about, Uncle Lonnie?" asked Nettie, patting Ali on the back and trying to keep him calm.

"Haven't y'all been watching the news?" asked Pops. "I'm sorry to be the one to tell you this, Nettie, but Rondell was found dead in the Florida Project with multiple gunshot wounds to the head."

"Oh, my God." Nettie held the baby against her shoulder and immediately fell into a hard cry. Kojack had a serious look on his face, like he was guilty as charged.

"Wait," I said. "And you think Kojack had something to do with this?"

"Why don't you ask him yourself?" Pops said. "If he didn't, I'm sure it's a hell of a coincidence, given how he felt about Rondell getting Nettie pregnant."

"Tell me you didn't do this, Kojack," Nettie said with tears streaming down her face. "Go ahead, man. Tell him you didn't kill my baby's daddy."

Kojack didn't say one word in his own defense but just stood there like a damn fool. Man, I couldn't believe this shit was happening, especially in Pops's presence—the one person who already thought the worst of Kojack in the first place.

"You know what, man," Kojack finally said, looking directly at Pops. "You gon' believe what you wanna anyway."

"You disgrace my precious and loving sister's memory!" Pops shouted in his face with a pained look in his eyes that could burn a hole inside a wall. Something inside of me burst, and I had a sudden flashback to my childhood. I was around five years old, and for some reason Pops was screaming at me with the same fury in his eyes he had for Kojack.

"You're not welcome in this house." Pops pushed Kojack against the door, and I went into another flashback. Memories collided with reality.

Pops was pushing and pulling on me, too. He was pushing and shouting something in my face, but I couldn't make out his words. They were muffled. His face was angry, though. Something serious must have gone down between us in my child-hood, but for the life of me I couldn't figure out what it was.

"You understand me?" Pops went completely ballistic on Ko-jack. "Don't you ever step foot in this house again. Ever!"

"For heaven's sake." Moms ran down the flight of stairs. "What's going on in here? I can hear y'all's voices from way up-stairs. Mama Eve is worried."

"I come home and find this man in my house," Pops said, "when I made it specifically clear that I did not want him com-ing here."

Both Nettie and the baby were now bawling out of control. As for me, I had a stupid-ass look on my face.

"Baby, calm down," Moms said to Pops. "There's no need for all the yelling. You're scaring the baby."

"Ma, I'm sorry about this," I finally said. "This situation is all my fault. I invited Kojack in despite your warning."

"You don't have to lie, dude," Kojack said to me. "Uncle Lon-nie ain't nobody but a man, just like me and you. He ain't God."

"Shut up, man," I said. "I'm trying to help you. Let me han-dle this."

"So, you're responsible for this, son?" Pops looked me straight in the eye with a look that I had gotten used to seeing from him over the years: one of total disgust and disappointment.

"Why don't you tell him your good news, Johnny?" Moms tried everything in her power to soften the tension, but there was nothing she could have said or done to erase the angry ex-pression off of Pops's face.

"Our son obtained his GED today," Moms said for me in-stead. "Isn't that wonderful news, honey?"

"That's all fine and dandy," Pops said. Man, this dude was unbelievable. His hatred for Kojack was more powerful than his love for and support of me. "But if he's hanging with this poor excuse for a human being then he can kiss his future good-bye."

"Don't say that Lonnie," Moms said.

"Let me get out of here, man"–Kojack opened the door–"before I say or do something I might later regret."

"Don't go!" Nettie cried out behind him, with the baby bouncing up and down on her hip like a seesaw. "We need to talk about this!"

"Come on, sweetie," Moms held Nettie from behind to keep her from going out the door behind Kojack. "This isn't good for you or the baby."

"He's not worth your tears, Nettie," Pops said. "You and your son will be much better off in the long run. Much better off indeed."

"You're a real asshole, man," I said, looking Pops directly in his face so he could see for himself that I meant every word. "A real asshole."

"Johnny," Moms said, "don't talk to your father that way."

But the damage had already been done, and no one could turn back the hands of time and make this moment into something beautiful when it was simply downright ugly. And that's just keeping it real.

"Thanks for standing up for me, dude," Kojack said as we cruised down the streets of the NO in a Lexus SUV with tinted windows and shiny-ass rims that got more attention than the goddamn car itself.

"I appreciate that shit," he went on. "Man, Uncle Lonnie be fronting on a brother. But it's all good."

"He went too far this time, man," I said. "Bringing up your mom's death and shit."

Kojack got real quiet on me and glanced out of the window. I couldn't help but wonder if he was thinking about Aunt Tina. Her passing away was something the two of us never talked about in the open.

"You all right, dude?" I asked. For a brief moment I could have sworn I had seen tears in my cuz's eyes. But you know that nigga would never have owned up to that shit, so I left well enough alone.

"I'm straight," he said. "Just got a lot on my mind."

"Was Pops right about you? Did you do something to that dude Rondell?"

"I think you already know the answer to that," Kojack said. "Ain't no nigga gon' mess over my sister and live to tell about it. And that's all I got to say about the matter."

On some level, I understood where my cuz was coming from. If some older dude had knocked my young sister up and then left her for broke, then I probably would have done something to his ass, too.

But murder? Not me, man. I couldn't take another human being's life. Shit, part of me wondered how Kojack could. You know, how one minute he could be loving and warm with his family and then be a cold-blooded killer in another instance.

"So, what's next on the agenda?" I noticed we were heading up toward Canal Street and couldn't imagine what business he had uptown. The extent of Kojack's power was in the lower Nine.

"I gotta stop over at Club Circus, this fag bar in the French Quarter," he said. "Bunch of punks, but don't be gettin' no ideas on me, nigga. My boss man owns the joint and me and him gotta talk some straight-up business."

Of course, you know my stomach was now twisted in knots upon hearing the news of our destination. Club Circus was James's hangout, and the last place I wanted to be seen. Too close for comfort.

"Sounds like some important shit." I forced a smile and kept my cool. "Talk to me, man. What's going on?"

"Some big-time player from the West Coast," Kojack said, "who goes by the name of Big Daddy Cane. Word out on the street is that motherfucker can't be trusted. That's why I need you to watch my back."

"Look, man," I said straight-up to him. "You know I got nothing but love for you, but I ain't trying to get back in the game for nobody—not even you."

"I know that shit, dude," he said. "You're about to go to college, and I dig that. All I'm asking is that you be there by my side this one time. It's that simple."

"If it's that simple," I said, "why you need me watching your back at all? Come at me straight, man."

"Okay, nigga," Kojack said. "I'm scared. You happy now? You got me to admit the shit out in the open."

Of course, I was blown away. My cuz was one of the toughest dudes I knew, and for him to be afraid of somebody must have meant this Big Daddy Cane person was a dangerous motherfucker. Thugs lived with fear, too.

"Man, you know you can tell me anything," I said. "You're not the first nigga to be afraid of something. What's the deal with this cat, anyway?"

"All I know from my boss man," Kojack said, "was that this

dude ran shit on the West Coast, and was known for smoking niggas without thinking twice."

"Then why you wanna get down with somebody like that?" I wondered. "Someone who can't be trusted?"

"Let's just say," Kojack said, "his business from the West Coast combined with ours down here in the dirty South will bring in major revenue for everybody. In this game you gotta take risks if you wanna be at the top and have worldwide pull. I'm trying to make big moves in 2004."

"So when is this deal supposed to go down?"

"This coming Sunday morning," he said.

"Man, that's the same day of your li'l nephew's christening," I said. "I thought you were trying to be there for that shit."

"Oh, I plan to be there, all right," Kojack said with a sinister look in his eyes. "Do you know if they still use that minichapel inside your pops's church?"

"I don't think so," I said. "Why you ask?"

"I'll tell you about my plans later," he said. "But right now I need to run inside this club and talk to my boss man. You staying in the car or what?"

I read the marquee sign and swallowed a shitload of spit.

PERFORMING TONIGHT IS THE ONE AND ONLY ARMARI ST. JAMES. The words were written in big black letters and surrounded by white lights.

"You all right, nigga?" asked Kojack. "You ain't never been around any punks before?"

"No, actually I have." I wiped that smile right off of Kojack's face.

"Say what?"

"I'm just kidding, dude," I said. "Now hurry up and handle your business so we can roll. I have to meet up with Tonya later."

"Now that's what I'm talking about." Kojack dapped me up real proudly. I wondered if he would have felt the same way had I told him about James and me. But, of course, I already knew the answer to my own question–not in this lifetime. My cuz was the most homophobic nigga I knew, yet his boss owned a gay joint. Now, how strange was that?

Kojack hit the "on" button on the CD player and gave me two bars. "This a new cut from Eminem. I'll be right back."

After which, I closed my eyes and swayed my body to Eminem's "Cleaning Out My Closet." If nothing else, his music relaxed me after such a long and twisted-ass day that only got crazier when Kojack's cell phone started vibrating on the seat beside me.

"Hello." The phone startled me, and I took the call more out of reflex than anything. "Talk to me."

"I need a hit," a man with a soft yet deep voice said on the other end of the line. "Tell me where I can meet you at."

"Who the fuck is this?" I figured the caller was one of Kojack's clients, so I changed the tone of my voice to sound more like his.

"Noxzema, motherfucker."

I suddenly felt like I had landed in a gold mine or inside a long field of never-ending dreams.

Part of me wanted to run inside the club and tell James the good news. But in the end, I decided to handle this one on my own.

{ 13 }

Tonya

"Girl, can you believe all of these faggots up in this motherfucking club, honey?" Latisha said, sipping on a cocktail and looking around at what used to be my old stomping grounds when Club Circus was a strip joint and completely straight before the gays took over and made it their own on Wednesday nights. "Now I see why I can't find me a man. Their asses are all up in here."

Me, Latisha, and Tamika, along with Peaches, was sitting up at the bar having drinks and waiting for the drag show to begin. We had basically gone down to Club Circus to scope out the place and to see if this drag queen, Armari St. James, was actually disrespecting Tamika's sorority, like Peaches's messy ass claimed.

"I told y'all to get ready for an unforgettable experience," Peaches said, dancing in the chair to the music that was bouncing off the damn walls. The club was packed with nothing but all kinds of gay men–some whom you would never even suspect of being that way. I'm talking about hard-core niggas with gold teeth from off the block.

Don't get me wrong. I knew we was inside of a gay bar so I

expected to see dudes dancing and kissing on other dudes. But not fine ass niggas with baggy jeans hanging off their waist and wearing Timberlands and shit. Needless to say, hanging out at Club Circus was an eye-opening experience for all of us. We was getting more than we bargained for.

"What time does this damn show begin?" asked Tamika. She was anxious and nervous, but I think all of us was a little un-comfortable being inside of a club where not one single nigga was checking us out or trying to holler. It was some strange and bizarre shit to say the least, especially given the fact that when I used to frequent the club back in the day, dudes were forever sweating me and trying to run wack-ass game.

"Hold on to your wig," Peaches said to Tamika. "Things should be jumping off at any moment."

Although the crowd had changed over the years, the club had the same makeup, with hip-hop, R & B, and reggae playing on three different levels, several open bars, a stage on the main floor, and mirrors everywhere. You couldn't go anywhere inside Club Circus without seeing your damn reflection. Once upon a time in my scandalous past, those mirrors came in handy when I was shaking and clapping for dollars. Sometimes I would catch my reflection in the mirror and say, "Damn, I really am hot and sexy, with a nice ass." Moreover, those mirrors gave me a natu-ral high that I can't even begin to explain, at a time in my life when I was making a living off of how I looked.

"Okay, everybody out there," the disc jockey said over the booming surround-sound system that was so loud, it pounded your damn eardrums. "Get your asses on the floor and show 'em what you working with. This that new joint by New Or-leans's own—Rico!"

Babee, that was all it took to get them faggots jumping

and rocking on the dance floor. Those dudes were up in there shaking and spinning and turning and twisting and working that shit out better than some women I knew. One thing I have to admit, though, was that those gay dudes knew how to party and have a good time. Although I was enjoying the show, Rico's song only opened up a can of worms and put the spotlight directly on me.

"So, girl, you never told us what happened the other day when you went to see Rico," Latisha said. "Was he really as sick as the news reported? Or was it just a publicity stunt to sell more records?"

"You know you can't always believe everything you hear," I said, thinking back to what went down between us. Let's just say that the shit I had to do in order to secure that dancing gig in South Africa wasn't something my mama would have been very proud of in the least bit.

"Earth to Tonya." Latisha snapped her fingers in my face. "So, he wasn't sick?"

"Yeah, but nothing that serious," I said. "He'll be back on his feet in no time."

"You still didn't answer the question," Peaches said. He was so raw and direct that it wasn't even funny. "What we basically want to know is, did you fuck him or not? And if so, was the celebrity dick as good as they say it is?"

"First of all," I said to him, "that's none of your fucking business. And where do you get off asking me some shit like that?"

"Okay, girl," Tamika said. "He was just asking you a question."

"No, hold up. I get sick and tried of this troll," I said, "getting up in my business like me and him got it like that. He needs to chill with that shit before he get his ass kicked for real."

"Girl, ain't nobody gon' be kicking nobody's ass up in here,"

Peaches said, trying his hardest not to tick me off, because he knew I'd go into beast mode in one-point-two seconds without thinking twice about it.

"But since you got all of this attitude," he continued, "I guess you just answered our question."

"Whatever, Ms. Wannabe Girl," I said. "You don't know what the fuck you talking about."

"Would the two of you stop it?" Latisha said. "And stay focused. Remember why we're here in the first place."

"Oh, my God," Peaches screamed, and covered his mouth with both hands like such a woman that I couldn't help but be tickled. "You would not believe who just walked out from the back of the club."

Of course, he now had our heads spinning and turning. Shit, there was so much going on inside the club that night I could hardly catch my breath for looking so damn hard.

"Who you see?" asked Latisha. "Tell us so we can get in on it, too."

"Look over near the stage." Peaches pointed. Babee, when I saw the person at the other end of his hand, I almost fell out of my chair from the shock alone.

"What the hell is Kojack doing up in here?" Tamika took the words right out of my mouth. "I know he's not gay, too. If he is, I'm through with all men, for damn sure."

"Please tell me I'm seeing wrong," I said, "and that's not Johnny's cousin standing over there in the corner and talking to that white dude."

"Well, I actually have a confession to make," said Peaches. "I'm really not surprised seeing Kojack in here."

"What the fuck you mean?" I asked with an attitude. Peaches and his games got to me like nobody's business and worked my last good nerve. "You already knew his ass was gay and didn't tell us?"

"First of all," Peaches said, "the man is not gay. That's the first mistake you made when y'all walked through the door. Not every person who goes to a gay club is necessarily gay."

"Okay, then," Tamika said. "Then why is he up in here?"

"That's what I'm talking about," I said. "Explain that shit to me."

"See the good-looking white man with the ponytail?" asked Peaches. "Dressed in the business suit and tie?"

We nodded our heads and waited for a goddamn explanation that made sense as to why a nigga like Kojack was running around in a joint like Club Circus on gay night, of all nights. If nothing else, seeing him only got me to thinking about Johnny and how we had been playing phone tag the last couple of days.

But I wasn't sweating it. I figured Johnny was busy with his family and trying to get on his feet after being on lockdown for so long. I knew it was only a matter of time before me and him sat down together and talked. Like I said before, that nigga was my heart, and he was always on my mind even when we wasn't around each other.

"That's his boss," Peaches went on to explain to us. "They slanging together. If you get what I mean. Kojack is one of his lead men on the streets."

"Okay. Now I feel much better," Latisha said with relief. Shit, all of us were relieved. One thing about sistahs: We don't wanna be hearing and thinking about our niggas being gay and fucking around with each other, especially someone we already knew who we couldn't picture being that way in the first place. Even if the dude happened to be a loser and a jerk like Kojack.

"Welcome to Club Circus." That white dude in the business

suit took the stage. He seemed to be in control of the crowd, the way he just stepped up and grabbed hold of the microphone. As for Kojack, he looked around the club as if he was completely lost up in that joint and totally out of his element.

"And to Armari St. James's Wonder Woman circus of gay fun," the white dude said, and the crowd went wild and crazy.

One thing I noticed from being inside of that club was that those gay men loved themselves some Armari St. James. The applause got so loud when they realized the drag show was about to begin. As for me, Latisha, and Tamika, we was waiting in the cut and seeing what was gone happen next. To be honest, I had no idea what we was planning to do if that drag queen said or did anything out of order to disrespect Tamika's sorority. We was simply taking things step by step as they happened.

"I'm sorry to inform you," the white dude said, "that Armari is not feeling well this evening and will not be performing tonight."

"Come on, man!" a skinny dark-skinned dude said sitting next to us. He was really not feeling the announcement—none of us was. Our whole purpose for coming to that club was to see the drag queen perform in person.

"Bring Armari on," the dark-skinned dude shouted at the stage. "Bring her on now!"

"I know this isn't what you guys want to hear," the white dude said. "But don't worry. She'll be back next week bigger and better than ever. Now enjoy the rest of your night and be good to one another."

After which, Kojack and the white dude disappeared to a private part of the club. To say the least, we was all disappointed.

"I can't believe we came down here for nothing," Latisha said. "What a waste of time."

"Not exactly," Tamika said, looking at Peaches to make the next move. "I say we go to plan B."

"Plan B is going to have to wait." My phone started vibrating. I had been waiting for this call all evening long. "This is Johnny. I'll be right back."

I stepped to a quieter part of the club near the women's bathroom and put one finger in my ear to drown out the noise. "Hey, baby!"

"Where you at?" asked Johnny. "I've been trying to reach you."

"I'm hanging out at this club with my girls." I switched the phone to my other ear. The music was blasting my eardrums. "What's up with you?"

"I'm handling some personal business." He chose his words real carefully. Johnny was up to something, and I imagined him at a jewelry store picking out my engagement ring. "Call me later after you finish kicking it with your girls. We need to talk."

"Damn it!" My phone went dead before I got a chance to tell Johnny how much I loved him. How much I was looking forward to our special evening together.

"What you smiling about?" asked Latisha. I joined them at the bar where her, Tamika, and Peaches surrounded me for answers.

"I think my baby is out getting my ring," I said with a wide grin on my face. "Girl, I really think he's going to pop the big question."

"I'm so happy for you, girl." Latisha hugged me. This was a shared dream of ours since we was in middle school. You know, to find a man who would one day get down on his knees and ask for our hand in marriage.

"Look, I'm happy for you and all, but do you think Johnny

can wait a few more minutes?" Tamika said. "So, don't even think about leaving me in this damn place by myself."

"Okay, girl," I said to Tamika. "Calm your ass down. I'm not leaving you, but I was simply letting y'all know that I do have other plans. So, what's the next move?"

"I'm gonna take y'all to Armari's dressing room," Peaches said. His smile was wider than a river. He knew a shortcut where we wouldn't get caught.

"So, this is it." He stopped us in front of a door with a drag queen's picture on it. The mystery was finally solved. Armari St. James was a tall man with beautiful skin and a wide, glowing smile that sucked you in like a magnet. "Armari's dressing room."

"What's up, Ms. Peaches, girl," a sexy-ass light-skinned dude opened the door and immediately said. What struck me the most about being inside of Club Circus was all the beautiful, fine niggas. Just one after another, like they dropped out of the sky or something.

"Hey, Jerome," Peaches said. "Some of my friends wanted to meet Armari. Is she around?"

"Armari is not seeing any visitors today," Jerome said. "She's not in a good mood right now. Why don't y'all come back another time?"

"Can you please tell her I would like to ask her a quick question?" Tamika said. "I promise not to take up too much of her time."

"Hon, who's at the door?" Armari suddenly appeared before us not looking anything like his photograph on the door, which fucked with my head big-time. You know, I thought he would show up wearing a wig and makeup like a drag queen, but instead he came to the door looking like a regular dude with a fade and a light mustache.

"Peaches and three pieces of fresh fish," Jerome said. "I already told them that you weren't feeling it tonight, but these girls weren't hearing it."

"What's this all about?" asked Armari. His body was wrapped in a silk robe, and he had a stocking cap on top of his head.

"I'm sorry to disturb you." Tamika took center stage. After all, this was her show. We was just there for backup. "But I had something I wanted to ask you."

"I'm listening," Armari said with an attitude. He must have caught the negative tone in Tamika's voice. She was not feeling him, and neither was I. "But make it quick, because like they told you up front, I'm not in the mood."

"First of all, my name is Tamika," she said. "And these are my friends."

"I see you know Ms. Peaches," Armari said, cutting eyes at him and gazing up in my face, too. You should have seen how he was all up in my grille, which made me very uncomfortable from the very beginning.

"Go ahead," Armari went on. "But if Ms. Peaches got anything to do with this, I already know I ain't gon' like it."

"I'm a member of Delta Kappa Zeta Sorority, Incorporated," Tamika said proudly. She loved and cherished those letters, for real. "And somebody told me that you be using our sorority as part of your act."

"Occasionally," Armari said. "But it's not out of disrespect or anything."

"All I want to say to you," said Tamika, her voice trembling and shaking, "was that I don't think it's cool for you to be using Delta Kappa Zeta as part of your act. My sorority is something that means a lot to me, and I don't appreciate anyone taking it for some kind of joke."

"First of all," Armari said, "I don't take your sorority for any joke. Like I said, it's no disrespect."

"Look, you don't need to be getting no attitude with my friend." I pushed Tamika to the side. The beast had been burning inside the pit of my stomach from the moment I locked eyes with Armari, and I simply couldn't hold my peace any longer. Armari St. James rubbed me the wrong way from the start. "She was just trying to get to the bottom of this."

"See you still got a lot of mouth, Ms. Girl," said Armari, staring me all up in my face.

"What the hell's that supposed to mean?" I said. "You acting like you know me or something?"

Silence swept the hallway.

"What's going on out there?" An older woman, maybe in her early forties, appeared in the doorway. She was stout and brown skinned, with a long grain of hair on her head.

"Honey, I don't know what the deal is with these girls." Armari pointed his finger at me, which only set me off even more. "But this fish right here working on my last nerve."

"Come on, Tonya, girl." Latisha took hold of my hand. She must have sensed some terrible shit was about to go down, for real. "Let's just get out of here."

I broke loose from her with a vengeance. "No way—I'm not running and letting somebody call me out of my name, especially some motherfucking faggot."

"Who you calling a faggot?" asked Jerome. I could tell he had a lot of love for this drag queen. "Bitch!"

"Hold up, Jerome. I got this," that older stout woman said. She got in between me and Armari. "Look, li'l girl. I don't know what rock you just crawled out from under, but you ain't gon' be calling my son out of his name."

"Lady, you ain't saying nothing but a thing. 'Cause we can take it to the streets."

Babee, before I could get another word out of my mouth, that woman had her hands around my neck and had done pinned me up against that goddamn wall. She had me in a choke hold.

"Talk your shit now," that woman said, with my back still against the wall. "You li'l motherfucking girls think y'all grown out here today, but you ain't run up on a real woman before."

Of course, it didn't take me long to figure out that I was dealing with someone from the same gutter streets I had grown up on, and to be honest I was scared out of my mind. That woman had some power and strength in her hands, like she wasn't even from this world.

"Get off of my friend." Tamika went to help me, but Armari and Jerome stopped her. Those faggots looked like they were ready to kick some ass.

"I don't think so, Ms. Girl," Armari said. "But if y'all bitches wanna take ten, we could all be scrapping out here, if that's how you want it to go down."

And it was about to go down, for real. That was, until we heard the sound of a gun being fired. Sometimes the person you least expect will come to your rescue.

"Get your motherfucking hands off of her," Kojack said with the gun pointed directly at that woman's head. That white dude was right behind him.

"Come on, Ms. Flo," the white dude said. If you could believe, that crazy bitch still had her hands around my throat. "Do what he says before someone gets hurt."

"Let her go, Ma," Armari said. "I know this li'l nappy-headed whore, and she ain't even worth it. Trust me."

At that moment, it was like a flood of memories came rushing over me like a big-ass wave, and I knew exactly who Ms. Armari St. James was. Years ago we got into a scrap outside of Club Circus—how ironic was that?—and it was an ugly situation where a girlfriend of mine died. Her name was Julie and she was a stripper. Of course, I was blown the fuck away, because I hadn't thought about that shit in such a long time until I ran into Armari face-to-face. Back in those days, he wasn't known as Armari but James.

"You all right?" Kojack asked, but I could barely catch my breath. That woman almost killed me.

"I'm fine," I finally said. "But shoot that bitch in the head. She's out of her motherfucking mind."

"Oh, you ain't had enough?" she said, looking like she wanted to grab me. I hid behind Kojack. "Because I got more where that came from, li'l girl."

"Get her out of here, and y'all can wait in my car," Kojack said to me, Latisha, and Tamika. As for Peaches, I looked around and noticed that he was gone. If you could believe, that scary bastard took off and left our asses high and dry.

"Johnny is outside waiting for me in the car," he went on. "Tell 'im I'll be right out."

"Johnny is here at the club?" Armari suddenly asked, and stopped everyone in their goddamn tracks. The way he said Johnny's name you would have sworn the two of them were close friends or something.

Moreover, I found it even stranger that Johnny didn't mention the fact of being outside of a club when I spoke to him on the phone earlier. Something was off, but I couldn't put my finger on it.

"What? You know him or something?" Kojack looked like he

was about to lose it, for real. I could tell right away that he had it in for Armari, and that the two of them hated each other with a passion. I never thought me and Kojack would find common ground.

"No, of course not," Armari said. "I thought you were talking about someone else."

Sometimes you hear what you wanna hear instead of trusting what you heard. And that was my biggest mistake of all.

Needless to say, I tried to put the situation out of my head as we headed out of the club.

"I thought he said Johnny was out here waiting for him," Latisha said, holding the car door open. Although Kojack's SUV was parked in front of the club, Johnny was nowhere to be found.

"Girl, let's just go home." I walked around the corner to my own car. Part of me was still holding out hope that Johnny was off getting me that engagement ring, which would account for his absence. "All of this drama done made me hungry. A bitch like me could now eat a horse."

"Let's get us a po'boy sandwich from We Never Close." Tamika sat in the front seat of my white Corolla. Latisha hopped in the back. "And try to forget this day ever happened."

I blasted the volume on my raggedy-ass CD player. Juvenile's "Slow Motion" was invading my speakers.

"That's my song right there!" Latisha said, snapping her fingers together. "Ooh, I like it like dat. Slow motion for me!"

For a brief moment our troubles seemed to melt away, because we had the one thing in the world that made perfect sense to us—that nobody could ever take away: hip-hop.

"Turn that shit up!" Latisha shouted.

PART TWO

No More Drama

{ 14 }

James

"Is this going to hurt?" I couldn't believe that I was actually allowing someone to stick a needle in my arm and draw blood from me. Yes, indeed, me and needles had never gotten along, and I hated small hospital rooms with white walls.

"Just stay calm and try to relax," Marvin said. He was the only doctor up there at Charity Hospital that I felt comfortable with and trusted with my life. "It's a piece of cake."

After running into Collen in the hospital the other day and discovering that he had full-blown AIDS, I knew I couldn't run or hide from the truth forever. The two of us had been intimate on many occasions and had not always practiced safe sex, which was a hard pill for me to swallow. Now in my twenties, I prided myself on being generally cautious when it came to my health and well-being.

"This is not going to hurt at all." Marvin tapped my arm in order to find a vein. He was such a gentle and sweet man. "Why don't you stare at the walls? That always seems to help people."

"Just take your time, hon, and don't hurt me," I said, reading several posters plastered on the walls. What those walls revealed about the reality of HIV and AIDS in the African American community, I would never forget.

"It's pretty grim when you think about it," Marvin said. He must have read my mind. "HIV and AIDS have gravely impacted our community. We've seen the highest rates in black men among any other groups of men, and it's the leading cause of death for black women between the ages of twenty-four and thirty-four."

"That's scary." My stomach churned and I took in a deep breath. "Some real scary shit."

"But you did the responsible thing, coming in and getting tested," Marvin said. His warmth and concern for other people made him so goddamn cute. "A lot of people in our community aren't being responsible enough."

"Why do you think that's the case? That so many gay dudes don't go and get tested?"

"First of all," Marvin said. He poked me with the needle. I cringed. "I wasn't only referring to gay people. I was talking about the black community as a whole. Don't get me wrong. We've made a lot of strides in bringing down the infection rate, but we still have so much farther to go."

"Said like a man who knows his stuff." I smiled. Although I was madly in love with Johnny, there was no denying that I had a crush on Mr. Doctor Extraordinaire. Although I told myself otherwise, the truth was Marvin had me from the moment I had opened the door to my dressing room and saw him carrying those lovely flowers for me. "You know, you're something else."

"What do you mean?" He placed a label around the tube that held my blood sample.

"I just never met a gay man like you before," I said, "who's attractive and smart and has his shit together."

"I'm no saint," he said. "I've done my share of wrong just like everybody else." He placed a bandage on my arm to cover up the tiny hole made by the needle. "But you're something else yourself."

"Who, me?"

"Yes, you. I've watched you onstage." He was looking me straight in the eye. "Your performances always leave me feeling so uplifted, like I could take on the world. And you're so funny at times that it's hysterical. I was so disappointed when you didn't perform last night. What happened?"

"Honey, you don't even wanna know," I said, shaking my head and thinking about Collen and what went down backstage. The very idea that someone would show up at my dressing room in order to check me over some sorority bullshit got me upset all over again.

Chile, I'm now talking about these three pieces of fish who showed up backstage with that ugly-ass lowlife Peaches. They got up in my face over using Delta Kappa Zeta as part of my act, which I had been doing for many years, mind you. Everyone knew I had nothing but love inside of my heart for Delta Kappas and that was just my way of honoring and showing the sistahs love. There was no intent on my part to disrespect anybody.

"Last night was one of the worst days of my life," I said, shaking my head.

"Why?" Marvin asked. "What really went down with you last night?"

Of course, the biggest surprise of all was coming in direct contact with Ms. Girl, Tonya, who hadn't changed one bit over the years. She still had way too much mouth and thought the world revolved around her. But one thing was for certain: Next time Tonya would think long and hard before stepping up to my mama again. Flo almost kicked Ms. Girl's ass the other night when she used the word *faggot* in the same sentence with my name. I told you from the beginning that Ms. Flo wasn't any joke, honey, especially when it came to her love and support of me. Nobody was gone disrespect her child, and Flo meant it.

"I was feeling under the weather," I said. "And worried about this test."

"So, the rumors weren't true about you getting into a fight with a bunch of college girls?"

"If you don't mind, let's change the subject," I said, rolling my sleeve down my arm. "So, how long will it take for me to get the results back?"

"With this new technology," he said, "I could have the results back to you within a day's time. If you're worried about anything, I could set you up with one of our counselors in the meantime."

"I'm all right," I lied like the ultimate performer. Although I was terrified of learning the results, I wasn't about to let Marvin see me vulnerable—him or anybody, for that matter. My reputation was built on being strong and resilient. "I just need me a cocktail and I'll be just fine, honey."

"Sounds like a good idea to me," Marvin said. "What are you doing later on?"

"I'm actually meeting with my attorney." I got the feeling he was trying to ask me out on a date, so I immediately changed the subject. "And I was so floored when I found out that the two of you already knew each other."

"Yeah, we go back a long ways," Marvin said. "Actually attended Harvard together. So, you guys are working on a friend's case? How's that going, anyway?"

As the days passed, I had become doubtful of proving Pandora's innocence. If the truth was out there, this would have been a damn good time for it to show up. With Noxzema still missing, I wasn't holding out much hope, though.

"Not good," I said. "We haven't been able to gain any solid evidence to get my friend out of prison. But I'm not giving up on her. That's my mother, and I love her to death."

"I hope it all works out then." Marvin looked directly into my eyes. "But I must say, you're in good hands with Debra. She's the best attorney in this city. What are you doing after you leave your meeting with her?"

"Hold that thought," I said. My cell phone was playing Alicia Keys's "Falling" from inside my pocket. I'd managed to scrounge enough change together to pay my bill and get my phone turned back on.

"Hey, there." It was Johnny, but I wasn't trying to throw him up in Marvin's face. "What's going on with you? I've been trying to reach you all night."

"Listen, I found Noxzema."

"What?" I screamed. "Don't even lie to me like that!"

"Meet me at the corner of Louisa and Chef by the Popeyes," Johnny said, "and I'll fill you in on everything."

"Honey, I'm on my way."

"Was that the boyfriend?"

"Actually, it was," I said, trying to avoid eye contact with him. "And funny how we were just talking about Pandora. I might have finally gotten the one piece of evidence to get my friend off the hook."

"That's wonderful," he said. "You have to keep me posted."

"I will," I said. "But I'm sorry; I have to get going."

"Very well then." Marvin turned completely professional on

me. "I'll have these results for you tomorrow. You probably have nothing to worry about."

"Thank you." I hopped off the examination table. "And I'm not just talking about for today, but also for how you took care of Ms. Wilson when she was here in the hospital. She told me how nice you were to her, and I appreciate it."

"Yes, I remember her. Such a lovely woman, and her grand-daughter..."

"Kelly."

"Yes, Kelly," he said. "What a sweet child. We had an insight-ful conversation and found out that we actually have a lot in common."

"You and Kelly?"

"Don't look so surprised," Marvin said. "I didn't grow up with a silver spoon in my mouth. I was raised by my grandma, too, in the projects. My parents died in a car accident when I was very young."

"I'm so sorry," I said. "I had no idea."

"It's okay," he said. "I was too young to even remember them. But how're Kelly and her grandmother doing?"

"Great," I said, thinking about Kelly's mom, Brenda, being out there on those streets on crack and neglecting that poor child of hers. If only I could get my hands on that woman, I would shake some sense into her. With Ms. Wilson being so old and now sick, Kelly needed her mom more than ever.

"They haven't had it easy," I went on. "But they're hanging in there. I'll tell them you asked about 'em, though."

"You do that." Marvin opened the door for me. "Take care, and I'll call you when those tests come in."

"Thank you again. And hopefully, we can still be friends." I didn't know what else to say. It felt like something beautiful had come into my life and was now slipping away from me. I hated the idea of losing out on something that might be good for me in the long run. Honey, mama was no fool. Although I was totally committed to Johnny, I was still playing my hand with a full deck of cards.

"I'm already looking forward to next Wednesday," Marvin said. "I wouldn't miss your Wonder Woman circus of gay fun for the world. Like I said, I enjoy watching you perform. You make me laugh, and that's not an easy thing to do."

I couldn't help but think that sometimes my best performances took place offstage. My most legendary one was hiding unexpected feelings for Marvin and being madly in love with Johnny at the same time.

"Where's Noxzema?" I asked Johnny as soon as I got off the bus.

"It's about time your ass got here." He was standing on Louisa Street by the Popeyes and across the street from a place known as the Crack Motel, a run-down building in the city where crackheads and drug dealers hung out.

"I'm sorry," I said. "There was a lot of traffic on the interstate."

"You gotta nigga standing out here in this damn heat." He wiped the sweat from his forehead. The temperatures were well into the hundreds that day, and Johnny had been baking in the sun for over an hour. "Where your ass was at, anyway? I've been trying to call you and you ain't been answering. You been acting secretive lately."

"Hold the fuck up. You don't handle me that way. I tried to call you back but your phone's been tripping. What's your goddamn problem?"

"Keep your voice down," Johnny said, looking at a crowd of

people at the Louisa bus stop. Yeah, they were all up in our grille, but you know what? I didn't give a damn who was around. I wasn't about to bite my tongue for anybody.

"I'm just asking you a question," he said. "That's all."

"I had some personal business to take care of." Part of me wanted to tell Johnny the truth about getting tested for HIV, but I knew he wouldn't understand. Trust me. He would have totally freaked out, and I saw no need to worry him until I knew for certain what I was dealing with myself.

"What kind of business?" he asked.

"Business that don't have nothing do with you," I lied. "If anybody's keeping secrets, it's you."

"What the fuck you talking about now?"

"I'm talking about Tonya," I said. "Have you spoken to her yet about us?"

He suddenly got quiet and took his precious time answering the question. "Not yet. But I'm getting around to it."

"Your ass been saying that same tired line since you got out of jail," I said. "And I don't have time for playing games with you. Keep fucking around and you gon' be left out in the cold."

"What you trying to say?" he asked. "You seeing some other nigga or something?"

"Let's just say you ain't the only one interested."

"Okay," Johnny said. "That's some cold shit. I'm breaking my behind out here trying to help your ass and you throwing some shit up in my face like that?"

"How you breaking your back, Johnny?"

"I've been out here all fucking night," he said, "watching this crackhouse and making sure your friend doesn't get away."

"You talking about Noxzema?" I said. "That ain't no friend of mine."

"No, I'm talking about the pope," he said. "Of course I'm talking about Noxzema. The person who set Pandora up all those years ago is right across the street in that building."

I felt the muscles inside my chest tighten. This was the day I had dreamed about for quite some time, and now it had finally come to pass.

"Are you sure it's him?"

"Of course I'm sure," he said. "He called my cuz's phone yesterday when I was outside the club."

"So, you were at Club Circus last night?" It dawned on me that Johnny had no idea what went down between me and Tonya.

"For a li'l while, anyway," he said. "How you know I was there?"

"Have you spoken to Tonya?"

"Briefly, but my phone has been acting up, lately, like you said, and we got disconnected," he said. "Why? Did something happen that I need to know about?"

"Let's not talk about it right now," I said. "We got bigger fish to fry."

Me and Johnny started toward the motel. As we got closer, we saw Ebony standing out front waiting for us.

"What the fuck my cuz's girl doing here?" Johnny wasn't totally comfortable around Ebony, and with good reason. She was a direct link between him and Kojack–the last person in the world Johnny wanted to find out about his sexuality. Kojack and Johnny were so close that it made me sick to my stomach.

"I called and told her to meet us here," I said. "She's been involved in this from the very beginning, so I couldn't leave her out."

"Hey, y'all," Ebony said. As usual, she looked as if she had just stepped off the cover of *Vibe*, wearing a pair of designer jeans and big loop Phat Pharm earrings. No matter what the circumstances were, Ms. Girl always had her shit pulled together. "You guys ready to catch us a criminal?"

"Girl, this is no time for jokes," I said. "Noxzema is real cutthroat, and you gotta be on top of your game around him."

"Don't worry. I'm ready." Ebony turned to Johnny. "You know, you could loosen up around me, Johnny. Your li'l secret is safe with me. I have no intentions of telling your cousin anything."

"I'm straight," Johnny said as he shouldered open the door to the motel. "Everything is all good between me and you."

"Do you know what room he's in?" I asked, looking around at how rundown and gutter the entire place was.

The paint on the walls was peeling, the carpet was soggy and smelled like a mixture of week-old garbage and a toilet full of urine. A light flickered off and on in the hallway. There was a woman walking toward us.

"Brenda?" I stopped in front of her. "I can't believe this shit."

"My name ain't no Brenda," she said, scratching and rubbing her arms. Her dark skin was greasy, and the clothes on her body were dirty. She smelled worse than that carpet in the hallway.

"You know this woman?" asked Ebony.

"Let's go," Johnny said. "We don't have time for this."

"Don't lie to me," I said to Brenda. "I recognize you from a picture that your daughter has of you."

"You got the wrong person." She was rubbing and scratching her arm. "Get out of my way."

"You ain't going nowhere." I threw her against the wall. "Don't you know what that poor child has been going through?"

"It's none of your business," she said.

"The hell it ain't! I've seen with my own two eyes what you've done to that child."

"Come on," Johnny said. "We don't have time for this, man."

I ignored him. Me and Brenda were locked eye-to-eye. She saw that I meant serious business.

"She's better off without me." She broke down in tears. "So just leave me alone!"

"I'm not leaving you alone"—I held her up against the wall—"until you hear what I have to say! Kelly has been worried sick about you, and your poor mama has been in the hospital."

Brenda couldn't even respond for crying so hard. It was so sad to see how drugs had completely taken over her mind. Poor woman didn't know if she was coming or going.

"Pull yourself together." I let go of her. Her nose was running with snot, and tears were falling from her eyes like it was painful. "And go home to your daughter. She needs you."

As she walked away sobbing, my only hope was that Brenda had taken what I said to heart. But with a crackhead, there was no telling.

"Don't worry, sweetheart." Ebony put her arms around me. I had tears in my own eyes. "I'm sure she'll be okay."

"I'm good," I said.

"You sure?" Johnny asked. "Because if you're not up for this . . ."

"Oh, believe me," I said, "I'm up for it. Now, what room you said that bitch was in?"

"Room One-oh-one," Johnny said, leading us down the hall. "He's been inside there all night. Why don't y'all stand back and let me handle this?"

Me and Ebony stepped to the side and allowed Johnny to take things to the next level. He pounded the door with his fist.

"Who's there?" My stomach began to churn from anxiety and anticipation. The voice belonged to Noxzema, and the idea of seeing him after all these years gave me an immediate rush.

"Yo, open up." Johnny sounded more like Kojack, which was kind of scary. The last thing I wanted was for my man to act anything like that no-good bastard cousin of his. My greatest fear all along was that Johnny would get sucked back into Kojack's drug-dealing world of thugging and killing.

"Who the fuck are you?" Noxzema said as the door opened a crack. But before he could say another word, Johnny pushed his weight against the door, knocking Noxzema on the floor. Me and Ebony were right behind him.

"Man, get the hell off of me." Noxzema put up a good fight, but Johnny proved to be the stronger of the two. He held Noxzema against the floor with both arms twisted behind his back. "Let go of me."

"Shut the fuck up"–Johnny pushed his face toward that nasty-ass carpet–"before I knock your teeth in."

Noxzema stared up in my and Ebony's faces, looking like he had seen a ghost.

"Well, well, well," I said with my eyes glued directly on him. He wasn't dressed in drag; he had on a pair of tight-fitting Levi jeans and a dingy white tank top. And unlike me, the years had not been too kind to Ms. Girl. Noxzema had cuts and bruises over his entire face, like someone had been operating on him without medical credentials. The life of a drag queen could sometimes be hard and brutal. "Noxzema Cartell. What's up, Ms. Bitch? Aren't you happy to see me?"

"James Santiago," he said with a wicked grin on his face, as Johnny lifted him off the floor. "I can't believe it."

"Well, believe it," I said. "And I'm sure you remember Ebony?"

"So, what is this? A goddamn reunion?"

"No, Ms. Thang," Ebony said. "We have unfinished business, like that murder outside of Club Circus years ago."

"Is that why y'all tracked me down?" He broke out in laughter. This was all one big joke to him. "To drag up old shit that happened a lifetime ago?"

"You killed that girl," I said, trying to hold back my emotions. This moment with Noxzema brought me and Ebony full circle. "And then left my friend to take the fall for it."

"First of all . . ." Noxzema tried pulling away, but Johnny had him in a tight choke hold. "I was only at that fucking club," Noxzema said, "because I was trying to help Ebony from getting her ass kicked."

"I didn't tell you to kill anyone," Ebony said. "So, don't be putting that shit off on me."

"This ain't my fault," Noxzema said. "And I'll be damned if I'm going down for this."

"You did the crime and now you gon' do the time," I said. "Because of your ass, my motherfucking friend is locked up in prison for something she didn't even do."

"It was an accident," he said. "And y'all know that shit. I wasn't trying to kill that girl, but just teach her a lesson."

"Tell that to the police," I said.

"Go ahead and call the police," he said. "You don't have any proof. It's my word against yours."

"Actually not." Ebony pulled a small recorder out of her purse and hit the play button. We got the entire conversation on tape. Our plan to bring Noxzema down was going smoothly, as planned. Now all we needed for him to do was confess to the police. "You've been punked, Ms. Thang. How does it feel?"

"You fucking bitches." Noxzema started going crazy, like a rabid animal. "You won't get away with this shit!"

"I think we already have," I said with a satisfied grin on my face. "Once the police get here and hear this tape, you're finished."

Ebony pulled out her phone and dialed 911. "I'd like to report a crime."

While Ebony talked to the police, me and Noxzema played catch-up.

"So, you've been living in Atlanta?"

"Fuck you."

Johnny twisted his arms.

"Wow," I said. "And to think we used to be such good friends."

"They're on their way," Ebony said. "And we can finally close this chapter and bring Pandora home."

"Look at you. You think you've won," Noxzema said with that same wicked grin on his face that gave me the chills. "But even if I go to jail, Mother Pandora won't be around to see me do any time. That girl ain't going anywhere but to an early grave."

"What the hell did you say?"

"Oh, my bad," Noxzema said. "You didn't know."

"Shut the hell up." Johnny pushed Noxzema's face against the wall. "You crackhead."

"I wish they'd hurry up," Ebony said. " 'Cause I really need to get home before Justin notices I'm gone."

"What the hell are you talking about?" I pushed Noxzema for answers.

"She's lying in a hospital, honey," he said. "Your precious

mother is dying, if not already dead. And so the world is rid of one more faggot."

"Shut up!" Johnny slapped Noxzema across the head. "Before I knock your teeth out."

"What is he talking about, Johnny?"

"Don't listen to him, man. He's a crackhead."

"I might be on crack," Noxzema said, "but I know what I'm talking about. You remember light-skinned Fred?"

"Of course I do," I said. Fred was once a member of the House of Craft, and my long-lost sister. Last I heard, he had been sent upstate to Sierra Leone for armed robbery. "What does Fred have to do with any of this?"

"He called me a while ago," Noxzema said with blood on his teeth. Johnny had really done a number on him. "And he told me everything about how Pandora had gotten sick with tuberculosis that's been killing them prisoners."

"Oh, my God." I cringed. "I can't believe this. What the fuck is going on here?"

"I'm so sorry, man," Johnny said. "I didn't want you to find out this way."

"You knew about this?" I said.

"She told me not to say anything to you," he said. At that moment Johnny seemed like a total stranger to me.

"I hated lying to you," he went on. "You have to believe me, man. It tore me apart to lie to you."

"Just shut the hell up," I said. "I have nothing else to say to you!"

"Hey, where are you going?" asked Ebony, as I walked out of the room. "Aren't you going to wait for the police?"

Johnny

When I pulled up to the Pontchartrain Lake and saw Tonya standing looking out into the water, I knew right then and there that telling her the truth about me and James wasn't gonna be easy. One thing about the lake was that it held a lot of special memories for us.

Back in high school we used to sneak away from everything and everyone to have what we called our li'l "us" time together. You know what I mean, man. We did a whole lot of fucking out there on the lake, and it was actually the place where I first told Tonya how much I loved her. Funny how shit changes over the years, though. The deep love I once had for her now belonged to someone else, and only the Big Man upstairs knew the torment I was going through, being out at that lake with Tonya and knowing in my heart that we could never be together.

"About time you got here, nigga," she said. Tonya had on a pair of tight blue jeans and a tank top that had her round, sexy titties peeping out at a nigga like a jack-in-the-box. Moreover, a light breeze was coming off the water, and her long hair was even blowing in the wind. It was during times like these that I wondered what the fuck was wrong with me, man.

Here I had a dime piece in front of me—a beautiful-ass woman with a cute face and a big butt—but my heart was longing for another dude. Sometimes I questioned myself, and wondered if there was ever a time that I had been truly attracted to women in the first place—to Tonya. Or maybe my attraction to her was something I made up in my head to please my old man?

In a perfect world, I should have taken Tonya in my arms and never let go of her. But this wasn't a soap opera where we could just run off into *Fantasy Island* bullshit. Like I said before, my heart belonged to James, and I wasn't gonna front about my feelings for him any longer. Lying and sneaking around was no way to live when you truly cared about somebody the way I felt about James.

"Sorry I'm running late," I said, putting my cell on vibrate and waiting for a call from my nigga. The shit hit the fan the other night between us when James found out in the worst possible way that I had been keeping Pandora's illness a secret from him. What should have been a celebration—we had finally captured this dude Noxzema and gotten him to confess to the police after many years of being on the run—ended up being my worst fucking nightmare. And to make matters worse, Noxzema was the one who dropped the ball about Pandora being stricken with tuberculosis, which caused all kinds of drama between me and James.

Of course, I was scared of losing him, man. Although I had apologized until I was blue in the face, that dude wasn't taking any of my calls.

"I had some shit to take care of for my moms." I took Tonya

by the hand and looked her dead in the eyes. "But, anyway, you look beautiful, as always."

"Thank you." She leaned against me, and her sweet perfume made the hairs in my nose stand up. Her skin was soft, like baby lotion. It would have been a romantic setting under different circumstances. "I tried to look nice for you, since I hadn't seen your ass in what seemed like forever. You've been avoiding me or something?"

"There you go," I said with a half-assed smile on my face. It was hard for me to front like I was in a good mood. "Talking out of the side of your neck. But I can say the same thing about you."

"Don't even try to flip the switch on me, nigga," Tonya said, "like I've been the one avoiding you. So, what's been up, for real? You ain't trying to hit this anymore or what?"

"We do need to talk. But I don't even know where to fuck-ing begin, so much shit on my mind."

"Maybe you should start right around the time me and you was in high school." Tonya smiled. She had to be thinking about the night of our homecoming dance, when I boned her in the backseat of Kojack's black Mustang. I'd borrowed it for the pure sake of getting the drawers from Tonya and laying that wood down on her.

"It was a night something like this," she went on. "I was so happy being with you. It was my first time. And you was so gentle and patient with me."

"You remember that shit like it happened yesterday."

"A girl don't forget her first time," she said. "Unlike you men, who don't care about that kind of shit."

"Yeah, that was a crazy-ass night," I said. Going back in time was my way of giving Tonya her props and respecting what the two of us once shared—one last go-round before I told her what was truly up with me. "We got so drunk and fell asleep inside the car."

"Which got me in a whole lot of fucking trouble, nigga," Tonya said. "Somehow Mama found out where we was and showed up at the lake the next morning. You know, she beat my ass from sunup to sundown over that shit. I get chills just thinking about it."

"You know your mama has always been off her rocker," I said. "Is she still mean with a foul mouth?"

Man, Tonya's mom, Ms. Vivian, was no joke when it came to protecting her daughter from dudes. That woman would get right up in your face and cuss your ass out without no shame. And for some reason, she never liked my black ass from the beginning. She told Tonya that I was too good-looking and slick. One day I would break her heart.

"Yeah, she just as controlling as ever," Tonya said. "Now that I'm older, though, I don't even pay that woman much mind. But I do need to be getting my own place. Maybe me and you should move in together?"

"How we suppose to do that," I asked, fumbling with a set of car keys, "when I don't even have a job and shit? I can't afford no apartment."

"Well, I can't tell, nigga," Tonya said, looking at the Rolex on my arm and admiring the sparkling diamonds up against my dark skin. She also noticed the keys to the smack-brand-new Mercedes-Benz. "An expensive-ass watch. And you come driving up in a Benz. You hit the lottery or something and didn't tell me?"

"Nah, it's not like that at all. The car is a loaner from my cuz, but the watch was a gift." I placed the keys in my jacket. The last thing I wanted to do was give Tonya any false hope of thinking that me and her was about to relive history in the backseat of another one of Kojack's rides. "The Benz has to be back to him within the hour."

"An hour," she said with both hands on her hips. "I know you ain't trying to put me on a time limit?"

"Girl, simmer down," I said. "I'm just telling you what's up with my man's ride."

"And I know you ain't letting yourself get sucked back into the game," Tonya said with a worried look. "You've come too far to be going backward," she went on, but she was soon interrupted by the ringing phone inside her purse.

"Aren't you gon' answer that?" I asked.

"They can wait." She took the phone out of her purse and placed it on vibrate. "Now, where was we at?"

"Nothing important," I said. "But like I was saying earlier, we need to talk—"

"Yeah, I remember," she cut me off. "We was talking about your cousin. But I almost forgot to tell you. You know he came through for me and my girls the other night? He ain't tell you about it?"

"Nah, we didn't really have that much time to talk earlier," I said, thinking about how nervous that nigga was when we last saw each other. Me and Kojack were at his crib chilling, and he was preparing for a big meeting with his boss man concerning a deal going down in the NO with that player from the West Coast that had all of them on pins and needles. This dude Big Daddy Cane was a ruthless and coldhearted nigga who was known for his double-crossing antics, and one of the only reasons I had agreed to cover my cuz's back when the deal went down. Nothing was thicker or more reliable than blood.

What the hell you thought? You know that nigga wasn't giving me diamond watches and letting me ride in his brand-new car for nothing. Although we were family, I still had to earn my way, just like everyone else out there on those streets.

"Well, I'm surprised he didn't tell you about the other night," Tonya said. "Because like I said, it went down, for real."

"What happened? Talk to me, man. Don't be holding back."

"Some punk down at Club Circus," Tonya said, "thought he could disrespect my girl Tamika, so I had to get up in his motherfucking face."

"I don't understand," I said, trying to hold a weak-ass grin on my face.

"Babee, it'll make a whole lot of sense once I finish telling you everything," she said. "This punk I was telling you about was using Tamika's sorority as part of his act."

"I'm still not following you." There was suddenly a river of spit inside of my throat. I took a long hard swallow and tried to keep my cool as much as possible, considering the circumstances. "What act are you talking about?"

"A drag queen, punk-ass motherfucker who goes by the name of Armari St. James. I had to get up in his face, but then some ghetto-ass woman got in the middle of things and caught me off guard."

"I can't believe this. All of this went down the other night?"

"Yep. It sure did," Tonya went on. "And that ghetto woman was trying to choke me, and Kojack had to pump her brakes. I never thought in a million years that a cousin of yours would ever come to my rescue, but I'm glad he did. That motherfucking woman had a set of hands on her, for real. I think somebody said that it was that punk's mama."

"This was not how I wanted things to go down. Definitely not like this."

"What the fuck is wrong with you, nigga?" Tonya had picked up on some weird vibes. "You act like you know this punk or something."

"Don't call him that," I said.

"Why not? That's exactly what he is. And why are you defending some goddamn punk, anyway?"

"I told you to stop calling him that," I said, looking around to see if anyone else was around us. Besides a few parked cars on the other side of the street, we were totally alone.

"Man, I can't do this anymore," I said with my fist balled up in a tight knot. "I can't do this shit anymore."

"You can't do what anymore?" asked Tonya. "You're not making any goddamn sense. What the fuck is you trying to tell me?"

"Why don't we sit down inside the car and talk." I reached for Tonya's hand, but she jerked away from me like she didn't want me touching her or something.

"I don't think so, nigga," she said. "Whatever you gotta say, you say that shit right here in the open, because I'm suddenly getting a funny feeling about your ass. I know you ain't trying to tell me you gay or something?"

I suddenly got quiet, like somebody put my ass on mute. Tonya looked into my eyes and knew the truth without me even having to say anything.

"Answer me, dammit!" Tonya screamed. That full moon sent her into beast mode. "Are you telling me you a faggot?"

"That's not what I would call it." I cleared my throat. "I really didn't wanna do it like this."

"You fucking bastard." She punched and then clawed me in the face with her long fingernails. Man, Tonya had completely lost it. She was punching and screaming and going completely crazy on me. "You motherfucking punk! How you gon' do some shit like this to me, Johnny? I can't believe this shit!"

She tried to punch me in my face again, but I caught hold of her wrists. Tonya had a set of hands on her like a dude, and those licks were beginning to hurt. "Calm the fuck down. I know you upset, but we gotta talk about this."

"Let go of me, nigga." She pushed me off of her. "We don't got nothing else to talk about. How long this shit been going on behind my back? Tell me that, huh? Since high school?"

"It wasn't even like that. In high school I wasn't fucking around on you with anybody."

"Whatever, nigga," she said. "Your ass is a liar, and I don't believe nothing else you have to say, so get your punk ass out of my face."

"Come on, girl. Don't walk away like this." I followed close behind her. She stopped and turned to face me. Pain and hurt were written all over her face. "Just give me a few minutes; that's all I'm asking for."

"I don't know what you can possibly say that would make this situation any better," she said. Then she paused and just stared at me. "I'm listening."

"For a long time, I was confused." I rushed my words like a speaker onstage pressed for time and under the gun. "I didn't know what I wanted. Man, I'm so sorry to hurt you like this."

"Hold on," Tonya said. Her cell phone was vibrating inside her purse.

"Let it ring." I snatched the cell out of her hand. "Whoever it is, they can wait."

"Give me my phone, nigga," Tonya said. "Me and you don't have nothing else to talk about."

I looked at the display window and couldn't believe my eyes when I saw the name on the caller ID.

"Rico," I said with the phone pointed at her. "I know this ain't the same Rico you messed me over with while I was serving time for your ass?"

"Yeah, nigga. It's him." Tonya tried reaching for the phone but I held it over her head like I was slam-dunking on her. "And he's more man than your ass ever was or could be. And I'm not playing with you. Now give me my damn phone!"

"You stink whore." Seeing Rico's name brought up old feelings of betrayal that had been deeply buried inside of me for years. "Here I'm worried about your feelings, and you still playing me behind my back."

"Boy, ain't nobody playing you." Tonya sounded completely out of breath. Trying to get her phone out of my hand wound up being a whole lot of work. "Give me my phone, Johnny. I'm serious."

I sent Tonya's phone flying into the air like a football—straight into the Pontchartrain.

"If you want that nigga," I said, hopping inside the Benz, "go get 'im, slut."

"Fuck you!" Tonya banged on top of the hood and stared in my face through the window.

I pulled into reverse.

"I hate your ass!" She kicked the side of the car. "You motherfucking punk nigga! I'm gon' tell everybody on the street about your ass, too!"

Without saying another word, I laid rubber and headed up the road like the NO police force was trailing my black ass. Getting out of Dodge as quick as I could was the only way I knew how to deal with the pain and hurt that were burning inside my chest like gas.

"How you doing, Ms. Maggie?" I poked my head in her office. She was a stout older woman with round eyeglasses who had been the church's secretary since I was a baby crawling around in diapers.

"I'm doing good, sugar," she said. "I was wondering when I was gon' see you. Look how handsome you done got. Come here and give Ms. Maggie a hug."

No doubt she was a sweet woman, man, who had always shown me nothing but love over the years. But that was how it was when I got out of the pen. A lot of them older folks up at Pops's church thought the world of me despite all the bad mistakes and wrong choices I had made over the years. Pops was the only one who couldn't seem to accept or deal with me on my own terms. That dude was full of judgment.

"We miss you around here," she said, looking me over like a proud mother. "You've been out that prison for weeks. Now, why it took you so long to come in see Ms. Maggie?"

"I've been busy, man," I said. "You know, trying to get my life together and do positive things."

"Well, I'm glad to hear that." She hugged me once again. I could barely catch my breath with those big breasts of hers pressed up against my chest. "You stay positive and keep God first. You hear me? Because ain't nothing out there in those streets for a young black man but trouble. Now, what brings you by here this evening?"

Mt. Zion Baptist Church was the last place I thought I would end up after my big blowup with Tonya. But the truth was, our argument shook a nigga to the core, and I needed some kind of reassurance that everything was gonna be all right in the end. One thing I could say without question was that church always brought on feelings like my troubles were only passing and not planning to stick around for the long haul.

"I was just stopping by to say hello," I said, looking out into the hallway and trying to locate the sound of gospel music that could be heard throughout the entire building. "You know, check out the old place."

"Well, you couldn't have come at a better time." Ms. Maggie led me into the main sanctuary, where the choir was practicing for Sunday-morning services. "I know how much you used to love to hear the choir sing. We've grown since then and have become one of the best in the city."

Ms. Maggie was actually being modest about the church's expansion and success over the years. Man, Mt. Zion was a pillar of the black community, and the choir was recognized not only in the city of New Orleans but around the country. While I was in the pen, they had once been invited to sing at a ceremony at the White House. No lie, man. And Pops had been recognized by a lot of important people as one of the top preachers in the country, including *Ebony* magazine. Pops was considered a people's pastor. Everyone loved his down-to-earth nature. Where some pastors might obtain wealth and success and then leave the community, Pops stayed right there in the Ninth Ward with the poor and working-class people.

Despite our problems, I couldn't deny that dude brought in folks from all walks of life to hear his powerful delivery of the word of God. Moreover, Mt. Zion was slowly becoming one of those megachurches you see on TV, and Pops was making big moves and buying up real estate around the church building so that he could further serve the community.

"Wow, man," I said from the doorway, with Ms. Maggie standing right beside me. The large windows inside the sanctuary were painted with different church symbols and angels. In addition, the pulpit where Pops preached from every Sunday morning was huge and fit for a king. The choir was directly behind the pulpit. "Man, a lot of things have changed. I don't know what to say."

The choir was singing one of my favorite hymns, "His Eyes on the Sparrow." They were one hundred strong and gave me goose bumps. Man, without a doubt, church music was one of the sweetest sounds in the world that always uplifted me no matter what I was going through in life.

"You stick around as long as you like," said Ms. Maggie. "But I need to get myself back to work. You gon' be all right?"

"I'm straight," I said, making eye contact with this dude on the choir stand who could hardly sing for looking at me. "It was good seeing you, though."

"Same here, sugar," she said, stepping out into the hallway. "You know your father is downstairs getting ready for the christening of your cousin's baby this coming Sunday morning. This must be an exciting time for your family. Everyone around here is thrilled, too."

No sooner was Ms. Maggie out of sight than I realized that dude in the choir was Jerome—one of James's house daughters.

Man, don't even act like you surprised. You know a lot of gay dudes be up in those church choirs shouting and screaming and blowing everyone away with their voices. Everyone knows that shit, but no one acknowledges it out in the open. In fact, if it wasn't for those gay dudes a lot of them choirs would be boring. But we gotta keep it on the hush-hush, 'cause church folks don't wanna be hearing nothing about no gay dudes singing in the choir. If nothing else, though, seeing Jerome up there on that choir stand got me to thinking about James, who, mind you, still wasn't taking any of my calls. Between him avoiding me and Tonya hating my guts, they were driving a nigga stone-cold mad.

"What brings you by, son?" Pops walked up behind me and startled my ass. "Ms. Maggie told me I could find you up here."

"What's up?" I said, taking my eyes off of Jerome for a moment. "I can't stop by my own church?"

"Of course you can," he said. I noticed he had a Bible. Pops never went anywhere without the Word. "I'm just surprised you're here. What's going on?"

"Ain't nothing going on," I said, avoiding eye contact with him. One look into my eyes and Pops would have known I was lying. That dude had a way of reading your spirit and pulling the truth out of you. "I just felt like stopping by."

"Then why do I feel like there's more to it than that?" asked Pops. "I've been trying to get you to come to church for weeks, and now you suddenly show up here out of the blue?"

"Well, aren't you the one who's always saying that the doors of the church house are always open?"

"If you're here for the right reasons, son." Pops raised his voice. We had to talk over the choir, which was now belting out another beautiful hymn. "Are you here to recommit your life to the Lord? Or is there something else going on?"

"Don't start with me, man!" I felt myself shouting, but quickly lowered my voice. "I didn't come here to pick a fight with you."

"You never did answer me," Pops said. "Why did you come?

Does this mean what I hope it means? You've decided to stop running with Kojack and are coming back home to do God's work?"

"First of all, I'm not running with Kojack! Unlike you, I can't cut my family off like they don't mean anything to me!"

"We can finish this conversation at home," Pops said. "This is not the time or the place for us to be talking about this. I hope you plan to be at Nettie's baby's christening tomorrow."

"I wouldn't miss it for the world," I said with a slight grin on my face. "Is that off-limits to Kojack, too?"

Pops shook his head as if he didn't know what to say or do with me. "You already know the answer to that. His presence here would only upset Nettie and the family, and I'm not going to allow anyone to ruin that baby's christening. I'll see you at home."

Like he had with every other member of the family, Kojack had now managed to put distance between him and Nettie, too. Her baby's daddy's murder was still a mystery. Nettie blamed Kojack, even though he never really owned up to killing anyone.

"Yo, Pops." I hit him from left field as he made his way down the hall. "Did anything ever happen to me when I was a child?"

Pops stopped dead in his tracks and faced me with the Bible clutched under his arm. "Happen like what?"

Pops had one of them nervous grins on his face, like someone just caught him red-handed.

"I've been having these nightmares," I said, "of someone taking me out of my sleep. Keep seeing the face of Jesus, too."

"I wish I could help you, son." Pops took a long pause, like he was choosing his words carefully. The choir brought the hymn to a satisfying end. "But I have no idea what you're talking about. All I could say is that God works in mysterious ways."

"Don't quote me no verses from the Bible, man," I said. "If something happened to me as a child, I wanna know about it."

"And like I said, son . . ." Pops lowered his voice to a whisper. A few of the choir members were walking down the hallway. "I don't have the answer you're looking for."

"Then why I feel like you're keeping something from me?" I said. "If there's something in my past—"

"Okay. I've had enough of this," Pops cut me off. "It's late. And I'm heading home to be with my wife—*your* mother, who's been worried sick about you ever since you came home. For her sake, I hope in the end you turn away from your wicked ways and do the right thing, son."

I watched Pops as he strode down the hallway with his Bible. I could sense that Pops was lying to me. But why? I had no idea. Sometimes the only way to discover the truth is to keep living and breathing and going on with life.

Anyway, I found my way downstairs to the prayer room, where the church held its Sunday-morning Bible classes. The room was like a minichapel, where Pops would practice his sermons and sneak away for private time. It was equipped with surround sound and a TV monitor that allowed you to view services from the main sanctuary.

Me and my brothers spent a lot of time inside of that prayer room growing up, so I knew of its existence long before any plans between me and Kojack were put into action. Since it was downstairs and quietly tucked away from the main church, it was the one place where you could have total privacy during Sunday-afternoon services. Kojack had planned to use the room to watch Nettie's baby's christening without anyone knowing that he was even in the building.

I dialed Kojack right away. "Everything looks good, man." After the christening, we would jet down the street to handle his business with that dude Big Daddy Cane. You heard me right, man. One of the biggest drug deals in the NO was going down only blocks away from my pops's church, and nobody was more worried than me. I must have been out of my mind to agree to any of this. "Catch you tomorrow, nigga, and remember this is a onetime deal."

{ 16 }

Tonya

"So, you playing it straight with a brother?" Rico held me close, with his hard dick rubbing up against my leg, and coughing out loud like he had a bad strain of the flu.

We was alone inside of my bedroom, and that freaky bastard had lust in his eyes, as usual. Sex was always on his brain. "And still planning on taking that trip to South Africa, so we can run around in the jungle butterball naked?"

"I told you I'm going, nigga," I said, turning my head so he wouldn't kiss me on the lips. Rico wasn't getting any more of this pussy until I had landed safely in South Africa. "Now chill out."

"Oh, so, you ain't trying to let me hit that again?" said Rico. "And here I thought this trip meant everything to you."

"Why you still questioning me?" I asked. "You know how much I love to dance and how badly I want this!"

"Well, I can't tell." Rico rubbed my arms. "Your ass ain't trying to put out."

"Don't start with that again." I pulled away from him and started throwing clothes inside of the Louis Vuitton luggage that was laid out across my bed like precious jewels—a gift from Rico for putting out the goodies the last time I visited with him at his crib. All I had to do was give that nigga a li'l piece of ass, and the world was mine for the taking. "Besides, there'll be plenty of time for that once we get to South Africa."

You heard right. I didn't stutter or trip over my words. Fuck what you heard. At this point, it was all about getting mine and ending up on top. But being a damn fool for love, I almost gave it all up—a mistake that I promised myself that I would never make again. After you hear what went down with me and Johnny at the Pontchartrain Lake, you should completely understand why I wasn't trusting niggas anymore or giving my heart to anyone.

"Now that's what I'm talking about." Rico licked his lips and held his dick. "But what about that loser jailbird?"

"I told you, me and him are over and done with." I sat on the bed and thought long and hard about the situation between me and Johnny. How he came at me with the most unbelievable and shocking news that blew my motherfucking mind into orbit.

Johnny had us meet at the lake—the most heavenly place on earth, where me and that nigga fell in love—just so he could tell me that it was over between us. But, babee, that wasn't the worst of it. Johnny wasn't leaving me for another woman—that I could have kind of understood—but he now claimed to have feelings for some drag queen—that punk-ass, faggot motherfucker, of all people, who I had a run-in with at Club Circus the other night.

"Excuse me. I'll be right back." I ran past Rico and headed straight for the bathroom. My stomach suddenly got weak just thinking about the idea of Johnny and that dude fucking around together. That shit was nasty and made me vomit.

"Oh, God." I leaned over the toilet and rested my legs on the cold white tile floors. "I think I'm about to be sick."

"You all right in here?" Rico followed me into the bathroom. "You need some medicine or something?"

"Wait for me in the bedroom." I slammed the door in his face and leaned over the toilet seat. All I wanted was to be left alone. Johnny had truly done a number on my head, and I was heartbroken for real, y'all.

I loved that nigga with everything in me that was good and honest. I truly did. When I met Johnny at the lake, I was planning on telling him the truth about me and Rico. How he wanted me to go to South Africa to dance in a hot new video and everything. You know, as a way to make a fresh start. But the kicker was, I had decided not to even go on the trip with Rico, because I had this stupid idea of me and Johnny moving into our own place and starting our lives together.

For heaven's sake, I thought Johnny was gonna ask me to marry him, and we was gone spend the rest of our lives together. Now, I wasn't certain about anything anymore but the pain inside of my heart that hurt so fucking much. My chest felt like it was about to cave in like an earthquake.

"Girl, what's ailing you?" Mama opened the door and found me on the floor with my back against the wall. My legs was wide open to the world. And you should have seen my hair. It was a mess, too. "And what's Rico doing in my house? Answer me, girl. What's wrong with you?"

I flushed the toilet and pulled my hair out of my face. The last thing I wanted was Mama all up in my business. She had a way of making an already bad situation worse with her cussing and fussing over nothing. "Nothing's wrong. I'm fine."

"Well, you don't look fine to me," Mama said as I stood on

my feet. Her work uniform was dingy and dirty. And she looked tired and beat-down.

"In fact, you look downright awful," she said. Yet Mama was the one looking bad lately. That made no goddamn sense to me.

Don't get me wrong. Mama was pretty, but she just wasn't into fixing herself up. After Daddy died she gave up on living. And when my brother Eric was killed, she finally gave up on being happy, too. I don't remember the last time Mama went out on a date. Although she got on my last fucking nerve, I still worried about her. You know, she was my mama, and I loved her despite our problems and hardships.

"Whatever, Ma." I walked by her and headed to the bedroom. She followed close behind me.

"Now where's Rico?" I looked around the room for him, but he was nowhere to be found. "I told his ass to wait in here for me."

"He just took off," Mama said, taking a cigarette out of her purse. "What was he doing in my house, anyway?"

"What did you say to him, Ma?" I wondered. "Did you tell him to leave?"

"And if I did?" Mama lit the cigarette and then took a long, casual puff, like she had all the time and freedom in the motherfucking world. She blew smoke in my face. "What your ass gon' do about it?"

"Girl, I see you in the mood for a fight." I walked over to the closet. "But I'm not even about to give you one."

"He mentioned something about y'all going out of the country and the limo picking you up at midnight." Mama smashed the cigarette underneath her dirty white shoes. "What the hell is he talking about?"

"I'm getting out of here." I placed the clothes on the bed and started shoving everything I owned inside my suitcase. "I'm tired of this fucking hellhole. Everywhere you turn you hear about somebody being shot or killed."

"I admit," Mama said, "these ain't no easy streets to make a living on, but I always did my best to protect y'all."

"Well, that's just it, Mama," I said, moving from the closet to the bed. "I'm grown. And I don't need your protection any-more."

"So, you gon' just run out on me?" asked Mama with a hurt look in her eyes. "Leave me behind like your brother Ricky did when he went into that white man's army?"

"At least Ricky had the good sense to get out of here before he got taken down on those streets like—"

"Don't you dare say it," Mama cut me off. "I don't wanna hear it."

"Hear what, Mama?" I asked, holding a pile of clothes in my hand. "That Eric is dead? But he is dead, Mama, and so is Daddy. You need to let them go, Mama!"

"Shut up!" She let out a loud scream. "You ain't nothing but a li'l whore walking around here high and mighty like you got it all figured out, telling me what I need to do."

"Mama," I said, more out of shock than anything, "why you talking to me like that?"

" 'Cause you sleeping and running around here from one man to the next," Mama said. "People talk, and it don't look good."

"You think I give a damn what these people say around here?" I snatched a blouse off the hanger and laid it across the bed. "I don't give a fuck about them. They don't know me."

"So, what happened?" asked Mama. "I thought you were all in love with Johnny?"

THREE SIDES TO EVERY STORY

"It's not gon' work out with us." I cleaned out my jewelry box and suddenly felt a sharp pull in my joints. The idea of leaving Johnny behind was killing me, and I could feel the agony way down deep in my bones. "I found out he's a punk."

"Girl, what the hell you talking about now?" asked Mama with a confused look on her face. "You talking about punk as in being weak like a punk? Or punk as in being fruity, with a li'l sugar in his drawers?"

"It's a long story," I said to her. "But all you need to know is that we ain't together anymore, which should make you very happy. I know how much you didn't like Johnny, anyway."

"I didn't have nothing against him." Mama was full of shit. She changed her mind from one minute to the next. "It's that Rico you gotta watch."

"And here I thought you liked him," I said. "He was your friend when he was giving you all of his money."

When me and Rico was an item, he would break Mama off with hundreds and thousands of dollars just about every other week. Sometimes she would get more than me, and I was the one fucking that li'l-dick nigga two and three times a day. But one thing about Mama: She had selective memory when it came to certain topics.

"Don't get me wrong. I appreciate everything he did for me, but he ain't no better than the rest of 'em," she said. "Left your ass for the first white girl who smiled in his motherfucking face. He's only gon' use you up, sweetheart, and then send you with your bags packing."

"You'll say anything to stop me from going." I sat on top of the suitcase in order to make room for more stuff. "But you can save your breath, Mama. I'm leaving with Rico and that's just all there is to it."

"I thought I raised you better than this." Mama shook her head. "Don't you have any kind of pride, taking back a man who left you high and dry?"

"Maybe I do. Maybe I don't." I rose up off the bed and got right up in Mama's face, with my chest sticking out like I was the only woman. "But at least I have the good sense to live my life instead of sitting around here wasting away and crying over dead people who ain't coming back!"

"You li'l rotten whore, you!" Mama reached back and slapped me so hard, I fell over the suitcase on the bed and landed on the floor, knocking the nightstand and lamp over.

"You think you a woman now." Mama started pounding me on top of my head with her black purse. "But you don't know a damn thing about being no woman!"

"Stop it!" I held my hands out in front of me. "Mama, what's wrong with you?"

"I'm tired of your damn mouth." She sent another blow across my head. "But I'm gon' show your ass who's really the boss around here."

Sad as this situation was, this was how it was growing up under Mama's roof.

"Oh, Jesus." She lowered her purse, and I wondered what was wrong. Why had Mama stopped beating my ass? I had become numb to the pain. "You're bleeding."

Her face looked like a goddamn ghost town.

"Somebody help!" Mama rushed me through the front doors of Charity Hospital. I had been bleeding from the time we left the house, and there was blood everywhere. Between my legs was where I felt the most heat. "Somebody–anybody–please help my daughter!"

"Tell me what's wrong." A nurse immediately came to our aid. When she saw all of that blood running down my legs, that nurse really looked worried–me and her both.

"The two of us got into it," Mama explained to the lady, as I could barely get a damn word out of my mouth. Now I knew what it was like to go into shock. "I'm her mother, you see. And I didn't mean to hurt her."

"Are you in any pain?" The nurse ignored Mama and focused her attention completely on me.

"Not really," I said. "But I can't stop bleeding."

"Just stay calm," the nurse said. She was a young black woman who seemed like she knew what she was doing. But it wouldn't have mattered. My brother died up there at Charity Hospital, and ever since then I hated the place–all hospitals, to tell you the truth. "Let's get you to an examination room."

Mama held me up by the arm as if I didn't have any legs to walk on my own–a far cry from the woman who was steady beating my ass earlier without shame.

"Just take a seat right here." The nurse led us into a small examination room with white walls. I suddenly got the chills. Eric had passed away in a room similar to that one. "You think you'll be all right while I go and find a doctor on duty?"

"I'm okay," I told her. "Just hurry, ma'am. I think something is really wrong."

She ran off and left me alone in the room with Mama. There was a hard moment of silence between us before she eventually broke down and said something to me.

"I'm so sorry, sweetheart," Mama said. "I don't know what

got into me earlier. If anything happens to you, Lord knows I couldn't live with myself."

"I don't wanna talk about it," I said, staring at the walls and avoiding eye contact with her. It hurt too much to even look Mama in the face. "But if you think this gon' stop me from going on my trip, you better think again."

"Okay. What seems to be the problem in here?" A handsome black doctor with a clean-cut face entered the room and interrupted us. His voice was sweet like candy. "I'm Dr. Marvin Holmes. The nurse said you were bleeding."

"Wait a minute," I said to him. There was something about his voice that made me very uncomfortable. "Are you my doctor?"

"Yeah, ma'am. I am," he said, rolling his eyes like he couldn't believe I had just asked him that question. "Is that a problem?"

"Yes, it is," I said. "I want another doctor. Find me somebody else."

"Tonya," Mama said. "Are you crazy? This man come in here to help you."

"Well, I don't want his help," I said, looking at him directly in his face. "Get me somebody else or I'm leaving."

"I'm so sorry, Doctor, for my daughter's rudeness," Mama apologized. Dr. Holmes looked like his feelings might have actually been hurt, but I didn't give a shit. I wasn't about to allow some sweet nigga with a soft voice to put his hands on me—not ever again!

"It's no problem," he said, removing a pair of white gloves and tossing them in a nearby trash can. "I will find y'all another doctor."

"What done got into you, girl?" Mama asked me as soon as that doctor left. "Saying something like that to that man."

I stared at the walls again and wondered how hot it was in South Africa. It was pushing ten o'clock in the evening, and the limo was due at our house at midnight. If nothing else, I was beginning to get worried about making it to the plane on time.

"What's taking them so damn long?" I wondered, but no sooner did another doctor enter the room. She was white, which wasn't much better in my eye.

"I heard there's an issue with blood," she said. "I'm Dr. Cramer. What seems to be the problem?"

"Damn. There ain't no black women doctors in this fucking hospital?"

"Ma'am, there's no need for that kind of talk," Dr. Cramer said. She seemed like the type of person who didn't take much shit from anyone, so I bit my tongue. You know I needed to get my ass out of there with a quickness. "We would like to help you, but we will not tolerate that kind of behavior in this hospital. Now I'm going to ask you again: What's the problem?"

"Out of the blue," I said, "I started bleeding."

"There was so much blood," Mama finished, "that we were both worried."

"Let me take a look." Dr. Cramer put on a pair of white gloves. "Why don't you lean back on the table and relax."

She lifted my skirt and looked between my legs. Mama stared down at me with tears in her eyes.

"Okay," the doctor said. "You can sit up."

"Can you tell what's wrong with her, Doctor?" asked Mama. "Why my girl bleeding so much?"

"I don't want to speculate." Dr. Cramer took off the gloves and placed them in the garbage. "When was the last time you had a checkup, Tonya?"

"A checkup?" I stared at her as if she was crazy. "I don't have no money to be getting no checkups."

"Who's your insurance provider?" she asked.

"Woman, are you hard of hearing?" I said. "I ain't got no insurance."

"Don't be disrespectful, Tonya," Mama said. "The woman is only trying to help."

"All I was trying to say was," Dr. Cramer said, "it's okay if you don't have insurance. Most of our patients don't. We have all kinds of payment plans."

"So, what's the next step?" asked Mama.

"I would like to do a complete physical and run some blood samples," Dr. Cramer said, "just to cover all bases. Including an HIV test."

"An HIV test?" I said with an attitude. "I don't have no fucking AIDS."

"Ma'am, I'm going to have to ask you again to calm down and refrain from using that sort of language with me."

"Man, you tripping for real," I said, thinking about Johnny and that dude James being together and putting my fucking life at risk. You damn right I was scared.

"I'm sorry, Doctor," Mama said. "She's just worried and stressed out."

"I'm only here to help, but I need permission to run certain tests," Dr. Cramer said.

They both were staring at me.

"Okay then. Fine," I said. "Run your stupid tests."

"I'll send a nurse in to take a blood sample," she said on her way out of the door.

"Thank you, Doctor," Mama said for both of us. I was staring up at the ceiling and trying to be brave. But the truth was, I was scared out of my mind.

Needless to say, the nurse took my blood just like Dr. Cramer said she would and then left. Me and Mama waited against the silence with the white walls keeping us company for little under an hour.

"I need to go and call Rico." I finally broke the mood inside of the room. Me and Mama was getting nowhere giving each other the silent treatment. "So the limo can pick me up here."

"You heard what the doctor said." Mama stood in front of the door like she was a bouncer at Club Circus. "You need to stay put until she comes back with the results."

"I'm going to Africa!" I screamed. "Nothing is going to stop me. You heard me, Mama. Nothing!"

"What's the problem in here?" Dr. Cramer said as she came into the room. "I could hear screaming down the hall."

"I need to get out of here," I said, getting up to leave. "I'm sorry, Doctor, but I gotta plane to catch."

"Tonya," Dr. Cramer said with seriousness in her voice, "I think you need to have a seat."

"Why I got to have a seat?" I felt the nerves in my neck jump.

"We ran your test sample," Dr. Cramer said, holding a medical chart in her hand. "And I have your results. I really think you need to have a seat."

"That was quick." Mama cut the woman off before she could get another word in edgewise. Dr. Cramer had a serious look on her face, like the stars had fallen out of the sky. "Please, Jesus—tell me my baby girl gon' be all right."

{ 17 }

James

"Are you sure you want to go through with this?" Ms. Boudreaux handed me a face mask to protect myself from the bacteria. She knew a judge that had strong ties with the warden, which ultimately led me to getting an early Sunday-morning visit with Pandora at Sierra Leone Infirmary, a dark, decaying warehouse where they quarantined inmates who had been infected with tuberculosis, so they claimed.

At the time of our visit, there had already been over fifty reported deaths. Something was definitely wrong with this picture, and I was determined to get to the bottom of it while I was up there. You best believe that, honey.

"I've never been more sure about anything before in my life." I placed the mask around my head and pulled at the loose straps to cover my nose. Fear suddenly overtook my body. I was going into the unknown.

"I gotta do what I gotta do," I finished what I was saying. "She's always had my back, and now it's time for me to be there for her."

"Well, you're a good friend." Ms. Boudreaux rubbed the side

THREE SIDES TO EVERY STORY

of my arm. "Wasn't your friend Ebony supposed to meet us up here, as well?"

"Chile, I wouldn't count on it," I said. "That girl has drama in her life and isn't reliable these days."

Ms. Boudreaux had a questioning look on her face.

"She's involved with a drug-dealing thug," I said, "who's beating her ass into the ground."

"I see," she said. "Well, I'll wait out front just in case she shows up. In the meantime, that will give you some private time with your friend."

"Thank you." I took in a deep breath and opened the door. An awful smell, like something dead and rotten, hit me from all corners of the room, and it took everything in me not to turn around and run back out of that door.

You see, when I walked out of this hellhole of a prison many years ago, it was my intention to never return, no matter what the circumstances were. Pandora was the only person who could make me break a promise to myself. My love for her was stronger than any amount of hatred or apathy that I had for the place.

"Let me see your ID and visiting papers." A security guard, who was eating doughnuts and drinking a hot cup of coffee, was posted at the front door. I guess he was immune to the smell.

"You straight." He handed my ID back to me. "Is this your first time in the infirmary?"

"Yes." I shivered from the coldness. It felt like an ice storm inside of that goddamn warehouse.

"Well, I hope you have a strong stomach," he said. "Just make sure you put these gloves on."

I followed his directions, and then another sliding door

opened and that smell got even stronger. Now it smelled like I was inside of a refrigerator with a month's supply of spoiled meat. But that wasn't the worst of it.

"Shit!" I screamed. A giant-ass rat ran across the floor right in front of me. No fucking joke. That bastard was huge and grown-up, like he had been a resident at the prison for years. Honey, I might have been cut from tough cloth, but I don't do rats.

"Excuse me, hon." I grabbed a frail nurse by the arm. She was carrying a tray of medical supplies and wearing a mask of her own. "I'm looking for a patient."

"Yeah, what's his name?" She sounded like one old country hick. Her hair was blond, loose, and wild, like it was thrown together at the last minute. Ms. Girl seemed stressed and over-worked.

"Alexandria Pandora Craft," I said proudly. "Legendary mother of the House of Craft."

"You're kidding me, right?" she said.

"You must not have worked here very long," I followed with an attitude. " 'Cause everyone knows the mother of all mothers."

"You're right about that," she said, struggling with the medical tray in her hands. "This is my first week. And it's a god-damn mess around here, as you can see."

"Well, I won't keep you, girl," I said. "I'm sure I'll find her somehow."

"I'm so sorry." She took off down the hallway and disappeared behind another door. There were a lot of goddamn doors to that awful, godforsaken place. I wondered how anyone could find their way without a map.

"James Santiago." An old white man with large round glasses and a beautiful set of blue eyes caught my attention. He was lying in a twin bed watching TV. "How long has it been?"

"Mr. Reynolds." I immediately made my way over and stared down at him in disbelief.

When I was an inmate, Mr. Reynolds had to be well over three hundred pounds. Now he was lucky to be over a hundred. Whatever kind of bacteria it was, that shit must have been lethal and ruthless to reduce grown men down to almost nothing. And I'm not just talking about Mr. Reynolds.

Alongside his bed were long rows—on both sides of the room—of weak and sick men who looked as if life had been zapped out of them without prejudice. On top of that, a blue light flickered off and on inside of the room. It suddenly dawned on me that these men weren't patients but specimens. Not one single person was on an IV or respirator. They meant for these men to die!

"Yeah. It's me, sweets," Mr. Reynolds said with a large smile on his face. One thing was for certain: That bacteria couldn't take the humor out of him. Mr. Reynolds had always been a nice and fun-loving old man. "It's been a while. How you been?"

"I've been fine, hon," I said. He couldn't see my huge smile from behind the mask, but my eyes proved my joy. "Just trying to keep my head above water. What about you?"

"I'm making it all right." He coughed uncontrollably. His bed shook against the hardwood floors. "Just trying to fight this fucking disease. Let me guess. You come here to see Pandora?"

"You know it," I said. "Nothing was gonna keep me away."

"She's the last bed at the end on the right." Mr. Reynolds pointed me in the right direction. "Make sure you stop by on your way out and say good-bye, okay, sweets?"

"I sure will." I grinned at him. That old man actually had a crush on me, honey. "You li'l devil."

What can I say? I was fabulous and desired even by the older inmates. If nothing else, though, running into Mr. Reynolds and being up there at Sierra Leone was bringing me back to another lifetime. Of course, I'm talking about Johnny.

"What's up, Ms. Pandora, girl?" When I saw my mother lying with her back toward me and looking so emaciated and decrepit, I knew forgiving Johnny probably wasn't going to happen anytime soon.

How could he have kept such a secret from me when he knew my mother's life was on the line? The hate built up inside of me like a volcano, just thinking about how his ass lied and deceived me.

"When I heard what happened"–I sat down in an empty chair next to the bed–"I couldn't stay away."

She finally turned to face me, and it took everything in me not to scream. Her once glowing skin was covered with large, black spots, and those gorgeous brown eyes that used to steal many hearts were now dark and lonely, like a bottomless pit.

"Well, you shouldn't have," she said in a raspy and weak voice that sounded like the pain beating inside of my chest.

"Why would you say something like that?" I tried to be more upbeat and positive.

"Because I don't want you here." She coughed, and her whole body seemed to shake against the building. "So go. Get out of here!"

She gripped the side of the bed and tried to raise her head off the pillow.

"You need to calm your nerves and get used to the idea," I said. "Because I'm not going anywhere."

"You've always been stubborn." She shook her head and surrendered. "You gon' force yourself on me."

"What did you think, hon?" I wondered. "That you could just keep this secret from me forever?"

"Don't you get it?" She started bawling right there in front of me, and I honestly didn't know how to handle it. For as long as I had known her, Pandora had always been the strong one that everyone else could depend on. "I couldn't stand for you to see me like this. I'm a mess. Now please just go."

"Stop it." I raised my eyebrows for optimum effect. "I love you, and nothing will ever change that. So, you better hear me, Ms. Girl, because I'm in this for the long haul."

I squeezed her hand and became a source of strength for the both of us.

"How have you been?" She talked her way through a river of tears. "What's been happening on the outside?"

"I've been fine," I said. "Just taking it easy and doing my thing, hon. You know how I roll."

"And what about the children?" Pandora pulled out a hand-kerchief and patted her eyes dry. "What I wouldn't give to have another spin on the dance floor at Club Circus."

"And one day you will," I told her. "You gon' get out of here, and we gon' dance like it's nobody's business. Let the children have it, honey."

She laughed. "Bitch. I see you still crazy as ever. What else you been up to? You and Johnny still together? I assume that's how you found out."

"Johnny wasn't the one who told me," I said. "But I don't wanna talk about him. He's on my shit list."

"Don't be angry with that boy." She sounded weak. It took a lot of strength out of her just to talk back and forth with me. "I made him promise me."

"Well, he should have known better," I said. "Now he's gotta pay the price and hope I forgive him."

"You keep playing games," Pandora said, "and one of those vicious children out there gon' be somewhere screwing your man. You can't turn your back on a fine-ass nigga like Johnny. Not for a minute, honey."

For that brief moment it felt like old times. Pandora was her strong and healthy self again, advising me on the gay lifestyle and how to deal with the children.

"Promise me you gon' call 'im," she went on. "Because take it from me: Life is too short to waste. Everyone can see you and Johnny belong together. Besides, I got a fierce Vera Wang gown for y'all's wedding."

"I think George W. Bush might have something to say about that," I said. "But I promise you I will call him, so stop worrying about us. You have enough to deal with as it is. So talk to me. What's going on around here?"

"They ain't giving us the proper medicines," Pandora raised her head off the pillow and whispered. There was an old, stout woman seeing to a patient across from us. "But they ain't gon' kill me."

I looked in her face and wondered. She lifted the sheet off the bed and stuck her hand inside a small hole on the right side of the mattress.

"I stopped taking these." She held a small blue pill in front of me. "You take these and die in a couple of weeks. I've seen it happen so many times."

"What are you saying?"

"I'm saying"—she forced herself to speak—"they killing us up in here—one by one."

"What about the bacteria?" I asked. "They're talking about it all over the news."

"They don't know what it is," she said. "Ain't one person run a single test on me to know what I got. I'm telling you, things done got worse around here since you left."

"Well, you hold on," I said. Pandora had suddenly become too exhausted to continue our conversation and stay awake. "Because I'm gon' get you out of here," I whispered. She was now in a deep sleep, but I finished what I had to say to her anyway. "We found Noxzema and got her on tape confessing to that girl's murder. We gon' get you out of this hell before it's too late."

After which, it took everything in me not to break down and cry. Seeing her in that terrible state was eating my ass alive.

"You hold on, Ms. Girl." I laid my head across her belly. "And you better not die on me."

I felt like singing, so I did. For some reason that precious hymn "Jesus Loves Me" was upon my heart. Given the circumstances and the fact that it was early Sunday morning, it seemed like the appropriate thing to do.

"Jesus loves me..." I cried through every single syllable of that song. "Yes, I know, for the Bible tells me so."

"I'm so sorry to interrupt you." I immediately felt a heavenly presence behind me and a warm hand on my shoulder. The gentle touch belonged to Ms. Boudreaux. "But your friend Ebony just called."

"What is that girl going through now?" I didn't take my eyes off Pandora, who was sleeping so peacefully.

"I have no idea," Ms. Boudreaux said. "But she did say it was urgent, concerning someone by the name of Johnny."

I prayed over Pandora that the gods would take good care of her in my absence and then got out of there as fast as I could.

"I'm so glad you come." Ms. Li, the housekeeper, met me at the front door. She was a petite Asian woman with a beautiful spirit. Why she was working for a man like Kojack was beyond me.

"What's going on around here?" I suddenly noticed the house was in disarray. Broken furniture and glass was at every turn of the three-story mansion.

"Mr. Kojack come home." Ms. Li was really worked up, which was unusual for her. On a normal day she would have been calm and mild mannered. "He be very mad. Start shouting and tearing the place apart."

"Did he hurt her?"

Ms. Li suddenly pleaded the Fifth. Her ass went silent on me with a quickness. That girl had to be thinking about her job security.

"If you like, I can take you to Ms. Sinclair," she said instead. "Follow me."

We passed the luxurious state-of-the-art dining room and took a long flight of stairs to the second floor. One good thing I could say about that low-life nigga Kojack was that he had great decorating skills and elegant taste. Every item inside of his home, from the linen to the furniture, was expensive and grand.

"Ebony. My God. What did he do to you?" I walked into the main bedroom and found Ebony sitting on the floor with an empty bottle of champagne next to her leg. The room looked like it had been destroyed by a category-five hurricane.

"I'm so sorry." Ebony burst out in tears. She was beaten

badly, visibly bruised over her entire body and face. "I didn't wanna tell 'im. You gotta believe me."

"What are you talking about, hon?" The poor girl was in such obvious pain that she could barely hold it together. I held her up by both arms. "Tell me what happened. That no-good bastard did this to you? Ebony, this has to stop. That nigga gonna wind up killing you."

"He knows," she blurted out from the corners of her full lips. "He knows everything. And I ain't never seen him this mad before."

"You're not making any sense." I tapped her on the cheeks. She was falling in and out of consciousness. "Who knows what? Are you talking about Kojack?"

"Listen to me," she said with urgency. "He knows about Johnny and you. I'm so sorry."

I noticed a picture frame shattered to pieces on the floor beside the bed. It was a childhood photograph of Kojack and Johnny. My heart began to race, and I feared the worst.

"Where's Kojack now?" I held her tight. "You tell me where he's at. And you tell me now!"

"He went down to the church," she said through bloody teeth. "He was drinking up a storm, and I don't know what he gon' do."

18

Johnny

Ali was the star of his own show. Moms and a bunch of her friends surrounded Nettie and the baby in the lobby outside of the main sanctuary. And my li'l man was soaking up the attention like sun rays on a hot summer day.

Man, to the tell you the truth, I was just glad the focus was on him and not me. My nerves were definitely shot and on edge, with me thinking about the drug deal with Big Daddy Cane that was about to go down within the hour a couple of blocks from Pops's church.

Moreover, how did I allow that nigga Kojack to convince me to sneak him into the prayer room downstairs so he could watch the baby's christening on TV?

"Look how handsome he is." Ms. Maggie played with the baby's feet as Nettie held him up in her arms for everybody else to see. Both her and the baby were dressed in white in honor of Ali's christening, which was due to begin at any moment. "He looks like a li'l angel."

Nothing was going as planned that afternoon. Earlier that morning, I had awakened out of another one of those nightmares of mine to the pounding of rain against the window. Waking up to dark clouds instead of sunshine on a Sunday of all days should have been my first clue that evil and goodness just don't mix. It was a bad omen from the beginning to bring the devil's work to God's house.

Plus, Kojack was running late and not sticking to the damn schedule. That nigga was supposed to meet me in the alley behind the church at a quarter to one so I could sneak him into the prayer room and we could strategize before our meeting with Big Daddy Cane at three P.M. All I could do at that point, though, was hope on a wing and a prayer that nothing went wrong, 'cause backing out on our arrangement was not even an option when dealing with cutthroat niggas from the streets like my cuz.

"Once we shake on this"–I recall Kojack saying to me days before the deal was to be sealed with a firm handshake. He handed me an envelope filled with hundred-dollar bills, which I had planned on using to make a fresh start–"there's no turning back."

Don't get me wrong. I still was going to college and fulfilling my dreams of becoming a football player, but with no job security or steady cash flow, a nigga was dirt broke. No one was rushing to hire an ex-con, and living with Moms and Pops for the long term was simply out of the question. I truly saw this opportunity as a win-win situation for everyone involved. If nothing else, this plan allowed me to watch my cuz's back and to honor our brotherhood.

"Come over here, my son." Moms took hold of my arm and dragged me away from the door. I was looking around for Kojack and staring outside at the rain. The heavy downpour mixed with the wind sounded like demons under the spell of the Holy Ghost. "I would like for you to meet someone."

"Is this your son, Johnny?" asked an attractive older woman. She was dressed in fancy clothes and had a large hat on her head. There was a younger fair-skinned girl standing next to her with a wide grin that made the rainy day seem less cloudy. Man, this girl was definitely a ten, with long, flowing hair and beautiful, soft skin.

"It sure is." Moms locked arms with me. She wanted them churchwomen to know that I was her son and that she was proud of me. "And isn't he handsome, honey?"

No doubt, that shit felt good, having Moms make a fuss over me the way she did, but I wasn't taking anything away from Ali. He still had his fair share of gorgeous-ass women admiring him, too. I could see Nettie and the baby inside of the sanctuary from where I stood with Moms, and they looked real happy together. Although my cuz was raising that baby without his pops, she was keeping her head up, nonetheless. I loved to see strong women raising their children.

"Well, it's so nice to finally meet you," the older woman said. The younger girl looked on with a slight grin. I think she had eyes for me. "You can call me Linda, and this is my lovely daughter, Carla."

"Nice to meet both of you," I said, trying not to make eye contact with that girl. You know, I didn't want to give home girl the wrong idea. Man, that was how it was up there at the church, though—nothing but single, beautiful black women all over the damn place. And they were up in that joint looking for a husband. With so many niggas being up there at Sierra Leone, which I knew from firsthand knowledge, sistahs for damn sure had it hard.

"Carla is a freshman at Xavier," Moms said. She was trying to set me up. Deep down, I don't think Moms cared for Tonya, anyway. She never said anything bad against her, but Moms had her li'l ways of letting me know that Tonya wasn't the right woman for me. With so much else going on, though, I didn't have the opportunity to give Moms the good news about me and Tonya being a thing of the past. My future was with James, but I didn't think Moms would have been ready to hear some shit like that either, so I basically kept quiet and pretended.

"What's your major?" I asked, looking around and staying aware of my surroundings. My ass couldn't keep still for nothing.

"Premed," she said in a sweet and low voice. If I wasn't into dudes, this girl would have definitely been my girlfriend.

"Wow," I said. "You must be smart."

"My Carla," Linda said, "is a straight-A student."

"Mama." Carla was now embarrassed. Both of our moms was pushing way too hard. "Stop it. I don't think he wants to know all of that."

"I was just letting him know," Linda said. "But anyway, Johnny, it was nice meeting you. I think we gon' take our seats."

Within a matter of seconds the church had filled, and there was still no sign of Kojack. Man, at this point I figured something went terribly wrong that prevented him from getting to the church on time.

"Sweetheart," Moms said as I walked away from the sanctuary. "Where do you think you're going?"

"I'll be back, Ma," I said with a nervous grin on my face. "I need to go downstairs and check on something right quick."

"No, you don't." Moms forced me inside of the sanctuary. "Service is about to begin."

We took our seats in the front pew beside Nettie and the rest of our family. Pops took the podium amongst a packed house.

"Praise ye the Lord, everybody!" he screamed into the microphone, and the congregation went wild. As for me, I kept watching the front entrance and looking out for Kojack. "This is the day the Lord has made, and we should rejoice and be glad!"

After which, the organ started up, and that was it, man. Those folks up in that church started jumping and running and falling out between the pews, which wasn't anything strange to me at all. Growing up in the black church, I was used to people catching the Holy Ghost. Me and my brothers got big laughs when church folks caught what they called "the spirit." Women were always more fun to watch than the men, 'cause they would lose their shoes and come out of their clothes praising the Lord. One time we even saw a woman's wig fly off.

Anyway, since everyone was caught up in the spirit, I slipped out of the sanctuary without anyone even noticing I was gone. There was no more time to waste. The drug deal was scheduled to go down directly following Ali's christening, which was about to begin at any moment. Kojack's ass had to be found, and that was all there was to it.

"Damn it." I reached inside my pocket for my cell phone and realized I'd left it at home. But I shouldn't have been surprised. Like I said earlier, nothing was going right for me that morning. The lobby was empty and still no sign of Kojack. I was heading into the sanctuary when I heard him.

"There he is, everybody." It was Kojack, but he wasn't his usual self. I found something about him strange right from the beginning. "Mr. T-Mack, the running mean machine."

Kojack had a bottle of whiskey in his hand and he was tripping all over himself. It didn't take me long to figure out that nigga was drunk.

"Man, where you been?" I asked him. "I've been waiting for you to show up for hours. Weren't we supposed to meet that dude right after church?"

"The plans changed." He stumbled over toward me and stood directly in my face. His eyes were bloodshot, and his breath smelled of alcohol. A woman with two kids rushed into the sanctuary. She closed the doors behind her and left us alone in the lobby.

"It went down early," Kojack finished what he was saying. "Without you."

"What the hell you talking about, man?" I couldn't believe what he was saying to me. Shit, my feelings were even hurt. You know, that he would cut me out of the deal without even letting me know ahead of time. "And what you mean, the plans changed?"

"Like I said," he went on, "things changed. I didn't need you."

"That's cold, man," I said. "That's real cold, but I'm glad you all right."

He took a pull from the bottle and looked out the door at the rain.

"Listen to that," he told me. His ass was acting and saying some really strange things. "You hear the rain?"

"Yeah, nigga," I said. The rain was pounding down on the roof, and the church house was rocking. We could hear them praising and shouting from behind closed doors. "Of course I can hear the rain. Your ass drunk."

"See, I don't think you're listening." He pulled a gun out of his pocket and pointed it straight at me. If this was some sort of sick game, I for damn sure wasn't laughing about it. "Because if you did, you'd hear what it sounds like. Now listen to it, nigga."

"Man, what the hell are you doing?" I said, backing away

from him and looking toward the sanctuary, hoping someone would open the door and see us. "Pointing that gun at me. Your ass done gone crazy or something?"

"Stop interrupting me, nigga!" he shouted at the top of his lungs. I couldn't believe some shit like this was even happening. Nothing about this situation was making any goddamn sense to me. "And listen to the rain."

"Okay." I played along with him. "I'm listening, man."

"Good," he said with the gun still pointed at me. "Now, what does it sound like?"

"I don't know, man," I said. "You tell me, and while you at it, put the gun away before someone gets hurt."

"I'll tell you what it sounds like." He took another swig from the bottle. "It sounds like pain. Like that rain had a hard time getting down here from way up there. You feel me, nigga? I'm in a lot of pain."

"I don't know, man." My voice began to crack under the pressure, and I had tears in my eyes. There was an evil look on Kojack's face that gave me the chills. This was no fucking game. He was serious as a heart attack and pissed off about something deep.

"Whatever you say, man," I said. "Just take it easy with that gun."

"Put your hands behind your head," he demanded, "and walk slowly to the exit."

We took the long flight of stairs to the basement and headed for the prayer room. It suddenly dawned on me that he might actually be planning on shooting me. Why else would he have been taking me to a remote part of the church?

"Are you gon' kill me, man?" I asked. Kojack had killed so many niggas in his lifetime that it would have been nothing for him to take another life. " 'Cause if you're trying to scare me, it's working."

"Get down on your knees," he said. "A position I'm sure you're real used to."

"What the hell's that supposed to mean?" I followed his direction and got down beside the pew in my nice blue suit that Moms bought me as a gift. "You obviously got something on your mind. Why don't you just say that shit and get it over with?"

"Shut the fuck up." He slapped me across my face with the pistol. I tasted blood on my lips. "And don't talk unless I tell you to speak."

"What the fuck done got into you, man!" I shouted at him. "Why you treating me this way? We family, man. Talk to me."

"How many times we played ball together?" he asked, with the gun pointed at the top of my head. The bottle of whiskey was still in his other hand.

"I don't know, man," I cried out like a bitch. "Hundreds of times. Why?"

"And how many times have you seen me in the shower naked?" He went on with one strange question after another. "And slept in the bed together when we was little?"

"Why you asking me all of this shit? You're my cuz, man. We spent a lot of time together growing up, but you already know that shit."

"Yeah, but what I didn't know"—he took a pull from the bottle—"was that you might be looking at me in that way."

"Man, you tripping," I said with my heart in my ass. Once things became clear to me, I was really scared then. "We family."

"Don't call me that." He placed the barrel of the gun at the top of my head once again. I was in full-blown tears at this point. "Ain't no family of mine a fucking punk-ass, sissy motherfucker."

"I'm still Johnny, man," I said. "Ain't nothing changed. Don't do this, man."

He tossed that bottle of whiskey on the floor, and it broke into little pieces like our brotherhood.

"Everything has changed, nigga." He cocked the gun. "And I'm gon' take you out of your misery and do God a favor. Now close your damn eyes and get ready to meet Satan in hell!"

"What the hell are you doing to him?" A familiar voice hit my ears and saved me from death. But this wasn't no heavenly blessing, 'cause things only got worse. The voice belonged to James. "Get away from him with that gun."

"Well, well, well." Kojack lifted the gun from my head and aimed it straight at James instead. My heart started to tick like a time bomb.

"Isn't this cozy?" He made fun of us out of pure pleasure. "Your li'l girlfriend has come to save the day."

"You're a weak-ass nigga," James said. "Why don't you put the gun down and handle your business like a real man?"

"What are you doing here?" I looked up at James with my hands still behind my head. "Don't say anything else. He's serious."

"I can't believe this shit," Kojack said, looking at me and then back at James. "The two of y'all are actually together, like boyfriend and girlfriend? This shit is unreal."

"Johnny is more man than your ass could ever be," James said. That dude had a mouth on him no matter what. "At least he don't beat up on helpless women. Now, you tell me who's the punk around here?"

"You know what? I've had enough of your ass!"

Kojack unloaded the gun. He ran off. There was suddenly blood everywhere. And then James was in my arms, bleeding and dying.

"Don't try to talk," I said to him. He had been hit with not one but several bullets. The blood from his wounds was all over my hands and clothes. "Oh, God. Why did you have to be so brave, man?"

"I see what you mean now." He forced himself to talk with blood running out of his mouth.

"Just hold on." I held him in my arms and looked around for somebody, but there was no one in sight. We were alone inside the prayer room, but I could hear footsteps running down the hall. Help was on its way. "Don't you die on me, man."

I placed my ear to his mouth, since he was determined to talk to me. That dude was stubborn even with gunshot wounds.

"I see that face of Jesus, too," he whispered into my ear, looking up toward the heavens. There was a painting of Jesus with His disciples at the Last Supper that took up the entire area of the ceiling.

When I saw that painting, my nightmares should have ended, but they didn't. James blacked out right there in my arms.

"Don't you die on me, man." I finally found the words that I had been searching for all of this time. And I really didn't give a damn who heard me, either. Pops and some of the church members found us on the floor with blood running between the pews.

"I love you!" I cried from the gut to him, and the words came together like a sweet melody. "I love you, man! I love you. I love you. I love you."

19

Tonya

"This is not the end of the road for you." Dr. Cramer gave it to me straight, without cutting corners or playing it safe. Tamika had her arms around me, and Mama stood next to the bed with tears rolling down her cheeks like raindrops. This was sad news to everybody. "Living with HIV is no longer a death sentence. You can survive this virus with proper treatment, exercise, and healthy living."

And so those were the hard-core facts in a nutshell. After all of the ups and downs I had been through in my life, the greatest battle was now happening inside of me. I had this fucking virus running through my veins that was gonna be with me for the rest of my life, and that was all there was to it. Once the bad news started coming, though, it kept going on and on, like the Energizer bunny.

"And what about the cancer, Doctor?" Mama had already lost a son, and the thought of losing another child to something like AIDS or cancer must have been a whole lot for her to handle in one sitting. She was taking the diagnosis harder than I was. "Is my daughter gon' be all right?"

Within a day's time, I had not only been told that I was HIV-positive, but that I also had uterine fibroids. You got me, too. I had no idea what the fuck that meant. But all I knew was that it wasn't as serious as it sounded in comparison to having something like AIDS.

"As you know we took a Pap smear," Dr. Cramer explained. "We were able to detect fibroids in the uterine wall, which explained the excessive bleeding. Now the good news is that the fibroids pose no threat and were safely removed during surgery. I've put her on medication, and we'll monitor the situation closely."

"Praise God. Thank you, Doctor," Mama said. She did all of the talking, while I just sat there and stared at the plain white walls, hoping that something or someone would come out from the other side and tell me that this was just one big fucking joke. But those walls didn't have nothing to say to me that could have helped in any way.

"Thank you for what you're doing for our daughter, Doctor," Mama went on. "The family really appreciates it."

She had gotten hold of kinfolks, and they had been stopping by the hospital all throughout the day. We might not have had a real close family, but when one of us got in a jam, we for damn sure came together.

"Tonya's brother, Ricky, is in Iraq serving his country," Mama said, running her hands through my hair and talking to Dr. Cramer and Tamika. For a minute, they forgot I was even in the room. You know, just going back and forth over my head. "He's really concerned about his li'l sister, so whatever you gotta do to make sure my daughter will be okay, by all means do it."

"I can't imagine what you're going through, having a son out of the country and a daughter in this condition," Dr. Cramer said. "I also have relatives over there. And it's scary not knowing if they're coming home safely. How old is your son, anyway?"

"He'll be thirty years old this year." Mama was finally able to smile for a change. That girl had been looking really sad and depressed from the moment we had arrived at Charity. "I'm so proud of him."

"I'm sorry, Doctor." Tamika interrupted them and wrapped her arms around my shoulders. She knew better than anyone how hard this situation was for me, and she meant for Mama and Dr. Cramer to get their asses back on track. "But is my friend gon' pull through this and be all right?"

After my brother Eric was killed, me and Tamika had spent many nights talking about death, and she knew how afraid I was to die. Meeting God simply wasn't something I was in a rush to do. Shit, to be truthful, I couldn't even remember the last time I had even prayed, let alone thought about going over to the other side. Moreover, if going to heaven was measured by the number of times a person got down on their knees and called upon God, then I knew my ass was heading straight to hell for real.

"Well, like I said, Tonya is not out of the woods yet." Dr. Cramer wrote something in my medical chart. "And that's why we're keeping her for a couple of days, to run more tests. I want to make sure the fibroids are a thing of the past. At this point I suggest a lot of bed rest. Later we'll send in a counselor to talk to her about the other matter."

Dr. Cramer rubbed the top of my leg. She was now talking directly to me, but my mind was completely somewhere else. You should have seen me staring out into space like I was in la-la land and my ass belonged on the third floor of Charity, which was where they kept those crazy folks with mental problems.

"And I'm not going to try to downplay the seriousness of what you're dealing with either, Tonya," Dr. Cramer went on to say. Despite what I had said earlier about wanting a black woman doctor, she ended up being all right by me in the long run. "You have a tough road ahead of you. But from what I hear from your family and friends, you're quite the fighter."

"You don't know the half of it," Tamika joked, rubbing the top of my head with tender loving care. She was trying her best to be strong and positive for me. "My motherfucking girl ain't no chump, baby. We gon' get through this shit like we got through everything else."

What can I say? Tamika was my girl, for real. And to know she had my back the way she did felt damn good, like cold water going down my throat when it was fucking hotter than hot outside.

"Yes, we will," Mama said with relief, too. You know she had to be somewhat happy that she wasn't to blame for my being up in the hospital after all. No amount of ass kicking she could have put down on me would have caused a situation like this one. The person to blame for my condition was Johnny, and I hated his ass for putting my life in jeopardy, fucking around with some dude.

"She'll be just fine," she went on in tears. "Gon' pull through this here thing with flying colors."

Dr. Cramer turned toward Mama. "I need to speak with you in private. Can you follow me to my office?"

"I'll be right back, sweetheart," Mama said. And then she and Dr. Cramer left me and Tamika alone inside of the room.

"So, what's up, girl?" Tamika took hold of my hand. "Talk to me. I can tell you got something on your mind."

"I just can't believe this is happening to me." I finally broke my silence and opened up to her. Although I loved Mama for her concern and everything, she wasn't my best friend. With Tamika, I felt totally comfortable saying what I needed to say. "That motherfucker gon' pay for what he did to me."

"You talking about Johnny?"

"I sure the fuck am," I said, trying to hold back the tears and be strong, but this situation was breaking a tough bitch like me down, for real. "That faggot got something coming to him."

"Well, whatever you need me to do," Tamika said. "You know I got your back, girl—me and Latisha both. She's holding down the salon, but sends her love, too."

"First thing I need to do is get myself together," I said. "I gotta get in touch with Rico and let 'im know what happened. I don't want that boy to think I just stood him up."

The hardest part for me was knowing that Rico's private jet took off for South Africa without me on it. What should have been my opportunity and big break turned out to be yet another letdown. It seemed like all kinds of shit was always getting in the way of my dreams and happiness, like I didn't belong on earth.

"Give me his number," Tamika said. "And I'll call 'im for you. The last thing you need is to stress yourself out. I'm sure Rico will completely understand why you couldn't make it. And besides, there will be other trips."

"I'm so glad your ass is here." I squeezed her hand. "Because I'm so motherfucking scared, girl. I don't wanna die, Tamika, but I have HIV. How I'm gon' live with that?"

My emotions finally got the best of me, and I started bawling and falling apart right there in front of her. "Oh, God. It hurts so bad, Tamika. It hurts so bad, girl!"

"Go ahead and let it out." Tamika sat beside me on the bed and gave me her shoulder to cry on. "But you gon' be all right, girl. You heard what that doctor said. This is not a death sentence."

"Oh, God," I said, with puffy eyes. "I think I'm about to be sick. Help me to the bathroom."

I pulled the sheets back off the bed, and Tamika gave me her arm for support.

"Take it easy," she said to me as we made our way slowly down the corridor. My body was in so much pain that I could hardly stand up straight. "We only got a few more steps to go."

"Tonya? Is that you?" someone called out to me, and I couldn't turn around fast enough to see who it was.

"Ms. Liz," I said, more out of surprise of seeing her than anything. Johnny's mom was the last person I expected to see at the hospital dressed in her Sunday-morning-going-to-church getup. Without a doubt, Ms. Liz was a class act, with the style and manners to prove it. Too bad for her she ended up with a son like Johnny, I thought to myself.

"Are you okay, sweetheart?" She had a funny look on her face, but so did I.

"Actually, I'm not," I said with an attitude. And the pain that I started down the corridor with was suddenly gone. "No thanks to your son."

Tamika pulled at my arm, heading off potential drama. "It was nice seeing you, Ms. Liz, but we really have to be going."

Ms. Liz just stared as me and Tamika struggled with each

other. Although I was feeling sick, I ended up showing the most strength. Nothing was gone stand in my way of letting Ms. Liz have it about her son.

"No, Tamika," I said, thinking about the events that had happened over the last couple of days. "Let go of me. I got something to say to her."

"What's going on here?" Ms. Liz clutched hold of her purse. "Does this have something to do with my son?"

"You damn right it does," I said from the deep pit of my gut. There was so much hurt and emotion inside of me that it was bound to explode. "Your son put me in this fucking hospital!"

"If Johnny's hurt you in some way," Ms. Liz said, calmly, never raising her voice beyond a whisper, "I would like to know about it, but there's no need for you to use that type of language with me, young lady."

"Let's just go, girl," Tamika said once again. "This ain't the time or place."

"Get away from her, Ma!" Johnny came charging down the corridor like a running back in the NFL. I don't know about Tamika and Ms. Liz, but he for damn sure caught me off guard. "Don't believe nothing she has to say!"

"Why not?" I started screaming out loud in front of everyone. As expected, doctors and patients at the hospital started staring in our direction, but you know I didn't give a damn. I had something on my mind, and no one was gone stop me from saying what I had to say, for real. "You don't want your mama to know what a trifling, no-good bastard you is?"

"Come on, Ma." He grabbed Ms. Liz by the arm. "Don't pay her any mind. Let's get out of here."

I noticed that Johnny was dressed in a suit with what looked like blood on his hands and clothes. But that wasn't getting that nigga any sympathy from me. Whatever business he had up there at that hospital didn't mean a damn thing to me, because what I was going through in my own life took priority over everything else.

"Why you running away now?" I asked him. "Your ass scared of your mama knowing the truth about you?"

"And what truth is that, young lady?" Ms. Liz wanted to know. "What exactly did Johnny do to you?"

"No, the question," I said to her, "is what he didn't do."

"Shut the fuck up!" Johnny got up in my face. "It's because of your damn mouth that my friend is lying up in this hospital fighting for his life in the first place!"

"What friend?" asked Tamika. Curiosity got the best of her.

"Stay out of this, Tamika," Johnny told her. "This don't have nothing to do with you."

"I don't think so, nigga," she said. "Whatever goes on with my girl has to do with me, too."

"Johnny's friend James," Ms. Liz said instead, "was shot earlier today at Mt. Zion. That young man is in ICU fighting for his life, so please, can we deal with this later?"

"Well, I'm sorry, Ms. Liz," I said, looking in Johnny's face. There was so much hatred and anger between us, like we became enemies overnight. "I wouldn't wish death on anybody, but maybe he got what he deserved."

"You motherfucking whore!" Johnny launched at me like a wild animal or something. If I didn't know it before, I for damn sure found out that day: Johnny had it bad for that dude, and his love for James hurt me more than any disease growing inside of me ever could.

"I hate you!" He tried to get at me, but Tamika stood between us. A tall white man with a strong build grabbed Johnny by the arm. That white man just came from out of nowhere.

"Hold it, fellow," this man said. He was a total stranger who was smack-dab in the middle of our drama. "I wouldn't do that if I was you."

"I hate you, too!" I shouted at him. Ms. Liz and Tamika got an earful along with a crowd of other folks who gathered around us to see the action up close.

"Because of your ass I'm in this hospital with HIV!" My finger was pointed in his face. "So, fuck you and your faggot-ass friend!"

"Okay, that's enough." A male doctor joined us. I recognized him from the other day. His name was Dr. Holmes. "This is a hospital, for heaven's sake. Now, what's going on over here?"

"She's crazy, Doc," Johnny said. He could barely catch his breath. "She got these people thinking I gave her HIV."

"Which simply isn't true." Ms. Liz stood up for her son, like what I had said didn't even matter. "My son doesn't have HIV or AIDS."

"No, he doesn't," Dr. Holmes said, looking directly in my face. I couldn't help but think that this was payback for the way I had treated him yesterday. "Johnny gave blood to this hospital for a friend of his and took an AIDS test. And I can assure you that he doesn't carry the HIV virus–or any other disease, for that matter."

"Oh, my God." Tamika caught me just in the nick of time. When that doctor told me the news, I almost hit the floor from total shock. "For God's sake. Don't just stand there. Somebody help her!"

———

"There's no need for alarm," Dr. Cramer said to Mama and Tamika moments later. She had given me some medication to calm my nerves that now had my entire body weak. "The medication should help her to relax."

"What were you thinking?" asked Mama, rubbing the top of my forehead. "Confronting Johnny and getting yourself upset like that. You gotta stay calm and listen to these doctors."

"I tried to stop her," Tamika said. "But she just flipped out and started going crazy."

I listened to them talk, drifting in and out of sleep. That medicine had me drowsy.

"Why don't you give me some time alone with Tonya," Dr. Cramer said.

"Sweetheart, I'll be outside in the lobby if you need me," Mama said, looking down at me and smiling. "Try and get some rest. I love you."

She kissed the top of my forehead. Maybe I should get sick more often, I was thinking to myself. Mama hadn't shown me that much love since I was five years old and had fallen off my bike. Back then she took me in her arms and rubbed my knees with petroleum jelly.

"I'll be in the lobby, too," Tamika said. "I ain't going nowhere."

Dr. Cramer waited until they were gone and then pulled a chair next to the bed. She looked like there was something really deep on her mind.

"I guess you're wondering why I sent your mom and friend away?" she asked with a warm smile on her face. For the first time I really noticed her. She wasn't all that bad-looking, and her teeth were a perfect shade of white. Her spirit was good, too, and I felt totally safe with her as my doctor.

"I figured you would get on me," I said now, talking a little funny, like something was caught in my throat. That medication she gave me was some strong and powerful shit. "But I'm not apologizing."

"Your mother just told me what's going on," she said. "And I'm not only concerned about your physical health but your mental state as well."

"Everybody around here acting like they understand what I'm going through," I said, reaching for the words from deep down inside of me. "But nobody knows what it's like but me. I got this fucking horrible disease to live with."

"That's where you're wrong," Dr. Cramer said. "You're not the only woman to ever find out that she's HIV-positive. This virus is everywhere—in every community."

"Well, I never thought this kind of shit would be happening to me," I said, holding back the tears once again. It was hard for me to talk about this situation and not get worked up with emotion. "So forgive me if I'm having a hard time with this. I know in your perfect li'l white world you don't know what it's like to go through some shit."

"That's where you're wrong again." She looked me in my eyes, so I could feel the weight of what she was saying. "I'm HIV-positive, and I have been for many years."

Of course, I was blown away, with my eyes big and wide, like Dr. Cramer had a third head attached to her body or something.

"But you don't look like it," I said with a stupid-ass look on my face. "You really got me with this one."

"I'm only telling you this," she said, "so you can understand what I'm trying to say to you."

"Okay," I said. "I'm listening."

"From what I understand," she said, "you thought you got the virus from a former boyfriend who's gay and didn't tell you. Am I right about all of this?"

"That's pretty much accurate," I said with a burning pain in my chest. Talking about Johnny wasn't good for my heart. "But I found out that he don't have it, which I don't understand, man. He gotta have it. How else I got this shit?"

"Seven years ago I was engaged to my high school sweetheart." Dr. Cramer started telling me a story out of the blue. "I came in for a routine checkup and found out that I was HIV-positive."

"Me and Johnny was high school sweethearts," I said to her. "But I'm sorry. I didn't mean to cut you off. What happened between you and your friend?"

"To make a long story short," she said, "I found out that he had been sleeping around with a lot of women behind my back and having unprotected sex."

"You sure it was only women?" I couldn't help but ask. "And not men?"

"Well, I only knew about the women," she said, "because they started showing up at my door. But that's the point. It doesn't really matter whether he was fooling around with men or women."

"I don't understand," I said. My head was beginning to hurt. "What you trying to get at?"

"As women we think we're safe," she said, "because AIDS is a gay disease that happens to someone else. Heterosexuals transmit the virus, too, which is not widely accepted in our society. But it's just that kind of thinking that is why we're seeing women diagnosed with HIV, especially women of color. We have to protect ourselves regardless, no matter how fine or gorgeous or straight the man may look—use protection always. How many times have you engaged in unprotected sex?"

"Shit, I don't know," I said. She now had me thinking about every nigga I had allowed to fuck me without a condom. Although it wasn't a lot of them, one or two was way too many given my current situation. "But it wasn't like I was no slut."

"Anyone within the last couple of years?" she pushed.

"Johnny, but he don't have it." I paused. "Well, there was someone else."

"Who's that?"

"This dude Rico," I said, thinking about the very last time we was together in his bedroom. We used protection. "But it was years ago that I slept with him without a condom."

"You see, it doesn't matter," Dr. Cramer said. "He could have been carrying the virus for years and not even known it. He could have given it to you years ago."

"But wouldn't I have given it to Johnny then?"

"Not necessarily," she said. "Some people sleep with someone with HIV the first time and get the virus. But I've heard of cases of someone sleeping with an HIV patient for years and not getting it. There's just no formula for who gets it or not. That's why it's important to protect yourself at all times."

"Man, this is too confusing." I suddenly got a headache. "I just want to go to bed."

"Well, I'll let you get some sleep then." She stood up to leave. "Consider what I said, and try to get some rest."

"So, how did you get through it?" I hit Dr. Cramer with one last question on her way out the door.

"With close friends, family, counseling, and faith," she said. "And a whole lot of prayer."

Dr. Cramer left me alone inside the room with nothing but my thoughts and broken heart. If nothing else, she got me to focus on something other than how much I hated Johnny's guts. Blaming him wasn't helping to uplift my spirit.

"Lord." I staggered out of bed and got down on my knees on that cold hospital floor, surprising even my own self. My hands was balled up in front of me in closed fists. "I know I haven't done this in a long time. But can we talk anyway?"

20

James

Waking up in that hospital bed with IV tubes inside of my veins and immediately hearing the wretchedness in Flo's voice, I almost wished that I hadn't woken up at all. Every bone in my body ached, and I had to strain my eyes just to make out the images in front of me. My arms and legs even betrayed me.

"Don't tell me to calm the fuck down!" Flo was going off on a young cop who was trying to conduct his investigation. Wearing a blue uniform, he looked like a schoolboy being scolded by his homeroom teacher.

"Some crazy-ass motherfucker done shot my son." She used her purse as an exclamation, pointing it in the man's face. "And now he's out there on the loose. You better believe I'm fucking upset!"

Flo's revelation ran through me like a bolt of electricity, and the horrible nightmare flashed through my head like a traffic light. I saw pictures in different colors that gave a snapshot of what had occurred: the Church, the gun, the blood—and a confession of love that I would never forget. It was a miracle to be alive and to know that Johnny truly did love me.

"Take it easy on the man, Ms. Flo," Jerome said. And thank God he was there to help keep that girl calm, honey, because Flo was totally beside herself. "They gon' catch 'im eventually."

"He's right, ma'am," said that cop—who, mind you, was tall, dark skinned, and fine, with thick arms and a solid chest. Shit, I wasn't so blind that I couldn't see that gorgeous specimen standing right there in front of me.

"We got every available cop out there searching for that bastard," he went on to say, and I could see Ms. Jerome checking him out on the sly. That girl didn't miss a beat, honey, when it came to putting the moves on trade. "And trust me, we will stop at nothing until he's apprehended and brought into custody."

"Well, y'all better do something, because if I get hold of his ass before y'all do, believe me, y'all gon' be handling a first-degree-murder case. And you can put that one on record, because I don't play when it comes to my motherfucking child. You better ask somebody around this bitch."

"I understand your anger and frustration, ma'am," the cop said respectfully. "There's way too much violence out there in those streets. These niggas—and excuse me for saying it that way—need to stop killing and acting like savage animals with one another."

"Sorry to interrupt." Johnny, my baby, poked his head in the door, with a nice-looking older couple following directly behind him. Right away I realized it was his parents, because Johnny was the spitting image of his dad, minus the light specks of gray covering the top of his father's head and his mustache. "But do you mind if we come in?"

"We're actually discussing personal family business," Flo said, real directly and with a bit of harshness. Her worst fears concerning my involvement with Johnny had come true, and she

was not going to make it easy for him to love me. "I would pre-
fer if you gave us some time alone."

"Don't go." I cleared my throat, catching everyone off guard.
Although it hurt to speak, I couldn't think of any better reason
to go through the pain than for the man I loved. "I want him to
stay."

"Thank you, Lord." Flo ran over to the bed and kissed me on
the forehead. Jerome followed her lead. The two of them were
both kissing and crying over me while Johnny and his parents
looked on in wonder. I noticed the cop quietly slipping out the
door. "You woke up," Flo said. "I've been so worried about you,
boy. Oh, God. Thank you so much."

"Welcome back, Mother Love," Jerome said. "I just knew you
were gon' fight your way back, honey."

"I'm sorry if I scared y'all," I said, looking at the IV tube in
my arm and the machine attached to my chest. Charity was
really taking care of me. "I didn't mean to."

"You don't have to apologize to us." Flo rubbed the side of
my face with her rough hands. "We just so happy to see those
pretty eyes of yours."

"Yeah, man." Johnny joined Flo and Jerome by the bed. He
was wearing a blue suit covered in what must have been my
blood. "It's good to see you awake. You had us worried for a
minute. I want you to meet my parents. They've been praying
for you, too."

Needless to say, I had always dreamed about meeting
Johnny's parents in person, and now that day had finally come.
And it was nothing like I had envisioned. Being half-dead inside
of a hospital would not have been my choice for a first meeting, but at least it did bring us together under one roof.

"My husband and I are so sorry for everything," Johnny's

mom said. She was sophisticated and elegant and spoke proper English. You know, like she was one of those rich white people on a soap opera or something. "And the fact that this incident took place at our church by the hands of one of our own relatives . . . If there's anything we could ever do for you—"

Flo cut the woman off. "We'll do just fine. Thank you."

"I appreciate that, ma'am," I said, breathing real hard. My heartbeat seemed to increase with every syllable. "I'm sorry we have to meet under these circumstances."

"You're definitely in our prayers, young man," Johnny's father said in a deep, manly voice. He sounded just like one of those Southern Baptist preachers. "And know that there is a balm in Gilead and that God is still a presence of help in the time of need."

Me and Johnny suddenly locked eyes, and it removed everybody from the room but us. Moreover, I looked into his big brown eyes and felt a calming peace, like a wave of water on a sunny beach. And that was all I needed to see, feel, and taste in order to fight my way back to him.

"I'm so glad to see you up and talking," Marvin said as he entered. And I was so glad—so relieved—that he was my physician. "How do you feel?"

"I'm okay." I frowned. A sharp pain caught me in the midsection. "Just aching all over."

"Is my son gon' be all right, Doctor?" asked Flo. "Because I need to know straight-up—good or bad."

Marvin checked my pulse and other vital signs. "We were definitely concerned about James being unconscious for such a long period of time. At least we're over that hurdle."

Everyone cheered like we were at a sporting event. Johnny's father was the only one who kept a cool and level head. The man was devoid of emotion, like he had a lot on his damn mind.

"Thank God." Flo held her fist in the air. "You just don't know how you made my day, Doctor."

"Hold up, everybody," Marvin cautioned. "James is not out of the woods yet."

"But I thought you said him waking up was a good sign?" asked Jerome. "Was there something we missed?"

"I'm just going to be honest with you." Marvin gave it to us straight-up. "James suffered major upper abdominal injuries with damage to both his liver and pancreas. For the most part, the surgery was a success, but there's been intense trauma to these areas and severe hemorrhaging. The large amount of blood lost and internal bleeding is our greatest challenge at this point, considering the fact that James has a rare blood type and we have been unsuccessful in finding available donors."

"But I gave blood earlier," Johnny said, with his moms's arms around him. His father stood far off in the background, observing everything from a distance. "I can give more."

"I gave some, too," Jerome said. "But you can poke my ass again right now, if that's what it takes."

"I know everybody has given blood." Marvin didn't sound all that hopeful, which only added to my stress and worries. It finally hit me that I might really die. And you're talking about a girl being scared, honey. I was out of my mind with fear.

"However, nobody in this room has been a perfect match." Marvin went on with nothing but more words of bad news after another. "But we will keep looking and monitoring the situation very closely. I say, do a lot of praying. We definitely need a miracle."

"Come on, man." Johnny took hold of my hand in front of

everyone. His emotions finally got the best of him, and the fact that his parents were in the room didn't seem to matter, either. "You're not trying to tell us he gon' die, because I won't accept that. I'll never accept that shit."

After which we heard the door flapping in the wind. Johnny's father couldn't conceal his feelings any longer. Two men expressing love for each other must have simply been too much for him to handle.

"I'm sorry." Johnny's mom felt a need to speak up for her husband's sudden departure. "Please accept my apology. This day has been very hard on him."

"It's been hard on him?" Flo went into beast mode. "My son is the one lying in this bed and fighting for his damn life. And you think I'm worrying about how he feels?"

Everybody in the room looked at Johnny's mom like she was the oddball, which made the woman very nervous and uncomfortable.

"I'm so sorry." She ran out the door like a drama queen.

"Now, Doctor . . ." Flo focused her attention on Marvin, who seemed truly hurt and upset by all of this, as well. I couldn't help but think that this was the man Flo would rather me date instead of Johnny. "Please tell me there's something we can do to help my son?" she finished.

"Get everyone you know on the phone," he said. "And tell them to come down to this hospital and give blood. Someone out there is a match, but do know that time is of the essence."

There was not a dry eye in the room after Marvin left. But everyone was on their cell phones making calls to friends and family members, hoping against hope that one of them might be the perfect match that saved my life.

———

"Finally, we're alone," I said to Johnny. Jerome and Flo were fast on the job of trying to find me a donor. "Mr. Lover Man. It took me almost dying for you to finally say those three words, huh?"

"So, you complaining, nigga?" asked Johnny with a smooth grin on his face. He made my toes curl underneath the sheets. " 'Cause you know I got more where that came from."

"Don't start nothing we can't finish." I struggled through every word with a shortness of breath. "But, seriously, I'm so glad you're here with me. I'm scared. I'm really scared."

"Come on, nah." Johnny squeezed my hand. "You gotta stay strong and positive. That's the only way you gon' beat this thing."

Johnny took in a deep breath, and sadness seemed to overtake his entire face like a long funeral procession.

"You all right?" I asked, looking up at him. "I know all of this must be hard on you, too. The two of y'all were very close."

"Man, I still can't believe he was gonna actually try to kill me." Johnny shook his head. "My own flesh and blood. For heaven's sake, it was his sister's baby's christening ceremony."

"People like him are sick in the head," I said. "You couldn't have known how far he would go. But Nettie and that beautiful baby of hers will be okay, because they have you to look out for them."

"Thank you for saying that," he said. "But that ain't gon' stop me from getting on you."

"For what?"

"That was a stupid thing you did," he said. "Spouting off at the mouth with a gun pointed directly at you. You could have been killed, man. I could have lost you forever."

"I'm sorry if I scared you," I said. "But when I walked in and saw him holding that gun at your head—"

"I know, man." Johnny cut me off after seeing how worked

up I had gotten over the situation. "You don't even have to say it. I felt the same way about you, too. Now all we can do at this point is hope the police catch up with his ass before he gets out of town."

I immediately changed the subject. "I hope your dad is all right. I thought he would catch a heart attack when you took hold of my hand."

"He'll be okay." Johnny dismissed it. "And if he isn't . . . oh, well. I'm over and done with living my life for other people."

"But you know, y'all do need to talk," I said to him, thinking about that painting of Jesus that I saw plastered on the ceiling inside of the church. It was the exact same one that Johnny had described in his dreams. I couldn't help but wonder if there was a connection. "That's the only way you're gon' heal from the past and put your nightmares to rest once and for all."

"Will you stop worrying about me for a moment?" He quickly switched the topic. " 'Cause I gotta surprise I've been trying to get to, but you keep interrupting a nigga."

"Okay, then," I said, looking around the room. "What's the surprise? Because I need something to uplift my spirits, honey."

Johnny walked over to the door and opened it. "Come on in. There's somebody in here just dying to see you."

"Mr. James!" Kelly blew into the room like a breath of fresh air. Her little innocent and sweet face was just what the doctor ordered. Ms. Wilson, who was walking with a cane, was right behind her. "You're okay!"

"Of course I am, hon." I rubbed the top of her head as she held my hand. "You know I couldn't let something happen to me and not see that pretty smiling face of yours."

She broke down in tears and got me all emotional, too. "I love you, Mr. James."

"We both do," Ms. Wilson said. "We've been praying for you something hard, and I just know in my heart that God gon' see you through."

"Thank you," I said, wiping gigantic tears from Kelly's eyes. This little girl was working me overtime, honey. I never realized how much she truly depended upon my love until then. "Now stop all of this whimpering, and show me some teeth."

She grinned wide as an ocean. "I don't have any cavities, either."

"Isn't that something else?" I squeezed her fat cheeks.

"Mama came to see me," Kelly blurted out. I searched Ms. Wilson's face for answers.

"She's telling the truth," she said. "Stopped by the other day, and even brought Kelly a gift."

"Look." Kelly showed me a beautiful heart-shaped pendant around her neck similar to the one Pandora had sent me in the mail. I started to cry.

"What's wrong, Mr. James?" Kelly asked.

"Nothing, hon," I said. "These are just happy tears."

"That's right," Johnny said, as I tried to pull myself back together. "Mr. James is just so glad you came to visit him."

"She told me what you did." Ms. Wilson squeezed my hand. "And I wanna thank you for how you've been there for my family. I'm glad to report that my daughter checked herself into rehab the other day. God is good!"

"All the time," I said with a full and joyful heart. "Y'all have made my day."

"Well, we're not gon' keep you too long," Ms. Wilson said. "I know you gotta get your rest. But if you need anything, don't hesitate to call. You hear me?"

"Yes, ma'am." I smiled up at her warm and gentle face. "I sure will."

"Bye, Mr. James." Kelly waved at me on their way out the door. She stole my heart with three words that I could never get used to hearing: "I love you."

"I love you, too, hon," I said, turning to Johnny after they left. "And I love you, too, Mr. You Got Me Good."

"I thought that might cheer you up." He ran his finger underneath my eyes. You should have seen me crying like a newborn baby.

"Seeing Ms. Wilson and Kelly," I said, "hearing about how Brenda went to rehab makes me feel hopeful about things. You know what I mean? Like anything in life is possible."

"Sorry to interrupt." A woman suddenly appeared in the door out of nowhere. She was dressed real fly, with high-heeled pumps and jeans, holding flowers in her hands. The visitors just kept coming one after another. "But I heard what happened to you, and I wanted to stop by and bring you these."

She set the flowers on the nightstand beside the bed. When she got closer to the bed I recognized her face. She was the sorority girl from the club—Tonya's best friend.

"Hey, Johnny," she said. "Don't look so surprised to see me."

"Well, I'm speechless," he said.

"So, the two of you already know each other?" I asked, looking up at her. She was kind of cute, with short black hair and full, sexy lips.

"Oh, yes, we do," she said to me with a slight grin. "Me and Johnny go way back to high school. I'm sorry for being rude, though. I'm Tamika, but you probably already know who I am."

"Yeah, I recognize you," I said. "And I must say, I'm surprised to see you here, considering the last time we saw each other."

"I wasn't happy about how any of that went down," she said. "We had no right to come at you that way."

"And I shouldn't have been so insensitive when it came to your sorority," I said. It felt good making amends with her. "Something that's obviously so important to you."

"Believe me"—she suddenly got real sad on me—on us—"there's been enough pain going on around here, and we don't need any more of it. I'm sure Johnny told you about my friend Tonya."

Johnny looked as if he was daydreaming. His body was there with us, but his mind was on the other side of town somewhere. Sweat was even popping off his forehead.

"No, he didn't tell me about your friend," I said, with my eyes focused completely on Johnny. "Why? Did something happen to her?"

"Nothing for you to worry about." Johnny finally came out of his trance and cut me off. "Thanks for dropping these off, Tamika. But this dude needs to get his rest. I'm sure you understand."

"Okay," she said. "I'll be going, then. Hope you feel better."

"Thanks again for the flowers," I said to her.

She opened the door and flashed a smile over at Johnny. There was something weird going on between them. "And I'll let Tonya know you asked about her."

"You do that," Johnny said facetiously.

"What was that all about?" I asked him. "What's going on with Tonya? And why didn't you tell me?"

" 'Cause you got enough on your plate," he said. "Stop worrying about other shit. Just drop it, okay? I don't wanna talk about it right now."

"Okay. I'll let it go," I said, coughing up a handful of blood, which was a sure sign that my situation wasn't improving. The internal bleeding must have been getting worse.

"Oh, my God." Johnny reacted strongly upon seeing that large amount of blood come up out of me. "You're bleeding! Let me go and get that doctor."

"No." I grabbed his arm.

"What is it?"

"Just hold me," I said. "No more doctors right now."

He lay next to me on the bed, and we gripped each other like our lives depended upon it for survival.

"James." A sweet voice landed on my sleepy ears. "Is it all right if I come in?"

Moments later I awoke, only to find the lovely and beautiful Debra Boudreaux staring down at me with glowing eyes. Her beauty was excruciating.

"I ran into Johnny in the hallway." She must have read my mind, because I was for damn sure looking around for him. We had fallen asleep in each other's arms. "He said he was going to find your doctor, but he'll be right back. How are you feeling?"

"I'm okay, considering I was shot," I said, trying to make out Ms. Boudreaux's facial expressions. You know, to see if I could figure out the reason behind her visit. The last thing I needed to hear was more bad news. "But it's good to see you."

"Sorry to just drop in on you like this. I know this can't be an easy time for you." She forced a smile. My heart rate increased slightly on the monitor. "But I thought you would want to know right away. I have great news concerning your friend Pandora!"

{ 21 }

Johnny

"Excuse me, ma'am." I stopped a stout black woman in the corridor. She was a nurse at the hospital. "I was wondering if you can do me a favor?"

"For you, handsome," she said with all thirty-two flashing in my face, "I'll do just about anything, as long as it's legal."

I pulled a white envelope out of my pocket and pushed it toward her. "Can you drop this off to the person in room Two-ten for me?"

"That depends. Is she a boy or a girl?"

I licked my lips and hit her with some game. You know women like that kinda shit. "It's a former old lady of mine, but she ain't got nothin' on you, sweetheart."

"Yeah, tell me anything, but I guess I'll do it." She took the envelope. "You seem like a nice young man."

"Thank you, baby," I said. "I appreciate it."

She took off down the corridor, and I waited until she entered the room. I peeped through the glass and put my ear up against the door.

"He didn't tell me his name," the nurse told Tonya, who had

296

been sitting on the bed and looking real depressed. "He just wanted me to give you this envelope."

Man, of course I couldn't forget about Tonya, even though she had embarrassed the hell out of me in front of everyone earlier. In these same corridors she'd told my moms and a bunch of other strangers that I was basically gay, which was true, so I couldn't hold that against her. But the thing was, Tonya went so far as to say I had given her HIV, too. Now, that was an entirely different matter. I may have kept the fact from her that I was interested in dudes, but I wasn't no cold, cruel motherfucker to give her some disease and then try not to own up to it.

Whatever the case, man, that girl was going through some terrible shit in her life. You know, finding out that she was HIV-positive, and not even knowing the bastard who had given it to her. No doubt, my heart went out to Tonya in a big way.

"Johnny." Someone slid up behind me like a sneaky rat. I turned around and saw that it was Dr. Holmes—James's doctor. Out of nowhere this dude started tripping on me for no reason. "What the hell do you think you're doing?"

"Excuse me." I frowned at him. He was a skinny, lightweight li'l motherfucker sporting round frames and a white lab coat. "I know you ain't talking to me like that, man. You better chill with that shit."

"First of all," he said, "do I need to remind you what happened earlier in this hospital between you and the patient in that room?"

We walked away from the door. "I was only stopping by to give her something. That's it, man. Why you riding me?"

"Because James needs you to be focused on him more than ever right now," he said. I got the sense that there was more going on here than met the eye.

"You act like you know him or somethin'." I gritted words between my teeth. "What's up with that?"

"Actually, I do." He pushed his eyeglasses up on his nose. "We knew each other from before."

"Come again?" I said with a hard face, letting his li'l educated ass know what type of real Ninth Ward nigga he was dealing with. "He ain't never mentioned you."

"Maybe he hasn't had time to," he said, "with so much other stuff apparently going on in your life."

Man, I couldn't believe this dude. His ass was really coming for me on the sly. But you know I wasn't gonna take his insults lying down.

"Look, man." I raised my voice. And there's no other way to put this—I was jealous. "You better explain what's going on here, 'cause I ain't feeling this shit, for real. What's up with you and James? And how y'all know each other?"

"Could you please keep your voice down?" He held his hands out like a school crossing guard.

"Man, you better start talking," I warned him. "How you know my nigga?"

"James and I are just friends," he said. "We met at the club."

"Just what I thought," I whispered. It was always interesting for me to discover other dudes who were down, too. Being totally gay was opening up a whole new world of dudes to me. "You down too?"

"Yes," he said. "Isn't that much obvious?"

"Hey, I didn't want to assume anything," I said. "But it's all good, man. You helping my nigga get on his feet, so you cool with me."

"I'm glad you approve," he said. "How's he doing?"

"He's hanging in there," I said. "Matter of fact, I was coming to find you to see if you found out anything."

"I don't wanna get your hopes up high," he said. "But we may have found a donor right here in the hospital."

"Man, straight. You for real?" I could hardly believe it myself. This was my nigga's life we were talking about, and I loved that dude. "I have to go and tell him the good news."

"No, wait." He suddenly stopped me.

"What's up, man?"

"Let's hold off until we get the test back," he said. "You know, just to be on the safe side. If I were you, though, I'd go downstairs to the chapel and pray this donor's blood matches up with James's. His life may very well depend on it."

Without delay I took the flight of stairs, but when I got down to that chapel my ass froze like I was stuck in time. And the gun went off in my head like a firecracker. Man, I would never be able to go inside of another church or chapel or sanctuary and not think about Kojack.

"Please don't go, son." Pops quickly rose to his feet when he saw me enter the chapel. But I made an immediate U turn and ignored him. He grabbed me by the arm and it felt like I had been electrocuted.

Suddenly me and Pops were in another time and place. I was five years old again, and we were inside a chapel similar to the one up at Charity. It was the prayer room at Pops's church, and it was lit with candles.

"Come out of him, demon!" Pops had me by both arms, shaking and slapping me across the face. "Come out of my son! You can't have him!"

"Stop it, Daddy!" I was screaming in my five-year-old voice, but Pops wouldn't quit, man. He kept slapping and shaking me so hard until I fell over the pew and hit my head against a table. Blood was running down the side of my face, and I was staring up toward the ceiling at a painting of Jesus.

"How could you do it?" I came back to the present moment and stared Pops directly in his face. He finally let go of me. You could hear a pin drop, it was so damn quiet.

"What are you talking about, son?" He looked nervous.

"I was just a fucking child, man!" I went ballistic, backing away from him.

"I know you're upset with me, son," Pops said. "But don't disrespect God."

"This coming from a man who lies and keeps secrets," I said to him. It took all the strength in the world not to haul off and punch Pops in his face for what he'd done to me. "Isn't that one of the top ten? And you talking about disrespecting God, man? What a joke."

"I never said I was perfect," he said, slowly walking toward me. "I'm only human."

"Don't come any closer," I said. Pops was suddenly like the devil to me, man. Like the fucking devil.

"You have to let me explain." He stopped a few feet in front of me. "I wasn't thinking straight."

Those nightmares I had been having for the longest time wasn't just me having a horrible dream. That shit really happened to me. Someone came into my room in the middle of the night and took me out of the comfort of my own bed, kicking and fighting.

"I'm so sorry, son." Pops broke down crying right there in front of me. The cat was out of the bag. He was the bogeyman in my dreams—my own pops, man. This was almost too deep and twisted to be happening in real life, to me, but it was. "I know I did a terrible thing to you."

"Just answer me one thing," I said. "Why did you do it?"

"You have to let me explain." His voice began to crack under the pressure. "Five minutes. That's all I'm asking for, son."

"You got three minutes," I said. "And then I'm out of here and out of your life for good."

"I think part of me always knew." Pops went straight into it. "Some things a parent just knows. But I never wanted to believe it—not about my own son. I was a young preacher trying to build a church. The last thing I needed was—"

Pops suddenly stopped short, like the words tasted like horse shit inside of his mouth and he couldn't bring himself to say it.

"Gay," I said it for him. "You didn't want your li'l church folks to know you had a faggot for a son."

"You're putting words in my mouth," he said. "That's not what I meant."

"Just say what you gotta say, man," I pushed him. " 'Cause I don't have all day."

"Your mom and brothers went up to Baton Rouge to see your uncle Leroy who was sick with cancer," he went on. "It was a hard time for the family."

"Get to the point," I said.

"The rain was coming down real hard," he said. "You could hear the trees howling in the wind, and that lightning outside of the window sounded like demons speaking to me in my head. I didn't wanna do it."

"You fucked me up in the head, man!" I shouted at him. "I trusted you!"

"Your grandmother was upstairs in her bed asleep," Pops went on, like he didn't even hear me screaming at his ass. It was like he was caught up in a trance or something. "I remember you were having a sleepover with–"

"Don't mention his name to me," I said. "As far as I'm concerned, that nigga is dead to me."

"Y'all were hugged up on top of each other," Pops said. "It just didn't look right. I got this funny feeling."

"We were kids!" I screamed. "Close cousins having a fucking sleepover! What the hell were you thinking, man?"

"Don't you think I know that now?" Pops looked dead at me. "I wasn't myself back then. You gotta believe me."

"So, those were your hands over my mouth?" I asked. All those bad memories were coming at me at once, and it felt like I was about to have a nervous breakdown. "I couldn't get Jesus out of my head."

"I thought once I got you down to the church," he said, "I could get 'it' out of you. The exorcism was the only way I knew how."

"I hate you, man!" I yelled at the top of my lungs. "Stay away from me. You sick bastard!"

"Don't say that, son." He reached for me, but I pulled away from him and ran out the door.

"You gotta forgive me, son," I heard him screaming. His voice followed me down the corridor. "I didn't mean it!"

I ran into the bathroom and vomited. All of those horrible nightmares went down the toilet. As far as I was concerned, that was the end of it. Pops was out of my life for good.

"There you are." Moms caught me in the corridor outside of James's room. "I've been looking for you. Have you seen your father?"

"Last time I saw him, he was down in the chapel," I said. "But he can be six feet under, as far as I care."

"Johnny, don't speak of your father in that manner, after everything he's done for you."

"What are you talking about, Ma?"

"That's what I've been trying to tell you, son." Moms rushed her words. "Your pops is a match."

I was now staring down the corridor with a blank look on my face. The shock alone left me paralyzed. I could no longer trust what I was feeling.

"Didn't you hear me, son?" asked Moms. "Your father's blood is going to be what saves your friend's life."

PART THREE

Around a Year Later . . .

$$\left\{ \; 22 \; \right\}$$

Tonya

"Your recent test results are looking good," Dr. Cramer said to both me and Mama. I had spent the last several days in the hospital being tested for minor bleeding and fatigue. "There's no sign of cancer cells anywhere in the body."

"Thank God for that." Mama squeezed my hand. The two of us had gotten really close over the past year. "I had been so worried."

"But Tonya, you're going to have to take it easy," Dr. Cramer went on. She was the one added blessing in my life, who had become like a guardian angel through this entire ordeal. "Your T cells are slightly lower this month, so I'm going to change your cocktail just a bit to strengthen your immune system."

One of the worst things about being HIV-positive is all the pills and medication they have you take. Cocktails is what they call it, and without them I don't think many of us diagnosed with the HIV virus would make it.

Babee, it's no joke: Living with HIV is an everyday struggle, too. Some days I feel so charged and energized, like I could take on the world. But then there are those times when I'm so sick and weak that I could hardly get out of bed. Being HIV-positive may not have been a death sentence—thanks to scientists and doctors and advances in medicine—but it was a battle from within. This past year I definitely found out what I was really made of.

"Please. No more medication," I said to Dr. Cramer. "I just want to go a week without taking any pills."

"I know it isn't easy," she said. Both me and her had that virus inside of us, and therefore we understood each other on a level that nobody else could—not even my best friends, Tamika and Latisha. Sometimes it's the people you least expect who wind up playing a major role in your life. "But you know the drill. We have to keep you healthy and strong."

"I know," I said. "But you know how it is?"

"Indeed I do," she said. "And I think you've done pretty well for yourself, considering the rough year you've had."

"Thanks to you, Doctor," Mama said. "And I know I've said it many times before, but I really appreciate how you've been there for my daughter."

"Oh, it was easy." Dr. Cramer took hold of my hand. "I like Tonya. And before I forget, I have something for you."

Dr. Cramer pulled a black jewelry box out of her white lab coat. "Happy birthday, my favorite patient."

"I can't believe you remembered my birthday, and brought me a gift, too." I opened the jewelry box and was blown away by a silver cross that could easily be worn as a necklace. "It's beautiful."

"Let me put it on you." Dr. Cramer placed the chain around my neck. "Perfect."

While she and Mama admired my cross, I couldn't help but

think about how much I had grown in my faith. Two days ago I was baptized for the first time in my life, which was a miracle, considering the fact that I had never been a religious type of person. Now you couldn't stop me from praising Jesus.

"Thank you." I hugged her and then raised my arms over my head. "And thank you, Lord. I give You the glory. Baby, I couldn't have made it without Him, for real."

"Amen," Mama said. "I couldn't have said it better myself."

"I'm sorry to break up this party, ladies," Dr. Cramer said. "But I have to run. I probably won't be able to check back on you, because I'm in surgery the rest of the evening, but hopefully you won't mind Dr. Holmes seeing after you. I'm just asking, because I remember what happened the last time."

"Of course I don't mind," I said. "But hopefully he don't mind, given how foolish I acted with him. But in my own defense, I wasn't myself at the time."

"I'm sure it won't be a problem," Dr. Cramer said. "But if you hadn't requested another doctor, you and I wouldn't have met. And that wouldn't have been good at all."

"Not at all," I said.

"Anyway, take care and get some rest," she said on her way out the door.

"She's such a sweet woman." Mama straightened the covers on the bed. "Taking such good care of you."

"So, did you pick up a copy for me?"

"Against my better judgment," Mama said. "Why would you want to put yourself through any more pain is beyond me."

"Just hand it over to me, Ma."

All of this back and forth between me and Mama was because I had asked her to pick me up a copy of *Vibe*. They were running a special issue and giving tribute to Rico, who had passed away a couple of months ago. His untimely death rocked the rap and hip-hop world.

"Thank you." I flipped through the pages, viewing one photograph after another from when Rico was at the height of his career. It was still so hard for me to believe that he was gone. Him dying so unexpectedly was really affecting me big-time. For the past couple of weeks I could barely eat or sleep, which was the reason my behind ended up in the hospital in the first place.

"I know what you're looking for." Mama stood next to the bed as I read an article on Rico. "But they didn't mention nothing about him being HIV-positive."

It was a cover-up that I'm sure his mom, Beverly, had a lot to do with. When Rico got back from his trip to Africa, his health took a turn for the worse. He collapsed onstage during one of his concerts and later died of complications with his lungs, which might have been true. But when I think about the last few times I saw Rico leading up to his death, he was losing a lot of weight. I straight-out asked him if he had AIDS and he tossed me out of his house. He even stopped taking my calls. His reaction basically told me everything I needed to know.

"I'm not surprised at all," I said to Mama, putting the magazine on top of the nightstand. "Beverly would go to her grave before she let something like that get out about her son. But that's okay. She and I both know the truth about Rico, and I don't need no test to prove it. The reason I'm HIV-positive is because of him."

Because of the accusations I had made against Rico when he was alive, Beverly refused to allow me to attend his funeral, which I didn't even fight her on. Losing her only child was hard enough on the woman without having me up in her face acting like a fool.

"Is it okay if an old friend stops by and says hello?"

"Reverend Lomack!" I yelled when I saw his warm face. "Come in. It's so good to see you."

"And same to you, darling." He placed a beautiful bouquet of flowers on the nightstand. "How are you ladies doing today?"

"Oh, we fine," Mama said. "Just trying to keep our heads above water."

"And how's our favorite patient?" Reverend Lomack gave me a fat kiss on the cheek. He was such a handsome and sweet older man, who reminded me so much of my own daddy. Both of them were just good people.

"I'm hanging in there." I touched the cross around my neck. "And keeping God first."

"Now, that's what I like to hear." He clapped his hands together. "You can't go wrong with a plan like that one. The rest of the family sends their well wishes, too."

"And how's Johnny?" Mama was trying to make nice. The mention of his name was a sore subject for both of us, though.

Don't misunderstand me. Me and Johnny was definitely in a better place, but no matter how hard I tried, I still couldn't stomach the idea of him now dating another dude. Last I heard, they was even living together.

Reverend Lomack cleared his throat. He had a bittersweet smile on his face. "He's doing good for himself, and recently started taking classes up at UNO."

"Well, that's nice," Mama said. "You must be real proud."

"Yes, Lord," he said, looking at Mama. "You know how it is. No matter how old they get, we still worry about them. But look, I'm not going to hold y'all long."

"Thanks again for stopping by." I hugged him. "And tell Ms. Liz I said hello."

"Will do, darling," he said on his way out. "And if there's anything we can ever do for you, please don't hesitate to call. You'll always be family to us."

"Why don't I walk you out?" Mama followed him out the door. "I'll be right back, sweetheart."

"Take your time." I loved Mama for standing by me this past year, but sometimes she could be overbearing. Babee, I couldn't go to the bathroom without her looking over my shoulder. You know, it was just good to have a moment to myself on my birthday.

"Happy birthday, girl!" Tamika and Latisha burst in on me with balloons and gifts.

"What are y'all doing?" You should have seen me just grinning and smiling. Hands down, I had the best friends in the world, who always lifted me up when I was down.

"You didn't think we would let your birthday pass and not celebrate, did you?" Latisha showed me much love, shaking me from side to side. "Happy birthday, and I pray God blesses you with many, many more."

"What's up, bitch?" Tamika said, grabbing me around the neck. "Oh, I forgot. Forgive me, Lord. I shouldn't have said that."

Since I had become a full-fledged, bona fide Christian, even my friends didn't always know how to act around me. I had given up all cussing and swearing.

"It's okay, girl," I said to her. "You can still be yourself around me."

"Sorry, I'm late, love." Peaches made his grand entrance wearing a pink shirt with a big collar and a pair of white Kenneth

Cole slacks. He had to give extra, as usual. But one thing that was different, though, was how me and Peaches related to each other. It was time-out on all the name-calling, hatred, and petty insults.

"Happy birthday, love." He kissed me on both cheeks and then put one hand on his hip. I noticed a white envelope in his hand. "How you be today?"

"Just fine, Peaches." I was tickled by his gestures. "Thanks for coming."

"Wouldn't have missed this party for the world, love," he said, pushing that white envelope toward me.

"I can't believe you brought me a gift," I said.

"Isn't that sweet?" Tamika said.

"It would have been," he said, "but I can't take credit for this one. Some woman was standing outside your door and asked me to give this to you."

Everyone suddenly got quiet as I ripped the envelope open. "Oh, my God!"

"Who's it from?" asked Latisha.

"It's a check from Rico's mom," I said with both my hands trembling. There was so many zeroes behind that first number that I could have screamed. "She sent me a note, too."

"That girl looked like she had coins," Peaches said, "with those diamond earrings that were screaming bling-bling."

"What does the note say?" asked Latisha.

However, I couldn't stop shaking, so Tamika picked up the envelope and read the note for me: " 'Thank you for honoring my son's legacy. Rico would have wanted you to have this. Take care of yourself. Beverly.' "

"What does she mean?" Everyone looked at me for answers.

Although I had confronted Rico about his HIV status, I

never told another soul about my suspicions, except Mama. You know I could have easily blasted Rico in public and told all of his business to the media. But I wasn't that type of cold-hearted person. Getting that check in the hospital only confirmed what I knew all along.

"What I wanna know is, how much is the check for?" Peaches said.

I slipped the check in my bra. "Wouldn't you like to know?"

"Oh, it's like that," Latisha said. "You ain't gon' tell us."

"Let me put it like this," I said. "Y'all go home and pack your bags, because when I get out of this hospital we're going to Jamaica!"

That news for sure sent all of them jumping up and down in the air. From the way they were screaming and shouting, you would have thought we was at a sporting event.

"What in the world is going on in here?" Mama walked in on us acting like plumb fools. "I could hear the commotion down the hall."

"We're rich!" Tamika said.

"Tonya, what's going on?" Mama had a confused look on her face.

"Ms. Beverly was here," I said.

"What did she want?" Mama asked with an attitude. She hated the way Beverly had treated me after Rico's death. Before I could answer Mama's question though, she cut me off.

"But you can tell me about it later." She was beaming with joy. "Because I have a surprise of my own."

"I don't know if I can take any more surprises," I said.

"Believe me, sweetheart," Mama said. "You gon' like this one."

She swung the door open and a tall, handsome man entered, decked out in a military uniform and shiny black shoes.

"Happy birthday, li'l sister."

"Ricky?" I couldn't believe it was him. Last I had heard, he wasn't sure he would be able to come home until the Christmas holidays. It was only July.

"It's me, li'l sister," he said. "In the flesh."

"Oh, God." Tamika held her hands up to her mouth. "This is so wonderful."

As for me, though, I was speechless.

"I mean, if you want me to leave," Ricky started fooling around with me, "I could come back another time."

"You better get your behind over here and give me a hug," I said to him.

He did, and it was the best one I had gotten all year.

"So, what does this actually mean?" Mama held my check in her hand. Tamika, Latisha, and Peaches had gone back to the salon, and it was just me, her, and Ricky. We was having family time together.

"What it means," I said to Mama, with Ricky holding my hand and smiling at me—the two of us just couldn't stop staring at each other—"is that you can take the next forty-something years off from work and don't have to clean nobody's floors."

{ 23 }

James

When the spotlight hit me, I glided down the runway with all seriousness and fierceness in my step. I wasn't only walking for myself, honey. This walk was for Pandora, who had recently passed over to the other side. Her long battle with tuberculosis ultimately got the best of her.

"Welcome, everyone, to Pandora's last dance!" I said to the cheerful crowd at Club Circus who were losing their gay minds, screaming and shouting, with thunderous applause. The children had come from near and far to show their support of a legend who had given so much to our community. But tonight was not only about performing and paying tribute, but also to raise funds for Pandora's funeral. She died without burial insurance, and there was no way I was gonna allow them to put my mother in a cardboard box six feet under. No, ma'am. No way, honey.

"Prepare yourselves for a night of grandeur, honey." I went on with my theatrics, wearing a long, flowing white gown and a pair of sparkling diamond earrings that stole the show. Of course they were knockoffs, honey, but the children didn't need to know all of my business. "For a grand diva who's no longer with us."

"We love you, Armari!" someone shouted out from the back of the crowd.

"And I love you, too, hon," I said. There was so much love bouncing off the walls that I could hardly stand it. "I just wanna take this time out to thank all of you for coming and supporting this cause for my mother, a strong and bad motherfucker who lived her life on her own goddamn terms. Ms. Alexandria Pandora Craft, of the legendary House of Craft, will forever live on in our hearts."

More thunderous applause.

"You know, it's so important for us to take care of one another." I immediately went back into serious mode. "That's what Pandora was all about, honey: gay sisterhood. The best way you could remember her is to look out for your fellow gay sister. Stop the violence. Stop the hating on one another. Let's start sticking together."

More applause and then dead silence.

"As many of you know, Pandora ran away from home when she was a teenager," I said, thinking about the last couple of days dealing with Pandora's brother and sister—her parents were deceased—who were two of the most ignorant-ass people I had ever met. They told me to do whatever I wanted with Pandora's body, because as far as they were concerned she had been dead to them for a long time.

"She grew up not having the love and support of a family," I went on. "Pandora never wanted any of the children to feel that kind of pain and hurt, and one of the reasons she started the House of Craft was to bring the children together in love and fellowship.

"So, in keeping with that idea, I plan to use some of the money left over from the funeral, along with private donations, to start a house for runaways and homeless gays who have nowhere else to turn. I will call this community-based home 'the House of Pandora.' "

This revelation was followed by the loudest outbursts and screams of the entire evening, which brought a smile to my face and lifted the heavy burden off my heart, honey. Losing Pandora was one of the hardest things I have ever had to go through in my life. If it wasn't for the love and support from the gay community, I don't think I could have made it this far.

"Some of those private donors are here today," I said, looking out into the crowd. "Come on up here, Marvin and Debra."

As those girls made their way to the stage, I did a Wonder Woman spin so the children could catch the back of my dress that was cut in a V shape, revealing just enough skin to be dangerous. It was my way of being silly and trying to add humor to an extremely difficult and sad occasion. My showcase was received with cheers and whistles.

"I thought you might like that," I said. Debra Boudreaux, who I was now on a first-name basis with, glided up beside me.

Ms. Debra really came through for us in the end, winning Pandora her freedom and allowing her to die in the comfort of her own home. Marvin even chipped in with free medical care when Pandora's illness reached the point of no return.

"Get to know these two wonderful people in our community, honey," I told the crowd, holding Debra by the hand. Marvin stood beside her. "They are the best of us—a doctor and a lawyer. But besides that, these two individuals are the nicest people I know in the whole goddamn world."

It took every ounce of strength in me not to break down and

cry in front of everyone, honey. This shit was so goddamn hard for me.

"I just wanted to thank the two of you," I said with mascara running down my face. "And my makeup is getting messed up, but I don't care."

"You're welcome, sweetheart." Debra kissed me on the cheek.

"You know we got your back," Marvin said with his arm around me. "I'm still your biggest fan."

"Give them another round of applause," I said as they made their way off the stage. "Okay. There's one last thing before I turn this stage over to our next performer. I want you to put your hands together for my man, who's a virgin tonight, honey. This is his first time inside a gay club."

I looked out into the crowd and saw Johnny. He was pulling his baseball cap over his face and trying to be inconspicuous.

"Hey, honey," I said, waving at him over near the bar. The only thing I got in return was a nod of the head. He was such a boy.

Me and Johnny had weathered a difficult year, but those trials and tribulations only brought us closer. We recently moved into our first apartment together.

"There's no need to be nervous, hon," I said to him with the spotlight still on me. The children were getting a real good kick over me going back and forth with Johnny. You should have heard the laughter up in that place. "You're among family. But you sissies better keep y'all's hands off my man, honey."

Much laughter from the crowd.

"I'm being serious," I said. "I know how some of you girls are, but we ain't gon' even go there tonight because this evening is all about unity. So in keeping with that idea, I bring to the stage our next performer, who's real fish, honey, but fierce. Put your hands together for my motherfucking girl, Ebony Sinclair!"

When the curtains were drawn, Ebony was standing center stage and wearing a two-piece black leather suit with a pair of high-heeled pumps for your mama's nerves. And she was quite the performer, I would soon learn. Ms. Girl let them have it that night with her own rendition of Mary J. Blige's "No More Drama." I couldn't help but think she picked the perfect song to express herself. You know, given everything she went through with that thug Kojack, who I am glad to report was out of her life for good, honey, and serving a life sentence up at Sierra Leone.

Thank God for one of life's little miracles. With him out of the picture, Ebony was able to focus completely on herself. She went back to college to study drama and music.

"Sounds like she's working it out there," Jerome said. I met up with him and Flo in the dressing room.

"Serving them from the hip, honey," I said, slipping out of my dress and getting ready for my next number. "The crowd is really feeling it tonight."

"This is a beautiful occasion," Flo said, with a cigarette up to her mouth. "I think everyone can feel that. Pandora would be proud."

"Oh, thank you, Flo, girl." I hugged Mama. "You know just what to say."

"Shit, I'm just speaking the truth." She took a puff from the cigarette and exhaled.

I sat down in front of the mirror and gave myself over to Jerome, who was about to tease my hair into a beautiful creation of art.

"Is it all right if I come in?" Johnny poked his head in the door.

"Yeah. Come on in," Flo said, moving her purse off the chair and making room for him. It felt so good seeing the two of them getting along. "And have a seat."

"What's up, Johnny?" said Jerome, curling my hair with the hot iron. "You all right tonight?"

"I'm straight," Johnny said, looking at me through the mirror and grinning. "I just ain't never seen this many people in one club before."

"I hope you weren't embarrassed earlier," I said.

"Don't worry. I'm gonna get your ass back for that one," he said. "But it's all good. Ain't that much different from being in a straight club."

"You like to dance?" asked Jerome.

"Nah, I'm not into dancing," he said.

"Well, honey, you ain't official," I said, "until you've had a spin on the dance floor."

"Well, I guess I'm gon' always be unofficial then." Johnny cut his eyes at me in the mirror.

Tony opened the door and peered in. We could hear the crowd going crazy over Ebony's performance. "Sorry to interrupt."

"You're okay." I turned to face him. "This night wouldn't even be happening if it wasn't for you letting us use the club. What's up?"

"There's a woman here to see you," he said. "Ms. Lomack."

"That's my mama." Johnny got to his feet. Ms. Liz walked in and surprised the hell out of all of us. Tony excused himself.

"Ma. What are you doing here?" He kissed her on the cheek.

"I'm here to offer my support," she said, pulling a white envelope out of her purse. "The church picked up a donation for your friend."

"Oh, that's so sweet." I walked over toward her with rollers dangling from my head. This was Ms. Liz's first time seeing me in drag, and I have to admit that I was a little nervous. You know, this was Johnny's mom, and I wanted the woman to like me. She kept her composure, along with a straight face. "I can't believe you did this."

"It was no big deal," she said, clutching her purse. Ms. Liz was anxious, but she was still handling my and Johnny's relationship with such class and sophistication. "I'm just glad we were able to help."

Johnny's father had come a long way, too. When we moved into our new apartment, he sent a housewarming gift by way of his wife. He and Johnny were even on speaking terms. As far as I was concerned, the man was my hero. If it wasn't for him giving blood when he did, I wouldn't even be alive today.

"You remember my mother," I said to Ms. Liz.

"Yes, I do," she said. "So good to see you again."

"Same here, baby," Flo said, holding another cigarette between her fingers. "We have to get together for dinner one of these days."

"I would love that," Ms. Liz said. "Well, I can't stay long. My husband's mother is celebrating her seventy-fifth birthday today."

"Thank you again, Ms. Liz." I hugged her. "Having your support really means a lot to us."

"You're very welcome." She turned to Johnny. "Would you walk me out, son?"

"I'll be back later," Johnny said.

"Wow." I took my seat in front of the mirror. "That was really nice of her."

"She's not as bad as I thought." Flo took a puff from her cigarette. "Although she's a little too bourgeois for my taste."

"Everybody can't be ghetto like your ass," I said.

"Whatever," Flo said. "You better be lucky I'm being nice to your mother-in-law."

"Mother Love..." Jerome finally finished beating my hair. He gave me one old ponytail that was sticking straight up on the top of my head. I noticed my exotic outfit with an avant-garde flair laid out across the ironing board. "I don't think the children gon' be ready for this one."

I was about to give those children something they had never seen before–drag in the new millennium.

{ 24 }

Johnny

"Look who I found," Moms said to Grandma Eve when we walked in the door. Her birthday party had already ended, and she sat on the sofa unwrapping gifts with Nettie. As for the rest of my peeps, they were long gone.

"Happy birthday, Grandma." I kissed her on the cheek. "I'm sorry I missed your party."

Moms showed up at Club Circus, where James was performing a benefit event for Pandora to raise money for her funeral. Of course, I was surprised, but happy to have Moms's support. We needed it, man.

No doubt, these were some hard times for James—he and Pandora had that close bond like me and Kojack used to have. But I learned the hard way that nothing lasts forever. I'm just glad the police finally caught up with Kojack's ass and put him away for life, so he wouldn't hurt nobody else. That dude was crazy, and as far as I was concerned he could rot up there in that prison.

"It's okay, sugar," Grandma Eve said, squeezing my hand and

looking up in my face. Her voice was real old and shaky. "I know you're a busy young man."

Man, the truth was, I had tried to avoid family functions since everyone found out that I was gay and had a lover. Don't get me wrong. No one had disrespected me or made me feel uncomfortable about it. It was just something I had to get used to for myself. Being out in the open was like having eyes on you twenty-four-seven, with no masks to hide behind.

"What's up, cuz?" asked Nettie. She and the baby were still regulars at my parents' house.

"Nothing much," I said. "Just hoping to get something good to eat."

"Well, we have plenty of food back there." Moms laid her purse on the table and joined Nettie on the sofa. Grandma Eve had so many gifts up in that joint that it looked like Christmas in July. "Go ahead and help yourself."

"You know, you could have brought your friend with you," Grandma Eve said. Moms and Nettie looked at each other.

"Thank you, Grandma," I said with an uneasy grin on my face. "But he was kind of busy tonight."

Me and James had taken things to the next level, with moving in together and everything. But it was all good, man. I loved playing house with him and being in our own li'l space. The only major problem we had was getting used to each other's habits. Where James was neat and organized, I was the sloppy one. We often argued about stupid bullshit, like me leaving a plate on the table or my shoes lying around on the floor. But we always had a good time making up.

"Where's Ronnie and Carl?" I noticed both their cars in the driveway when me and Moms drove up.

"In the backyard shooting hoops," Nettie said. "You know, the usual. Uncle Lonnie is upstairs in his study."

"You should go up and say hello," Moms said. "I'm sure he would be glad to see you."

"I think I'll do that." I took the long flight of stairs.

"I thought I heard you down there." Pops looked up from his desk when I walked in. "I'm glad you made it. I know it means a lot to Mama when y'all come around."

"Yeah, I had to show my support," I said, looking around Pops's study. He had a mountain of books and looseleaf paper on top of his desk. This room was where Pops came up with his sermons for Sunday-morning services. "And my love, too."

Pops removed his reading glasses. He yawned. "It's been a long day."

"Moms was telling me in the car," I said, "that you went to see Tonya the other day."

"I sure did," Pops said. "She's hanging in there, and she told me to tell you hello."

Me and Tonya hadn't spoken much over the past year. I figured we both needed some time to heal before we could even think about being friends. She still had a lot of hurt and bitterness toward me and James. I wasn't about to push our relationship in her face, especially given everything that girl was going through with her health.

"I'm glad you stopped by to see her," I said. "That was real nice."

Me and Pops paused for a moment and just looked at each other.

"Look, son," he said. "I know we've had our fair share of problems—"

"That's water under the bridge," I cut him off.

Once I found out that Pops came through for James in the hospital last year, I saw that dude in a whole new light. And the shit that went down between us in my childhood was in the past, and that was where I wanted to keep it buried. Forgiving him was the easy part.

"Let's just focus on the present," I said.

"You know I'm trying to accept things"—he cleared his throat—"with you and your friend."

"I know it ain't easy for you," I said. "You got your beliefs, and I respect that."

"But still," Pops said, "I'm your father, and I want you to feel like you can always come to me."

"I appreciate that," I said.

"What's up, dude?" Ronnie walked in and interrupted us. He was carrying a basketball in his hands and looking all sweaty. His T-shirt was dripping. "I heard you were here. How you feeling?"

We dapped each other up.

"I'm cool, man," I said to him. "What's up with you?"

"Chilling, man," he said. "Out there whipping your li'l brother's behind."

"Y'all been at it for a while," Pops said. "You need to pick on somebody your own size."

"Is that a challenge?" asked Ronnie.

"It's whatever you want it to be," Pops said.

"Okay, then," Ronnie said with his hand on my shoulder. "Me and Johnny against you and Carl. Losers have to buy dinner."

"That's if your brothers are up to it," Pops said.

They both stared at me.

"What's up, dude?" Ronnie asked. "You down or what?"

"Count me in."

1. *Three Sides to Every Story* takes on many cultural stereotypes, including effeminate gay men, angry black women, and ruthless drug dealers, to name a few. Were any ideas you have about particular types of people or situations challenged? If so, how?

2. In *Three Sides*, author Clarence Nero reminds us that many social and economic forces affect the lives of people living in the Ninth Ward of New Orleans. What are some of these forces that the characters contend with?

3. How does materialism influence the characters of Tonya, Johnny, Kojack, or others? Imagine yourself in some of the predicaments in which they find themselves: fresh out of prison, no college education, tempted by the lure of easy money, and so forth. How would you respond? If you've ever been in a similar situation to the characters, what did you do? How did you cope?

4. This novel portrays troubled relationships between parents and their children, whether it is because of abusive parenting,

neglect, abandonment, or the untimely death of a mother or father.

Think about the mothers in the novel. Tonya's mother is bitter and violent; Kelly's mother is a drug addict; Johnny's "sophisticated" mother submits to her husband's bullying. "Mother" Pandora St. Craft–the male leader of the House of St. Craft, a nonbiological family of gay people–might be considered the finest example of motherhood in the book. What can Pandora teach some of the other mothers who appear in the novel? What can these families referred to as "houses" teach us about family?

5. Think about the recent frenzy surrounding "down-low" men and the misconception that they are the main culprits for the spread of HIV in the African American community. When Tonya discovers that she is HIV-positive, she presumes that Johnny must be the source of her infection because he is gay. It turns out that Johnny is HIV-negative and that Tonya's other ex-boyfriend, Rico–a straight and very promiscuous hip-hop star–has probably infected her. How does Tonya's infection challenge generalizations about HIV transmission in the African American community (and, furthermore, in all communities)?

6. Homophobia runs rampant in the community portrayed in *Three Sides*; Reverend Lomack's fire-and-brimstone religious beliefs, Kojack's anti-gay actions, Tonya's accusation, and Johnny's self-loathing are all forms of homophobia. Some critics point out that in light of such homophobia, it is no wonder that black men who have sex with other men are scared to come out. What responsibility should communities take for creating a climate in which gay or bisexual men–fearing for their safety and their lives–pretend to be straight or try to become straight?

7. Johnny's secret desire for other men is central to *Three Sides to Every Story*, but it is not the only secret in the novel. Others keep secrets too: Reverend Lomack of the attempted "exorcism" of his five-year-old son, James of his acquaintance with Tonya, Tonya of her fling with Rico, and Johnny of Pandora's illness, to name a few.

Are there times when people should keep a secret at any and all costs? When should one break a vow or come clean? Consider, for example, that Johnny vowed to keep Pandora's illness a secret. This promise placed Johnny in a bind. On the one hand, he could keep the vow he made to Pandora. This would protect James from the painful knowledge that his mentor was deathly ill, but it would also keep James from seeing Pandora in what might have been Pandora's final days. On the other hand, Johnny could have broken his promise to Pandora and disclosed the illness to James. There is no simple solution to this predicament. What would you have done, and why?

8. Fueled by pain, anger, distrust, and frustration, many of the characters in the novel spend a lot of time reacting to each other with their words and actions. Yet it's only toward the end of the novel, when Johnny and Tonya are honest with each other and are forced to chill out because both James and Tonya are in the hospital, that their lives seem to take a very different direction. What is the author showing in the novel about the effects of people reacting angrily toward one another versus being calm and still?

9. Much of New Orleans—particularly poor, predominantly African American communities—was ravaged by Hurricane Katrina. Though *Three Sides* is a work of fiction, it is inspired by

real people and lives, and it serves as a testament to the community devastated by this disaster. Imagine how the individual characters in the novel might be affected by Katrina and how they would cope as survivors. Take into account the specific aspects of their lives and lifestyles.

10. *Three Sides* touches upon many important social concerns: the spread of AIDS, domestic violence, homophobia, injustice in the criminal justice system, drug abuse in poor and African American communities, even high blood pressure among black Americans. Jot down some of the issues examined in the book and consider them in relation to current events.

ABOUT THE AUTHOR

Clarence Nero grew up in New Orleans and earned a B.S. degree at Howard University. His first novel, *Cheekie: A Child Out of the Desire*, received an endorsement by renowned poet Dr. Maya Angelou and won wide critical acclaim. He is currently an M.F.A. candidate at Louisiana State University. He lives in Baton Rouge.

Printed in the United States
by Baker & Taylor Publisher Services